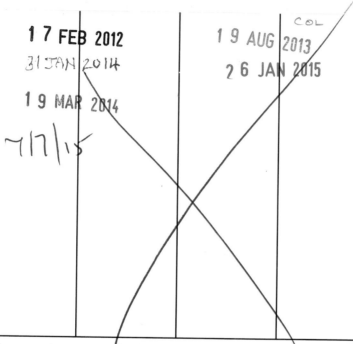

WHERE THE BODIES ARE BURIED

WHERE THE BODIES ARE BURIED

Chris Brookmyre

WINDSOR
PARAGON

First published 2011
by Little, Brown
This Large Print edition published 2011
by AudioGO Ltd
by arrangement with
Little, Brown Book Group

Hardcover ISBN: 978 1 445 85748 0
Softcover   ISBN: 978 1 445 85749 7

British Library Cataloguing in Publication Data available

Printed and bound in Great Britain by
MPG Books Group Limited

In memory of Gerry Haetzman

ACKNOWLEDGEMENTS

My thanks to: Marisa and Jack for their understanding and indulgence; Andrew Torrance and Steve T for their technical insight; and Frightened Rabbit for the soundtrack in my head.

THE LONELINESS AND THE SCREAM

It didn't seem like Glasgow.

There was a mugginess in the air despite its being a clear night, not a wisp to obscure the moon and stars. Not like last night, when the clouds had rolled in on top of a sunny day like a lid on a pan, holding in the warmth, keeping hot blood on a simmer. It was warm on the street at nine o'clock that morning, and now, past eleven, it felt as though every molecule of air was drunk and tired. If a clear night wasn't cooling it down, then the next clouds were going to bring thunderstorms.

The inside of the van had been stifling, smells of sweat and aftershave battling it out with piss and blood. When Wullie stepped out on to the gravel and weeds, the horseshoe of the quarry walls like an amphitheatre around him, he had expected to feel the welcome relief of a freshening breeze, but the temperature drop was negligible. Only the smells changed. There was a sweetness in the air, scents from the trees you never smelled in the cold and rain, mixed with the charcoal and cooked meat of a thousand barbecues wafting from the city below, warm smoke, warm smells borne on warm air.

No, it really didn't seem like Glasgow at all. Apart from the guy lying on the deck in the advanced stages of a severe kicking. That was as authentically local as haggis suppers and lung cancer.

Jai didn't struggle as they hauled him out of the van. All the fight had been booted out of him long

1

before that point. He half-lay and half-sat on the ground in a disjointed and blood-soaked heap, like a big pile of washing. He was shaking with shock and fear, making it look incongruously like he was shivering. If anybody could be cold right then, it would be him: cold in his fear, cold in his isolation: the loneliest man in Glasgow. He knew he had nobody, and making it worse, he knew what to be afraid of, because he had been among those dishing it out plenty of times in the past.

Nobody thinks it'll ever come to them, especially once they've found themselves with a bit of clout. Money in their pocket, fancy motor, smart threads, folk fearfully averting their eyes when they walk past, others kissing their arses any chance they get. Dodge a couple of prosecutions because nobody will talk, or somebody down the food chain takes the fall, all of a sudden they think they're invincible, and that's when they get greedy, that's when they get careless. They think they can take on the bigger guys, think that just being young and hungry gives them some kind of edge, forgetting that a lot of folk have been young and hungry at some point; forgetting that the guys at the top are where they are—and have stayed where they are—for a reason.

Jai made no attempt to get up, most likely in case it was interpreted as flight or resistance, but just as possibly because he couldn't. He kept his eyes down, but they were still scanning back and forth, checking the positions of his captors. They stood in a triangle around him, Big Fall just climbing out from the front cab to make it a square.

It was the arrival of a fifth that was going to

2

answer all his questions. If Jai thought he was broken and defeated before, then he was a proper Pollyanna compared to how he'd feel when the self-styled Gallowhaugh Godfather made his entrance.

He was just arriving now, in fact. He'd followed the van at a necessarily careful distance, but now that he'd parked, he was deliberately taking his time, making their captive wait. Making *everyone* wait. Prick. If conceit was consumption, Wee Sacks there would be dead.

He slammed the door of his big BMW to herald his arrival, alert their prisoner that there was more to this than he had already understood, as much as you can understand anything when you've been ragdolled around the back of a van by three guys battering your melt in. Then he walked across slowly, taking the long way around the side of the van to further protract the anticipation before he would make his presence known to the poor bastard quivering in the dirt.

Wullie detested him, always had. Gallowhaugh Godfather? Gallowhaugh Grandfather more like. All right, the guy was only about forty, but he was always wearing gear that was too young for him, which had the paradoxical effect of making him look older even than his scarred and lived-in face would indicate; a face you would never get sick of kicking.

Wullie resented being here, dancing to the jumped-up old throwback's tune. It was one thing playing along to keep the peace, but that wee cock just loved this all too much. The bastard should watch his step, see he didn't make the same mistake as his ex-pal lying on the deck. Seemed to

3

think he was gangland royalty because he'd been around the game for a while, saw himself as 'old school' and somehow more respectable than the new breed. He shouldn't forget who was the biggest gang in this city. Just because they found it expedient or mutually profitable to help you out didn't mean you could take liberties or start kidding yourself about the nature of that relationship. Wee Sacks thought Big Fall had come to him because he ran Gallowhaugh. Truth was, Wee Sacks ran Gallowhaugh because it suited Fall to allow him to.

That the wee shite had insisted on being here tonight said it all. Small-man behaviour. He should have risen above it, just been content in the knowledge that the problem was being taken care of, discreetly too, ensuring no uncomfortable fallout. Not Wee Sacks, though. He was taking unnecessary risks simply because he had to let Jai here know he'd got the last word, that it had been trying to put one over on the mighty Godfather that had sealed his fate.

He wanted to sing when he was winning.

Jai lifted his head at the sound of this unexpected late arrival. The intended response was etched large upon his bloodied features: a mixture of confusion and despair as he tried to work out how this was possible then calculated the implications for his own chances. He said nothing, incredulity at the revelation of this unholy alliance giving way to a grim resignation as the true nature of things made itself unforgivingly clear. Jai thought he was the one who had been fly, doing secret deals with his boss's enemies, but now he was seeing who was truly fly, and why his boss was the boss.

Jai truly, inescapably, knew the score, and that should have been enough. But not for Wee Sacks. He pulled out a gun, even though that part was meant to be left to Big Fall's crew. He was using it as a prop, milking Jai's fear as he started spelling everything out, starting with a potted history of their relationship so that he could ham up his claims of hurt at Jai's betrayal.

He held the gun to Jai's forehead. Jai closed his eyes, as though he could shut out what was to come. He squeezed them tighter and tighter as the moment endured and the shot didn't come, tears eventually seeping from them as he broke down. Then the wee prick took the gun away again and started talking some more, further elaborating upon his indignation. He was getting too much from this to have done with it quickly, although not in some sadistically frivolous way. There was boiling fury in him, incredulous outrage at Jai's temerity. It was as though this moment was not reparation enough, killing him merely the once insufficient vengeance. He would kill him over and over if he could, and this was as close as he could get to doing that. He was an angry wee dog, barking all the louder in rage against his size.

Fall wasn't having it, though. The big man had heard enough. He took out his own gun and barged the yappy terrier aside.

'Don't kick the arse oot it,' he warned, and shot Jai through the head.

Jai slumped backwards, his head haloed on the ground by a spreading arc of blood as the shot reverberated like a ricochet around the walls of the quarry. It seemed to echo back upon itself,

5

sustained like a feedback loop; then, as the report
of the gunshot slowly faded, Wullie became aware
that within the reverberation was a second sound:
a human scream.

It wasn't a healthy sign that it took his initial
surprise to remind him that most normal people
still found this kind of thing shocking.

JASMINE SCREWS UP

'Subject vehicle is taking a right right right on to
Byres Road. Foxtrot Five make ground. I'm letting
him run straight on at the lights before subject
becomes able to draw my face from memory.'

'Yes yes,' she replied, feeling her heart speed up
far faster than the little Renault was accelerating.

She had eyeball now.

This time, Jasmine Sharp vowed to herself, I
won't screw up.

She watched Uncle Jim's car—no, *Delta Seven*'s
car—veer left ahead of the junction, heading west
along Dumbarton Road, and found herself
suddenly closer than she intended behind the blue
Citroën minivan. She had to step on the brakes
quite stiffly, her anxious literal response to the
'make ground' command causing her to forget that
the subject would be slowing to a stop as he waited
to turn right. She hoped he wasn't looking in the
rear-view, as nothing grabbed the attention quite
like the appearance that you weren't going to stop
in time, especially with this guy.

Jasmine watched him indicate, almost
hypnotised by the blinking light, focusing on it so

that she wasn't tempted to look at his rear-view mirror.

It took seven or eight oscillations before she realised that she'd neglected to indicate herself. She corrected her omission, feeling as she always did on this job that she had too many balls in the air, and that her efforts to get the procedure right were in danger of causing her to forget to take care of the basics. It was bad enough when she was the secondary in a two-car surveillance, but when it was she who had eyes-on, she kept expecting at any second to stall the engine, if not smash into a lamp post, pedestrian or double-decker bus she had failed to notice due to her attention being so singularly directed at the subject vehicle.

I won't screw up, she vowed. I won't screw up. Not again. Not like the previous vehicle surveillance, in Paisley last week, when she lost the subject in the cinema car park. Not like Duntocher the week before, when she managed to get burned by following the subject twice around a roundabout. And not like Monday. Sweet Jesus, no, please, not like Monday. She'd be feeling embarrassed about that when she was vegetating in some old folk's home, in her dotage: embarrassed for herself and mortified about how badly she'd let Jim down. She could feel her cheeks burn just thinking about it.

The minivan slowed and it looked like he was about to pull in and park. He was a jammy sod finding a space on that stretch of Byres Road at this time of day, which meant the chances of her finding one an acceptable distance ahead were vanishingly small. She could be looking at setting a new personal best for eyeball time prior to losing a

7

subject, at well under a minute. Not entirely her fault, circumstances outwith her control and all that, but having blown surveillances as often as she had, even genuine excuses rang hollow.

Oh, thank you. Magic. He wasn't parking: it was the car in front of his that had been jammy enough to find a space, and he'd been forced to stop while it reversed laboriously into the gap.

She sighed, trying not to dwell upon how ill-suited she must be for this job if she could get so het up over every minor or even just potential hiccup.

She reached down and pressed the push-to-talk button mounted on the gearstick, the corresponding microphone embedded in the sun visor.

'Uncle Jim . . . I mean Delta Seven, permission?'

'Delta Seven, go ahead. You don't need to ask permission when you're eyeball. And for the umpteenth time, it's your own call sign you say, not mine.'

'Sorry. I mean Foxtrot Five, sorry. Just wondering where you are.'

'My *location* is Hyndland Street, north towards Highburgh Road, where I'll be hoping to make ground and re-obtain the subject vehicle when it reaches the lights.'

'Yes yes,' she said, though it was his reminder that she had once again failed to use appropriate terminology that she heard most loud and clear. How much patience could the man have? He deserved better: much better.

'Subject is approaching the junction with University Avenue,' she relayed. 'Lights are red and he's not indicating. Anticipate subject going

8

straight on straight on straight on in the direction of Great Western Road.'

Straight on straight on straight on. That couldn't be correct, surely?

Her doubt precipitated a gut-tightening recollection of Monday. A disaster on that scale usually prompted a telethon.

It hadn't been a difficult task. It was an 'establish', nothing more: the proverbial barn door from six feet. Monday's subject had been a small businessman who had done a runner while in heavy debt to one particular supplier. Rather than declare bankruptcy and go through insolvency proceedings, he had flown the coop in the knowledge that the supplier was in major financial difficulties arising largely from this unpaid debt. Put simply, if he stayed out of sight long enough, the supplier would go bust and his debt would disappear.

The supplier had made inquiries of his own, but had passed the matter on to professional investigators Galt Linklater, in order to ensure that all evidence obtained was legal, above board and admissible in any court action. Galt Linklater had in turn subcontracted part of the job to Sharp Investigations, as they often did when their caseload exceeded their personnel.

Sharp Investigations was known less formally, to Jasmine at least, as Uncle Jim. He was an ex-cop, who had set up as a private investigator upon his retirement from the force. He'd been offered jobs with a few agencies, Galt Linklater among them, but for 'reasons of professional experience' that he was reluctant to elaborate upon, he preferred to be his own man. Sharp Investigations had thus always

9

been a solo operation, and a successful one at that. How its scope and effectiveness might be improved by employing a nervous and clumsy young woman with no experience and even less natural aptitude was something Jasmine was still waiting to discover.

'Foxtrot Five. Lights through to green no deviation Byres Road,' she said. *That* was it. Why did these things come out right when she wasn't thinking about them?

'Delta Seven,' Jim replied. 'I am approaching the junction of Byres Road and Highburgh Road. Lights are red. I will be baulked.'

The fugitive businessman from Monday's ghastliness had been named Pete Harper. He was from Kilwinning but had disappeared from his home six weeks before, and according to his landlord he had cancelled the direct debit that paid his rent. The supplier had provided a list of possible addresses where he might be lying low. Galt Linklater needed an establish: proof that he was living at a certain address, best obtained by doorstepping the guy with a hidden video camera recording the happy event.

This kind of job, Jim had explained to Jasmine, was precisely why he needed her on the firm.

'Guy like this is going to be skittish at the best of times,' he said. 'So he'll be hyper-suspicious of anybody asking questions while he's doing his invisible. He'll smell polis coming off me from a hundred yards out. Sees me through his window or the peephole in his front door and he's not even going to answer the bell. That's why Galt Linklater farmed it out: all their guys have ex-polis stamped on their foreheads. Fresh-faced young woman, on

10

the other hand, different story.'

The logic was inarguably solid, but despite that, it just sounded to Jasmine all the more like he was taking pains to avoid admitting the real reason he'd taken her on.

'Delta . . . I mean Foxtrot Five. Subject is indicating right right right on to Great George Street but is blocked by oncoming traffic.'

Shit. She should have said 'offside indication, held due to oncoming traffic'. She was supposed to be practised at learning lines, for God's sake.

Strictly speaking, there was no need to keep confirming call signs on a two-man follow, but Jim had insisted upon it to get her into the habit. At this rate, she'd have it down by around this time next year.

'Delta Seven, yes yes. Making ground. I can take eyeball when he turns.'

Looking conspicuously unlike a cop or an ex-cop, and bearing no resemblance whatsoever to a private investigator (particularly in the way she practised her new-found profession of private investigation), it had been Jasmine's job on Monday to hit the front doors.

It had happened at the second address. The first address was a dud: the ex-girlfriend who was meant to be living there had sold up two years back. Jim had had his doubts about it in any case, but they'd given it a shot as it was en route to the place on which they had the soundest intel. Technically, the second address was actually addresses two through ten, as it was a three-storey tenement in Partick and they only had the number of the building, not the flat.

'Foxtrot Five. Subject vehicle has turned right

right right and is proceeding west on Great George Street. Subject vehicle now indicating offside. Over to you, Delta Seven.'

'Delta Seven confirms the eyeball. Subject vehicle entering Lillybank Gardens, which is a one-way crescent. He's looking to park.'

'Yes yes.'

As Jim had explained, you need a story when you're going around knocking on strangers' doors, asking after people who don't want to be found. Most people will just tell you—truthfully—that they don't know who you're talking about, but occasionally they'll want to know why you're asking, because they *are* the subject, or because they know the subject personally. You need to keep it simple, avoid extraneous detail and extrapolation. It was much the same principle as something she'd been taught at drama school, regarding acting on film or television: never do anything you can't repeat precisely for ten more takes.

Jim had fed her a solid, time-proven script that he assured her would serve her for most occasions. She was looking for someone who had served in the navy alongside her father. The old man had retired a few months back and was trying to organise a reunion among the old shipmates with whom he had lost touch. When she eyeballed the subject and he confirmed his name, her out was that she had the wrong Peter Harper, this one being evidently too young. Sorry to trouble you, then out the door with the establish committed to the hidden video camera's electronic memory.

After a catalogue of screw-ups, Jasmine had been determined to get this establish right, particularly as it was a subcontract from the firm that provided so much of Jim's business. She decided it would be wise to plan contingencies, and concocted a second, back-up story to be on the safe side.

'Delta Seven. Subject vehicle turning left left left into the car park Ashton Lane. That's a stop stop stop. I have one vehicle for cover. Foxtrot Five park and deploy.'

'Foxtrot Five. Yes yes.'

The address given by the supplier had been number 315. There was a main-door flat at 313, occupying the whole of the ground floor, so the first three possibilities were on the level above it, accessed by the close next door. Jasmine had rung the doorbell on the left-hand flat, which was answered by a hunched old woman, eyeing her suspiciously through the narrow crack permitted by her security chain, a Westie yapping and panting excitedly at her ankles.

'No, never heard of him,' the old woman answered.

She got the same at the middle flat from a harassed-looking mum with a baby over one shoulder and a streak of fresh creamy sick across the other. There was no reply at the right-hand flat, so she climbed the stairs and started again on the next landing, where she struck out for a response at the first two doors. She'd try them again on the way back down, just in case.

How did she find herself here, she'd asked herself, as she rang another bell and stood waiting for a response: knocking on doors to empty flats in search of a man she didn't know, who didn't want to be found? It was like something out of Beckett.

Where along the road had she ended up in this lane and missed the turn-off for a place in a regional rep or even a half-decent touring company? Well, she knew the answer to that one, didn't she? No mystery there.

She was about to ascend to the next landing when her reverie was interrupted by the door being opened. Her surprise at this belated response was slightly jarring, but nothing like as jarring as being confronted by the subject. Pete Harper, despite being a slippery customer, was evidently no master of disguise, having gone to precisely no trouble to alter his appearance from the two-year-old photo the client had provided Galt Linklater with.

'Delta Seven. Subject is out out out of the vehicle and walking still walking towards Ashton Lane. Foxtrot Five confirm you are deployed on foot in a position to follow.'

'No. I mean: Foxtrot Five no no. Still trying to find a non-permit-holder space.'

'For God's sake, just pull in any . . . Radio silence.'

Jasmine pulled her hand away from the PTT button as if stung by it. Radio silence. Subject must be close to Jim. She wasn't going to push the button, wasn't going to forget procedure, wasn't going to screw up.

Harper had exhibited an agitated air that instantly put her in a state of unease: the demeanour of a man who had already given her two last warnings to stop annoying him. He seemed to be almost buzzing with latent aggression, and she felt as though he was staring right through her, able to read her purpose and intentions as clearly as though they were printed on cue cards in front

14

of him. It struck her with full force that she wasn't just doorstepping a stranger under false pretences, but doorstepping a stranger of whom it could reasonably be inferred, from the very purpose of her visit, that he was a bit of a crook. The possibility that this bristling individual might do her physical harm seemed palpable; further upsetting him strongly contra-indicated.

'Can I help you?' he asked in a monotone grunt, Jasmine interpreting the enquiry as sincere only insofar as he was wondering whether she might require assistance in being imminently strangled and buried.

'Ehm, it's, well, sorry to trouble you, I'm, ehm, I'm looking for a man . . .'

Harper's eyes narrowed in deeper scrutiny and his nostrils flared. Jasmine's knees started to feel wobbly.

'He was, ehm, you see, my dad retired and, ehm, he was in the navy, and he was trying to get in touch with some of the guys he served with, but no, I can see that you're too young, so you must just have the same name as the guy I'm—'

'I haven't told you my name. Who is it you think I am? Where did you get this address?'

Oh God oh God oh God oh God.

Jasmine remembered that the guy was lying low here, and the whole point was that nobody had him listed at this address. It suddenly seemed imperative to give him a different name, in order to allay his suspicions and extricate herself from the situation as quickly as possible.

'I, ehm, the name I had was, ehm . . . Hayley,' she said, the first name that came to mind. Then she realised it was a girl's name. 'William. William

15

Hayley.'

'That's not me,' Harper said.

He began to close the door again, which was when it body-slammed her that she had just completely blown the establish.

'Oh no, wait, Peter Harper,' she blurted.

'What?' he demanded, now looking as suspicious as he was annoyed.

'I'm also looking for a Peter Harper.'

'Also? A second ago it was William Hayley.'

'That was the name . . . I mean, there's more than one person I'm looking for . . .'

'Aye, and you just said I'm too young to be who you're looking for, so why are you patting more names at me? Who gave you this address?'

Jasmine was collapsing so completely inside that she feared for a moment she was about to just burst into tears. She had to hold it together. She thought of her back-up story and grabbed on to it like it was a branch in the rapids.

'Well, you see, I've moved into this new flat and the girl there split up with her boyfriend, and there was mail for him and she doesn't want to see him so she asked me to track him down to wherever he's moved, and see, it's his name that's Peter Harper, so . . .'

'You're looking for your flatmate's ex-boyfriend *as well as* your dad's old shipmate?'

Jasmine felt her eyes widen involuntarily, perhaps to take in the full scale of the catastrophe that was unfolding before them.

'Yes, but I got mixed up, and the first one, Hayley Williams . . .'

'You mean William Hayley,' he said, almost helpfully.

16

'William Hayley, yes, I shouldn't have been asking about him here, because he lives in Hyndland and that's where I'm going next.'

'After you've tracked down your flatmate's boyfriend.'

Jasmine's throat went so dry, she couldn't even mumble a mortified 'yes'. It must have been the fierce heat radiating from her cheeks that parched her.

'Peter Harper, you said his name was?'

She nodded meekly.

'Never heard of him,' Harper said, then slammed the door.

Jasmine pulled over into a permit-holders-only space, figuring that a parking ticket constituted a low level of collateral damage compared to her track record.

'Delta Seven. Subject just walked past as I was getting out of my car and gave me a definite funny.'

'Are you burned?'

'Just a bit warm. I avoided eye contact, but I'll need to hang well back. Need you to get eyeball ASAP. Subject is walking still walking along Ruthven Lane in the direction of Great George Street.'

'Copy that.'

'You mean yes yes.'

'Sorry sorry,' she offered.

Jasmine felt her legs become heavier as she spoke, precipitately burdened by so much responsibility. The subject had looked at Jim, given him a 'funny', and they could not afford to let this guy know he was under surveillance. It was all on her now. Jim wasn't burned—the subject hadn't

17

sussed that he was being tailed—but he would have to keep sufficient distance now that this was effectively a one-woman follow.

'It was a partial establish,' Jim had assured her on Monday as she blubbed in the passenger seat of his Peugeot, parked around the corner from the Partick tenement where she had so comprehensively failed to get Peter Harper to acknowledge his own name, while all but spelling out to him that he was under surveillance.

'We've confirmed where he's living, at least,' he went on. 'Albeit he'll probably now only be living there for the time it'll take to pack a bag and make a few phone calls.'

He gave her a smile, letting her know that he was saying this in good humour, although he wasn't joking.

'I'm so sorry,' she told him.

She had fallen apart the moment Harper looked at her. It reminded her of the first time she got called upon by her teacher to answer a question in primary school. The establish hadn't gone quite as badly as that, but it clearly wasn't a great result when the best thing she could say about it was that at least this time she didn't pee herself.

Didn't say much for her acting aspirations either. For what was the job Jim had set her, if not acting? For goodness' sake, it was one of the fig leaves he had given her in order that they could both pretend this wasn't a charity gig: that he needed someone who could act. He'd even provided a script. Unfortunately, Pete Harper took about half a second to penetrate the fourth wall, and nothing she had learned in college was able to rescue her.

18

'Don't worry about it,' Jim assured her, handing her a bunch of paper hankies. 'It's early days. Nobody just clicks into this first time.'

Poor Jim. He was so kind, so generous and so fooling nobody. He kept claiming he needed her, but it was obvious that if he genuinely did need an assistant, he'd be better with a personnel deficit than with Jasmine on board. She was the one who needed him: since her mum died, she'd had nobody else.

'Delta Seven. Subject is walking still walking, approaching Cresswell Lane, and I am struggling to maintain line of sight. Do you have eyeball?'

'Yes yes,' she confirmed, having just turned the corner back on to Great George Street.

Following her mother's death, Jasmine had spent months living in a state of numb subsistence, losing track of the hours, the days and even the weeks. She barely left the house and ceased to function according to normal rhythms, finding herself staring into darkness on the living-room settee far into the night and sound asleep on it throughout the day. She gave no thought to the future, unable to visualise herself doing anything other than crying, sleeping and staring into the unanswering blackness.

At times she could barely remember being the girl who had once known what she wanted to do with all the life that was in front of her. Or rather, she could recall the memories, but they felt like they had belonged to someone else. She felt utterly disconnected from that person, as though she had died too and now Jasmine was this other being who only shared her past, not her path to the future. In this respect, she believed bereavement must be easier if you had a job, a career, a husband and kids, as all those clichés about life going on would apply. There would be a template for how to spend your days: commitments and obligations to supersede the desire to pull the covers back over your head and stay in bed for ever. You'd know what to do, even if you didn't much feel like doing it.

She didn't have a life yet. There was no saddle for her to get back into.

Jasmine had just started her final year at drama college when Mum got her shocking, unreal diagnosis. Pancreatic cancer: late-presenting, fast-spreading.

Jasmine never knew her father. He had died when she was just a baby, and her mum had never married, never even lived with anyone else. They only had each other, and suddenly they only had months left together.

Jasmine dropped out. She had to move back in with Mum in Edinburgh, had to be close, had to be home. She didn't think about her education or her ambitions. They became instantly irrelevant, abandoned as unnecessary baggage she could not afford to carry on this most arduous of journeys.

When she contemplated them again, after Mum was gone, it was like happening upon a box of toys that had meant a world of pleasure and possibility to her as a child, but held no appeal to an adult harshly schooled in the realities of the world. The same strangeness had assailed her when she re-entered her flat back in Glasgow, the trappings of the existence she had suddenly suspended all still right where she left them: the *Mary Celeste* two flights up on Victoria Road.

Very gradually, however, she had begun to accept that, despite her devastation, she was nonetheless a twenty-year-old woman who needed to construct some kind of life for herself. As well as the long-term future, there were the immediate practical considerations of earning a wage and paying the rent. Mum wasn't there any more to hold her hand and wipe her tears. Even if she had been, this was the point when she had to make her own way in the world, and it struck her harshly that her previous choices had left her in a position whereby there were very few things she was cut out or qualified to do. Acting, therefore, quickly recovered its lustre, though she ceased thinking in terms of vague, dreamy ambitions and more in terms of a purposeful way to fill her days and score a pay cheque at the end of them.

Good job for her nobody else had the same genius idea.

'Foxtrot Five confirms the eyeball. Subject is walking still walking along Cresswell Lane in no apparent hurry. Stopping to look in a shop window ahead.'

'He's probably looking out for me. Overtake him if you have to, then pause for some window-shopping yourself.'

'Foxtrot Five. Yes yes.'

She halted and stared into the window of a craft and jewellery shop, her focus on the reflections in the glass rather than the goods beyond it. She was angled so that she could see the subject, but caught a glimpse of herself, one of those sideways snapshots that reveals all the more for its brevity and obliqueness. She was attired as smartly as Jim insisted, in a jacket and trousers like some proper, grown-up professional, but all she could see was a little girl dressing up as something she was not, for play. Short, slight, a little underfed of late, the clothes wearing her rather than the other way around. Her hair was swept back by an Alice band for better peripheral vision, but at a cost of more starkly exposing her face, the myriad sun-prompted freckles upon it making her look about thirteen. She was twenty. When she *was* thirteen, she thought she'd be looking back at a woman's face, something more like her mum's: not this eternal teenager who was going to get carded in pubs until the year 2020.

The subject started moving again, albeit at a dawdling pace, Jasmine about fifteen yards behind. Walking down the street alone, ostensibly talking to herself, she was grateful for the advent of Bluetooth and hands-free kits, wondering how her predecessors remained inconspicuous on a follow while updating their colleagues over the radio.

Foxtrot Five: that was the call sign Jim had given her. It was in reference to her birthday, February fifth, but it had taken on a different significance for Jasmine. It made her think of *Fox Force Five*, the cancelled TV pilot mentioned by Uma Thurman's character Mia in *Pulp Fiction*. It had been aspiring actress Mia's one and only role: the big break that came to nothing.

The reality of finding work had nagged at the back of her mind at college, as it did everybody, but it was always a worry for the future, something she couldn't afford to dwell upon, otherwise what was the point of training?

Dropping out of the course hadn't done much to help her chances. Nonetheless, failing to finish a

22

drama degree wasn't like dropping out of medical school: if somebody liked her audition, they weren't going to ask to see any certificates. The problem was, by dropping out of college she had also dropped off the radar, losing touch and losing contacts. People had heard what happened—yes, poor girl—but they didn't just think she had quit her course: they seemed to regard her as having dropped out of existence, given up for good.

It was slow going to even get auditions. You had to be animated beyond the point of pushy in your networking in order to know where the openings might be. So far she had notched up four callbacks but no jobs.

The only glimmer of light was a director called Charlotte Queen and her company, Fire Curtain. Jasmine had got a callback from Charlotte after auditioning for Fire Curtain's touring production of *Top Girls*. She didn't get the part, but Charlotte said she might be right for Miranda in the production of *The Tempest* that they were planning for the Edinburgh Fringe in a year's time. Okay, it would probably be in a converted garage in Newington, but it was more true of acting than any other job that it was easier to get work when you were in work. If she got the part, then as well as a pay packet, it was four weeks of exposure, increasing the chance that someone might see her and think she'd be right for another role.

Charlotte Queen was already something of a legend in Scottish theatre. She had dropped out of drama school too, though in her case it wasn't personal tragedy that precipitated her exit, but impatience, as she told interviewers. She felt restricted, she claimed, and decided to start her own company at the age of twenty-two. She was, by all accounts, a force of nature, though some observers noted that it didn't hurt that her dad was Hamish Queen, London West End director and impresario: meaning she was as connected as she was rich. That said, Charlotte had easier paths open to her that she decided not to take. She had partly grown up at her family's Highland retreat, where she saw touring shows by the RSC playing in local community centres and sports halls. She reasoned that the local punters weren't simply turning out because it was the RSC. To an extent they were, but only because the brand guaranteed certain production values. Charlotte believed there was an untapped provincial audience for live theatre, and after a shaky start she was vindicated, as Fire Curtain became a popular and critically esteemed touring outfit.

Jasmine knew it was a big deal to have made any kind of impression on Charlotte. She was reputed to be flaky, capricious and egotistical, but if she took to you, she would draw out the best of your abilities and make you look brilliant on stage. It was said she truly valued her actors, made them feel magnificent, but that their job was always to be remarkable planets in orbit around her sun; that she had an indisputable eye for recognising talents, but only insofar as envisioning how they would augment her own. Jasmine didn't care. Getting an audition for Fire Curtain had been a boost, getting a callback massive, and the possibility of a part in their Fringe show so tantalising that she couldn't allow herself to think about it past ten at night or she would never get to sleep.

However, it was only a maybe, and it was a

maybe for *next* August. She had to get real about the here and now, which was where Uncle Jim had stepped in.

Jim was her mum's cousin, so not strictly speaking Jasmine's uncle, but that was what she had called him since toddlerhood. He and Mum had always been close, but not exactly in each other's lives all the time. Nobody was in Jim's life, in fact, largely down to him letting it become consumed by work. His police career had contributed greatly to the break-up of his marriage, and when he got maudlin after a few whiskies, he would confess to having failed his wife and in particular his three kids by always being busy at work when he should have been there for them. He was a grandfather now, five times over, and had vowed to make himself more available to help out looking after the young ones, but the demands of running a one-man business had him breaking his promises all over again.

It was therefore a double-edged attempt to do the right thing that had led him to employ Jasmine. He knew she needed a job and he deeply wanted to help out in his cousin Beth's absence. If he could train her up, he explained, then once she got the stabilisers off, it would free him up more often to see his family.

It was an honourable sentiment, Jasmine thought, and a far more convincing way of selling the job to her than his claim that an out-of-work actress with no experience was just what his business was lacking.

'Delta Seven. Look, I've just had a very important call about another job. I'm no use on this one with the subject giving me that funny. Can

I leave this in your capable hands?'

Oh God, please, no, no.

'Yes yes.'

She remembered the things she had told herself when Jim first took her on, barely a couple of months back. He had explained that this wasn't a Saturday job for pocket money, and required commitment. He knew she was hoping to find work in acting but assured her that once she was trained up, it would be a good fallback when she was 'resting'. He was smart that way: he wasn't asking her to choose, not offering a 'real' job to help her get over her silly ideas.

It would do to tide her over, she decided. It was money in her pocket, and it was just for now. It was better than bar work: it paid more, and it involved a kind of acting. Valuable experience as well, good for the CV. Yeah: all the things every would-be actor probably told themselves when they started the job they ended up doing for life.

She wondered whether this fear—that before she knew it she'd be thirty and still doing this job 'just for now'—was what was causing her to screw up. Subconsciously, did she want to fail so that Jim would take the choice out of her hands?

No, she wouldn't deliberately do anything to let Jim down. She just sucked, was all, which meant she was in an impossible situation: landed with a job she couldn't do but couldn't do without.

The subject stopped again. She didn't figure him for a window-shopper, particularly in a lane specialising largely in interior furnishings and decidedly girlie knick-knacks, so there was a strong possibility that he was checking his six. The likelihood was that he was on the lookout for Jim, but with his suspicion piqued, she couldn't afford to be noticed. Without a back-up to take over the follow, the procedure was to walk past and stop to look in another window, waiting for him to overtake again. She kept her head down as she passed him, but in her need for reassurance that she wasn't being noticed, she stole a glance to see where he was looking—just as he turned to check back along the lane. Their eyes met. She kept walking, feeling her cheeks burn and her stomach leaden with that familiar feeling of having blown it.

Jim had this sun-yellowed cartoon on the wall of his cluttered and poky little office in Arden on the south side. It showed a geeky-looking guy standing in his place as part of an orchestra. He was holding a cymbal in his right hand, and in a thought bubble he was saying to himself: 'This time I won't screw up, I won't screw up, I won't screw up.' It was only when you looked more closely that you noticed that in his left hand he was holding nothing at all. It was captioned: 'Roger screws up.'

That was how Jasmine felt every day on the job. It felt like the harder she tried, the more she found new ways to blunder. Even now, as she coached herself to stay focused, as she determined not to screw up, she feared that simply by doing so she was diverting her own attention from the fact that she was missing a cymbal.

She had to rationalise, though. Their eyes had met, but it wasn't strictly speaking a funny. She wasn't burned, but she was on a yellow card. She had been noticed, so he'd recognise her if he found her looking again, but right now she was just a girl who'd caught his eye, and he hers. He was kind of leery anyway: he probably got clocked eyeing girls

27

every time he walked down a street.

She crossed the lane and looked in a window of her own, her pulse rising as she waited, hoping, to see him pass in the reflection, all the more desperate to get a result because Jim had been forced to leave it in her 'capable' hands.

They were running out of time and running out of chances on this particular case, and it wouldn't only be Jim she'd be letting down if she dropped the ball today.

'The subject's name is Robert Croft,' Jim had explained to her. 'He's a thirty-seven-year-old plasterer from Clarkston. The client is Hayden-Murray Solicitors on behalf of Mrs Dorothy Muldoon, a retired widow from Giffnock. In December last year, Mrs Muldoon runs into the back of Croft's Escort van at a roundabout in Pollokshaws. Minimal damage, she accepts it's her fault, expects to pay the excess on a wee bit of panel-beating and a skoosh of spray paint. Unfortunately the observant Mr Croft has noted that Mrs Muldoon has run into him in a Lexus, and the cogs have started to turn inside his grasping wee heid.

'Couple of weeks later, she gets a notice saying she's being sued for long-term loss of earnings because Mr Croft sustained an injury in the accident and can no longer wield his trowel. The letter is from a company called Scotiaclaim.'

'Is that the ones that have that tacky advert on the telly? The personal injury mob?'

'Aye. And this shower would give ambulance-chasers a bad name. They advertise on daytime TV partly because it's cheaper but mainly because their target market is shiftless bastards who believe

28

something's owing to them despite sitting on their fat arses all day when other folk are busy at work. Soon as I heard that's who was representing him, it told me all I needed to know. Suffice to say, Hayden-Murray are sceptical as to the veracity of Mr Croft's claim, especially as they have learned he has successfully made a similar claim before. Unfortunately, that's not admissible in court, but it tells us plenty.'

'What about doctors? Doesn't he need a medical report?'

'Oh, dodgy lawyers often have pals who are dodgy doctors. They can always source a diagnosis favourable to their position. But even if Hayden-Murray are able to secure an independent examination, Croft will have been made aware—if he wasnae aware already—of how to cite some conveniently non-specific and non-testable symptoms.'

The court date was fast approaching, and so far they had nothing. They had tailed him twice before: once being the occasion Jasmine lost the subject in that cinema car park in Paisley. On the other, he had raised their hopes by going into a health club: some footage of him swimming or working the weights would be all they needed. It turned out he was seeing a physiotherapist, most likely as another witness who could testify to having treated his nebulous injury. The only plus was that up until now he didn't appear to be aware that he was under surveillance, though he was bound to have been informed by Scotiaclaim that it was a possibility. As it stood, there was still a chance, albeit slim, that they could catch him doing something he shouldn't be.

'It's Last Chance Saloon now,' Jim had confessed. 'With a very strong possibility that he's playing it canny and we won't get a thing.'

'Do you still get paid?'

'Aye, but it burns to see a guy like this get away with it. Plus, if you don't get results, the lawyers will say they understand, but the likelihood is you won't get hired again.'

Jasmine watched Croft's reflection pass across the window, this time resisting the temptation to look at his face for assurance that he wasn't looking back. She turned her head slightly, enough to keep him in her peripheral vision until it was safe to commence walking again. She allowed him a longer lead than before, conscious of having had that almost-funny.

'Subject is turning left left left on to Cresswell Street.' She kept up the commentary even though Jim was off the follow. She was recording her progress on the bodycam, so it was partly for the benefit of the tape (or rather, memory card) and partly just for practice.

Jasmine felt anxiety seize her as she approached the end of the pedestrianised lane, in anticipation of what she might see—or more pertinently not see—when she turned on to Cresswell Street. It must be a documented phenomenon, she thought: the foot-follower's fear of the corner. It was so piercingly acute that in recent days she'd been experiencing it even when she wasn't on a follow, turns on busy streets becoming a Pavlovian trigger for a tightness in her chest.

When she turned this particular corner, the sight that met her truly was grounds for dismay. It wasn't that she'd lost the subject: Croft was visible twenty yards ahead, approaching the junction with Byres Road. It was what else she could see. Charlotte Queen was sitting at a table outside a deli-café on Cresswell Street, she and two friends enjoying the atypically summery weather by sipping their coffees al fresco, and she was looking Jasmine's way. Their eyes met: only fleetingly, and at a distance, but it was definitely reciprocal.

Croft was almost at Byres Road, a T-junction, and by some distance the busiest street in the West End. The lead she had given him was acceptable on back streets, but very risky on a bustling main drag. Making ground was strongly advisable; allowing him to gain any more seconds potentially calamitous. She had to hurry, but she couldn't do anything conspicuous like run.

She increased her walking pace and locked her gaze on Croft, acting as though she had barely registered the group outside the café. Charlotte had only glanced at her for a moment, so there was every chance that she didn't recognise her, or didn't remember her out of context.

She was five yards from the table. Brisk and purposeful, come on, focused and in a hurry, mind *obviously* elsewhere, *clearly* not ignoring the brilliant but flaky, capricious and egotistical . . .

'Jasmine? Jasmine Sharp?'

It felt like time stood still. Jasmine was suddenly presented, in one precipitate moment, with making a decision that could lay down a path before her for the rest of her life.

She knew she could not stop to talk. Nor did she have time to explain, even with the utmost brevity, precisely *why* she couldn't stop to talk. A quick 'oh, hi' as she walked on by would also look

31

unacceptably dismissive when she was being personally hailed by someone well used to having people in her thrall.

It was a stark, unavoidable choice between losing the subject, leaving Jim with nothing to give Hayden-Murray, and blanking—in front of her friends, no less—the one person who could yet offer Jasmine an acting break.

Jasmine looked deep into herself in that moment, asking not merely what she really wanted, but what she truly believed she could be.

She continued—walking still walking—saying nothing as she passed Charlotte's table, so close she could smell the fumes from their espressos, all the time keeping her eyes on the corner. There were tears forming in them by the time she had turned right on to Byres Road. It took her a moment through the throng and the mist of tears, but she could see Croft ahead, passing the bollards at Vinicombe Street. She picked up the pace.

'Making ground,' she reported, swallowing. 'Subject walking still walking towards Great Western Road.'

This job was real. It was paying a wage. She couldn't be a little girl any more. Mum was gone. Dreams were gone.

She kept walking.

Croft was approaching the junction of Byres and Great Western Roads, where Oran Mor looked across at the Botanics; Oran Mor, where, when she could afford it, she spent lunchtime enjoying A Play, A Pie and A Pint for a tenner, telling herself that one day she'd be the one on stage.

Croft glanced back before reaching the corner, just a casual look but potentially suspicious.

Jasmine not only got her head down but checked her pace and stepped out of sight behind a gangling art student toting a big black portfolio. She was already envying him his aspirations, the fact that he still had them.

The traffic on Great Western Road bustled left and right across her path directly ahead. Another corner, another pang of anxiety about what was around it, the dread possibilities of which had just been given a whole new depth of scope back on Cresswell Street. Everything was simpler now, though: she only had one thing left to lose. Around this corner, as long as she saw Croft, then she could live with that.

Unless, of course, it was his face she saw, coming straight towards her.

Shit.

He had performed a reciprocal, doubled back: always a sure sign that the subject suspects he's being tailed. He was looking right at her too; an unqualified funny, which she promptly escalated into direct eye contact: as in can't-look-away, rabbit-in-the-headlights eye contact.

She was burned liked a vampire on a sunlounger. At noon. In the desert.

Verbal challenge coming too, by the looks of it. Oh God, what if he got violent? Jim was miles away by now.

As he opened his mouth to speak, Jasmine got in ahead of him.

'You're a plasterer, aren't you?' she blurted in her panic: the only thing she could think to say.

It set him on the back foot for a moment, but only in a manner sufficient to prompt the obvious question.

'How do *you* know?' he demanded.

Jesus, why not tell him it's because she's working for a private investigator hired by Dorothy Muldoon's lawyers: she'd already given him everything else. How *would* she know?

Then inspiration struck.

'You did my auntie's kitchen. Don't know if you remember? It was on the south side, a wee semi. Used to be Artex on the ceiling and you smoothed it away.'

His brow wrinkled in concentration, searching his memory as she sold him a tale from her own. She didn't leave him to search long.

'I'm not stalking you or anything,' she added with a nervous laugh. 'It's just, when I saw you back there, it took me a minute to place you and then you were away. The thing is, I've moved into this flat with my boyfriend, up in Hyndland, and there was this damp problem, but thank God that's all sorted, fingers crossed.'

Suspicion was replaced on his face by confusion as she babbled away.

'Anyway, the living room's a state, so's the bedroom, they both need a whole new . . . I don't know what you call it.'

'A skim,' he prompted.

'Yeah. A new skim. But we just can't *get* anybody. They say they'll do it and then they don't turn up. I mean, they're quoting like a thousand pounds because it's two big rooms, high ceilings, and my boyfriend's happy to pay it just to get it done, but they still end up leaving you hanging. When I realised who you were back there, I just wondered if it was worth asking whether maybe you could do it? It would be cash in hand. Michael

34

withdrew it to pay this other guy who let us down.'

Croft was already nodding. She saw his eyes flash when she mentioned the price quoted, and if there was any question of him squirming on the hook, it evaporated with the words 'cash in hand'.

'Aye, I could manage that.'

'Could you do it for the same money?'

'Sure, aye. Sounds fair enough. Unless it's like a mansion or something.'

'I wish. But see, the other thing is when. After all this time, as you can imagine, we're just sick looking at it, so the sooner the better. I don't suppose you could manage next week?'

He glanced away a moment, calculating. He wasn't much of an actor.

'I'd have to move something, but I could manage next Monday.'

'Oh, thank you, so much,' she gushed, with not entirely fake sincerity. 'You've really bailed me out of a hole.'

They traded mobile numbers and she gave him the address. What she had from the bodycam was probably plenty, but if that wasn't enough, it would definitely sink him to turn up with all his kit next Monday at Jim's flat in Hyndland.

As she watched him walk away, continuing as he had originally intended along Great Western Road, she felt this almighty endorphin rush, which combined with everything else that had flooded her system over the past five minutes made her whole body thrum. Suddenly, everything seemed possible. She could do this job. Not only that, she could act: she could play a part under pressure, she could improvise, anything.

She found herself hurrying back along Byres

Road. She would join Charlotte and her pals at their table and explain. Charlotte would lap it up too: it was an amazing—and true—story, one that showed what a colourful character Jasmine was, someone with background and depth, someone who was acting on a razor's edge like none of them had ever experienced.

She broke into a jog, then almost a sprint, slaloming pedestrians, giggling to herself as she turned the corner on to Cresswell Street.

The table was empty. Charlotte and her friends had gone.

Of course.

Jasmine screws up.

WHODUNIT

'Mum, what does whodunit mean?' Duncan asked, as Catherine tucked his Ben 10 duvet tightly around his shoulders.

'I'll tell you in the morning. Time for you both to go back to sleep.'

'It's who *did* it,' corrected Fraser, fifteen months his junior and ever eager to imply that he was smarter than his big brother.

'I know it's who did it,' Duncan retorted with a tut. 'God, I knew that when I was a P3. That's why I'm asking why people talk about a whodunit. What does it mean?'

Amazing how garrulous they became in the middle of the bloody night, Catherine thought. You could ask them a dozen questions throughout the day and receive one-word answers, and as for what was happening at school, it was easier persuading suspects to open up in interviews than to get an expansive answer on that subject. Yet when the time drew near for lights out, or when they had managed to snag a parent in the small hours with the had-a-nightmare routine, they invariably became quite the little interlocutors, keen for all manner of broad discourse. Perhaps she should give it a shot down the cells.

She sighed. Sometimes a bit of chat at this time made them feel they'd got their money's worth and they'd go back to sleep without a fuss; other times, of course, you just whetted their appetites for more attention.

'It means a story about a murder, where the detectives have to work out who was responsible.'

'So why is it not who *did* it?' asked Fraser.

'Don't the detectives have to work out who did it in every murder?' enquired Duncan simultaneously.

'I don't know why people say "whodunit".' She answered Fraser first, knowing that his older brother tended to have a little more patience. 'I think it was the Americans that coined it.'

'They spell colour wrong too,' Fraser observed sagely.

'*Mum*,' Duncan insisted, growing dismayed at Fraser's success in diverting the conversation.

'Sorry, pet.'

'And favourite,' Fraser continued.

Catherine had to stifle a laugh, aware that she had better give Duncan an answer before he leapt across the gap between the beds and chinned his brother.

'You're right. The detectives have to establish

37

who was responsible for a murder, but it's not always a mystery. When it *is* a mystery, that's when the story is called a whodunit.'

'What about in real life? Is there a name for when it's a mystery?'

Aye, Catherine thought: a pain in the arse.

'Do you have to work out who done it, I mean who did it?' Fraser interrupted again. 'Is that your job, Mum?'

'Do you catch murderers?' Duncan trumped.

'Have you seen a dead body?' bid Fraser.

'Have you ever caught the wrong man?'

Catherine was actually relieved when she heard her mobile ring from her and Drew's bedroom across the hall, even though it had to be work calling, and even though she was technically still on holiday until tomorrow morning.

Drew was beside her in moments, passing her the phone and holding open the door to let her out, an unspoken team tag. He'd been awake anyway from when Fraser came in and played the bad-dream card. Drew knew that any call on her mobile could be his cue to take over bed- or bathtime supervision, and at three in the morning it was a certainty that the child-comforting baton would have to pass to him. How he must hate the sound of her ringtone, she thought. If it wasn't waking him up in the middle of the night, it was heralding an evening in on his own and frequently the waste of whatever he might have spent two hours cooking.

He seldom complained, though sometimes she thought it might be reassuring if he did. Nobody could be that tolerant without having some ghastly hidden dark side to compensate, could they?

38

Perhaps periodically getting sole custody of the Sky remote for the evening was compensation enough. It probably helped that the boys tended to act up less whenever she was out of an evening. They seemed to understand that if they were down to one parent, they'd better stay onside. That was how it worked for him, anyway. The novelty value of a night when Daddy was out and just Mummy was home tended to bring out the wee chancer in both of them.

She walked down the hall, out of earshot of the boys' room, before answering the phone. It was Sunderland. The Almighty.

He gave her the script, staccato and succinct as only a detective chief super could be when he was delegating decisively in order to get back to bed.

'I appreciate you're not officially back yet, but I'd a notion you'd want this one,' he said. 'There's certain of your peers want you on it too, but don't ever let on I told you that.'

She felt her mouth go dry as she processed the details, simultaneously wondering why he was buttering her up. Could be in compensation for the late call when she was still on leave, but it was seldom that obvious with Sunderland. Why would her peers—whoever he might be talking about—particularly want her on this case, and why would he be so indiscreet as to relay this tacit (and doubtless private) vote of confidence? She shook it off. No point dwelling upon the vicissitudes and outright caprice of a man like Sunderland, especially as that might be precisely what he intended. When it came to that level of police politics, she had long since adopted the wisdom of the big computer in *War Games*: 'the only way to

39

win is not to play'.

'Laura Geddes is on her way,' Sunderland informed her. 'She'll pick you up in five. Don't say I'm not good to you, McLeod.'

She was trying to think of a polite but spiky response when he rang off.

Drew stuck his head out of the boys' bedroom door, his sandy hair looking endearingly unkempt. Actually, everything about him looked that bit more attractive when she was being dragged out of the house in the small hours.

'Work?'

'I'm sorry. I know I'm still on leave, but . . .'

'I'm guessing it's something big.'

'Somebody seems to think so.'

She threw on a suit, tied back her hair into something that would pass for order at this hour and allowed herself a quick check in the mirror. Ostensibly this was for reassurance that her appearance was professionally acceptable before leaving the building, but that was the only issue it offered any reassurance on. It was never the best time to judge these things, but she thought she looked old. Grey flashing at the roots, and the rest of it never the silky black it had once been without the help of her colourist. She was overdue a trip to the salon, something she'd put off until after her holiday, sunshine, sand and seawater never doing much for her coiffure.

Her eyes looked a little puffy, though the consolation was that the minor swelling stretched the skin and concealed a few wrinkles. Drew always said he thought the lines gave her eyes an intensity, but he was the one who referred to her nose as being aquiline when a less indulgent

40

individual would probably have settled for big. His testimony was far from objective, especially considering that it was frequently offered in the service of improving his chances of a shag, but she liked to hear it anyway.

Catherine slipped out quietly, her sons' queries still resonating despite the gravity of the development that had interrupted them. Whodunit. She didn't want to go there. She avoided talking shop around the boys, but the truth was they couldn't get enough of it. All the things that she feared might disturb them were the very things they most craved to hear about. Evil little changelings: where had they come from? What had happened to the guileless wee innocents that she used to pick up from nursery?

She always thought she'd have daughters. There was no rational basis to believe this would be the case; it was simply how she had imagined motherhood, probably influenced by her own upbringing. She'd have little girls who liked scrapbooks and horses and dressing up; she'd read them Malory Towers and *Heidi*, and tell them about the games she liked to play when she was a girl. Instead she'd got two boys and was utterly outnumbered in her own home, the only female. No scrapbooks, no horses, just guns and swords, fake wounds and plastic dog turds. Instead of Malory Towers and *Heidi*, she was reading Mr Gum and Captain Underpants, and instead of her telling them about innocent childhood days on a farm, they were asking about dead bodies and whodunits.

That said, she'd be more comfortable telling them about the smelly corpses than about 'solving' the murders. Guts and gore they were fine hearing about, as evidenced by the Horrible History books lining their shelves, but the squalidly mundane realities framing the deaths were another matter. The Putrid Present was maybe a bit much for wee boys to cope with.

The very word 'whodunit' put her in mind of her one-time boss and mentor, Moira Clark, whose mantra—often restated bearing the added emphasis of a clout to the back of the head with a file folder—was simply: 'This is Glesca.'

The first time Catherine heard it was in direct response to her suggestion that a case was 'starting to look like a whodunit'.

'This is Glesca,' Moira told her. 'Any time you're confused, take a wee minute to remind yourself of that inescapable fact: this is Glesca. We don't do subtle, we don't do nuanced, we don't do conspiracy. We do pish-heid bampot bludgeoning his girlfriend to death in a fit of paranoid rage induced by forty-eight hours straight on the batter. We do coked-up neds jumping on a guy's heid outside a nightclub because he looked at them funny. We do drug-dealing gangster rockets shooting other drug-dealing gangster rockets as comeback for something almost identical a fortnight ago. We do bam-on-bam. We do tit-for-tat, score-settling, feuds, jealousy, petty revenge. We do straightforward. We do obvious. We do cannaemisswhodunit. When you hear hoofbeats on Sauchiehall Street, it's gaunny be a horse, no' a zebra, because?'

'This is Glesca,' she answered.

Catherine was still closing the car door as Laura pulled away, never mind waiting for her to clunk-click. The girl was keen, give her that, but the guy would still be dead when they got there.

'What are we dragging you away from?' Laura asked. 'A night in front of the telly? Dinner for two and a bottle of wine with the kids tucked up?'

'Laura, it's ten past three.'

'Christ. Sorry.'

'Been there.'

And she had, many times. It was easy to lose track of normal people's schedules when you were on a run of shifts. You remained aware that you were out of synch but became vague about by how much, and would take a random stab on the basis of whether it was dark or light. At least it assured Catherine that she wasn't sporting that conspicuously dragged-out-of-bed look.

Laura, for her part, had an animated eagerness about her that suggested she really needed to cut down on the coffee. She could come across like a probationer as a result, despite being an experienced DI. This girlish keenness was at odds with her dress, too, which seemed sober to the point of austere. Catherine couldn't decide whether she seemed like a young girl dressing primly to look older or some wild child trying too hard to rein in her natural instincts.

'Heart-starter that call in the dark, eh?' Laura stated. 'You never get used to it.'

'I was awake anyway. Fraser had a bad dream, and of course as soon as I appeared, Duncan woke up as well. They were giving me a grilling, so I was saved by the bell. I hate it when they ask me about my job. The other night Duncan wanted to know where gangland was. I think he'd seen it on a newsagent's billboard. I had to stop myself telling him it was a theme park, just to see the look on his face. "Aye, they've got the nuttercoaster and the joyriding dodgems, but watch yourself on the shooting gallery, because they shoot back."'

'I always thought it sounded like a shop,' said Laura, accelerating through a set of lights as they turned amber. 'You know, Gangland: your one-stop for all your criminal needs. What did you tell him?'

'I told him he couldn't find it on a map.'

'Can find it on my sat nav tonight, though. Capletburn Drive, Gallowhaugh. Think it's a light industrial estate. Appropriate. Nobody lives in gangland: they just work there.'

'No,' Catherine disagreed. 'Plenty of people have to live in gangland. Just none of the gangsters.'

They drove along the dual carriageway, heading east through Shawburn, grim tenements and post-war mid-rises on either side. It all seemed so placid, so still, and at such times Catherine couldn't help but wonder about the lives that were led behind all those closed curtains.

Laura was glancing left and right with eager curiosity at what flanked her route. She had not long transferred from Lothian and Borders, her command of both the local geography and local colour still in its rudimentary stages.

'You been to Gallowhaugh before?' Catherine asked her.

'No. What's it like?'

'You ever come across a place that looks really depressing and run down, then you hear people say it's a real shame what's happened to it, because it used to be so much better?'

44

'Aye. I grew up in one.'

'Well, nobody says that about Gallowhaugh. It was always rough as a crab's arse. Apache territory for decades.'

Laura had programmed the address into her sat nav, but there was no need for precision navigation to isolate the locus. Never mind GPS systems, there was so much illumination around the spot that it was probably visible to the naked eye from space. The place was lit up like Blackpool, the oscillations of blue lights on the tops of police cars sparkling amidst the white glow of portable floods. The crappy wee sixties-built parade of shops must never have looked so interesting, especially from the rear, where the action appeared to be. The floodlights were set up in a lane running parallel to the parade, backing on to a quadrant of converted garages that constituted the light industrial estate Laura had referred to.

The lane was wide enough for a single vehicle, even if, as was probable, that single vehicle happened to be a bin lorry. A brick wall separated it from the industrial units, while to the south, on the Shawburn Road side, the shops' back doors opened directly on to the thoroughfare. It ran roughly east-west for a hundred and fifty yards, exits either end, no direct access to the converted garages unless you had a ladder.

Laura parked across the road from the Capletburn Drive end of the lane, having carefully steered her vehicle around the two squad cars that were blocking access from the main road through Gallowhaugh. There were two uniformed officers further securing the entrance, albeit crowd control was not going to be a problem up a back alley in

45

the early hours of the morning. There was one male and one female officer. The latter was just a young girl, not long in the job. She was trying to look professional and composed, and earning pass marks from Catherine, who was sharp enough to recognise the tear-streaks on her face. She'd been there herself, once upon a time. You learned to put on your game face, especially as a female officer, hiding your true responses, scared that people would think you couldn't handle it. Then after a while, you no longer felt a response worth hiding, and you realised that what you should have been scared of was discovering just how much you *could* handle.

'First cold one?' Catherine asked her, offering an inviting smile.

She responded with a shy nod.

'Not exactly vanilla,' her older colleague added by way of support and explanation. 'She's doing fine. I'm PC Jim Keeney, by the way. My colleague's PC Jacqui Malone.'

'I'm Detective Superintendent McLeod. This is DI Geddes. Men in white here yet?'

'Ten minutes ahead of you,' Keeney reported.

'Who is it? Cal O'Shea?'

'Couldn't tell you, ma'am.'

'Short guy, looks a bit like a corpse?'

'I'd really rather not—'

'Was he eating?'

PC Malone nodded, looking queasy at the thought. 'Mars bar. Don't know how anyone could.'

'No, me neither, but that'll be Cal.'

Catherine saw Bill Raeside approach from further down the lane, silhouetted theatrically against the lights in a tableau of dramatic portent that seemed to be straining the bounds of incongruity. Raeside's presence usually served as a comforting reassurance that nothing either dramatic or portentous was going to happen, and that if it ever did, he'd be an incidental background detail rather than bathed in light at the centre of the picture.

She had often heard Raeside referred to as 'part of the furniture' in CID, which she took to indicate both his longevity and the apparent absence of career momentum. The piece of furniture he made her think of was a slightly careworn but particularly comfy old couch. He was a human comfort zone: dependable, predictable and unflappable, a safe pair of hands but not exactly the lateral thinker who could make a crucial connection, or the driving force whose infectious enthusiasm could reinvigorate a flagging investigation. His easy-going (some would say over-easy-going) nature meant he wasn't resentful at being overtaken on the career ladder, and he never had a problem taking orders from younger officers, male or female. She'd heard it uncharitably suggested that he'd be happy taking orders from a nine-year-old as long as it meant he didn't need to make a decision, but from what Catherine could see, he was just a guy who liked doing his job and didn't want that job to change. Poor soul had lost his wife to cancer a couple of years back, and a few people had expected him to take an early retirement package, but many that knew him were unsurprised when he stayed on. With his kids having grown up and left home, he had very little else, apart from an Alsatian dog named Fritz, to keep him company.

It was serendipitous that he'd been the first available CID officer on scene, as this was the ideal kind of job for him: no initiative required, just calm management of the situation until superior officers took charge.

'Guy from the Chinese takeaway found the body about quarter to one,' Raeside said, escorting Catherine and Laura along the lane on quiet feet, like it was a church and he an usher. They were still twenty yards away, but Catherine thought she could feel the heat from the lamps, supplementing what was already a muggy August night.

'He was emptying his bins, getting ready to lock up for the night. Thought it was a jakey dossing down. Turned out it was a bigger sleep than that. I was in the area, so I've been here since about fifteen minutes after the initial call. I IDed the guy right away. That's why I sent it up the chain. This is no jakey. Aftershocks could be seismic.'

'Who's the lucky winner?'

Raeside stopped next to a roller-shuttered rear doorway and turned to face Catherine.

'One James McDiarmid, esquire.'

'As in James McDiarmid, first officer of the Fallside Fleet?'

'If Gallowhaugh's own Patrick Steel is the admiral, aye.'

'You absolutely positive?' Catherine asked, requiring confirmation before she let her mind begin to race.

'I've been lifting him since he was in short trousers, and he was a bam even then. He's not looking like his passport photie, I'll grant you, but it's him, no question whatsoever: James Allan

48

McDiarmid. Aka Jyzer, aka Jai.'

'Nobody in Glasgow gets called Jimmy any more, eh?' Laura asked.

'It doesn't appear to be on-trend these days,' Catherine replied. 'Our apologies. It's a scunner when a place doesn't live up to all the things you've heard about it. I'll never forget how crestfallen I was the first time I went to Edinburgh and I never got to meet Harry Lauder.'

'He used to be known as Jammy when he was younger,' Raeside added, resuming progress along the lane. 'Wasnae very jammy tonight, by the nick of him.'

Catherine was only a few yards from seeing for herself. The floods were trained on a concrete enclosure for housing the parade's bins, a sour scent of rotting vegetables wafting on the warm air. She was grateful for the brightness of the lights, which always gave an artificially clinical appearance to a corpse, like she was already seeing it on a slab. The true horror was always in the context: death where there should be life, the puddle of blood on the living-room carpet, the body in the long grass next to the swing park. Lit up harshly, a murder scene looked like a murder scene, a place of work for Catherine, the start of a new journey.

Her view of the locus was obscured by two Forensics personnel in white oversuits. One of them alerted the other to her approach with a slight nod and the second turned around, giving her a drily ironic grin, the closest thing to a formal greeting she could expect under the circumstances. It was, of course, Cal O'Shea, accompanied by Aileen Bruce, and Cal was, of course, chewing.

49

There was once a time when Catherine would have considered it unthinkable for anybody to eat in the presence of a corpse, in or out of a pathology lab, but she had become used to the sight of Cal munching his way through snacks and sandwiches as he updated her on his findings. He was shorter than her by a good three inches and built like a whippet, yet he always seemed to be hungry. Must be the permanent motion, she reasoned. He was never still, a mercurial, restless energy about him that presumably burned up a lot of fuel. Either that or he had a whole colony of tapeworms.

Cal took a step to the side, away from Aileen, and thus revealed the main attraction.

'Some state for one guy, eh?' Cal suggested.

'That your professional assessment?'

'No. Speaking as a doctor, I have to confess I fear the worst.'

McDiarmid was lying in a heap between two bins, like another piece of trash waiting to be disposed of. Catherine had often taken an odd kind of solace from considering her job analogous with that of the binmen in Glasgow. No matter how hard you worked, there was always more waiting for you to clear up when you went back in the next day. That thought could sometimes wear her down with fears that her efforts were futile, but then she'd remember that if nobody showed up to do her job, or the binmen's, the whole city would become choked with garbage, poison and disease.

McDiarmid's legs were splayed beneath him like a marionette at rest. He looked so much smaller than Catherine remembered, devoid of the energy and latent aggression that must have amplified the

50

impact of his presence. She thought of how tiny her boys always looked when they were sleeping compared to when they were bouncing off the walls during the day, then promptly tried to banish the image. Not here, not now.

Too late.

Have you seen a dead body?

Fraser's voice got into her head before she could stop it, in the same way that the worst possible thing you might say could sometimes leap to mind in a sensitive situation. She had read that certain mechanisms of the brain could not distinguish between positive and negative, so the very awareness of what it was she didn't want to think about would in fact provide the impulse that conjured it up. This scene was everything she wanted to protect her boys from, everything she didn't want them to know about the world and, most particularly, about herself.

'Single shot to the forehead,' Cal told her. 'Close-range, execution-style, resulting in an exit wound you really don't want to see. No ligature marks or other evidence of restraint but plenty of facial injuries and defensive bruising to the forearms. He had the resistance beaten out of him instead, so he'd sit nice for the man with the gun.'

'I'm guessing very little blood?' Catherine suggested. 'Indicative that they had their party elsewhere and just dumped the empty back here when they were finished.'

'Spookily prescient, Superintendent McLeod. As ever.'

Cal liked to remark that Catherine 'creeped him out' with certain of her deductions, and tended to sound like he was only half-joking when he did so.

51

He wasn't referring to Holmesian leaps of logic or an ability to observe what others had missed, but the insights she often gleaned merely from imagining the view from inside the killer's head. Catherine had subsequently made a point of playing up to this, endeavouring to turn a half-joke into a full joke. It seemed the best way of covering up the fact that she was a little uncomfortable about Cal alluding to her having such a facility. A guy who spent all day around dead people finding *you* creepy was wisest written off as a joke. The other implications were best not dwelt upon.

'Hardly,' she replied. 'You don't light a guy up on a dry summer's night around the back of a shopping parade that houses two takeaways and a late-night supermarket. Somebody's bound to notice something, even in Gallowhaugh.'

'And yet by the same token, even abandoning the body here exposes the perpetrator to a measure of risk. Are we to ascertain that there was some benefit or significance accruing from the choice of location?' Cal was speaking rhetorically, familiarly hamming up the professorial patter as though to patronise the daft polis.

'He owns the tanning salon next door to the Chinese,' said Raeside. 'He was dumped next to his own bin.'

'Ah, so the deceased was in the health and leisure industry?'

'Tangentially,' Raeside replied. 'More the pharmaceutical end. The salon was a money-laundering front. Punters pay cash, you inflate the number of punters, suddenly your drug takings are legit.'

'You're right, of course, Cal,' said Catherine.

52

'They could have dumped him anywhere. Burnt him, buried him, made sure he was never found. Instead they left him round the back of his own premises, like rubbish for the borough men to lift.'

'You know,' Cal observed, 'there are a select few semiologists who might be able to decode some kind of message in that.'

This is Glesca, Catherine thought. We don't do subtle.

'Aye,' said Raeside. 'Somebody's telling Paddy Steel his tea's oot.'

'Begging the question, Bill, given that a blind man could see this is gang-related, when you sent this up the chain, why didn't you take it to Locust?'

Raeside wrinkled his nose, a sour look instantly coming over his face.

'Abercorn,' he said with a scornful hint of laughter and a slight shake of the head, simultaneously an answer to her question and an indication that he found the very notion absurd.

She stiffened a little inside, as she did any time a colleague mentioned Abercorn to her in less-than-respectful terms, since their scorn bore a tacit acknowledgement of her having been overlooked for his position. Unfortunately, Abercorn was seldom referred to in anything *but* less-than-respectful terms, so every mention of his name was like a little aftertaste of the disappointment and shame she had felt when she didn't get the nod.

Abercorn was the head of the Organised Crime Unit Special Task Force, set up almost two years ago specifically to target gang-related criminal operations. He had been preferred to Catherine for the post despite her greater experience, higher conviction rate and then superior rank. All of the

53

reasons she considered herself the better-qualified candidate therefore became the reasons her rejection felt all the more humiliating, and it served to remind her that her colleagues were aware of that humiliation whenever they disparaged Abercorn.

The Organised Crime Unit Special Task Force was often decried as having a name longer than its list of convictions. It was officially known as Locust, a quasi-acronym that ignored the final F and added an L at the front in order to accommodate a word invoking parasites and pestilence, presumably to describe its targets rather than itself. This being the Glesca polis, the cops weren't long in coming up with their own alterations and definitions. It was frequently claimed that the missing F was to represent the complete absence of force the unit had proven to wield, while the redundant, makeweight L was variously suggested to stand for lame, lazy, lackadaisical, lamentable and languorous, among others. However, the most damning slight in circulation was in the 'backronym' that had been coined to suggest what Locust really stood for: Letting Off Criminals Under Secret Trades.

'We want bodies for this,' Raeside said. 'Not bargaining chips.'

'So who do you reckon? Frankie Callahan? Stevie Fullerton? The Cassidys? Maybe the McLennans?'

'Take your pick. It's been brewing, though. Anybody could see that.'

'They've all taken some hits lately,' Catherine agreed. 'Trouble is, we put a few of them away and the others just think that means there's more of the pie up for grabs. Could be a show of strength by somebody to demonstrate that they're back off the canvas. Could equally be the strongest of them making a play while their rivals are vulnerable.'

'If it's the latter, I'd be looking at Callahan,' Raeside suggested. 'Word is he's the only one whose supply lines haven't been disrupted in recent months. If he fancied muscling in to Gallowhaugh, now would be the time. The former is the nightmare scenario. Wounded animals taking bites out of each other. That's when you get weans hit by stray bullets and folk stabbed because they look like somebody else. Either way, we need to nail this down quick with proper police work: show these bampots that we're in charge before it escalates.'

Catherine glanced again at what used to be James McDiarmid. Raeside was right: the aftershocks would be seismic. Nothing said 'game on' quite like somebody abducting your right-hand man, beating him into submission, blowing his brains out and then bringing his corpse right back home for everyone to hear about. Paddy Steel would have to strike back.

Raeside said they wanted bodies for this. It was polis-speak for arrests, but either way, from where Catherine was standing, bodies were guaranteed.

THE PRESENCE OF ABSENCE

Jasmine was only moments in the door of Jim's office when she was beset by a shuddering sense of unease.

55

Out of nowhere, she went from her usual Monday-morning condition of mild anxiety at how she might screw up today, mixed with the growing comfort she was starting to enjoy at having a wage-earning purpose to her days and weeks, to being blindsided by a quite startling feeling of certainty that something was very wrong.

It wasn't transient or merely some disturbing passing thought: it had physical symptoms, like she'd just received an injection or eaten something to which she was allergic. She felt a twisting, hollow sensation in her stomach like she was inside a falling elevator, all her hairs prickling on her skin and a frightening awareness of being fragile and vulnerable. She had an urge to lock the door, offset by an equally unfocused concern that whatever was scaring her might be inside the office.

She immediately began trying to rationalise and deconstruct it, knowing from experience that finding sources for this sudden onset of fear would help it to dissipate. The first, albeit the least specific, explanation was simply recurrence. Since Mum had died, she had been prone to these sudden feelings of the floor having dropped from under her, accompanied by an acute, vertiginous insecurity deriving from having nobody left to turn to. Once in a while, some part of her remembered that she was all alone, that the person she had always been able to rely upon in times of anxiety, of trouble, of precisely this kind of scared vulnerability, was no longer there. It was as though the sense of devastation had been so large that her mind would only admit a little of it at a time. One of the things it had deferred was the fear, but the valve was loose from pressure, and every so often there was a leak that left her feeling this way.

On this occasion, it was more than mere insecurity. She was rattled by a profound fear that something had happened to Jim. It was absurd, she knew: totally unsubstantiated. In fact, it was probably just what her greater fear had latched on to: with Mum gone, he was the person she could least do without. The fact that he wasn't in yet this morning had sparked off a paranoid dread of losing him too.

He was usually here by this time, which must have piqued her sense of something being askew. Jasmine had keys to the office, but she had never had to open the place first thing in the morning. Jim was always there before her, even though he lived on the other side of the river. He usually closed the place too, returning to write up all the paperwork no matter how late or how far the field work had stretched. Perhaps there was heavy traffic; there was work starting at the Kingston Bridge to do with the M74 extension, so maybe that had led to increased volume through the tunnel, which was Jim's preferred route across the river from Hyndland.

No, *that* was it, she thought. Not traffic: Jim's flat. He wasn't coming into the office this morning because he was waiting in to film the not-so-disabled Robert Croft showing up with all his gear in expectation of carrying out a plastering job.

She worried for a moment that she was supposed to be there too, but then remembered Jim telling her it was safest she stay at the office in case Croft got nasty. Despite her excitement at successfully drawing their subject into a sting, she had all but forgotten about the subsequent arrangements, because it had been several days ago and she hadn't spoken to Jim since Thursday. He had told her he didn't need her to come in on Friday as he was working on something 'a wee bit sensitive' that for reasons of discretion he had to handle alone. Jasmine had tried not to interpret this as actually meaning that it was something he couldn't afford to have her ballsing up, and gratefully welcomed the prospect of an extra day of doing anything other than blundering around feeling hopelessly out of her depth.

She felt a vibration through the handles of her bag a moment before her ringtone began to play, and reached in to retrieve her phone, expecting to see Jim's name on the screen. She didn't: it was an unrecognised number.

Her voice was a little shaky and quiet as she answered, still feeling the effects of being spooked. They didn't ease at hearing Robert Croft on the other end, and in fact worsened as she learned that the plasterer was calling because he had turned up to the address she had given him only to find there was nobody at home to let him in.

She felt her previous relief contract into a hard little knot. There's nothing worse for your peace of mind than an irrational spooky fear being given substantive grounds by unfolding events. At least if it turned out she had a sixth sense, it would constitute *one* thing that might qualify her for being an investigator.

'I'm really sorry,' she replied. 'It's my uncle . . . There's been an emergency and I've had to come here and I forgot about waiting in for you.'

Croft's tone changed from challenge to concern.

'Is everything okay?'

58

'I don't know yet,' she answered honestly.

'Well, don't worry about me. You just let me know when would suit. I take it the job's still on?' he enquired, obviously thinking of that thousand-pound bait she'd dangled.

'Yes. I'll give you a ring in a few days. I'm really sorry.'

'Never bother. I hope everything, you know.'

'Yeah,' she said, hanging up.

He had bought it, which she could hardly congratulate herself upon, as it was something of a Method performance. Trembly voice, near-apologetic absence of certainty, authentic sense of events having overtaken her schedule. No acting required.

It was one thing Jasmine forgetting that Jim was supposed to be waiting in to film Croft, but there was no way it would slip Jim's mind. Unless *his* schedule had been overtaken by events, perhaps on another investigation, more important than this. Maybe that was it: there was a late-breaking development on whatever he'd been working on over the past few days and he had decided that the tape of Croft accepting the job would be good enough for Hayden-Murray.

Her mobile still gripped in her left hand, she speed-dialled Jim. The ringing tone pulsed in her ear for a few seconds, then stopped for a brief moment, just long enough for her to excitedly anticipate the sound of his voice. Unfortunately, the ringing tone resumed after its short pause, accompanied by the trilling of the office phone, which she was on her way to answer when she realised she would be talking to herself. Jim's phone was on divert back to here.

59

He could be on a follow, she reasoned. A van surveillance could sometimes require silence. If the subject was walking past or out in his garden, you didn't want him realising that the van with the tinted windows parked close by was actually occupied by a PI with a video camera. Had she seen the van parked outside on her way in? She couldn't remember.

She walked out of the office and looked through the window in the back stairs. Jim's van was sitting in its usual spot in the car park. Shit.

She returned to the office, where she was acutely conscious of its emptiness, its unaccustomed stillness. She began to deduce that this was what had unsettled her in the first place. It wasn't the first time she'd been in here alone: she'd manned the phones a couple of times and been sent back to retrieve equipment or paperwork (possibly as a means of getting her out of the way for a couple of hours while Jim calmed himself or repaired the damage she had just done). The place hadn't felt like this then, though. Something was different. She wasn't simply conscious of being the only person here: she was subconsciously aware of being the only person who had been here in days.

Whenever you returned to a place, there were changes that let you know instinctively that someone else had been there, things that you didn't even consciously register but which your brain took note of and compared to its equally subliminal record of your last visit. It could be big things, like an item of furniture having moved or tea cups having been rinsed out at the sink; more subtle changes, such as which folders were open on a desk, which newspapers were in the bin; maybe

60

even right down to the water-level indicator on the kettle. Rather like when she had first returned to her flat on Victoria Road after having temporarily gone back to live with Mum, in the office that morning she had been confronted by a sense of absolute stasis, of nothing having changed.

Despite taking her on ostensibly to allay his workaholism, she knew that Jim still usually put in a few hours over most weekends. A quick look around showed her that the bin hadn't been emptied and the most recent newspaper in it was Wednesday's.

She looked at the files and paperwork on his desk while she waited for his computer to boot up. Jim logged everything by date and time, in keeping with decades of police work. Nothing had been added since Thursday. It was possible he hadn't been back here since taking off and leaving her to complete the Croft follow in the West End.

She ran a file search by date on the PC. No files had been accessed more recently than Thursday morning. The cold, unambiguous certainty of the digital figures seemed to lock in her sense of dread.

Time passed slowly, every minute stretched out like an unceasingly extending corridor in a dream. The hollow feeling of restless worry refused to fade, nor did she have any means of distracting herself from her concerns. Without Jim to tell her what to do, there was nothing to occupy her, no autonomous tasks to get on with while she waited for the phone to ring or the sound of his feet on the stairs.

Her loneliness was exacerbated by the burden of being the only person who suspected that something might be wrong, but she knew she ought not to phone Jim's family in case she worried them unnecessarily. Perhaps there was a simple explanation she had overlooked, some message that maybe hadn't been passed on.

Her resolve on that score held out until about lunchtime, after a call from Harry Deacon at Galt Linklater. Jim hadn't dropped in at eleven as arranged to discuss the details of a new subcontract they had for him. That was as concrete as the evidence from the PC. Galt Linklater was Jim's biggest source of work, and no late-breaking lead, no silent surveillance or any other professional circumstance would cause him to blank a meeting there without getting in touch to say why.

She called her cousin Angela, Jim's eldest, whom Jasmine had always deemed most likely to have a nose in Jim's business. She posed the query neutrally, disguising her concern, playing up her own scatterbrained disorganisation as the most likely reason she didn't know where Jim was.

Angela reported that she hadn't spoken to her dad since the preceding weekend. She didn't seem concerned, but then her dad not being around when he was supposed to be was a circumstance Angela had grown up with.

Putting down the handset and being once again confronted with interminable silence, Jasmine decided she could no longer tolerate this state of limbo. She had to do something, take some form of action, to dispel this feeling of being helpless.

She got in her car and drove across to Hyndland. In the early-afternoon traffic it took about twenty minutes to reach Jim's address, the time of day also contributing to her unaccustomed ease of finding a space to park.

As she turned off the engine and glanced across at the door to Jim's close, she felt sick. She could see so vividly what might be about to unfold. She would walk up there to the second floor and ring the bell, then, when there was no answer, she would peer through the letter box. That was when she would see him, maybe just an arm or a leg, motionless, dead on the carpet. She didn't think she could take that. She had seen Mum slip away by small increments, fading from normal life to exist only among drips and monitors. Mum was still warm the last time Jasmine touched her. She still took comfort from that. If Jim had been lying there for days, then no, she really didn't think she could handle it. Somebody had to, though, and she needed to know.

She closed her car door, looking again at the unfamiliar plethora of available parking spaces, and realised the purpose of her visit was moot. She wouldn't find Jim in the flat, dead or alive, as his car wasn't here. Just to be sure, she took a walk back and forth along Jim's street and then a good hundred yards around the corner, in case he had last come home at a busy time and been forced to park further afield, but his Peugeot was nowhere to be seen. Grateful for this minor relief, she decided to check out the flat anyway for what little information she might be able to glean.

She felt oddly self-conscious about ringing the doorbell in the near-certain knowledge that nobody was going to answer it, but felt she had to go through the motions anyway, like some vestigial religious rite the origin of which even its believers had forgotten. It sounded disproportionately loud, perhaps because she was imagining the emptiness of the flat causing it to echo, though the absence of the normal ambient noises of an occupant probably did amplify it. Truth was, when you rang a doorbell, you could tell when nobody was home, perceive the emptiness behind the door. Croft had, she bet. He hadn't phoned her because he thought she might have been in the shower or not heard him for the radio. He knew the place was empty.

Jasmine pushed open the letter box, confidently unafraid of what she might discover. The sight that greeted her wasn't comforting. She saw a scattering of mail and a couple of newspapers. Her angle of view only showed what had fallen a foot or so away from the door, so she retrieved a compact mirror from her bag and held it through the slot. There was a third copy of the *Evening Times* resting near-vertically against the inside of the door. Subtracting Sunday, when it didn't print, that meant three deliveries since Jim was last home. She didn't know if his paper-boy had been yet today. If he had, then at the absolute latest, the last time Jim was home was some time before his *Times* got delivered on Friday; and if Monday's paper wasn't one of the ones on the floor, he'd been missing for four days.

LIES OVER BREAKFAST

They found Paddy Steel where their information had indicated: jogging around Strathclyde Park in the morning sunshine, his pace being dictated by the two burly minders accompanying him every step, neither of whom could be said to have a runner's build.

Catherine and Laura watched the troika from the Bothwell end of the loch, their car parked a few spaces from Steel's Hummer.

'He likes to keep himself fit,' Catherine remarked. 'He's here most days, hits the gym too for his weight work. Guys like that, it's the alpha male thing writ large: they need to know they could take a guy half their age, theoretically anyway. In practice, the challenger wouldn't get near them. Most other mammals don't have security personnel.'

'Or MAMILs,' Laura observed. 'Middle-aged men in Lycra. He's not exactly cut down in his grief, eh? Either he doesn't know about Jai McDiarmid yet, or he's dealing with his sorrow through the reassurance of the familiar.'

Catherine let out a dry chuckle.

'Oh, he'll know. Just check the nick of the minders. Do they look like they jog every morning? Paddy might not be on a war footing yet, but he's moved to DEFCON Three. He'll be loving the fact that the minders cannae hack it, though. Lets them know he's not the boss just because he's got good connections and has made a few bob.'

'He won't tell us anything, will he?'

'Course not. It's the Glasgow Omerta: the silence of the bams. But sometimes you can work out that there's something specific they're not telling you. Besides, that's only part of the game here. Mainly I want him to know we're watching him, so that he thinks twice about launching reprisals.'

Laura made to get out of the car as the trio ambled towards the car park, the sweaty minders now at walking pace with the end of their ordeal only yards away.

'Hang fire,' Catherine told her. 'He'll be going into the restaurant for his power breakfast. We'll let him order, then I'll undo a couple of buttons and bat my lashes and ask if we can join his table.'

'Power breakfast?' Laura asked, confused and betraying the years between them. Catherine just hoped the DI realised she was joking about undoing a couple of buttons too.

'Paddy Steel was a skint up-and-comer during the eighties,' she explained. 'His aspirations got jammed back in adolescence. Now that he's got the money, he thinks he's in *Miami Vice*.'

They found him at a big corner booth with a dual-aspect view through floor-to-ceiling windows, no doubt his regular spot, given that it was unquestionably the best table in the house. Catherine hadn't doorstepped him here before, but she wondered whether he wasn't sitting a little further in from the glass than normal.

He was smaller than she'd expected. She hadn't seen him up close in maybe a year or so, but her impression was always revised the same way. He grew in the mind over the intervening period so that the real thing always literally came up short. It wasn't just a proportion thing, given his muscular build; he really was two or three inches smaller than Catherine. You don't have to be big to be the big man, however. His presence was still a powerful one, with a brute fortitude and strength of will crackling off him like you were standing under a pylon.

66

He looked up neutrally as they approached, maintaining the same expression to hide his recognition and whatever else he felt and deduced regarding the arrival of two polis. He was tucking into an omelette, polka-dotted with red, green and yellow peppers, a pint glass of fresh orange juice next to his plate. His minders clearly felt they had earned the right to a more traditional indulgence, each tackling a fry-up of quite heroic proportions.

'Can we help you?' one of them said gruffly, speaking through a mouthful of black pudding.

'It's all right, Bobby,' Steel told him. 'These ladies are just here to offer their condolences. Aren't you?'

'Quite,' said Catherine. 'I don't mean to intrude. I can see you're all devastated.'

'Loss affects people in different ways,' Steel replied, still poker-faced. 'Bobby and Big Nige here are comfort-eating.'

This drew a grunt of laughter from Big Nige on the right, while Bobby on the left just eyed them warily and kept chewing.

'You knew James McDiarmid what, twenty-odd years?' Catherine said. 'Since you were both in your teens.'

'Aye, what aboot it? Is this grief tourism or something? Are you all put oot because you've come doon here and you're not getting to see any grown men cry?'

'As you said, Mr Steel, it affects people in different ways. I just thought, given the length of your relationship, you'd be keen to assist our efforts in bringing your friend's killer—or killers— to justice.'

'If I knew anything, you'd be the first person I'd

67

tell,' Steel replied, before taking a sip of juice. 'Unfortunately, I'm totally in the dark here.'

'Can you think of anybody who might have wished Mr McDiarmid any harm?' Laura asked, playing the game by responding in kind.

'I'll not lie to you, hen, we're nane of us nursery teachers. I don't doubt Jai had enemies. But this came out of the blue, and that's gospel.'

Catherine clocked Steel eyeing the salt, about to reach for it, but she got there first, picking it up as though absent-mindedly.

'You're telling us you've no idea what this might be about?' she asked, toying with the object between her fingers. 'There's nobody you're worried about making a move on you, given that they've just taken out your right-hand man?'

Steel put down his fork, a sour look on his face. He wasn't going to enjoy his breakfast now until he'd got rid of her, and he certainly wasn't going to enjoy his omelette until he'd got the salt back.

'You need to stop reading the *Daily Record*,' he said. 'Until I read aboot it, I wasnae aware I had a right-hand man. Aye, we did business, and aye, we ran aboot together when we were kids, but we don't have a gang hut any more. I don't know what Jai was up to seven days a week, any more than I know what Bobby and Nige here have got planned for this afternoon. Jai got himself in bother, obviously, the worst kind, but it's nothing to do with me.'

'When did you hear?' Catherine asked.

'Back of seven.'

'Not a nice way to start the day. Woken up with that news.'

'I was awake already. I'm an early riser.'

'And what was the first name that popped into your head?'

'I was too shocked to think about anything like that.'

'Bollocks you were. Gut instinct: who did you think about?'

He took another gulp of juice, buying time. This told her that whatever name followed would be a lie, but more importantly that there had been a name he didn't want to give her.

'Tony McGill,' he said, prompting a snort of amusement from both his dining companions. 'I just thought, maybe the auld bastard's still trying to keep the drugs out of Gallowhaugh.'

'Aye, very good,' Catherine said with a measured lack of interest. 'So you won't feel it's incumbent upon you to respond on the late Mr McDiarmid's behalf, or be worried that you might also be under threat.'

'I'm keen that justice is done, and I've every confidence that you'll see it is, Officer . . . ?'

Nige reprised his grunt. He thought his boss was a riot, clearly. He was easily pleased, although not so easily sated, going by the damage he had inflicted on the buffet.

'McLeod,' she stated. 'Detective Superintendent.'

'McLeod, aye. And no, I'm not worried. Like I said, I don't know what this is about, but it's nothing to do with me. Now, would you mind passing the salt?'

Catherine motioned to toss it. Steel cupped his hands. She deliberately threw it a little too hard and a little too fast for him to catch. It hit him in the chest, bouncing off his sweatshirt with a

69

percussive sound that Arnold Schwarzenegger's pecs couldn't have made, even in his prime.

'Not worried, aye,' she said. 'That's why you're out running between two fat bastards, getting jogger's nipple off a bulletproof vest.'

MACHINERY

Sergeant George Collins had the polite and slightly disconnected air of giving a well-rehearsed speech. The effect was dishearteningly like speaking to an advanced but no less impersonal answering system. For missing persons, press one.

'You see, Miss Sharp,' he explained, 'our resources are finite, so it's incumbent upon us to prioritise them appropriately. For that reason, unless we have solid evidence that a crime has been committed, we can't act upon a report of a missing person.'

Jasmine felt stupid now, but only because, deep down, she had known this was how it was going to play out. It was only just gone eight o'clock, meaning she had to admit to the cop that she had first noticed Jim missing less than twelve hours ago, not even overnight.

Determined to be able to tell the police that she had exhausted all reasonable avenues open to her as a civilian, she had opened the *Yellow Pages* with the intention of checking the local hospitals. When she saw the list, she realised that she could be at it a while, which was when it struck her that this normally worked the other way around. If Jim had been admitted somewhere, then the staff would have attempted to get in touch with his relatives. Nobody else had wind that anything was wrong, which meant the onus was on her to raise the alarm.

It had originally been her intention to sleep on it and go to the police in the morning if there were no developments, but she knew she wouldn't be sleeping on it so much as lying awake all night worrying on it. Having spent all day doing just that, she needed the assurance that some kind of process was under way. She was also impatiently aware of police statistics dictating the importance of the first twenty-four hours after someone had gone missing, with the likelihood of success dwindling rapidly after that period had been breached. Or was that to do with solving murders? She couldn't remember, but either way, she felt it was imperative she act fast.

Besides, it wasn't less than twelve hours in reality: only twelve hours since she'd noticed. A check of that day's *Evening Times* back page matched none of those on Jim's hall carpet. He hadn't been home since Thursday.

'I understand,' she pleaded. 'His front door hasn't been kicked in or anything, but I really feel very strongly that something is wrong. He didn't show up to a very important meeting today. He is a very meticulous and conscientious person. He wouldn't just drop off the map like this, I promise you.'

The officer on the front desk had been quietly spoken and reassuring, showing her to a small room just off the station's main reception area, where he offered her a cup of tea while she waited. She declined, then wished she hadn't, as it would have passed the short but fretful period before his colleague, Sergeant Collins, showed up. For some reason she had expected a plain-clothes detective, though that was an expectation coloured largely by optimism. When she saw the uniform, she was a little disappointed, but unsurprised. It immediately gave her the feeling of being processed, among a hundred other miscellaneous and trivial issues this man would deal with over the course of his shift tonight.

'Miss Sharp, I appreciate that you are worried for your uncle, and I am well aware of how distressing that can be. You're not the first person to be sat in front of me saying the same thing. But that is also why we can't take any action right now. I understand that this is uncharacteristic for your uncle, but that in itself doesn't constitute grounds to suspect a crime.'

'I don't care whether there's a crime involved. I just need some help because I think something must have happened to him. Why would he not show up to work? He had a meeting that was crucial to his business. He's not been home in days, his phone is just diverting . . .'

Sergeant Collins nodded patiently, waiting for her to let it all out. He really had heard this a hundred times before.

'It's difficult to accept, but it's a hard fact that sometimes people *do* uncharacteristic things. They most frequently go missing simply because they don't want to be found.'

'But he would have no reas—'

'And those closest to them,' he interrupted this time, 'have had no idea, no inkling about the reasons that were leading up to it. It can be money,

72

it can be to do with relationships, but from a police point of view, unless some law has been broken in the process, they have a right to do just that.'

Jasmine could feel her eyes tearing up as she ran out of reasons to throw at Sergeant Collins' polite implacability.

'It's very early days, Miss Sharp,' he assured her. 'I'm sure you've thought yourself that there could be a simple explanation and it'll all be resolved in a couple of days, even a couple of hours.'

'But what if it's not?' she demanded, her voice close to breaking.

'Well, when people are trying to find someone and it's not appropriate for the police to get involved, they often consider going to a private investigator, though that can be expensive.'

This put the tin lid on it. Jasmine broke down into sobs, her face in her hands. Sergeant Collins put an arm around her shoulders and offered her a paper hanky.

'Don't upset yourself,' he intoned calmly. 'Like I said, it's early days. I only mentioned private investigators as something hypothetical for the future.'

Jasmine lifted her head and fixed him with a red-eyed but determined glare.

'You don't understand. My uncle *is* a private investigator. He's an ex-cop: detective sergeant, retired, after thirty years' service. If you can't push the boat out for him, then who the hell *can* you help?'

Sergeant Collins bridled a little in surprise, then straightened his posture as though standing to attention. His tone remained professional, but there was now a softness to it. Sadly for Jasmine, it spoke more of regret than intention.

'As far as missing persons go, our hands are very much tied by law and policy, but you're right: this is a wee bit different. I'll flag it up on the system that he's a retired officer and we'll see what we can do.'

THE LONG VIEW

Catherine was eating a sandwich at her desk when she saw Abercorn through the glass partition. He was talking to Sunderland, but she had little doubt that he was here to see her. She hadn't officially informed Locust of the murder investigation (though it was genuinely on her to-do list—albeit quite far down) but there was no doubt Abercorn would have become aware of it first thing that morning. That he was equally aware that nobody directly involved in the investigation had bothered to contact him was a given too. How he would choose to react to that was anybody's guess, but guilt trip, tantrum, humility or trade-off, it would be a precisely calculated response.

She brushed some crumbs from the sheet of paper she'd been writing on. It was a list of names: Frankie Callahan, Stevie Fullerton, Grant Cassidy and Craig McLennan. She told herself she was contemplating which one had really popped into Paddy Steel's mind when he first heard about Jai McDiarmid, but in reality she knew an interruption was imminent and was trying to compose herself so that it wasn't obvious to Abercorn that she had seen him coming.

74

She moved the sheet of paper to one side with a tut, annoyed at herself for acting like a daft wee lassie. She always slapped on a fake smile and played nice for Abercorn with the same politic insincerity she did for the likes of Paddy Steel. Unlike with the crooks, it wasn't calculated. She couldn't help it. It felt stupidly imperative that she not give off any sense of grudge or bitterness regarding the fact that he had been preferred for the job of heading the task force; doubly stupid given how it had subsequently worked out for their respective stock. The problem was, she was trying to kid a ninth-dan black-belt kidder, and feared that her attempts to appear magnanimous merely enhanced his impression that she had an even lower professional opinion of him than did her colleagues.

In the immediate aftermath of the decision to appoint Abercorn, unable to challenge her superiors for an explanation lest she look even more of a clown, Catherine had gone to Moira Clark instead. Moira had retired by this point, but was on so many panels and committees that she knew more about what was going on now than when she was still serving.

'You're too useful at bringing in bodies,' Moira told her, over morning cappuccinos in a noisy café just off Byres Road in the West End. 'There's no greater impediment to career mobility in this line than making yourself invaluable at a particular task. If I was in Sunderland's shoes, I must confess, I wouldn't have given you my vote for this either. Your conviction rate has an impact on the stats that no chief super is going to be selfless enough to sacrifice. Catherine, believe me, the brass know

75

your worth. In fact, among the senior officers, your ability to spot a murderer runs a fine line between earning admiration and creeping them out.'

'Thanks,' Catherine told her. 'That really makes me feel better.'

'It's the truth, hen.'

'I know. So now we've got the sugar-coated bollocks out of the way, do you want to tell me the real reason?'

Moira had taken a sip of coffee and nodded, an ironic smile acknowledging that she'd been nailed.

'You wanted it too much,' she stated, her eyes meeting Catherine's unflinchingly, which told her not only that Moira agreed with this assessment, but that she suspected Catherine would too. 'That's the feeling. It made them uncomfortable. You hate these people, Cath: the Stevie Fullertons of this world, the Frankie Callahans, the Paddy Steels. Don't pretend otherwise, and don't kid yourself that it doesn't go unnoticed. The brass know what you're good at and they know how you operate. They were worried that you'd be happy to keep bringing in heads when you're dealing with a hydra. They want to construct an anatomy of the monster. Supply, distribution, revenue collation, where the money goes next, how it's laundered, how the deals can go down without money or goods ever seeming to change hands. To do that, there might have to be some unpalatable compromises.'

Moira didn't need to spell it out any further. Catherine could see clearly why she had never had a chance of getting the post.

'They needed a political animal. Somebody dispassionate and pragmatic.'

76

'Abercorn's young and ambitious,' Moira confirmed. 'He'll be autonomous without going off the reservation; do what he's told but won't need his hand held.'

'A yes man.'

'More somebody who's smart enough to know when to give his best *impression* of a yes man. For dispassionate read "sly"; for pragmatic read "sell his granny".'

Moira was the first person to slag off Abercorn in an effort to make her feel better, but in truth Catherine now understood why they had made their decision, and it burned all the more because she knew they were right. She did hate these people, and her feelings could influence her judgement and have a deleterious effect upon her professional patience. When she had scum like Paddy Steel in her sights, she found it very hard to pull back and look at the whole battlefield.

Abercorn's patience, by contrast, seemed limitless; so much so that he wasn't perceived to be in any great hurry to actually prosecute any criminals, hence the derision that tended to accompany any mention of him or his unit.

He tapped on the glass gently and gave an almost apologetic wave by way of announcing his arrival. Huffs and tantrums must have been contra-indicated by his profiling of forty-one-year-old mothers-of-two.

As usual, he looked like he had spent ten minutes in the toilets preening himself before strolling up and attempting to look nonchalant. There was not a hair out of place on his sculpted coif and he was slickly dressed, his suit immaculately turned out and guaranteed bobble-free. Some might say smartly dressed, even suavely, but for Catherine, slick was the apposite term, the others lacking the necessary connotations of oil. She would admit she could imagine other females finding him good-looking, though maybe not other female cops. Abercorn reminded her a bit of Don Draper in *Mad Men*: attractive in a classical way, but the wrong side of polished for her taste. Not enough rough edges: all surface, no feeling.

'Sorry to interrupt your lunch. I heard about James McDiarmid and just wanted to offer any information or insight I might be able to provide.'

Which translated as 'I'm over here seeking to hoover up any information or insight your investigation might provide *me*.'

Actually, it might not even mean that. Abercorn was even harder to read than Sunderland, but the one thing you could be sure about was that there was always an agenda. The guy couldn't ask you the time without there being a subtext in play.

'I appreciate it,' she said, trying not to sound too sugary. 'Any kind of background will be welcome on this one. The door-to-doors are under way, but right now we've little more than a body and all the colourful context of the late Mr McDiarmid's lifestyle.'

'Now that is a broad canvas, isn't it?'

'Very. I spoke to Paddy Steel. He's claiming he has no idea what it was about and that it came right out of the blue.'

Abercorn pursed his lips.

'I don't know about the first part, but he's definitely lying about the second. There's been a lot of tension lately: suspicion and counter-suspicion. The equilibrium's been upset since the polis poked the nest. I know it's not a popular opinion, as it was high-fives all round at the time, but the recent spate of scalps taken from the drug world may prove counterproductive in the long run.'

Catherine knew she shouldn't bite, but there was something insufferable about the piety with which he said this, as well as the insult to her intelligence that he thought she couldn't see how he was disparaging other officers' successes in order to put a fig leaf on his own unit's failings.

'I'm unable to see how getting drug dealers off the streets can ever be counterproductive to anybody but drug dealers. Indeed, there is a school of thought around here that would point to the fact that Cairns and Fletcher secured more convictions in the space of a few months than Locust has managed since its inception. It's one thing talking about a long game, but people need to see results or they start to lose faith.'

'I know it must sound like sour grapes,' he conceded, with that indefatigable air of reasonableness and fair-minded calm that sometimes made Catherine want to scream. 'We're all polis, we all know how good it is for morale to put a few bodies away. Cairns and Fletcher chalked up some scores, and I'm not trying to take that away from them.'

'Good. Because they did it through a couple of unfashionable old-school policing methods known as hard graft and initiative.'

'They cultivated some well-placed and reliable sources, and fair play to them for that. But it's a harsh truth that if they'd shared that information

79

with my unit, we could have got a lot more from it than merely banging up a few mid-level faces and providing drugs-on-the-table photocalls to maintain the public's faith, as you put it.'

Catherine could have slapped him for that one. At least he had the decency to be self-conscious about the name Locust. It was on all the forms and posters, but he was clearly embarrassed to refer to it as such in front of proper, growed-up polis, referring to it instead as 'my unit'. She couldn't see herself saying it with a straight face had she got the gig, so kudos to him for that much, but he was still an arrogant tosser, and she'd dearly love to hear him say what he just had to Cairns' and Fletcher's faces. She took a moment to calm herself, but didn't quite make it.

'I wasn't talking about the public's faith. Us polis need to see results in the short term too. Even the medium term appears to be beyond Locust. You've come a long way in a short time, Dougie, so maybe you don't realise how it looks to guys like Cairns and Fletcher, who have been doing the job on the street for decades. Fletch's mother's got senile dementia and he's spent everything on her care. Bob Cairns put three kids through uni. There's a lot of cops just like them. They've done their thirty, they're approaching retirement and they're skint despite working hard all their lives, yet every day they see these chancers driving about in their pimped four-by-fours, spending money like water. They need to put away a few "mid-level faces", if that's all they can get, in order for the job to make any bloody sense.'

Abercorn nodded sagely, a look of appeasing humility coming over his face. It might have been a precisely calculated look of appeasing humility, but it was an olive branch nonetheless.

'I get that,' he said, but Catherine wasn't sure he really did, or ever would.

'So who do you fancy for it?' he asked. 'McDiarmid, I mean.'

'Well, as you said, we poked the nest and upset the balance. Fullerton, Callahan, Cassidy, McLennan: any of them could have decided the time was right to make a move, and equally someone could just have lashed out. Bill Raeside seemed to think Frankie Callahan was a good shout. His set-up is in better shape than most, and Gallowhaugh would be all the more lucrative for him if Paddy Steel's hand was weakened.'

Abercorn screwed up his face, not impressed by what he had heard; or at least wishing to convey that he wasn't impressed by what he had heard.

'Callahan's operation is in rude health, but that's precisely why the idea of a turf war strikes me as rather one-dimensional logic.'

'I did say it was Bill Raeside,' Catherine conceded. 'He's not exactly renowned for thinking outside the box. But what's inside the box makes sense to me. What's wrong with it?'

'This is not about territory, that's what's wrong with it. We're not dealing with street gangs any more. It's entirely about having product. You don't need to control anywhere if you've got something the market wants. The product lets you control the territory, not the other way around. That's why the myth grew up around Tony McGill back in the day that he was an old-school gangster with a code of honour who was using his clout to keep drugs out of Gallowhaugh.'

'You mean until he got sent down for being in possession of enough smack to stone a herd of diplodocuses,' Catherine responded, though she was impressed that Abercorn had researched his local history.

'That's why I said it was a myth, but that's just the point. Tony McGill didn't have a line on a supply, and he understood that those who did were a threat to his power base, which is why he fought tooth and nail to keep the dealers off his streets. He lost in the end, though, because the product controls the territory.'

'So who would you look at for this? Gut instinct.'

Abercorn paused and glanced away, buying time just like Paddy Steel had bought time.

'I honestly couldn't say. I don't see how this is strategic for anybody, and both my instinct and my experience tell me that an *absence* of strategy better fits the standard MO. These folk generally don't plan very far ahead when it comes to bloodshed. You get wars of attrition that span decades and even generations, but never over anything so abstract as a commodity. It's always personal. Always petty. So if you don't have an old-fashioned motive for Frankie Callahan, I'd look elsewhere, because these days he's too busy making money to be bothered with the hassle.'

He shrugged regretfully.

'I'm sorry I can't offer you something more concrete,' he said, 'but if you want to run anything by me, don't hesitate. My door's always open.'

'Sure. And don't apologise: you *have* given me something to chew on,' Catherine replied, reaching for the sheet of A4, on which she firmly circled the

82

name 'Frankie Callahan'.

A WHOLE CHILD AGO

Jasmine was with her mum again, and it was warm and beautiful and safe. No, not with her *again*, because in the dream her mum had never gone away, and Jasmine wasn't the Jasmine of now, but the many little girls she had been, long before she had been forced to think that she'd ever be without her mother.

She was with her in a dozen places—in the first home she remembered: a cosy wee flat in Comely Bank; in Granny's living room; in that static caravan on holiday in Nairn; in the new house in Corstorphine—yet they were all one place. They changed from one to the other, but they were all the same: warm and beautiful and safe. And the reason they were all the same place, all warm and beautiful and safe, was purely because Mum was there.

Then she was gone, and Jasmine was lonely and lost and scared. She was standing rooted to the spot, surrounded by shapes and nothingness and walls and strangers. She just stood there crying, not knowing what to do: a scared little girl, not even school age, helpless and heartbroken and utterly terrified.

She was crying in the dream, but it tapped into emotions so close to the surface that she began crying when she woke up too. Not a good way to start the day, as the song went. Reaching for a hanky from the box, she caught a look at the clock

83

and saw that it was after nine thirty. She had been lying awake, tossing and turning, until close to four. Eventually she must have nodded off and had overslept. She didn't set an alarm these days, because it was summer and the light tended to waken her around seven, but not when she'd only been asleep for three hours.

The dream had felt so real, both parts.

She dreamt of Mum a lot. Sometimes it was a comforting place to go, and other mornings it left her all the more bereft, because it had reminded her so vividly what it felt like to still have what she'd lost.

The second part, though, was new. She hadn't had that dream before, and its impact was so profound because it wasn't merely a dream. It was a memory. There were few details, because it had happened when she was just turned four. She only remembered feelings and impressions, not specifics. She had been somewhere with her mum and become distracted by something. She remembered holding a doll with a missing hand. It wasn't hers; she had found it and been playing with it. Then she looked up and her mum wasn't there. She couldn't see her, couldn't hear her voice. She remembered just standing there and crying: utterly bereft, her worst fear, a fear she hadn't known she had until that moment, so completely realised.

It probably only lasted a few seconds, she didn't know. Then her mum came back, all of a sudden. She comforted her, but she sounded a little firm too.

'Why didn't you come and look for me?' she asked.

Jasmine remembered her relief being slightly

soured by her disappointment at the gentle chastisement implicit in the question. She felt it was unfair. It hadn't even occurred to her, because she didn't know how, or even that it was an option.

'Why didn't you come and look for me?'

She might as well have asked why Jasmine didn't rise up and fly.

She stumbled blearily through to the kitchen and put the kettle on, then opened the fridge. The milk was almost finished, and the shelves were close to empty; certainly there was nothing that might constitute the basis of a proper meal later on. The sight used to really stab at her, prompting an immediate worry about running low on funds, which in turn piqued a deeper concern about her longer-term prospects. That, at least, had been one relief of recent weeks, but this morning the sight of the empty fridge precipitated a realisation of disturbing practicality. She had paid off a couple of debts and indulged in a few treats of late, allowing her bank balance to run perilously low in the reassuring knowledge that she was due her month's salary this Thursday. If Jim wasn't there, she wasn't getting paid.

This seemed to add an entire new level of starkness to her situation. It wasn't just a matter of being worried for her uncle and scared of dealing with more pain, more grief.

She recalled the regret in Sergeant Collins' expression. She didn't doubt he would do his bit, but he hadn't looked hopeful that his bit would lead to much. It wasn't just his hands that were tied. He was going to 'flag it up on the system', but what if nobody took any notice, or they had their plate too full with prioritised duties to be able to give something so non-urgent their attention?

'Why didn't you come and look for me?'

She couldn't stand there crying, waiting for her mum to come back or for another grown-up to take her hand and sort it all out for her. She was an adult with a job to do. It was time to go to work.

MOTIVES

'All right, victim, James McDiarmid: how's his background profile coming along?' Catherine asked, by way of drawing the incident room to attention. She was on her fourth cup of coffee to get through this, having been on her feet for around fourteen hours. Just the kind of first day back that served to rapidly erase all memory of your holiday, not to mention much of the restorative benefit.

She used to feel uncomfortably schoolmarmish when she was first in charge of these gatherings. This had been largely salved by reaching the understanding that the true value of such meetings wasn't for the team to report their findings to her, but for her to assure herself that everybody knew what everybody knew. Assumed knowledge—and in particular the mutual assumption that the other person had passed something on—was a hazard that grew in direct proportion to the size of an investigation.

'Well, they won't be putting up any plaques in his memory,' responded Anthony Thomson, who had been charged with this particular task. Beano, as he was known, was the baby of the bunch, an inexperienced but enthusiastic DC whose eager professionalism was borne out by the fact that he was sitting there with his leg in plaster from ankle to hip. He'd broken it in several places falling off a garage roof in pursuit of a suspect, but had insisted on showing up to work every day, taking on any station-bound task, however menial or tedious.

'He was an eyewateringly vicious individual, even for Gallowhaugh,' Beano went on. 'Started off as a debt collector for Tam Beattie back in the early nineties, along with his pal Paddy Steel.'

'Aye, that was the local equivalent of a YTS in those days,' said Raeside.

'Fond of his blades, liked to say he'd marked more men than a tattoo artist. Not just a slasher, though. Stabbed Arthur Lafferty to death inside the Caplet Arms pub in February 1996 in front of roughly thirty witnesses, none of whom saw a thing. The case remains officially open. The dogs in the street know who did it, but McDiarmid walked away clean. Same deal again in July 2004, when he killed Paul McGroarty, reportedly over an unpaid drug debt. McDiarmid fronted a quantity of heroin to McGroarty on tick. Problem was, McGroarty got lifted and his stash pochled by the polis. McDiarmid discovered that the value of your investments can go down as well as up, and acted with a view to ensuring greater probity from any future venture-capital beneficiaries. He killed McGroarty in broad daylight: went up to him while his car was stopped on a red, reached through the open window and stabbed him through the throat. This time there were civilian witnesses, but by the time the case was due to reach court, none of them were prepared to give evidence.

'These are just the greatest hits, and the ones we know about. He's locally believed to have accounted for at least two more murders, as well as having a noted predilection for abduction and torture if he felt he needed to make a lasting impression on somebody but still wanted them alive. It's actually a bugger he's dead, because my sister and her husband were looking for a babysitter.'

'What about Lafferty and McGroarty?' Catherine asked. 'Any family or friends possibly been biding their time?'

'Lafferty was a thirty-five-year-old father of three with no criminal connections, just a guy in the wrong pub at the wrong time who didn't know who he was up against when he got into a drunken argument. McGroarty, though, had a younger brother, Charles, who has been known pretty much from birth as Chick. Which is a shame, as Charlie would have been a serendipitous choice of name for a Class A dealer specialising mainly in the eponymous. More significantly, Chick has in recent years mixed business with pleasure sufficiently to have ended up marrying Evelyn Cassidy, youngest sister of Michael, Gerard and, of course, Grant.'

'Ooh, said the crowd,' Catherine remarked, making a note. Beano grinned boyishly, appreciative of the pat on the head. She'd task someone to follow up his information later.

'Now, what do we have on the timeline?' she asked the room.

'It's coming into focus,' said Laura. 'Albeit by degrees. I talked to McDiarmid's girlfriend, Arlene Ross. She was weeping up a storm—"How could this happen, why would anybody want to hurt my

88

Jamie?"—in complete and utter denial about who he was. She was tearing into me for the polis harassing him in the past, telling me he was a legitimate businessman, making money's not a crime, works all the hours, keeps a close eye on the salon and the taxi firm he owns, blah blah blah. In between bouts of greetin' her eyes out and reapplying mascara, she gave us the last time she saw him, and his intended destination. He left just after ten, heading for the gym, goes there every day she said, and then to his tanning salon afterwards, which doesn't normally open until twelve.'

With this, Laura gave a rather girlishly conspiratorial cue to DC Zoe Vernon.

'I checked with the gym,' said Zoe, 'which has a swipe-card system, and according to their log, he's only been in once in the past month, just under two weeks ago. I spoke to the manageress at the tanning salon, Lisa Bagan, and she told me he put his head around the door most days, but not yesterday. However . . .'

'I also spoke to McDiarmid's ex-wife,' resumed Laura. 'Paula Graham, her name is. I reckoned she wouldn't be playing keeper of the flame. Sure enough, the scales have long since fallen from Paula's eyes and she was a lot more forthcoming. She said it was true he'd been spending a lot of time at the tanning salon, but only because he was pumping the manageress.'

'Armed with this wee snippet, we went back together and had another pass at Ms Bagan,' said Zoe. 'Amidst copious tears and earnest entreaties not to tell anybody—so everybody hold your ears, because we promised—she admitted that

McDiarmid's morning workout tended to be at the salon rather than the gym. They would have a wee sesh before the place opened, then he'd pop in later in the day, all business, acting like nothing was going on. Yesterday morning apparently went to form, except that when McDiarmid nipped out the back door for a post-coital fag, he never came back in. Lisa thought he had just taken off because it was getting on for opening time and they didn't want to risk being seen together out of hours, as it were.'

'Because of Arlene?' Catherine asked dubiously.

'No,' said Laura. 'Because Lisa Bagan is in an on-off relationship with Gary Fleeting: Class A drug dealer, Class A bampot and long-term close associate of one Francis Callahan.'

'Is she now?' said Catherine, glancing down at the name circled on her list. She wrote Fleeting's name next to Callahan's, but something about the former jarred for reasons she couldn't quite recall.

'Lisa seemed to think it was their big romantic secret, but it appears they weren't quite as discreet as they thought. Everyone in the salon knew. In fact, according to Paula Graham, the only two folk in Glasgow who *didn't* know were Arlene Ross and Gary Fleeting.'

'And perhaps in light of developments, we may have to revise that estimate down by one,' Catherine stated, though there was something about this latest revelation that still didn't sit right. She couldn't place what it was, but there was definitely a reason it didn't quite fit the picture. It was like trying to remember what other film an actor was in before the days of the IMDb.

'There's a strip of parking bays in front of the

parade of shops,' Laura went on. 'According to Lisa, McDiarmid parked there when he was popping in on business. For his more discreet morning visits, he parked on Capletburn Drive or Langton Drive, which are connected by the back lane running parallel to the parade. We found his Audi Q7 parked on Langton Drive, about sixty yards north of the entrance to the lane. Lisa puts his post-shag puff at around eleven fifty.'

'It seems reasonable to infer that he never made it back to his car,' Catherine said. 'And if so, it's quite possible he was abducted from the same lane as he was later dumped in. Someone get on to Fleeting. Find out what he's been up to over the last twenty-four hours.'

That was when she remembered what was wrong.

'Hang on, didn't we just bang him up recently? He's on remand, awaiting trial.'

She saw Raeside shaking his head; she assumed in disappointment or frustration.

'All the more reason why he wouldn't be happy, with McDiarmid shagging his girlfriend while the cat's away,' Laura suggested. 'He might not be without means on the outside.'

'The cat isn't away,' stated Raeside with a bitter, bronchial laugh. 'Fleeting got out couple of weeks back, while you were on holiday.'

'Bob Cairns busted him for about twenty grand's worth of smack,' Catherine said. 'How the hell can he be out?'

'Better ask Cairns about that,' he replied. 'Although I would imagine it's a sore point.'

*　　　*　　　*

91

Cairns had left on a call by the time all ongoing duties had been assigned, but Catherine bumped into his buddy Fletcher on the way down to the car park, from where Laura was going to drive her home. Fletch and Cairns had been a mutually reinforcing grumpy double act for as long as Catherine could remember, so even when they weren't working together, one could usually be relied upon to know what was going on with the other.

It wasn't all they could be relied upon to know: everybody else's business was a specialist subject too.

'I gather you got a wee visit from Abercorn,' Fletch said, before Catherine could venture any questions of her own. 'Sniffing around that psycho McDiarmid's murder. Was he lifting his leg, or just begging for scraps?'

'Detective Superintendent Abercorn has a unique way of making one appear to be the other,' Catherine replied, a non-committal response that Abercorn himself would have been proud of. 'He spoke well of you,' she added mischievously.

'Aye, I'll bet he did. Did he give you the speech about us old throwbacks just swatting mosquitoes while he's trying to drain the swamp?'

'Not as such, but I think he alluded to the principle. We discussed the respective merits of the longer- and shorter-term views.'

'Aye, the long-game speech. Heard that one as well. Cracking excuse for not lifting anybody. Wish I'd thought of it years ago.'

'Now, now,' Catherine chided.

'Cheap shot, I know. He's making a rod for his

own back, though. I'm not such a dinosaur that I cannae see what he's trying to do, but the problem with the long game is that the game keeps changing. Abercorn's spinning a lot of plates. It's my guess he's jumpy about what you might uncover in case it brings a whole bunch of them crashing to the floor.'

'Funny you should say that. He seemed keen to ward me away from Frankie Callahan's mob as a route of investigation, yet the early leads are pointing us towards Gary Fleeting. I thought he was on remand, but I'm informed otherwise.'

'Aye. Procurator Fiscal's office have dropped the charges. Bob was spitting feathers.'

'Was there a technicality? Wouldn't be like Cairns to drop the ball.'

'No, not at all. That's *why* he's spitting feathers. Shrouded in mystery, now you see it, now you don't. But get this: Dom Wilson was the junior fiscal dealing with the case.'

'Dominic Wilson? You don't think his old man . . .'

'Not in this heat.'

Laura looked puzzled.

'He means it would take a cold day in hell,' Catherine explained.

'Why, who's Dominic Wilson?' Laura asked.

'The only son of Ruaraidh Wilson. As in Ruaraidh Wilson QC.'

'Oh God almighty.'

'Actually, in Ruaraidh's case I think you're looking for the other end of that spectrum,' Catherine said. 'Though it would normally take an act of God for young Dominic to let go of a prosecution once he's sunk his teeth in. He's twice

93

as tenacious as any other fiscal in the place; take your pick whether it's because he wants to prove he didn't need any help from his father to get where he is, or because he's determined to be as effective at securing convictions as his old man is at thwarting them.'

'His old man could have played a hand,' Fletcher mused. 'Stranger things have happened. Not much stranger, I grant you, but legal politics can trump family politics sometimes. Probably the only thing more complex and sensitive.'

'Well, the practical upshot of it is that it puts Gary Fleeting well in the frame. Nothing solid yet, but it's early days. He'll do to be getting on with.'

'I heard you doorstepped Paddy Steel,' Fletch said with an approving grin. 'What was he saying to it?'

'The usual: Sitting Bull routine. Emphasis on the bull. He's acting like him and McDiarmid were passing acquaintances, but he's plonked there eating his three-pepper omelette with a Kevlar vest on.'

Fletcher let out a dry laugh.

'Did you ask him who he thought done it?'

'He said Tony McGill.'

Fletcher looked confused and even a little shocked for a moment, until the absurdity hit him and he got the joke.

'Still trying to keep the drugs out of Gallowhaugh,' Catherine added, which seemed to fairly crack him up.

Polis humour, she thought. You really did have to be there.

Their exchange apparently ending on this light note, Laura proceeded towards the double doors

94

ahead, pushing open the one on the left and holding it for Catherine. As she did so, Fletcher gave Catherine a subtly beckoning look.

'I'll catch you up in a minute,' she told Laura, who understood that she was being temporarily dismissed and proceeded into the car park.

'Not in front of the children?' Catherine asked.

Fletcher had a strained look about him, as though torn.

'Just a more candid word of warning about Abercorn,' he said. 'Particularly given where your investigation might be leading you.'

'I'm listening.'

'You've heard the joke about what Locust stands for, I take it. Well, many a true word and all that. There *are* secret deals get done. Always have been, and there's none of us so stubborn and idealistic that we don't understand why. When it's a non-stop war, you have to choose your battles. You cannae fight on every front. You need treaties. You need alliances. Now, you know me, I don't like to be telling tales . . .'

Catherine had to restrain a smile. Fletcher liked nothing better than to be telling tales. He was a three-decades cop and a gossiping sweetie-wife to boot, but his info was usually reliable.

He dropped his voice, though there was no one in the corridor to hear.

'There's a few folk wondering at what point the line between gaining somebody's trust and being in somebody's pocket starts to blur. I'm not one of them, by the way. I'm not saying Abercorn's bent or he's turned Indian, but as the boy Nietzsche warned, there's a feedback effect if you spend too long staring into the darkness. I'm just saying, be

95

wary of Abercorn until you know what game he's really playing. And more importantly, whose side he's on.'

BABY STEPS AND DAINTY FEET

Jasmine stood in the silence of the office and warded off the voice that was asking her just what the hell she thought she was doing. She didn't feel freaked by the place this morning, so that was progress, but the sense of forthright determination that had whisked her up and driven her here was in danger of running into a brick wall now that she had arrived. She had a choice of brick walls, in fact, none of them very far away in the cramped little suite.

She had been working as a private investigator, or at least a trainee private investigator, for a few weeks now. It wasn't much, but it was more than most people. She had to think like an investigator. More specifically, she had to think like Jim. What would that be? She tried to remember, came up with methodical, plodding and a little dull. No, not dull, that was unfair. Dispassionate. Level-headed. Unflappable. Yeah, right, no bother. These past twenty-four hours there had been little but raw emotion going through her mind, so logic had no chance, like trying to do algebra while your sailboat sinks in a hurricane. She had to deal in facts and data, not shock and anxiety.

Daunting as it was, above all she needed to put names to her fears, and thus if not contain them, at least quantify them. The first was that Jim was dead, lying undiscovered somewhere, either waylaid or having met with an accident. These possibilities were supported by the fact that he hadn't been home in days, but then so was the other hypothesis, that he could be in hiding. Militating against this primary fear was the fact that his phone was still working. She had tried it again this morning, not with any measure of optimism, but just in case. It was still ringing and still running active diverts. If he was dead in a ditch, would the battery have run out by now and would she be getting a recorded message saying it was switched off? She didn't know.

This left the theory that he was in hiding. He had wanted her out of the way on Friday. Was this to lengthen the time before anyone noticed his disappearance, or had he anticipated dealing with something dangerous that day and didn't want her in the firing line?

Sergeant Collins had suggested that such disappearances were often about relationships or money, which was hardly news, as the files on Jim's missing-person cases would unanimously testify. She couldn't really see either of these applying, although as Collins had said, people often concealed these problems as an overture to their disappearance.

Did Jim have debts nobody knew about? Hardly. He'd given Jasmine her first month's salary in advance, an astute move because she doubted she'd have stuck it out if she wasn't beholden by having already banked (and largely spent) the money. Relationships offered even less in the way of likelihood. That normally meant another woman. Jim was already divorced, so he didn't need to hide a relationship from anybody. Besides, his only true, dedicated long-term relationship had been with his work, first in the police and later as a PI. This, of course, brought her to the possibility that Jim was in hiding from somebody for reasons precipitated by one of his cases. If she was going to find him, she had to work out what he was running from.

There were three areas that might offer her some directions: the case files that were open or at least piled on his desk, the computer files most recently accessed, and the phone.

She began with the desk. First she took note of which folders were open, as opposed to merely teetering in piles, then she sorted through the lot, listing the subject and client names in the same order they were stacked, assuming it to be indicative that the most recently accessed would be on top. Next, she booted up the PC and cross-referenced her list with another search hierarchy prioritising recently amended files. The information Jim kept on the computer largely duplicated his cardboard folders, as he preferred to keep hard copies of everything as backup. These printouts were supplemented by letters, receipts and any other documentation not rendered in electronic form.

Her cross-check threw up two anomalies. She found several recently accessed computer documents pertaining to the same case, but no hard-copy folder on Jim's desk. The invoicing information stated that the client's name was Anne Ramsay.

As though to balance this up, she also found a hard-copy folder whose electronic counterpart did

98

not appear on the list on her monitor. The subject was listed on the folder in Jim's all-upper-case register as 'GLEN FALLAN'. Rather oddly, the invoice tag stated simply 'CLIENT: YES'. She scrolled down and down, past last week and into last month, still not seeing a record of it. Just to make sure such a file existed, she ran a search for the subject name. To her satisfaction, there was a relevant folder, in the Missing Persons section, but it hadn't been accessed in ten months.

Jasmine got a fresh sheet of paper and wrote out the list of cases again, this time grouping them by type. She was familiar with most of them on a first-hand basis, either having had a limited role in the field, or at least having processed some of the paperwork, and even the ones she'd never heard of slotted into the same bread-and-butter categories: insurance follows, missing persons/absconders, and serving writs; plenty of writs. She couldn't see anything potentially perilous in that lot, otherwise why would Jim have thrown a novice into dealing with them? It was always possible that somebody could get nasty when you were serving court papers, or bear a grudge over your role in exposing a fraudulent injury claim, but surely Jim wouldn't have to go to ground to avoid the likes of Peter Harper and Robert Croft. If low-life chancers like that made a threat, he could just go to the police.

Her next task was to sit down with the telephone and make a note of the numbers. Jim's office handset had a little colour LCD screen that allowed you to list the last ten calls, incoming and outgoing. She started with the former, but had only written down half the list when her endeavours were interrupted by the phone trilling into life.

Jasmine surprised herself by remembering to answer 'Sharp Investigations?' rather than the tentative 'Hello?' that she would have managed had it been her mobile.

A woman's voice asked if Jim was there.

'Can you tell me who's calling?'

'It's Anne Ramsay,' the voice replied.

Jasmine felt herself stiffen, as though her senses were making themselves more alert.

'He said he might have some news for me early in the week. I didn't hear from him yesterday, so I'm just phoning to see if he's got . . .'

She sounded barely more optimistic than Jasmine, somebody who was used to being disappointed. Jasmine could feel those same senses lapse as though being ordered to stand down. The caller was in the same boat as herself, someone expecting to hear from Jim who was wondering why he hadn't got in touch.

Nonetheless, now that she had her on the line, she should try and find out a bit about her case, as it appeared to be something Jim had been working on without making any mention of it to Jasmine. Was this, in fact, the case that was 'a wee bit sensitive' and that had thus led to Jasmine being given the day off on Friday?

'I'm afraid Jim isn't in the office just now.'

'I know. It was his mobile number I was calling.'

'Oh, I see. Well, he's got it on divert at the moment. Can you tell me what it was regarding?'

'It's Anne Ramsay,' the woman said, a little insistently. Jasmine was just slightly too late in interpreting from her tone that this alone was supposed to answer her question.

'Yes, but can you tell me what your case was

100

concerning?'

This time there was little chance of Jasmine missing any nuance to her manner.

'Christ alive, you have got to be kidding me,' she hissed, sounding caught between anger and tears. 'You have got to be bloody . . .'

There was a brief silence, during which it sounded like her words had choked in her throat, then the line went dead. She had hung up.

Way to go, girl, Jasmine thought. At least it proved she was becoming more autonomous in her work. Even with Jim not around to help her, she was able to obtain the same result: Jasmine screws up.

She pushed the red button to disconnect her end of the call and went back to listing the numbers. Anne Ramsay's was now top, and would have automatically bumped the tenth most recent from the memory. She realised that her own diverted calls to Jim's mobile would have accounted for another two, and was grateful she hadn't let it ring out every time she had tried him.

She completed her lists and set about putting names to the numbers. The incoming column was two shorter than the outgoing because strictly speaking the handset recorded calls, not numbers, so those made from behind large company switchboards came up as 'number unavailable'.

The second most recent incoming call was from Galt Linklater yesterday. She saw the number twice on the outgoing list and put the initials next to each instance. This prompted her to check Hayden-Murray's number too, which accounted for more listings in either column.

Once she had subtracted her call to Jim's

daughter Angela, she was left with four incoming and five outgoing numbers she still had to identify. For what it was worth, she put them all into Google, which identified one more, another law firm that Jim must have done some work for.

Her next task would be to cross-refer them against any numbers found in her list of recent case files. After that, if she still had a few question marks, she'd have to just try phoning them and asking, though this really would be the last resort. If they were up to no good, they were hardly going to cooperate. Actually, even if they were perfectly innocent, who would let a stranger put a name to their number in this day and age, unless they were lonely and wanted to spend a lot of time talking to double-glazing salesmen and debt consolidators.

She looked at the stack of files. Cold-calling suddenly seemed a more appealing prospect than sifting through that lot, but at least it would keep her occupied, keep her kidding herself that she was engaged in a purpose.

She made herself a cup of tea and got busy: methodical, plodding, dull.

She was about forty minutes in when she was interrupted by the arrival of a visitor. It didn't so much distract her from her task as almost yank her from her chair.

He was just standing there like he had materialised halfway into the office. Jasmine shuddered and recoiled, causing the chair to roll back on its wheels, and the visitor looked a little startled himself.

The door was hidden from where Jasmine sat at Jim's desk, the filing cabinets and the sink partitioned off by a wall that created a small corridor and rendered the office L-shaped. He hadn't buzzed to be let into the building, perhaps having come in as someone else left, and Jasmine hadn't heard him open the office door. His progress from there must have been muted and tentative; he gave the impression that by the time he turned the corner, he hadn't expected to find anybody, most probably because the place was monastically silent.

He put a hand to his chest to acknowledge his own fright, and laughed a little at their mutual shock.

'I'm sorry, the door was open and then it was so quiet . . .'

'Can I help you?' Jasmine recovered enough to ask.

He was an older man, maybe around Jim's age, possibly a little younger. He wore a grey suit that was smart but far from fashionable, unbuttoned at the front so as not to encumber a protuberant stomach that had presumably been a lot smaller when the jacket first left the tailor's. He was tall and broad in the shoulders, a little jowly about the jawline, but surprisingly light on his feet, as proven by his near-silent approach.

He flashed a warrant card, at which point Jasmine could have kicked herself. Jim kept going on about hiring her because cops and ex-cops were so obvious to the trained eye. This proved her training was still in its early stages.

'Detective Sergeant McDade,' he said.

Jasmine felt a cold dread for a moment as she briefly considered the possibility that he was the official bearer of bad news, but she just as quickly dismissed it. They wouldn't send a cop to her, but to Jim's ex-wife or to Angela. Plus, he wouldn't be making light of anything upon his entrance.

'I believe you made a missing-person report? Your uncle?'

She stared blankly at him in disbelief, a little thrown that such a senior officer would be looking into it, and so soon after her being given short (but polite) shrift at the station.

McDade seemed to interpret this as confusion.

'You are Jasmine Sharp, aren't you?' he checked.

'Yes. Sorry, I just . . . Sergeant Collins didn't give me the impression that I should expect much of a response.'

McDade nodded as if to say fair enough.

'Aye, ordinarily. But I saw the report flash up and I recognised the name. I checked, and when it turned out it was the same Jim Sharp, I thought I'd better look into it. I worked with him, you see. Not often. Different divisions, but our paths crossed. Sergeant Collins said you reported that it was uncharacteristic for him to drop off the radar, and from what I knew of him, I'd concur.'

Jasmine felt a glimmer of relief that her report was being taken seriously by the professionals, diluted within a greater volume of anxiety at this confirmation that the professionals considered it a matter they ought to be taking seriously.

McDade pulled up a chair and sat opposite, scribbling in a notebook as he got her to go over the details again for him. Every time he asked her a question, even the clarification of a minor point, he fixed her with a penetrating stare that seemed to look right inside her. It almost made her want to make up more dramatic details in case he concluded that she was wasting police time. She could easily imagine suspects wilting under that gaze during interview. She wondered how many years on the job it took to develop, while the actor in her wondered how difficult it might be to fake.

He didn't give her any feedback, not even the occasional nod. Just always that stare, probing, evaluating. This would not be an easy man to lie to.

'So, is that anything to go on?' she asked, feeling an unusually strong need for affirmation.

He made the slightest grimace, but not enough to indicate whether his sour look was because she'd given him nothing or because what she'd given him made him fear the worst.

'I would suspect you know more than you're saying,' he said, which immediately made Jasmine feel both guilty and rattled. 'It's okay, I don't mean you're being deceitful. It's just that in cases like this, there's often things people are reluctant to say, maybe because they don't want to sound daft or because they don't think it's relevant, or they don't want to place suspicion on somebody unnecessarily. But the reason those very things are on their minds is often significant. So with that in mind, is there anything you think this could be related to? Maybe something Jim was working on, anything?'

'I've been asking myself that all morning, and nothing's leapt out. The recent files are all here, if you want to have a look. You'd probably know better than me if there's any names in there that ring alarm bells. It's fairly standard stuff, though. The only ones that stood out were a couple of missing-person cases, and they only stood out inasmuch as I wasn't aware of them before. The main one was for this woman Anne Ramsay. Jim gave me the day off on Friday, and I think it was because he was working on this. He said it was sensitive. I don't know anything about it, though.'

McDade nodded sagely, as much of a response as any of her information had elicited.

'You know about it?'

'Everybody knows about it who's past a certain age. You're a bit young yourself. Tragic story. She was effectively orphaned when she was about four. Her parents and her baby brother disappeared one day and us polis were never able to shed any light on the mystery. Now that she's all grown up and presumably got the money to do so, she must have hired Jim to look into it again. We found nothing at the time, so it's hard to imagine it would be any easier twenty-five or so years later.'

'She was on the phone this morning, though. She said Jim had suggested he would have some news for her early this week.'

McDade gave a small, sad laugh, simultaneously sceptical and regretful.

'I very much doubt it was "news" news. Unless I've badly misread him, Jim never struck me as the type to take advantage of someone as desperate and vulnerable as that, though there's plenty would. They'd just keep stringing her along with titbits until the money ran out. I'd imagine he was planning to let her down gently. That's what I would hope, anyway.'

'But if he wanted me out of the way on Friday, why did he tell her he'd have news this week?'

'Maybe that wasn't why he wanted you out of the way on Friday,' McDade suggested. 'Either

106

way, it's a dead end. What was the other case?'

Jasmine cast a glance at the pile of folders.

'Oh, that one I only noticed because Jim had the file out, but it's not a live case per se. The last action on it was back in October. Missing person. Somebody called Glen Fallan.'

This time there was an unequivocal reaction from McDade, the genuine surprise of hearing something quite unexpected.

'You recognise the name?' Jasmine asked rhetorically. 'Who is he?'

'Bad news,' McDade replied, that slight sourness returning to his expression, as though the words themselves were bitter in his mouth. 'A mercilessly brutal man. Debt collector, enforcer, torturer, hit man. Ice-cold killer, and when I say that, I mean like the ice doesn't feel anything when it freezes you to death.'

Jasmine could actually feel cold on her neck as he spoke, a moment of chill combined with that same exhilarated sense of connection she'd experienced the moment Anne Ramsay announced her name.

'So he would definitely fit the bill, then,' she suggested.

'He might if he hadn't been dead for twenty years.'

'Twe . . . So why would someone be hiring Jim to look for him?'

'First question I asked myself when you mentioned his name. A wee bit of the Elvis syndrome, I think. Somebody famous—or sufficiently infamous—shuffles off and some people cannae quite believe it. He was an extraordinarily dangerous individual: he lived by

107

the sword and he almost certainly died by it. In this case, there was a basis for the ambiguity in that there was never a body to bury, but that was no surprise, either to us polis or to the folk in the circles he moved in.'

'Why not?'

'In his world, people disappear with depressing frequency, especially back then. It muddies the waters if their bodies are never found: no corpse, no crime. It also means no closure for their relatives, which is particularly cruel. No opportunity to mourn. Nobody would have been mourning Glen Fallan, though. Only heart disease has killed more men in this city, and if someone hadn't ended him, he might well have overtaken it.'

'But if Jim was looking for him, wouldn't that expose him to, you know, dangerous elements?'

'You said yourself the last action on the case was ten months ago. To be honest, the only motive to harm Jim that I can derive from this evidence would be envy.'

'Envy? Of what? By whom?'

'Retired cops and other private investigators. He appears to have cornered the market in getting paid by the day to look for people who will never be found because they've been dead for decades. Nice work if you can get it.'

Presented with that impassive face and that stare, it took Jasmine a few seconds to realise McDade wasn't serious.

'I'm just kidding, hen. Relax. You can leave it in our hands now. And I'd strongly request that you *do* leave it to the professionals. I realise you want to help, but when you don't know what you're doing, you can end up causing more harm than good. Tramp about where you're not meant to, even with feet as dainty as yours, and without realising it you've contaminated the trail.'

*   *   *

Any reassurance Jasmine derived from having successfully got the police involved seemed to evaporate as soon as DS McDade departed and she was left alone in the office once again. It was as though the last hour had never happened, or at least that it might as well not have. She had this impression, this quite irresistible impression, that despite his parting pledges, she wouldn't be hearing from McDade again. More than that, she had the unmistakable deflated feeling of having been dismissed. He'd all but patted her on the head, treating her like a daft wee lassie. Fair enough, when it came to this stuff she *was* just a daft wee lassie, but not so daft that she hadn't noticed a jarring shift in his behaviour.

It was that change of manner, that stark contrast between the man who had entered the office and the one who had left it. As he questioned her, McDade had seemed formidable, an intense and intimidating presence, marked by that near-disapproving absence of levity that she had seen Jim train on people when he wanted them to know he meant business. Then all of a sudden he was making light of the situation and patronising her, treating her like a silly schoolgirl who shouldn't be bothering her pretty little head.

She deduced that he had been there to satisfy himself about something, not to assist her. Once he had found out whatever that was, he was suddenly

109

at ease.

That was when she realised her mistake: she had assumed that cops such as Collins and McDade would be more likely to help her once they learned that Jim used to be on the force. She'd forgotten that any such loyalty would be to Jim first and foremost. McDade might just as easily want to prevent anyone looking into Jim's whereabouts if he thought Jim was trying to stay hidden. She had no idea what the DS had gleaned from his visit; he could have sussed precisely what it was all about, to his own reassurance and satisfaction, but he wasn't going to share it with her.

McDade hadn't troubled himself over the bizarre question of why Jim would be looking for a long-dead gangster, nor even to enquire who had been paying him to do so. Maybe Jasmine didn't know what she was doing, but that struck her as an odd thing to so quickly dismiss—unless he had some undisclosed reason to believe it wasn't relevant.

Or perhaps he wanted to give her the impression it wasn't relevant so that she wouldn't look deeper into it and 'contaminate the trail'.

She opened the Fallan file and leafed through it, struck immediately by how few pages it contained and what little information was on them. There were no invoice copies, no client details, only that rather redundant affirmation on the folder that there *was* a client. All the other case files contained the most pedantic and pernickety stage-by-stage progress notes, every phone call, visit, name, address and physical observation logged meticulously.

Jim's case notes were like maths papers: it

seemed imperative that he show his working, so that he could retrace his steps if need be, whether to see where he took a wrong turn or to check the veracity of his conclusions. In the Fallan file, however, this scarcity of information, this conspicuous absence of detail, made it look like he didn't want anybody to be able to follow his footsteps or to see how he had reached his conclusions.

Yet the conclusion itself was noted: or at least the last point his calculations had led him to. There was a name—Tron Ingrams—and an address in Northumberland. The file stated, in Jim's block capitals, that he had contacted Ingrams ten months ago, which appeared to have been where the investigation ended, as supported by the computer records.

Back off, McDade had instructed her. Leave it to the professionals. When you don't know what you're doing, you can end up causing more harm than good. Well, if it wasn't relevant, then she couldn't do much harm delving a little deeper into why Jim had been looking at this file shortly before his disappearance. And if it was the case that McDade didn't want her poking her nose into this particular area of investigation, then that was the first place this daft wee lassie was going to look.

HIGHER POWERS

'What's the view like from your front window?' Catherine asked.

They were parked opposite the Bay Tree

restaurant in Thornton Bridge, a prosperous suburb to the south-east of the city that was still clinging on tenaciously to the term 'village' for its property-value mojo, despite the ongoing housing sprawl that was directly resultant of the same. New-build developments snaked out like spider legs along all the roads in and out of the tiny core of nineteenth-century affluence that constituted the original Clydeside settlement; indeed, the newest ones stood closer to the centres of neighbouring towns but were still advertised as Thornton Bridge addresses.

Catherine remembered being brought to the Bay Tree as a wee girl, for birthday teas and other enjoyable family treats. Her first-year report card: that was one such memorable occasion, the pleasure of the meal augmented by her sense of having earned it, by getting the best grades in her year. Her dad insisted it was for hard work rather than coming first. She understood his sentiment, but he was on to a loser either way, given the level of competition: she'd have gotten the best grades in her year whether she had worked hard or not. Her diligent industry merely enhanced the margin. In fact, simply picking up a textbook and reading it, rather than hitting a fellow pupil with it, would also have enhanced the margin at a failure factory such as Calderburn High.

The restaurant had been very different then: small, cosy and probably well on the wrong side of twee, but heavenly back in a time when she considered scampi-in-a-basket and pear belle Hélène the height of sophistication. It had looked like a little cottage in those days, with tie-back curtains on its three little windows, and seemed to be staffed entirely by bustling middle-aged women who made her think of the three good fairies in Disney's *Sleeping Beauty*.

'Much the same as the view from the windows opposite,' Laura replied. 'I can see a sandstone tenement boasting varied but inconsistently successful examples of modern soft furnishings. If I go up inside the bay and look hard right, I can just about make out a wee bit of Queen's Park, but that's at the price of also being able to see the flat at the far end with these honking green curtains, eh? Why d'you ask?'

Catherine looked across at the Bay Tree again, partly by way of overture to her answer but mostly so that Laura didn't see the smile that crept across her face. She was still getting used to the girl's idiosyncrasies, one of which was undoubtedly her Edinburgh accent, which tended to rise in tone at the end of every sentence, as though it was a question rather than a statement. This effect was cemented by her further habit of adding 'eh?' at the end of certain remarks, as though requiring affirmation.

Upon reflection, Catherine had realised that Glaswegians often did the same thing, adding 'know?' at the end of half their utterances, but her relative unfamiliarity with Laura's accent made her invitation to agreement sound all the more genuine, albeit she couldn't decide if it was needy or merely polite.

Maybe it wasn't just unfamiliarity, however. Aside from the fact that the Glaswegian 'know?' was most definitely not the offer of an opportunity to dissent, there were other aspects of Laura's manner that tended to give the impression she was permanently apologising for herself. It was to be expected, perhaps, Catherine thought. New city, new force, new bosses. She'd be treading very lightly for a while yet. It just didn't quite tally with the reports of a headstrong and spiky young DI that Catherine had both heard and read ahead of her arrival.

'I ask because I remember what this place used to be like, and I was feeling for the folk in those two semis opposite. They used to look across the street to a homey wee cottage that looked like something out of a seven-year-old girl's painting. Now every time they open their venetian blinds, they get confronted with twenty or thirty folk stuffing their faces.'

Catherine was referring to the Bay Tree's twenty-first-century makeover, expanding it all the way to what was once the bounds of its front garden by means of a huge all-glass extension running the full breadth of the premises. The renovation job was rumoured to have cost close to seven figures, but had paid off by transforming a glorified tea parlour into a glitzy restaurant and bar, ideally situated to sell Thornton Bridge's aspirational new denizens an expensive but satisfying helping of lifestyle. The only bustling middle-aged women to be found there these days were seated at rather than waiting the tables: all push-up bras and blonde dye-jobs, Botoxed to the max.

Catherine didn't imagine they were doing high teas any more, but she wouldn't know. She'd never been in and nor would she spend two bob in the place, for the simple reason that it belonged to Frankie Callahan, and that alone would make the

114

food taste like ashes.

'Is it a money-laundering front?' Laura asked, glancing at the busy scene behind the glass.

'Not strictly speaking. Not in the short term, anyway, but it's a front, all right: a front for Frankie's public perception, and it's money-laundering inasmuch as it's all part of the process of turning his dirty-money past into a clean-money future.'

'An investment kind of thing?'

'That's the strategy now for these guys. Make your money in drugs and other scams, then buy your way into the legitimate game. Some of them miss being the big man, but once they reach a certain age, they can't be doing with the hassle. They just want the cash and the kudos: the new kudos of being a respectable man of means. They've already had the kudos of the notoriety trip, and the smart ones don't kick the arse out of it. Frankie here laid down a lot of money to renovate the Bay Tree, then ran it at a loss for a couple of years.'

'Tax write-down?'

'For sure, but that was just a fringe benefit. The real pay-off was what you're seeing now. An ordinary Tuesday night and every table is full. It's always mobbed. He took a hit to keep the prices down and the quality high until it became *the* place for an evening out or a lunch-time meeting in what is a very salubrious wee part of the world.'

'And once you've established that kind of popularity, you can invert the ratios, eh?'

'Not to mention branching out. He owns two other restaurants now, but he's also got a catering supplies and ancillary services company: Top

115

Table. They supply breads, pizza bases, pastry and other sundries to restaurants all over the place, and they've got a laundry sideline that collects and cleans all the tableware as well.'

'I'd imagine he's been very resourceful and competitive in tendering for contracts, though. Buy your bread from us or we'll burn your restaurant doon. Let us wash your napkins or you'll be using them to mop up your own blood, eh?'

'That's merely the entrepreneurial spirit, DI Geddes; see, if you'd grown up during the Thatcher years, you'd understand that. The legitimate part of Frankie Callahan PLC is ever-expanding. That's why if we don't get him in the next few years, we never will.'

'He'll get away clean. Like one of his tablecloths,' Laura suggested. Catherine could tell she was concealing a smirk, tipped off by the lack of an 'eh?'.

'He's not quite ready to ditch the core activities yet. Still makes too much from heroin to give that up, especially when smack is proven to be so much more dependable in volatile economic conditions. The Bay Tree is the apple of his eye, though. He lives just around the corner from it: a big original Thornton Bridge mansion house, you understand, not one of the ultra-modern footballers' wives' pads along in the new estates with a four-seater jacuzzi in the en suite and a plasma telly in the bog.'

'Aye, I'd heard a few of the Old Firm players live here. Is that right?'

'They do, and they often stop in at the Bay Tree, which considerably adds to the allure both for the clientele and for Frankie. He gets to be the genial host, friend of the famous, successful businessman and popular restaurateur, as opposed to back-stabbing, heroin-peddling murderous scumbag.'

'Have to imagine a man like that wouldn't want the polis making themselves conspicuous on his premises of an evening, eh?' Laura suggested, clearly understanding why Catherine had waited until now to pay him a visit.

'I find blokes like Frankie are less inclined to amuse themselves by dicking you about and playing wee power games when it's their own precious time they're wasting. You get more straight answers when they cannae wait to get rid of you. Besides, we'll make up for any potential embarrassment with the air of class the pair of us will bring to the establishment.'

*   *   *

Callahan read the situation expertly, Catherine had to give him that. He must have clocked Catherine and Laura showing their warrant cards to the waitress who met them near the front door, and he swept through the restaurant to intercept them before they could make themselves any more conspicuous, all the while composing himself in preparation for dealing with them. He concealed whatever anger he felt at the deliberate timing of the intrusion, perfectly aware of the effect Catherine was hoping to have, and escorted them briskly but politely to the Bay Tree's private dining room, out of sight of the other diners. If anyone caught a glimpse, they might well assume the two plain-clothes officers were there at his bidding, so calm was his demeanour.

117

Everything about Callahan was calm, in fact. In contrast to the way Paddy Steel exuded aggression like a Van de Graaff generator exuded static, Francis Callahan, as he liked to be known these days, did not exude, more absorb. He gave out nothing, the kind of man who, had he been a cop, could have elicited confessions merely by sitting there in unnervingly still and profound silence.

He sat them both down but didn't offer them a drink, eschewing the charade of disingenuously genial host. No games; or at least, no easy ones. There was a deep sincerity about him, though it was not to be confused with solicitousness or empathy. It was the kind of sincerity with which a judge addressed the dock once the black cap had been placed on his head.

If Callahan told you he meant you harm, you would worry. That kind of sincerity.

'You're here about Jai McDiarmid,' he said, soon as they had taken their seats. He was trying to steal Catherine's thunder again, skipping past the formalities of pretending he had no idea what the police might possibly want to talk to him about. It was probably intended to surprise her, but Catherine took it as a vindication of her own strategy: he wanted them out of the place as quickly as he could.

'Why would we want to talk to you about that?' she replied, reciprocating his gambit by being the one pretending to be surprised.

'You don't, specifically. You want to talk to Gary. Jai was carrying on with Gary's girlfriend behind his back. I'll get him for you. He's upstairs in the office.'

Callahan addressed her with no edge, no

118

irritation or sarcasm. He spoke as though he had nothing whatsoever to fear from this investigation because it simply didn't concern him. He gave off no hint of grudge or even the weariness that some men of his ilk displayed at enduring this mandatory occupational inconvenience.

He summoned a waitress with the subtlest of nods. The girl must have been in eyeshot the whole time, Callahan having seated himself in sight of the open door to the bar. The glass expanse of the dining area proper was a further remove from the private room, which occupied a space to the rear of the original property. There was even one of the little windows Catherine remembered from her childhood, though the tie-back curtains had long since been replaced with a trendy vertical blind. Callahan spoke softly to the girl and she walked away again, smartly but unhurried.

'Did you know him?' Catherine enquired.

Callahan nodded, eyes wide with that sincerity but unreadable as to whether he'd sincerely hated McDiarmid or sincerely wanted him dead. He wasn't going to volunteer anything else.

'What did you think of him? Did you have dealings? Cross swords?'

'I didn't know him personally. I knew what kind of man he was. I knew some of what he had done, and what he was said to have done.'

That was about as expansive as he was going to get, Catherine assumed. Even when he did offer a few words, they were unfailingly neutral, like his statements had already been lawyered before they came out of his mouth.

He glanced away towards the bar as they waited for Fleeting, not so much looking impatiently for

119

his man to appear as further demonstrating that he had nothing more to say to his guests and it would be impolite to sit and stare at them.

Catherine felt less constrained by any need to feign propriety, and took the chance to study Callahan's face, understanding that he would be entirely aware of this. Despite his status and notoriety, she realised she had never been this close to him. She had encountered him in the flesh only once before, at least ten years back and only momentarily, as he was being escorted through the teeming chaos of a police station on a Saturday night. Their paths were thereafter unlikely to cross, as she mostly dealt with murder and he mostly had other people deal with that on his behalf.

In the growing silence, Catherine was unsettled to catch herself contemplating whether she might, under other circumstances, have considered Callahan attractive.

He was early forties, looking good for his age, as opposed to young for it, the lines on his face etching evidence of his years but not speaking directly about how he had spent them, unlike so many of his counterparts, who might as well have had 'gangster' tattooed on their foreheads. If she didn't know more about him, she'd have taken him for a successful tradesman, perhaps a man who had his own business but earned the better part of its profits from the sweat of his own brow and the skill of his hands. She wondered distantly if that was how he could have turned out, under other circumstances; whether the brutality in his spirit had been put there by his experiences, or whether that spirit had picked out his brutal path.

He was slim and suntanned, a light and authentic holiday bronze as opposed to sunbed orange, dressed in a short-sleeved lilac shirt that complemented his skin tone. His hair was a silvery mixture of grey and white, trimmed neatly at the back and sides, lightly gelled to keep it in place on top. He had downy blond hair on his arms that seemed jarringly incongruous, as she normally associated it with the softness and fragility of her sons' skinny limbs. He was short too; shorter than her anyway. She preferred men shorter than herself, though at five-nine that didn't narrow the field too much. Callahan couldn't have been more than five-seven. Amazing how often, in Glasgow gangland, the big man was actually a wee man. Napoleon complex. Bantams and terriers.

His clothing was expensive but understated. Tasteful.

Not flash.

With that thought her reverie evaporated. Flash Frankie. That was what they used to call him, but not because he was ostentatious in his appearance. It was a name conferred by his criminal peers due to the fact that one minute you were just talking to him and then in a flash he had opened your face.

This was why his calmness made him a far more intimidating presence than Paddy Steel. Steel gave off so much energy that it was easy to detect changes in the atmosphere. By contrast Callahan, as many had found to their considerable cost, was impossible to read.

He relaxed a little in his chair, Catherine's first indicator that Gary Fleeting was about to enter the private dining room. Callahan wasn't quite getting up and leaving them to it, but there was a further

121

air of detachment about him now that his lieutenant had arrived.

Where Frankie was calm and unemotive, Fleeting was rangy and bristling, with a restless physicality about the way he composed himself, or rather didn't compose himself: not for more than three seconds at a time anyway. Catherine knew instantly both why Lisa Bagan had been trysting with Jai McDiarmid and why she had been anxious to keep it a secret. Fleeting struck her instantly as the kind of guy who would 'rather fight than fuck' if both options were on offer; someone who quite possibly got more of a thrill from learning that another bloke was shagging his girlfriend than he got from actually shagging her himself.

'Gary, these ladies are from CID.'

Catherine was aware that Callahan hadn't had the chance to prep him, having spoken only very briefly to the waitress who had been sent upstairs. She waited for him to further contextualise their visit in order to provide a heads-up: even just a terse 'They're here about Jai McDiarmid', heavy with hidden emphasis and discreet import.

Callahan, however, added nothing. Was he confident that Fleeting had had no involvement in McDiarmid's murder, or merely confident that Fleeting would know exactly why she and Laura were here?

'It's about James McDiarmid,' Catherine said. 'I believe you had a mutual acquaintance.'

'What aboot him? Any news, or is he still deid?'

Aye, he knew fine why they were here. He was aiming for feigned lack of interest, but didn't have his boss's emotionless intensity. Plus, he couldn't resist acting the big man. Put him in a room with

122

polis and he would come over all cocky no matter the circumstances. It was bred in the bone. She'd have said it was in his mother's milk, but the chances of finding a breastfeeder in Fleeting's infant-years postcode would have been roughly the same as finding a virgin in his school's fourth-year netball team.

'Where were you on Sunday, Gary? Between around half-eleven in the morning and midnight?'

'That's a big window, is it no'?' he asked, ostensibly of Catherine but clearly for the benefit of Callahan. 'Christ, the Gas Board give you a smaller time frame than that when they're coming round to fix your boiler.'

Callahan cracked a hint of a smile, genuine amusement rather than a gesture of solidarity. Catherine detected a hint of impatience too, as if he didn't fancy the prospect of Fleeting stringing them along. It was like he really couldn't be bothered with this, had better things to do.

'Well why don't you start filling that big window in?' Laura responded, an acidity to her patronising tone that conveyed unmistakably how unimpressed she was with his humour and with Fleeting in general.

'Where were you?' Catherine reiterated.

'Sunday?' He shrugged. 'I was in my bed until lunchtime, close on one, maybe later. Pulled a wee durty up the toon Saturday night.' He looked to Laura as he said this, mock conspiratorially, like she would approve or even identify. 'Nothing to write home aboot, but your hole's your hole. I went out and had a bit of brekky doon the boozer watching the game. That's me till aboot six-ish. Went hame, freshened up, got changed and came here. Bar was short-staffed, too many folk away their holidays. I was helping out Mr Callahan here as a favour. Closed up about quarter to one. Does that fill your windae enough?' he asked, giving Laura a sneer.

'Would this "wee durty" have a name,' Catherine asked, 'so that we could maybe get hold of her to verify her part of your alibi?'

'I think it was Lynn, though it might have been Lyndsay. Like I says, no' very memorable. I mean, she was pretty dirty, but maist birds are these days. Take it all ways, like wee porn stars, so they are.'

Catherine was doing better than Laura at not rising to the bait. Maybe it was her greater experience and maybe it was that the bait wasn't being cast for her. She wondered distantly whether to be insulted by this implication that she was too old to be worth bothering about.

'Aye, well if it turns out she doesnae remember you either, that's not much of an alibi, eh?' Laura responded.

'I'm sure she'll remember enough. She was at my flat. She gave me her mobile number. I'll write it doon for you,' he told Laura. 'Or if you give me yours, I could text you it.'

'Which pub were you in?' Catherine asked.

'My local. The Raven's Crag. You know it?'

'Aye,' Catherine confirmed with a small sigh. 'It's a popular spot for alibis. Did anybody see you there who hasn't served a minimum of five years?'

'Well, I couldn't say for the Raven's, but there must have been a good few dozen in this place saw me Sunday night, and I don't think you would be casting aspersions on the Bay Tree's clientele, would you?'

124

'Gary was here from about seven onwards on Sunday,' Callahan interjected with that intense, almost overstated conviction. 'I've still got the bookings list if you want to speak to individual diners. Their contact numbers are on the sheet. I'll have Gillian photocopy it for you,' he added, summoning the waitress.

He got to his feet as he gave her his instructions, his body language and demeanour indicating that he expected everyone else to rise likewise, because as far as he was concerned, business had been concluded.

'There must have been sixty or seventy people saw him,' he underlined. 'Regular customers. Local residents. Doctors, lawyers, teachers. I think even Marghrad Bell, the area's MSP, was in with her family on Sunday. You're wasting your time here, believe me.'

That neutrality of tone again, that conviction and sincerity. There was no smugness, no goading. In contrast to the walking taunt that was Fleeting, it almost sounded like Callahan was trying to help her here.

Right enough, Fleeting was offering enough smugness and goading for both of them. He folded his arms with a silly smirk as she and Laura stood up from their chairs.

The waitress, Gillian, returned with a copy of the restaurant's booking sheet from Sunday night. Catherine got Fleeting to dictate the phone number of Saturday's one-night stand and wrote it down on the same sheet, sparing Laura the task. She looked on the verge of doing or saying something rash. Catherine wasn't happy either, but she wasn't done here yet, and she knew to bide her time. Callahan wasn't getting to manage her from entrance to exit, and nor was he going to succeed in keeping this visit entirely discreet.

She waited until they were in the bar area, ostensibly headed for the main doors, then stopped and turned on her heel with a hammy pirouette, the better to attract the notice of any customers potentially in earshot. She was probably out of range of the dining area, but there were at least a dozen drinkers seated in the environs of the bar, including a tableful of precisely the sort of glammed-up young women Fleeting no doubt enjoyed impressing when he was on the premises.

'Mr Callahan, I've got one last question for your associate, Mr Fleeting, and it's this: why aren't you in jail? I mean, admittedly that sounds like a very general question, one that must go through most people's minds when they meet you, but I mean specifically. You were apprehended with a sizeable quantity of heroin not two months back and were remanded pending trial, yet here you are, free as a bird, getting "your hole", as you put it, from undiscerning wee birds who, in your words, "take it all ways" but are otherwise "nothing to write home about". What gives?'

This earned Catherine the satisfaction of seeing Fleeting glance anxiously at the table of young women and the smug look wiped off his face, but any further response was muted by Callahan's subtlest of touches to his arm.

'I'd rather my customers weren't exposed to this manner of discussion,' Callahan said, eyeing her fixedly but not angrily. 'So if you wish to continue this conversation, it would be courteous to them to do so outside.'

126

He did not attempt to further usher them towards the doors, but instead stood with a blankly silent expression communicating that no answers would be forthcoming from either of them until the party had vacated the bar. Catherine clocked him giving the merest shake of the head to the waitress, Gillian, who had gone to reopen the door to the private dining room. Such courtesies were no longer being extended. Nonetheless, while they would have to continue outside, she did not envisage that it would be an old-fashioned rammy in the car park. Callahan would ensure voices weren't raised. Not on his side anyway.

'Okay,' Catherine said, once they were on the forecourt cum disabled ramp leading to the main entrance. 'How come you're street-side, Gary?'

He smiled.

'Wouldn't you like to know.'

'Quite. I'm curious. Was it a wee technicality? A lawyer deal? Curious as to why you're being coy, too. You'd normally be crowing about it. Did you grass somebody? Is that it?'

'Let's just say it concerns matters way above your pay grade, hen,' Fleeting replied.

Having succeeded in keeping her emotions largely in check so far, Catherine could feel her anger rising, all the more so because it was largely at herself. She should have let her question in the bar hang unanswered and left it at that; left Fleeting to sweep up the damage. Instead she'd tipped her hand, let him see there was something he knew that she was out of the loop on, and given away just how much this was bothering her.

Callahan wasn't slow in registering it either.

'That must fuck you off,' he said, his eyes

127

burning with that penetrating, bloodless sincerity. 'Does it not? You do your bit, try your hardest, and some decision gets taken above your head . . . It must really fuck you off.'

Neither his tone nor his expression betrayed any sense of satisfaction. It was almost as though he was concerned for her. There was no hint of goading in his face, and yet that made it all the more effective, for goading it unquestionably was. At least it let her know she had riled him that much.

'The only thing that fucks me—off, on, up, down or in any other manner—is my husband,' she replied.

'Rather him than me,' said Fleeting, under his breath but intentionally loud enough for everyone present to hear.

'I don't doubt it,' Laura responded. 'If a silly wee lassie like Lisa Bagan's more your type, you must be shit scared of a woman who isn't shit scared of you. And yet you weren't enough even for a silly wee lassie like that. She had to go to Jai McDiarmid to get some proper service.'

Fleeting just laughed: a smirking, spurting, snottery effort.

'Need tae try harder, hen. You think I was that bothered aboot her? She was the one kidding herself there was still anything going on. Far as I was concerned, that was over. A lassie that's shagging somebody else isnae worth a fuck any more, and a fuck was all she was worth in the first place.'

'Well, she was certainly a fool to pass you up, you silver-tongued devil,' said Catherine, drawing it to a close, acutely aware that there was no profit to be had in tarrying any further. 'I'll be speaking to you both again,' she added, by way of taking her leave.

'I doubt it,' said Fleeting, predictably seizing the last word as a waiter rushed to hold open the doors for him and Callahan.

Laura was fizzing as they crossed the street to their car, her face flushed and thunderous.

'Quite the Renaissance man, Mr Fleeting, isn't he?' Catherine remarked, trying to defuse the mood.

Laura simply shook her head, as though too mad to speak and attempting to shake off how she was feeling. She got into the car and closed the door with a slam.

'Prick,' was as much as she could manage.

'Prick with a bastard of an alibi,' Catherine reminded her, bringing it back to business.

The thought seemed to clear the fog of anger and focus Laura's thoughts.

'It's a *complicated* alibi,' she opined. 'In bed with some lassie who might not have woken up until after the time of the abduction. Then he's down the Nutters and Cutters all afternoon, *he* says, but let's face it, aside from the reliability of the witnesses, he can make sure he's seen at the bar around kick-off, then again at full-time, and that still leaves a big gap to get busy in between. He was way too eager to account for his time. They both were, eh?'

Catherine couldn't disagree. Callahan might be disconcertingly unreadable up close, but when she took a step back, there was definitely something to be gleaned from his demeanour, from his unreadability itself. That impression of dispassionate, functionary cooperation, that very air of indifferent tolerance and unemotional disengagement: there was more to all of that than the manifestation of his stony and disciplined single-mindedness. He was a career criminal, someone who had been taking shit from the polis since he was in short trousers. They had turned up to question one of his main men and he knew either that Fleeting was totally covered or totally innocent. Both ways, the cops were facing the custard-pie treatment. That should have been a sweet wee interlude for him, yet never mind milk the moment, he didn't let a smile of satisfaction cross his lips, didn't 'lay the smack down', as she had recently overheard Duncan say to one of his toys, when the polis were there on a plate.

Why wouldn't he?

Because he wanted them gone. He didn't want to do anything that would draw out the visit or engage them unnecessarily. The only tiny hint of provocation had come when he had the assurance of knowing they were already out the door. Whether or not he was covering up McDiarmid's murder, Frankie Callahan had something else in the pipeline, something far more important.

Something way above her pay grade.

ASYLUM

Jasmine was almost simperingly grateful for the sat-nav programme Jim had politely insisted upon installing on her phone, not least because her Glasgow geography was sketchy at best, especially

130

outside her comfort zones of the West End and South Side. Understandably, her Northumberland geography was non-existent, and she very much doubted she'd have found this place with a road map. Even using her phone, she had driven past it twice, assuming the software was wonky or the triangulation off track.

The address said 14 Hexham Road, Tolheaton, a town or village that appeared to be a good couple of miles away yet. At the device's insistence she had doubled back on herself, but twice failed to put her faith in the flashing dot that appeared to be sitting in the middle of a field off the north side of the road. On her third pass she saw the narrow gate, little more than a single car's width, among overgrown hedgerows and a canopy of trees. There was indeed a rusted number attached to the weather-worn right-hand gatepost, identifying it as number fourteen. Number twelve was presumably not exactly a next-door neighbour in friendly cup-of-sugar-borrowing distance.

She switched on the hazard lights and checked her mirrors before climbing out of the car. It was a narrow little B road, on which she had barely seen another vehicle for the past few miles, but the gate was in sight of a bend, and in her mind's eye, the quieter a road, the more easily she tended to imagine rally cars hurtling along it.

She had driven down in her beloved red Civic, keeping a worried eye on the fuel gauge and specifically the rate at which it was descending. She had gone to a cash machine first thing that morning, and though she hadn't quite used the last of her drawings filling the tank, if she had to top up again before she got home, it could have serious ramifications for what she would be eating by the end of the week.

She was already considering how she might raise some cash in the short term, mercilessly triaging which possessions would have to go on eBay. She hadn't even looked up what she might get for the Honda, however. She'd go on the game before she gave that up. She'd run it until the wheels fell off. It had been a comfortable, dependable part of her life longer than most people, longer than any school or college, longer than any house or flat she'd lived in.

It had been her mum's, the closest Beth Sharp ever came to owning a new car. She had bought it when Jasmine was seven, this sleek, low-slung mid-nineties model that Jasmine considered as exotic and sporty-looking as any Ferrari. It was second-hand, but barely a year old and with a mileage suggesting a quarter of that. According to the dealer in Abbeyhill, along near Easter Road, it had belonged to an English professor at Edinburgh University, one of whose books was a prescribed text up and down the UK. This meant that he got a healthy royalty cheque with each year's new intake of students, part of which he spent annually renewing his car. In this particular year, however, they had changed the model, which greatly devalued its predecessor.

Jasmine couldn't understand why they'd changed it. The new one looked nondescript and fuddy-duddy, while she was in agreement with her mum that theirs was the most beautiful car in the world. It was built to last too, conscientious servicing and maintenance keeping it going all these years until eventually it outlasted its owner.

Mum had left it to her, and the first time Jasmine sat behind the wheel, she collapsed in tears. She could smell her mum all around the interior, like she had just nipped out of the vehicle to get something and would climb back inside any second. It wasn't Mum she smelled, though, just that she had come to associate the smell of the car with her.

After all these months, it still felt like her mum had recently been in it. Sometimes that caused her to weep again and sometimes it was a comfort, but either way it was a feeling she wouldn't be without.

She unlatched the gate and dragged it open, revealing a single track of compacted dirt. It led through a short belt of mature woodland, then opened out to reveal a large house across an expanse of coarse but well-managed grass.

It was a gloomy and forbidding structure, too big to be the home of an individual or even a family, surely, but insufficiently grandiose to constitute any kind of stately manor. The word 'convent' came to mind, but only because it was the first one she could think of to dislodge its predecessor, which was 'asylum'. It certainly looked like the kind of place that would have a mad woman in the attic, though this thought was probably coloured by having seen signs for Rochester on the drive here. Her impressions were doubtless also coloured by the awareness—wilfully suppressed for most of the journey but growing irresistible over the final miles—that she was approaching this place in order to doorstep someone who was somehow connected to an infamously brutal and prolifically murderous criminal.

What kind of person lived in a place like this?

she asked herself as she stopped the Honda, trying not to dwell upon how much 'a deranged serial killer' sounded like the right answer. It really didn't help that she could hear a mechanical buzzing from somewhere beyond the building that could well have been a hedge-trimmer, but in her imagination was undoubtedly a chainsaw.

As she walked up the steps to the front door, it occurred to her that nobody knew she was here. She could be murdered and buried in the grounds by teatime—right alongside Jim, perhaps.

She rang the doorbell and felt an enveloping sense of relief when she heard a rapid beating of feet accompanied by the exuberant energy of children's voices. They sounded Scouse. Jasmine had a keen and reliable ear for accents, and could often detect traces of multiple dialects in just a few moments of conversation, not that such subtleties were required for the voices behind the door.

She heard them called back from the entrance and told to go upstairs by an older-sounding woman with a more neutral middle-class English accent, though Jasmine detected a base of Brummie lightly flavoured with a more local hint of Tyneside.

She waited as the sounds of the children's voices receded. They weren't just being told to keep their distance; the woman was waiting until they were well gone before opening the door. Jasmine was reminded of a friend's house where the family's Alsatian had to be locked in the back room before they could let in any visitors. In this case, however, she soon understood whose protection the exclusion was in aid of.

The door was opened by a woman in her late

forties or early fifties. She was about Jasmine's height and build, but Jasmine had the impression the woman could pick her up and throw her like a wrestler if she needed to. She wore her hair tied back behind a headband; her face bore not a mote of make-up, yet it was undeniably attractive in a distinguished, unashamedly mature kind of way. It was the kind of face that Jasmine imagined people meant when they said 'handsome' of a woman. It was also, she inferred, not a face to be argued with.

'Can I help you, dear?' the woman asked. 'Do you know where you are, or are you lost?'

It was an oddly worded question, even for out here in the back of the Northumberland beyond, almost like a code. Jasmine picked up a conflict of nuance in her tone and expression. The woman came across as guarded but not wanting to sound guarded; protective without wishing to thus betray that there was something here worth protecting.

'I'm not lost, no. My name is Jasmine Sharp. I'm a private investigator.'

Jasmine felt like she was delivering a line, except that she tended to feel less self-conscious on stage, where you weren't trying to kid anybody that it was true—least of all yourself.

The woman's face dismissed any conflict of nuance, all defences mustered and the drawbridge pulled up in response to these last two words.

'What do you want here?' she asked.

'There's someone I need to speak to, and this is the address I've been given.'

The woman said nothing. There was no overt hostility, but Jasmine could feel suspicion trained on her like arrows through cross-slits.

'His name is Tron Ingrams,' she explained.

135

At this, the defences came down, though only a little. The suspicion remained, but not the defensiveness. Whoever this Tron Ingrams was, it wasn't him the woman was protecting.

'What do you want to speak to him about?'

'I'm looking into a missing-person case, and I believe he was helpful when my colleague made an earlier inquiry, back in October. I'm hoping he wouldn't mind answering a few more questions.'

Jasmine had gambled that by making it sound like a rapport had already been established with this Ingrams character, she would get the green light, but the woman still looked intractable.

'Who's missing?' she asked. 'What's the name?'

'Glen Fallan,' Jasmine replied.

The woman shook her head, but it was to register a lack of recognition, not a refusal of help. Despite this, something in her seemed to soften.

'Why don't you come inside and wait. Tron's out the back working at the moment, but he's due a break. It's getting on for lunch.'

She opened the door a little wider and stepped to the side.

'I'm Rita, by the way,' she said. 'Rita Cranleigh. Have you come far?'

'Down from Glasgow.'

Rita led her into the hallway, which was dark after the bright sunshine outside. There was oak panelling on the walls, absorbing a lot of the light, and causing both of their footsteps to reverberate from the varnished boards below. Jasmine could see a staircase leading to a gallery above, three doors visible along it. They were all firmly closed. She thought she could still hear the children's voices, somewhere behind one of them.

Rita caught her glancing upwards, detecting her curiosity at her surroundings. She led her beyond the staircase, past more closed doors, and on into a huge kitchen towards the rear. Jasmine could hear the chainsaw louder and closer, though she couldn't see who was wielding it; despite the allaying of her unease, she was now actually pretty sure that a chainsaw it was.

'You're wondering what this place is, aren't you?' Rita said, sounding strangely assured by Jasmine's curiosity.

'I'm not here to pry,' she insisted politely. 'Well, not into that, I mean,' she added with a self-conscious giggle. (Because I'm an investigator, me. Really, really, really.)

'It's a refuge,' Rita told her neutrally. 'A safe house. The women here generally don't want their whereabouts to be known, so you'll forgive me if I was a little defensive earlier.'

'Not at all. Under the circumstances, I don't suppose I could actually have said anything worse than that I'm a private investigator.'

'No,' Rita agreed, offering a wry smile as she filled the kettle. 'Although the likelihood is that a private investigator come in search of one of our residents wouldn't announce his or her profession up front.'

Jasmine worried for a moment that this was Rita's way of saying she had seen right through her as a shambling amateur, which was probably why she offered a renewed reason to suspect her by way of response.

'Could always be a double bluff. Allay your suspicions by asking after a man.'

'No,' Rita replied, almost amused by the notion.

137

She opened a large double-door fridge-freezer and took out a carton of milk, placing it on the kitchen table next to a sugar bowl. 'They wouldn't know to ask for Tron Ingrams. He's discreet about his involvement with us. And believe me, they wouldn't be asking for him by way of subterfuge. He'd see through them in a twinkling.'

'What is his involvement with you?'

'He works here on a voluntary basis, when he can. Gardener, handyman, courier, just whatever needs doing to keep the place shipshape. He was in the army. Kind of bloke who could demolish a shed for you in the morning, then use the parts to build a bridge in the afternoon. I don't know how we ever managed without him, to be honest, though we still have to at times. He's often away, out of the country.'

'Doing what?'

'Work.'

Jasmine wondered whether it was worth probing for a more specific answer, unable to decide whether Rita was being vague because she didn't know or because she wouldn't say.

She heard an interior door open somewhere beyond the kitchen, then close again a couple of seconds later.

'They won't come out until you're gone,' Rita said, lifting mugs from a shelf. Jasmine was simultaneously expectant and apprehensive to count three. 'They don't want anyone to see they're here in case it gets back to the people they're trying to escape from. We take every precaution, but it's not fail-safe. People let things slip, or they trust the wrong person with information. We've had quite a few husbands and partners turn up here over the years, and it's very distressing, not just for the women concerned. It shatters the sense of security for everybody.'

'What do you do then?'

'We have to call the police.'

She made this sound more trouble than it was worth.

'They warn the blokes off, escort them from the premises, but they come back. Once they know their wives or partners are here, they always come back. Except when Mr Ingrams is available,' she added, arching her eyebrows. 'When *he* warns them off, they never come back.'

Jasmine heard the buzzing sound cease outside as Rita poured hot water into a capacious and seasoned-looking teapot. She had just set it on a low heat upon a gas hob when the back door opened and Ingrams came in. He was dressed in dark green camo pants and a sleeveless black T-shirt, a pair of protective goggles fixed around his eyes by an elasticated strap. He had an unmistakably military bearing about him: tall, toned and muscular, his skin tanned and weathered, indicative of spending a lot of time outdoors in warmer climates.

He took the goggles off as he tugged the door closed, which was when he appeared to notice that Rita had a visitor. He fixed Jasmine with a stare from the doorway that made McDade's gaze seem like an ambient mood light by comparison. It was a look so deeply scrutinising that she felt pinned to her chair by it until he looked away again, glancing to Rita for explanation. He seemed discomfited by the sight of this new presence, but Jasmine guessed that this was his default position regarding

139

strangers here until Rita vouched for them.

Jasmine put his age at early forties, but allowed for a margin of five years either side; he was clearly a man who kept himself fit and healthy, yet something about his face suggested a very hard paper-round. His eyes gave the impression of having seen a great deal more than he would have liked. There was a stillness about them that hinted at chilling cold and perilous depths, where something truly frightening lurked beneath the surface.

'Ah, Mr Ingrams,' Rita said familiarly. 'This is Jasmine. She's down from Glasgow. She's a private investigator and she says you spoke to her colleague a while back regarding a missing person. She'd just like a little of your time to ask some questions.'

Ingrams stared at Jasmine again, a trace of confusion playing briefly across his face before it returned to its previous look of suppressed hostility. This time, she really didn't think she was being paranoid to suspect that the confusion was born of his failure to equate the words 'private investigator' with what he saw in front of him.

'I don't have anything to tell you that I didn't already tell your colleague,' he said. 'And I didn't have anything to tell your colleague.'

He walked straight to the sink and poured himself a glass of water, standing with his back to Jasmine as he gulped it down. Closer by, Jasmine could see the wetness that was hidden by the black of the T-shirt and a thin film of sawdust adhering to his skin, held there by a layer of sweat. His hair was close-cropped, shaven in tight at the back and sides, pale lines of scars amidst the salt-and-pepper

140

dots like the canals on Mars or fragments of crop circles.

She glanced anxiously at Rita to see how she was taking his response, in particular the indication that he hadn't been quite so helpful to Jasmine's 'colleague' as she had implied.

'I don't imagine Jasmine's travelled all the way down here if there weren't perhaps some new questions to ask,' Rita said, giving her an apologetic but unsurprised look. He might be Mr Sun-kissed, but clearly he was seldom Mr Sunshine.

'I don't have time,' he replied. 'I have to go to Heddon to the garden centre, plus the wood-shredder's finally given up the ghost, so I need to pick up a replacement.'

'Well, why doesn't Jasmine accompany you and she can ask her questions on the drive? That way you'd be killing two birds with one stone.'

It would have been hard at that moment to know which of them fancied that idea less. The main difference was that Jasmine had to disguise her misgivings at the prospect of letting Ingrams drive her off into the unknown behind a mask of gratitude for Rita's helpful suggestion. Ingrams was not constrained by any such dichotomies and thus shot Rita a glare that would have had most people whimpering.

The fact that Rita seemed mildly amused by it told Jasmine that there must be a great deal of trust between them. Rita would not have presumed to impose upon him in the face of such obvious reluctance, and equally Ingrams would not have responded with a look like that if they didn't both understand that she was immune to its threat.

141

Ingrams gave a sigh and muttered something about leaving in two minutes, before stomping back through the outside door again with unapologetically bad grace.

Jasmine had no reason to believe that she shared Rita's immunity, but she couldn't see how she could back out of this without making it obvious that she believed she had something to fear from him.

Rita seemed to read her apprehension. She patted Jasmine's hand.

'Make sure he buys you a cuppa at the garden centre, seeing as he's hauling you away from this one. And don't worry: his bark's worse than his bite.'

Jasmine was reminded of dog-owners who said things like 'he won't touch you' as their horribly befanged hound bounded towards her in the park, regardless of the fact that they would have precisely no control over the slavering beast if it decided to have her leg off. This woman, who ran a refuge, thought highly of Ingrams and thoroughly trusted the man, and that in itself was a kind of endorsement, but by her own admission there were plenty of things she didn't know about him. Like whether he had murdered Jasmine's uncle and was about to do the same to her. Either way, Jasmine really wished that Rita hadn't used a phrase that included the word 'killing' when she made her helpful suggestion.

THIS DARK PLACE

'What time will you be clear?' Drew asked, as Catherine indicated to pull in at West Street underground station.

'How long is a piece of string? You know what court's like.'

'You know what I mean. You sure you'll be done in time for the boys?'

'Of course. Don't worry about it. You take all the time you need.'

Catherine gave a small laugh as she spoke, trying to sound reassuring, but it was as much to cover her resentment at the implication that she might not be free in time to pick up Duncan and Fraser from school. Drew was going through to Edinburgh for a project meeting and then dinner with his colleagues. As he mostly worked at home and it was usually down to him to cover the school run, he could get anxious when it was left to Catherine, allied to a certain prickliness over the fact that though such instances were few, they were often nonetheless fraught with complications. He didn't spell it out, but she knew it pissed him off. In Drew's mind, given that he constantly and invaluably accommodated the unpredictability of Catherine's schedule, it was only fair that on the rare occasions when he needed her to reciprocate, he should be able to ride off relaxed in the knowledge that there weren't several variables in play that could potentially screw the whole thing up.

Catherine understood why it annoyed him, but

she still considered it unfair. Admittedly there had been a few mad dashes and some last-minute contingencies worked out, but neither of the boys had ever been left standing at the school gates, and nor would she ever have allowed that to happen.

Drew knew that, and he wasn't really implying that there might be a problem, either. He was angry with her about something else, but there wasn't time to talk about it, far less do anything about it (which was itself the rub).

'Okay. I'll phone around teatime,' he said, opening the passenger-side door. The rain chose that moment to progress from heavy to torrential, yet he seemed in a hurry to get out into it.

'Enjoy yourself. Give me a kiss.'

She feared for a moment he was going to say no, maybe use the rain and the fact that he was halfway out the car as an acceptable reason to just hurry off. Instead he leaned in and gave her a rather cursory peck on the lips, pulling away even as she was trying to prolong it.

'I'll see you about ten-ish.'

'Don't rush. Late as you like. Love you.'

He didn't reply: simply gave her a weak smile and then hurried off across the pavement, holding his wee man-bag over his head as cover against the downpour.

Catherine watched him disappear inside the station, her auto-responsive windscreen wipers thrashing like a pair of turbo-charged metronomes. She gave a sigh and indicated to rejoin the traffic, heavy and slow because of the rain.

It was a real 'party's over' moment, in her mind heralding the death of the summer. The weather had broken, an Atlantic low-pressure system

144

blowing in to quench the heat of a sustained sunny spell, the majority of which had happened, typically, during the fortnight Catherine had spent on holiday in Menorca. Now the holiday was finished, the sunny spell had been washed away, the schools were back and she was knee-deep in another murder case. It felt like summer was over and she didn't quite know where it had gone, or what she'd been planning to do with it anyway.

Catch up, that was what she had wanted to do. Get off the belt, step back. Now the belt was whizzing away again, everything the way it always was, except maybe faster. Fraser was starting Primary Two, yet some mornings over the school holidays she had caught herself wondering why Drew wasn't getting him ready for nursery. Duncan was starting Primary *Four*.

Then there was Drew, the main reason she had wanted to get off the belt.

They hadn't had sex in six weeks. He probably didn't think she was counting, but she was, and she knew for a fact that he would be. He probably thought she wasn't that fussed either, but he was wrong about that too, acutely.

It wasn't the kind of thing you could confide in anybody because they would jump to the wrong, overdramatic conclusions. To most outside observers, six weeks without sex would automatically indicate a rough patch in a marriage. Most outside observers without two kids and two jobs between them, that was. It wasn't indicative of a rough patch at all: it was just practicalities, complications. Everything else was fine. That, in fact, was perhaps what made it all the more of a strain that the physical side was so neglected. Drew

145

was understanding, up to a point. Going by his demeanour this morning, sealed with a cursory kiss, she could assume that point had been breached last night.

She wasn't withholding from him. It was just bad luck. Circumstance. Things had been chaotic and exhausting in the lead-up to their holiday, ironically because she was trying, prior to their departure, to free her mind of the kind of clutter that might be an impediment to relaxing. Hence she had been hammering it a bit at work, trying to tie up loose ends so that she wouldn't end up distracted by thinking about them when she went abroad. She knew she was knackering herself and consequently neglecting Drew, but the holiday was going to be a watershed. She and Drew would have time for each other, time to talk about something other than work and family arrangements. They'd talk about the future, what they'd like to change. They'd talk about sex, and they'd *have* a lot of it.

Bad luck. Circumstance.

Fraser got freaked out by the unfamiliarity of the villa, and in particular how dark it was at night compared to home, where the street lights were a permanent glow behind his curtains. He kept reappearing during the late evening, then kept them up half the first couple of nights as he grew overtired, irrational and consequently unable to sleep. Having barely slept since their arrival, she and Drew were both zonked out by about nine the third night. This left them well rested and refreshed in time for Fraser to tag his brother, so that the evenings and overnights were then dominated by dealing with Duncan's upset stomach. By the time that had finally abated, and

146

another embarrassingly early night had allowed Catherine to catch up on her sleep, they were already eight nights into their holiday, at which point Duncan briefly passed the baton, and the tummy bug, back to his younger brother. Fraser recovered quickly, but that still only left four nights of their stay, at which highly inopportune time Catherine's body committed a grave act of betrayal and commenced her period a full five days early, leaving her feeling lousy, cheated and utterly non-libidinous.

As John Cleese once said, it's not the despair, it's the hope I can't stand; thus Drew seemed to be less frustrated after that point, when he knew there was no opportunity being passed up. Drew was a man who looked at the long-term view of everything. It was how he worked. He was realistic, philosophical and very patient. Up to a point.

He had cooked her a meal last night: three courses, candles, gone to a lot of bother. She had got home later than planned, but that was all right as far as he was concerned: he had already got the kids bathed and pyjamafied. Relax, he said. Sit down, have some wine, eat. She managed the eating and drinking parts, but as she had come straight from the Bay Tree, not the relaxing bit. She could neither think nor talk about anything else; or not talk so much as rant and seethe. Sex was on her mind, but in the most negative way. She kept thinking about Gary Fleeting and his leery conduct towards Laura, his one-night stands with 'wee durties' who 'took it all ways'. She tanned far more than her share of the bottle, then, as her anger burned out, she found that so had all her energy. She barely remembered Drew coming

147

upstairs, though it could only have been five or ten minutes after her, and she was asleep before he'd even got into bed.

He was a little brusque in the morning, and as the fog of sleep lifted, she knew why. He wasn't in the huff about last night, or even the past six weeks. It was the future that was bothering him. Drew always looked at the long-term view, and he didn't like what he was seeing.

In the shower that morning, Catherine thought about what she ought to say to him, maybe tonight if he wasn't home too late. She'd apologise for last night, acknowledge the situation. They'd had a lot of bad luck, she would say. She would joke about it, tell him that they were like the IRA: they only needed to be lucky once. Or at least that they couldn't be unlucky all the time.

But were they just unlucky? she asked herself. Truth, girl. Truth.

No. And it wasn't just a lack of sex that was bothering Drew about last night. It was what lay behind it, what they might have got away from on holiday but what would always have been waiting for them upon their return.

Catherine had vowed to him that she wouldn't become a stereotype: a senior police officer consumed by her job, slowly alienating her spouse. And on the whole, she wasn't. Most of the time there was balance in their lives, and they were a normal, functioning, loving family. She wasn't obsessed by cases, she wasn't a workaholic and she wasn't drinking away the fears, horrors and regrets every night. But there was no getting away from the fact that it was a demanding and unusual job, witness on a regular basis to the worst days of

148

other people's lives, and dealing with the worst deeds of the worst people.

It waxed and waned. There were times when it had a cumulative effect, but rather than alienate her family, those were the times when having Drew and the boys helped her keep it at bay. There was something else, though. Drew had learned to recognise its advent at earlier and earlier stages, but was as powerless to stop it as he was to comprehend it. Catherine regretted the former impotence but was enduringly grateful for the latter.

'There's this dark place you go,' he told her. 'You're angry on the road to that place and you're unreachable when you get there. But what's hardest is you're numb for days afterwards.'

He had recognised the anger last night, and so had she. Other people could see it too.

You wanted it too much . . . You hate these people.

Moira Clark had recognised it, as had Graeme Sunderland. Not to mention Cal O'Shea, and Catherine really didn't want to spend time pondering what else the pathologist had noticed.

They all saw it but none of them understood its true nature.

Drew thought that her job sometimes took her to this dark place and made her forget she was a wife and a mother. The secret truth was that her job was what had kept her out of the dark place long enough to *become* a wife and mother.

She cast a glance at the station as she waited for a gap in the traffic, half-wishing that she would see Drew rush back out despite the rain to complete that kiss, and to hear her assurance that it constituted unfinished business. Instead she saw

149

only a flash in her rear-view, as a Corsa driver gave her the okay to pull away.

There was a fear she did not like to admit at times like this, as though refusing to name it would keep it from her head, far less from happening.

It was that Drew might stray. Not hypothetically either, at some non-specific time in the future, but tonight: that something previously only dreaded was a tangible possibility in the here and now. He could have a few too many and do something silly but perhaps understandable. A little drunk, more than a little angry with her, feeling sorry for himself, feeling in need of reparation: Catherine knew enough about the way people justified their transgressions to be afraid.

He was coming home, though, she remembered with relief. A big meeting with the inner circle and then dinner, after which he'd be on a train from Waverley to Central. It wasn't an overnight thing.

Games designers weren't exactly rock stars, but they weren't school librarians either. They transected certain circles, socially and economically. Where Catherine's own professional Venn diagram overlapped criminals, doctors and lawyers, Drew's brought him into occasional contact with more glamorous spheres. Two guys from *The Wire* had done voice talent on *Hostile III*. Rock bands were queuing up to get their tracks licensed on games for the kudos and exposure it delivered. And of course there were the aspiring cover girls providing eye-candy at the launch events.

Drew was nine years younger than her, and she couldn't be the only one who found him irresistibly attractive in a just-the-right-side-of-geeky way.

150

Therein lay the real root of her fear: sometimes she thought he was too good to be true. Too good for her, anyway. Attractive, bright, successful, considerate, affectionate, a loving and dutiful dad: what the hell was he doing with a crabbit older woman who complicated the hell out of everything and could go weeks without shagging him?

And what about that lack of shagging? Didn't they say where there's a will, there's a way? Why the lack of will, in that case? Did she just lose sight of it at times, on the road to and from that dark place? Or was she pushing him away, the scared part of her that believed he was too good to be true attempting to hasten his inevitable departure from her life, all the time preparing herself so that it didn't shock or hurt so much when it happened?

She slowed down at an amber light. She would have been through it before it turned red, but there was congestion on the other side of the junction anyway. It was a sensible, level-headed decision, and she needed sensible, level-headed thinking. These were stupid thoughts. She was overanxious because there was tension between them, and it wouldn't be outlandish to suggest that the lack of a damn good fucking wasn't helping her own head state either. Drew had never given any indication that he was likely to do anything rash, far less that he was unhappy with his life. He was kind, solicitous, selfless and loving. He was hers. But she was still very glad he wasn't staying in a hotel tonight.

VIEW FROM A DEAD END

Sitting in the front of the Land Rover, a vehicle as rugged and weathered-looking as its driver, Jasmine found her fear partially supplanted by a mortifying self-consciousness. She couldn't decide whether it was being fuelled by her feelings of vulnerability, or the other way around, but either way she felt quite literally exposed as Ingrams drove her along the winding rural lanes.

Her mind had been on other things when she came out of the shower this morning, and it was only striking her now that the bra she had put on was one she normally wore under blouses and other looser-fitting items, as opposed to the part-Lycra top she had stretched over herself in a caffeine-deficient semi-trance. Her nipples were showing through the material; not in a transparent way, but their topology was vividly described. This was something that, in Jasmine's experience, tended to be circularly reinforcing: once she was aware of it, it made her skin crawl with goose pimples, a tautening effect that had particular ramifications for her chest. She hadn't been aware of it while with Rita, but up close in the front of this Land Rover she felt acutely conscious of the masculinity in her presence. It was mostly olfactory: a smell of the outdoors and of fresh sweat, masked by a receding hint of shower gel and deo.

She folded her arms across her chest, but by this point she felt so self-consciously conspicuous that she felt self-consciously conspicuous about doing

152

that. She unfolded them again and tried to make herself appear relaxed, unworried, professional.

Ingrams, for his part, didn't appear to have noticed anyway: his focus was on the road, and when he briefly turned to address her (only at junctions), his eyes were locked strictly on hers, something for which she was not entirely grateful. If he was being gentlemanly, then it was the only thing he was doing to put her at her ease.

'I hope you enjoy the ride, because it's the only thing you're going to get from this trip. I don't know anything about this guy you're looking for. I've nothing to tell you.'

'I haven't told you who I'm looking for. And you don't know whether you've nothing to tell me until I ask you some questions.'

Ingrams just sighed, though coming from his frame it was close to a growl, a kind of ominous rumbling more associated with plate tectonics. Jasmine decided to play the only angle she felt she had.

'You know, your friend Rita gave me the impression that she expected you to be more polite.'

Ingrams raised his eyebrows at this.

'You think you made an ally back there?' he said. 'Believe me, you didn't. Rita just suggested you come along with me because it was the quickest way to get you out of the house. She doesn't like anybody snooping around, and neither do I.'

Jasmine was determined not to let him rattle her. It also occurred to her that if he really had nothing to say, he wouldn't be acting so put out. He had been evasive since the moment he clapped eyes on her. Then there was that accent. It initially reminded her of hearing tennis players and golfers being interviewed: people who spent much of their time on tour, permanently surrounded by a babble of voices speaking English as a second language. However, the more he spoke, the more she began to identify inconsistencies in his pronunciations and inflections, and to her ear, attuned by a couple of years of drama school, his accent sounded suspiciously put on.

He kept checking his rear-view mirror, and eventually Jasmine twisted in her seat and looked through the Land Rover's back windscreen. It was a left-hand drive model, indicating that Ingrams had acquired it overseas, and she found it a little disconcerting to be in the right-hand seat without a steering wheel in front of her, particularly when they passed oncoming vehicles. She could see a black Audi A4 behind them, driven by a bloke wearing a baseball cap. In her experience, such attire worn *inside* a vehicle did often mean 'wanker', and Ingrams might well have reason to be wary of some imminent act of highway stupidity, but he seemed to be giving it undue attention.

He took note of her turning, aware that she had picked up on his vigilance.

'This guy's been following me for about four miles, through three crossroads and two roundabouts. Is he with you? He needs to work on his technique if he is. Not exactly inconspicuous.'

'No, he's not with me. Just looks to me like someone who's not been able to get a clear stretch to overtake you. Are you always this paranoid?'

'I am when private investigators front up asking questions about dead people I've never met. More

154

so when it happens twice, despite it being obvious the first time that your colleague was barking up the wrong tree.'

Jasmine didn't respond for a few seconds, letting him think he'd made his point. In truth he had only made her all the more sure that he was hiding something, and she was going to show him why.

'Have you had a bad morning, Mr Ingrams? Get out the wrong side of bed? Football team lose last night?'

'No, but my pet goldfish snuffed it and my application for ballet school got turned down. On top of that, my shredder packed in, but I'd have to say that all of the above pale into insignificance compared to the irritation of being asked questions I've already answered, especially when the subject is something I know nothing about. It's bordering on Kafkaesque.'

'Hardly, Mr Ingrams. In fact, the reason I asked is that you strike me as acting disproportionately grumpy, and I'm inclined to ask myself why. Being asked questions by someone who mistakenly thinks you're informed is not the biggest imposition in the world. I think you're protesting too much.'

Ingrams gave an exasperated laugh.

'So if I'm pissed off at being asked questions I can't answer, that proves I *can* answer them? "Only the true messiah would deny it." Like I said: Kafkaesque. And why did the other guy send you anyway? Is it Bring Your Daughter To Work Day?'

Jasmine felt her cheeks burn and experienced a horrible combination of embarrassment and defeat. He had seen right through her.

There was a little ember of indignation burning in there too, though. For all she disliked working

155

as a PI, she was surprised to discover that she hated someone who knew nothing about her implying that she was rubbish at it. There was a voice inside her saying, 'Just wait, I'll show him,' but unfortunately it was a tiny little squeaky voice with absolutely nothing else to say. Under the circumstances, she felt that the truth was her only way forward.

'My boss has disappeared. He's been missing almost a week now, and I'm trying to find out what's happened to him.'

Ingrams took his eyes off the road for a fraction of a second, long enough to turn and give her a very curious look: partly incredulous, partly suspicious, partly guarded, but wholly surprised. Wherever he thought their little interview was going, this wasn't it.

'I'm trying to look deeper into the jobs he was working on. The Glen Fallan file was open on his desk, one of the last things he must have been looking at.'

Ingrams gave a small sigh: frustrated rather than petulant.

'At the risk of invoking your "only the true messiah" principle, what was there in that file that would make you come looking for me? I'd have thought I would be listed as a dead end.'

'Because your name and the refuge's address were just about the only things *in* that file. Which, and forgive me for getting all Kafkaesque, does make me wonder why my boss would possibly be looking through it if you were a dead end who had told him nothing. Did he come and see you again?'

'Yeah. That's whose body I was dismembering when the shredder packed in.'

'Listen, I'm just trying to work out where he might have gone, establish a timeline. He's been missing since possibly Thursday. If he was here on Friday, for instance, that would be a start.'

'Well, he wasn't. I haven't heard from him since he came down here last year, and I don't know how he got my details that time or what led him to think I could help.'

Ingrams glanced in the rear-view again. Jasmine didn't bother looking round. She hadn't seen the Audi overtake, so it was presumably still there. Perhaps the road had been too winding and hilly even for a boy-racer to risk it. Maybe he'd forgotten to wind down his windows and turn up the dance music.

'Here's the funny thing,' she said. 'Normally I'd be able to tell you all that: how the trail led to you, what source supplied your name, where it fitted into the wider investigation. I'd have had questions based on why Jim . . . my boss was interested in you. But all of the background information is missing from the records. My boss is normally meticulous beyond the point of pedantic about those things, yet on this one file, all such details were missing. So either somebody removed all the other documents from the folder, or you, Mr Dead End, were the alpha and omega of a completely fruitless investigation. Which would bring us back to the question of why . . . my boss would be digging out the folder.'

Jasmine winced, hoping Ingrams had missed the significance of her last stumble, then hoped he hadn't noticed her resultant expression. She had felt it inexplicably important not to reveal that Jim was her uncle, as opposed to merely her employer.

157

It may have been a natural caution against giving anything of herself away before she had succeeded in learning something about Ingrams; but just as likely she feared it would further underline that it was only because of nepotism that she was doing this job. However, it belatedly struck her that there was no reason to be quite so coy, and by trying to avoid mentioning Jim's name altogether, she may have tipped her hand.

'Your guess is as good as mine,' Ingrams replied. 'And on the subject of your guess, if this folder was so uncommonly light on information, what drives you to the conclusion that it's that particular case that is connected to your boss's disappearance?'

Jasmine feared for a horrible moment that she was going to fill up. It felt like Ingrams was not in fact obstructing her progress so much as merely pointing out the brick wall she was up against.

'Nothing in particular,' she admitted. 'I'm just looking for clues, exploring the possibilities. I'm worried . . .'

She was going to add 'for him', but pulled up short, once again concerned at divulging the nature of their relationship. Conveniently, she had an alternative motive she could plausibly offer.

'My salary is due at the end of this week. If I don't find him, I don't get any wages.'

She sounded desperate and pathetic, she knew.

'Jesus,' Ingrams said. 'Talk about performance-related pay. At least that explains why someone like you is doing this.'

'What do you mean, someone like me? A woman?'

'I mean someone your age. No offence, but you're not exactly what they call "hard-boiled".

158

What do you normally do for your boss: are you the secretary?'

They slowed to a near-stop at another junction as he spoke, Ingrams turning his head to scan left and right, his eyes looking past her and out of the side window as he checked for oncoming traffic. From his expression she could tell he wasn't being cheeky or patronising. He was asking honest questions, a hint of sincerity and even concern visible in his face. In a way, that made it worse.

She felt her cheeks burn again, that sting of shame at being found out mixed with a knot of anger. In her cringing self-consciousness she went to fold her arms yet again and once more stopped herself, as she knew it would look all the more girlie and pathetic.

She dearly wanted something to throw back and suddenly realised that she had it.

'No, I'm not the secretary,' she said, with a measured degree of distaste stopping well short of huffy indignation. 'I'm an investigator. I'm not the standard ex-cop model but I do this for a living. And I'm better at reading people than you would imagine. You've a daughter around my age, haven't you? Maybe a little younger.'

She spotted a twitch of a reaction, but it was too neutral to infer anything from, especially with his eyes flitting between his rear-view and the road. Nor was his response indicating either way.

'How do you work that out?' he asked.

'Is it true?'

'Tell me why you think so and I'll tell you if you're right.'

Ingrams accelerated the Land Rover steadily but unhurriedly away from the junction, aware of

159

another sharp bend coming up ahead.

'It would explain why you might more comfortably think of me as a secretary than an investigator. You would find it difficult to accept the idea of someone your daughter's age doing a job you associate with older people, older *males* at that; particularly a job you might consider unpalatable for a young woman.'

This sounded reasonable enough, but was only a more polite manifestation of the principle underlining Jasmine's deduction. The primary rationale behind her assertion, which she was not about to share, was that she had been shoogled around in this contraption for about twenty minutes and hadn't once caught him sneaking a look at her tits.

Ingrams said nothing, just drove on, hugging the bend, his eyes still flitting back and forth to the rear-view mirror.

'Well?' she eventually asked.

'Hm?' he responded, as though he'd bloody forgotten. 'Oh, I see. No. I don't have a daughter,' he told her, matter-of-fact to the point of distracted.

Christ, she thought. You go, girl. That showed him.

'Look, this guy in the Audi, is he with you?' Ingrams asked, like their previous exchange had never happened. 'I need you to be honest here. It's no big deal if he is.'

Jasmine glanced in the wing mirror. The Audi had rounded the bend and was gaining on them at pace. The road ahead was clear and straight, though: no dips, no climbs, no oncoming traffic.

'No, he absolutely, honestly isn't. He's

overtaking now anyway. See?'

Ingrams eased off on the accelerator to let the Audi pass while the road ahead was straight and clear. He turned his head slightly as the Land Rover slowed, his eyes directed south of Jasmine's neck for the first time; or at least the first time she had noticed. With the coast clear and the road straight for a stretch, he was finally taking the chance to grab an eyeful. She twisted to face him, thinking of something acerbic to embarrass him with, which was when she observed that he was actually gazing intently in the passenger-side wing-mirror.

Jasmine was about to turn and inspect what it was when Ingrams jolted the gearstick forward into third and slammed down his right foot, pinning her against the seat and throwing her head back. In almost the same moment, so close to simultaneous as to sound like the sudden ferocious gunning of the engine had caused it, both of the rear side-windows exploded.

Jasmine felt fragments of glass spray and ping around the interior, like she was inside a violently shaken snow globe.

She looked left through her window and saw the Audi accelerate to come alongside again. The driver's window was open and there was a passenger leaning across him, pointing a shotgun towards the Land Rover. She hadn't noticed a passenger before. He must have been bent down, out of sight, then leaned across and taken aim as the vehicle overtook. If Ingrams' sudden acceleration hadn't jerked them forward a couple of seconds ago, her head would have been blown apart.

161

She felt an almost convulsive panic, a primal terror mixed with the coldest dread. Not disbelief, not confusion. She knew the man with the shotgun was real, the threat was real, that everything was exactly as it seemed. Once, she would have constructed a hundred alternative explanations in her head that avoided accepting that something like this was happening to her. Mum's illness and death had completely changed her perspective. She knew that your worst fears could come true, and she knew that just because something awful happened to you, it didn't mean you would be spared something worse.

The Audi was faster and more agile over short distances than the bumpy old Land Rover. Ingrams couldn't possibly outrun it. She could feel shock turning very quickly to a helpless fear, the whimper of a lost little girl escaping from her mouth.

She was transfixed by the sight of the Audi pulling alongside, gaining excruciatingly incremental degrees of angle for the kill shot in what felt like slow motion. Then Ingrams jerked the handbrake, changed down again and turned hard on the wheel.

The Audi seemed to shoot forward out of sight like the Land Rover had opened a parachute. The world spun sickeningly before Jasmine's eyes and she was tugged roughly towards Ingrams as their vehicle lurched and skidded across the narrow two-lane road. Ingrams wrestled the steering wheel and elicited pained screams from both the engine and the tyres as he pitted them both vainly against the laws of motion. The Land Rover continued its sideways skid across the tarmac and on to a narrow stretch of coarse grass before slamming to a halt against a tall hedgerow.

The impact smacked Jasmine's head against the door frame, shaking loose glass fragments from her hair. There was blood smeared on her fingers. She was bleeding but she didn't know from where, the adrenalin surge preventing her from feeling the pain quite yet. It was worth it, though: the Land Rover was facing back the way they had come.

She looked frantically into the rear-view mirror. About seventy or eighty metres along the road, the Audi had stopped and was starting to reverse towards them. That was when she became aware that despite the roaring of the engine, the Land Rover wasn't moving forward.

'Drive,' she urged Ingrams, bouncing in her seat like an impatient toddler. 'Go. Why won't it move?'

'If we're unlucky, it's because the front wheel arch is jammed in the hedge. And if we're really unlucky, it's because the axle's broken. Either way we're not going anywhere. Shit.'

With that, Ingrams undid his seat belt and opened the door. Jasmine gripped the handle on her side, but the door was wedged up hard against the hedgerow.

'Don't leave me,' she pleaded, her desperation making her unashamed of her tearful supplication.

'Keep your bloody head down,' he retorted. His accent had changed. It didn't sound put on any more. It did still suggest someone who had lived in a lot of different places, but more specifically a Scotsman who had lived in a lot of different places.

She sank down in the seat, then briefly reached back up to adjust the rear-view mirror so that she could see the road, her heart going like a double-

163

kick drum. The Audi was closing in, the whine of its reverse gear getting louder as it approached. Fifty yards. Forty. She could see the driver and the passenger, both turned around to look through the rear windscreen. They were wearing latex masks, the driver's still topped with the baseball cap he had been wearing to disguise his disguise. Presumably he had guessed that the sight of Richard Nixon's face behind the wheel in Northumberland would have been more than enough to tip off somebody as paranoid as Ingrams.

She stuck her head up a little to look for him, expecting that he would be wrestling with the front wheel on her side of the vehicle. He was nowhere to be seen. Suddenly, though she wouldn't have considered it possible, she felt worse, more afraid. Why had he left her? Where the hell was he?

Then she both heard and felt a metallic clunk from somewhere beneath her.

The Audi had stopped about twenty yards away. The passenger-side door swung slowly open and in the rear-view mirror she saw a figure, also in a Nixon mask, emerge slowly and deliberately, holding a pump-action shotgun.

Jasmine shuddered and screamed as the first of a series of bangs assailed her ears. When she looked in the mirror again, however, she saw that the figure in the Nixon mask was empty-handed, his shotgun now lying on the road. He scrambled towards it, which was when Jasmine was shaken by a second bang from close by, resulting in the shotgun flipping and spinning across the tarmac like it had been yanked on a string.

She sat up a little straighter and turned to look

out of the driver's-side door, where she saw Ingrams alongside the Land Rover in a kneeling crouch. He was holding an automatic pistol in both hands, his face stony with concentration as his finger worked the trigger.

She heard a slam as the gunman closed the Audi's passenger door behind him and a screech of tyres as the vehicle accelerated away. Ingrams kept firing, taking out the Audi's rear windscreen and drilling some holes in its bodywork as it zoomed off like a startled rabbit.

He fired six shots in total, but kept the gun trained on the Audi until it had disappeared around the next bend, maybe quarter of a mile away. Only then did Jasmine feel she could breathe out.

Throughout the Audi's retreat, she hadn't wanted him to fire again, partly because of the jolting shock of the reports, but mainly in case he hit the tyres. She didn't want the car to stop, didn't want the gunman to have any reason to get out and return fire, just in case they had more than one weapon on them.

Having watched Ingrams train the pistol intently upon the escaping car without his trigger finger twitching again, she appreciated from the minutely calmer position of retrospect that he had never had any intention of precipitating such an outcome. He was scaring them off, not trying to draw them back into a fire fight.

Ingrams dropped his aim and walked calmly forward to retrieve the abandoned shotgun, picking it up by the trigger guard. The stock looked as if it had been shattered by his bullets, twisted and dangling like a broken limb. Jasmine watched all of this in a state of numb disbelief, like the little rectangle of the rear-view mirror was the screen on a smartphone or a portable DVD player, showing scenes far removed from her reality. Then she came back to herself, feeling stings and throbbings of pain that had been anaesthetised by fear.

It suddenly became imperative that she get out of the Land Rover. Despite the danger receding, she felt a compelling need to escape from this rickety metal box and put her feet down on the ground. She clambered across the driver's seat and hopped unsteadily on to the road.

The air outside was hot, warmer than the fan-cooled interior of the vehicle. Jasmine felt her head swim as she stood upright, the mugginess an unpleasant disappointment. For some reason she had expected to feel cold air like water to the face, sharpening her up, helping her shake off the effects of what had just happened. Adrenalin was still thrilling through her and her ears were ringing from the noise of Ingrams' pistol shots. Once again she felt tears begin to flow, but to her surprise, the upsurge she was feeling turned out to be as much anger and frustration as anything else.

'You all right?' Ingrams asked, thumbing the safety catch on his weapon and tucking it into the waistband of his trousers.

She watched him lean into the rear of his vehicle and flip open a storage bin, into which he carefully placed the damaged shotgun. His question hung in the air like it was a far more complex query, one Jasmine realised she didn't have a simple answer for.

'What constitutes all right, under these circumstances?' she asked, struggling to find her voice.

'Standing on two feet is usually a positive indication,' he replied.

Something about this infuriated her, quite volcanically so, and she was so shocked by the ferocity of her feelings that it took her a moment to realise why. It was that he was so calm, so matter-of-fact. It was that this wasn't new to him. He had brought her into his world.

'I'm standing on two feet, but I'm far from all right,' she said, a tremor in her voice that was one part aftershock, one part lingering fear and one part boiling rage. 'You've been acting shifty and evasive since we met and now you've almost got me killed,' she went on, fighting hard to keep her words coming steady and clear as she spoke. 'I think you owe me some straight answers. You're this Glen Fallan guy, aren't you? That's why there's nothing else in the file.'

He shook his head solemnly.

'My name is Tron Ingrams. I can show you my passport, my army discharge papers, anything you like.'

'So who the hell is Tron Ingrams? You go from driving like a pensioner to driving like something out of a stunt show. You've got people in masks shooting at you, you've got guns hidden under your car.'

'*A* gun. Singular,' he clarified.

'One gun is lots, okay? To normal people. One gun is plenty.'

She was babbling, but she was well past caring what kind of impression she was making. She didn't care if she was acting like a hysterical girl: she had every right to be acting like a hysterical girl, and her previous air of detached professionalism had got her nothing.

'What kind of a name is Tron, anyway? How did you know that gunman was even there? Why have you got a gun under your car when you work at a women's refuge? Who were those men? Oh yeah, and why were they trying to *kill* you?'

Ingrams made a placatory gesture with his hands, asking her to calm down. She thought for a moment that he was about to touch her, grab her arms, maybe hold her like she was going to cry. She stiffened, ready to bat away any contact, yet part of her deeply wanted it to happen.

'I realise you're pretty shaken up,' he said, 'and I apologise in advance for answering a question with another question: but could you please tell me precisely why you think they weren't trying to kill *you*?'

THE MERCY OF THE COURT

Catherine crossed the river on Gorbals Street and proceeded along Bridgegate, heading for the car park at St Margaret's Place. It was early enough to get a space, for which she was grateful on a morning like this. A train rumbled across the bridge overlooking the car park, making her wonder briefly where Drew was by now. Coming up the stairs at Buchanan Street underground, perhaps, maybe already inside Queen Street, getting a coffee for the train.

She hurried along the pavement and beneath the shelter of the cylindrical plinth that fronted the

High Court building. Supported by half a dozen columns, it always made her think of a gigantic occasional table, the kind of thing her great-aunts might have sat the telephone upon. Like every public building these days, the entrance was lightly shrouded in smoke, but the real mystical portals lay beyond. For some, the door they left this place by decreed where their future lay, sometimes for a decade or more.

Catherine had never been at the mercy of such a fate, but the interior of the building never failed to make her uneasy. It had been the scene of many satisfactory results, but in the way some people said the mere sight of a police officer made them feel guilty, court buildings had a similar unsettling effect on cops. It was the same principle: the awareness that you were subject to a higher power over which you had little control or influence, whose fleeting caprice could affect you disproportionately, irrevocably and unaccountably. In Catherine's case, though, it went a little deeper, a little more personal, to an anger that still simmered and a shame whose flame still flickered in the dark somewhere in her mind, never quite quenched despite the smallness of the source and the passing of the years.

It hadn't been this court, but just across the river at Carlton Place. Nonetheless, Sheriff Court or High Court, the memory could sometimes creep up on her as soon as she saw the liveries, the benches and the briefcases.

She was a little more than two years into the job at the time. Not a wide-eyed probationer but definitely still finding her feet. They wouldn't have asked a probationer to do this, and they bloody

169

well *shouldn't* have asked her. It was their mess, their pit, and they dragged her down to help them keep digging.

It happened on an otherwise quiet Thursday night, at her first station, Barnes Street over in Braeside. The officers concerned were Roddy Howard, an authoritarian automaton who was born forty-five, and the willing young Padawan to his Yoda, Mark McLean, whom even the young Catherine could tell wore his insecurities brightly on his sleeve.

Howard was classic constable-for-life material. Every station needs one: straight as a die, unquestioningly dutiful, humourlessly literal-minded, and thick as mince. McLean was not so much someone who was bullied at school as someone who had wanted to be doing the bullying but had never been hard enough. Now that he had the full force of the law as backup, he was fast making up for lost time.

According to the defendants (and Catherine now unequivocally accepted the three adolescents' version of events), they were walking back from the pub at around eleven o'clock when two of them, Anthony McGuire and Allan Reilly, decided they couldn't hold back the tide long enough to get home. It was, as stated, a quiet night. The streets were all but empty; indeed, the street they were walking along—Barnes Street—was completely devoid of life, otherwise they would have kept their legs crossed for another quarter-mile, what with the polis station being just across the road. However, with nobody in sight, they both nipped into a narrow passageway between the bank building and the tenement block next door while

170

their stronger-bladdered mate, Steve Gallacher, waited on the pavement. They were mid-pee when Howard and McLean came around the corner from the Main Street in a police van. Noticing Gallacher loitering on the pavement, they pulled in to investigate, at which point they noticed two figures along the dark passageway. One of the cops shouted 'Hoi!' prompting the pair of them to swiftly get off their marks, zipping up as they ran out the back of the passageway and into the bank car park.

As McGuire later told the court, when they heard the shout, they assumed that it was either an irate resident or, just as plausibly for Braeside, some heidthebaw wanting a bit of late-night action. Either way, they didn't hang around to find out. Then, when they saw two polismen enter the car park from the far end, they ceased running. Reilly stated that at the time he was actually relieved.

This was where it should have ended: a wee word of warning. Any decent cop would have clocked what he was dealing with. They weren't blitzed, they weren't rowdy and, most significantly, they weren't familiar. Howard, however, decided to lift the pair of them, then went for the hat-trick when Gallacher made the mistake of expressing his incredulity that they were being arrested for pissing up a lane already full of dog shit and broken glass.

They all spent a night in the cells before being charged with breach of the peace and resisting arrest. 'The polis breach', the former was known as: a catch-all charge that, with two cops as witnesses, made for a fait accompli, one many folk grudgingly learned to take on the chin whether they merited it or not. Resisting arrest, also engaging the mutual corroboration, was often thrown in there to seal the deal.

For the defendants' part, had they been blitzed, had they been rowdy, and significantly, had they been frequent fliers, they would quite probably have left it at that: taken the fine and put it down to experience. But they were none of the above: they were three respectable lads who had never been in bother with the law before. They knew the breach charge was an abuse of power, but it was the resisting part that really pissed them off, because it was an outright lie.

They disputed all charges and consequently the case went before the Sheriff Court. That was when Catherine became involved. It wasn't Howard or McLean who brought her into it, though: it was her sarge, Donald Morrison, someone she had already come to look toward for guidance. He didn't ask her to do it; he told her she *was* doing it.

'We need to nail this,' he said. 'Be good experience for you, getting you in the box.'

Catherine was rattled. It wasn't the end of the innocence, some epiphanic moment of disillusion, but it was still a shock to the system to be so matter-of-factly told to lie in court. However, the Sarge stiffened her resolve by giving her an unmistakable impression regarding two things: that to do this was no big deal; but to refuse was unthinkable.

You always back up your colleagues. It's the golden rule.

She was coached what to say, and assured she'd be in and out of there in no time. It was a formality, they told her.

They were right about none of this. The only part that took no time was for the defence solicitor to recognise not merely that she was the weak link, but precisely the tactical misjudgement the police had made, a recognition assisted by having been informed by his clients that none of them had seen her there that night.

'I was inside the van,' she explained, as instructed, this issue having been to some extent anticipated. 'In the front cab. They were making so much noise that I couldn't tell how many there were, and I was scared. PC Howard told me to stay in the van, because he feared they might get violent.'

In support of the resisting-arrest charge, she told the court: 'PC Howard and PC McLean got the defendants into the back of the van, but not without a struggle. They were kicking at the doors, thrashing around, trying to prevent themselves being forced inside. I've not been on the job very long and I found it terrifying.'

She got a subtle wee nod from Sergeant Morrison, who had come along for moral support. Good girl. She had done well. She was pleased. But then the defence lawyer got up.

'What kind of noise were they making?' he asked. 'Could you be a little more specific?'

It sounded like a curious little query, but she understood later that it was in fact his declaration that he knew she hadn't been there. The key word was 'specific': he knew she'd been put up to this, and specifics were where it would fall apart.

'Shouting and singing,' she replied, this much having been discussed between her and her colleagues. 'All at the tops of their voices, which

173

can happen when you're drunk. You forget how distressing that can be for everybody else— especially on a quiet night in a residential area.'

'But what were they shouting? Or singing? Can you give me some examples?'

'I—I can't really remember. I just remember how loud it seemed on a quiet night.'

'Just one thing would suffice. Maybe a name they were shouting, a phrase that stuck in your mind? A sentiment, maybe?'

She caught herself looking at Howard and McLean, then at the Sarge in the public seats.

'I can't remember,' she said pathetically. She wanted to pull her coat over her head and disappear.

'Obviously it was such a traumatic experience that your subconscious has blanked it out rather than relive the nightmare,' the lawyer said scornfully. 'An effect that presumably did not extend to all of your sensory recollections. Indeed your visual acuity seems to have been positively enhanced by your state of terror. You explained how you were cowering in fear in the front cab, keeping yourself out of sight of these noisy and potentially violent young men. This being so, could you explain how you managed to witness their titanic struggle to remain outside the van?'

It was a disaster. The case wasn't just thrown out: the sheriff tore strips off them for wasting the court's time and castigated Catherine in particular for 'having not a shred of credibility'. She felt her cheeks burning as he spoke, and it was only by some miracle that she made it out of the courtroom before breaking down in tears of shame and humiliation.

Her colleagues' responses were more measured, to say the least. Win some, lose some seemed to be the attitude, which told her that this kind of thing was standard procedure, culturally ingrained. They went to the pub later and most of the station turned up. Everybody bought her drinks, patted her on the back. Even officers who thought Howard and McLean were wankers. They thought she'd done well. She'd stood up, proven her loyalty. That was more important than a bollocks wee breach-and-resist case. Nobody regarded it as cause for embarrassment, just a hazard of the job.

They were acting like she had passed a final test and trying to make her feel accepted, but Catherine didn't feel as though what she was being accepted into was somewhere she wanted to belong. She felt used and she felt compromised. It wasn't about solidarity, it was about coercion, about being forced to submit your will. And once your integrity had been proven malleable, you were in a weak position to ever rock the boat.

On the plus side, it did provide something of an immunising dose. She vowed that nobody was going to make her lie for them again, no matter the consequences for her status among her peers. Maybe it was indeed a test, a rite of passage, and maybe it was the vibes she thereafter gave off, but either way, as it turned out, nobody ever asked her to.

She wouldn't have anybody lie for her either, which sounded an easy principle to enforce by mere omission, but was far more complicated in practice. It was generally accepted that gilding the lily was the right thing to do if it meant a guilty man didn't wriggle free with the assistance of a smart lawyer. Catherine wouldn't have it on her cases, though. It was one thing losing a trumped-up charge because of lying in court, but losing a genuine, solid conviction because some over-enthusiastic fib had undermined the whole case's integrity was a possibility she simply could not tolerate.

There was an argument for playing the percentages, but Catherine was never a gambler. Besides, she didn't want to be justifying her conduct to herself on the grounds that she was better than the scum she put away. She wanted to know she was better than the scum she put away because of the way she conducted herself.

Catherine made her way across the lobby to check the screens and confirm which court was hearing Crown versus Agnew that morning. This was not one she expected to be on tenterhooks about, nor remotely fearful of fleeting caprice.

Sammy Agnew had been rescued from the chill waters of a canal back in April, having been discovered clinging on to a drainage outlet by two early-morning joggers. He was suffering symptoms of hypothermia but was most likely unable to distinguish between those and the symptoms of having been drinking for upwards of seventy-two hours prior to his plunge.

Catherine never ceased to marvel at how many murder cases involved what was described in court as 'a three-day drinking binge'. These days she could barely manage three hours. A couple of glasses of wine once the weans were in bed and she was pleasantly on her way to unconsciousness.

On a recent visit to the pub, she had overheard one young reveller prevent his mate from ordering a burger and chips from the bar on the grounds that 'eatin's cheatin'.' Even twenty years younger, she could not have related to that mentality. For guys like Agnew, however, 'abuse' seemed too ordinary a word to describe what they did with alcohol. It probably took less time and commitment to condition the body for Olympic competition than to be able to endure that volume and longevity of drink. Sammy wouldn't be getting a medal, though.

Around about the time he was warming up in hospital, his nominal best friend and fellow bevvy-athlete Peter Leckie was being fished out of the same canal. Peter hadn't been so lucky, his chances of escaping the treacherous depths and the low temperatures greatly reduced by having been dead for several hours before he ever hit the water.

Sammy's defence was that he and Peter had been out for a late-night stroll when they were set upon by some local neds. They had chucked Sammy into the canal, but Peter had initially fought them off, his bravery earning him a severe kicking when the neds eventually got the upper hand. This accounted for the multiple blunt-trauma wounds to Peter's head, but there were a few pernickety details outstanding. Such as Sammy being caught on CCTV taking a trolley from the nearby Morrisons supermarket, and being seen by several witnesses later the same night pushing a lifeless body towards the canal, making 'wheee' noises in order to give the impression that he and his companion were engaged in some harmless fun.

The bloodstains all over Sammy's house were a puzzler too; presumably he had been intending to

177

clean up when he got back. His ingenious plan had evidently been to dump the body in the canal and make it look like an accident: two pals whose drunken high jinks had ended in tragedy. The saddest thing was that at the time, it probably all made sense inside Sammy's booze-pickled mind. Unfortunately, aside from his failure to anticipate pretty much all modern forensic and criminal investigation techniques, as he was still utterly blitzed, the stupid bastard had fallen in right behind his deceased ex-pal.

It was presumably a testimony to his resourcefulness in sourcing alcohol while in jail awaiting trial that he was still maintaining a plea of not guilty. People would laugh when she told them about it later, but to be honest, it was pissing Catherine off. She knew that due process had to be observed, but she wondered what it was costing the public in order to reach such a foregone conclusion. More than this waster had cumulatively earned, she bet. The bugger knew fine he was guilty, knew he was going down, but he was getting everyone else's money's worth.

There was a gaggle of people in front of her, checking the cases, the hanging monitors as always perversely reminding her of departure boards. When Sammy's flight was called, he'd be going for a very long holiday indeed. As she scanned the screens, looking over a host of heads, she spotted a familiar figure walking hurriedly along the corridor, carrying a sheaf of files under one arm. It was Dominic Wilson, the young anointed of the Procurator Fiscal's office and scion of that same office's most formidable adversary, Ruaraidh Wilson QC. He was wearing a three-piece suit just the silvery side of charcoal, the effect both a little flamboyant and at the same time prematurely ageing. It reminded her of something and she could have kicked herself that it took a second or so to work out what. He was affecting his old man's style. Was he taking the piss, some kind of calculated insult, or was it indicative that he was a little closer to his father than some people wanted to believe? Possibly a bit of both. Had there been a rapprochement? Or can you just not escape what's bred in the bone?

His head was down and he didn't appear to have seen her; or just as likely his head was down because he had seen her first. This would indicate he didn't want to talk to her, and if that was the case, then it confirmed her suspicions that there was something specific he didn't want to talk about.

'Good morning, Dominic,' she said, stepping into his path to intercept him.

He pretended to act surprised.

'Oh, hi, Catherine. How you doing? You here for the incredible floating jakey?'

'Yes, I—'

'Break a leg,' he interrupted. 'Sorry, I can't stop. Got a case myself this morning.'

'Aye, but the courts are that way,' she reminded him, glancing back over his head. 'You're off outside for a last fag, and that means you've got five minutes. Come on, I'll keep you company.'

'Bollocks,' he said with a sigh, before resuming his progress towards the main doors with huffy bad grace.

She waited for him to light up and have a draw, conscious that she'd get nothing until the nicotine hit.

'Know who I was talking to last night?' she asked. 'Gary Fleeting.'

He rolled his eyes, confirming that he knew this was coming.

'And how was he?' he said through gritted teeth.

'Well, for a bloke who got lifted in possession of that much brown, I'd have expected him to look, I don't know, a bit more prisony. What happened, Dom?'

'Scottish justice moves in mysterious ways,' he said wearily. He closed his fist then opened it again, palm up, a gesture of something disappearing or flying away. Catherine recognised the mannerism, having often seen Ruaraidh Wilson do it in court, usually as he was making some key piece of evidence suddenly seem tangential or irrelevant. For a guy who was supposedly determined to be unlike his father, he was helluva like his father. The apple clearly hadn't fallen far, which rather made a nonsense of the jokes and innuendo suggesting that his becoming a zealous prosecutor was proof that he was actually the product of an affair. It was the kind of thing cops told each other to make themselves feel better about Wilson Senior's occult powers thwarting their best efforts.

Indeed, the same embittered cops peddling this stuff had previously been happy enough to identify Dominic as his father's son during more troubled times. In his teens and student years, he had threatened to go seriously off the rails, reputedly due to his stormy relationship with Wilson *père*. There had been problems with drink and hard drugs, resulting in several arrests.

180

They might also have resulted in a few convictions and more than a few lurid headlines had it not been for surprising levels of compassion and discretion on the part of certain senior police officers. At the time, Catherine was a shade resentful of a poor little rich kid being indulged, wondering how often such understanding was extended to those from less esteemed backgrounds. However, she would have had to concede that being the only child of a phenomenally successful but slightly strange and unquestionably workaholic individual such as Ruaraidh Wilson QC must have brought its own difficulties.

In time, she came to respect her senior officers for it. They could easily have used his son's difficulties to embarrass and undermine Wilson, or even just for plain old payback, but they didn't, and when Catherine thought about why, she came to understand that, like it or not, they were all part of the same process.

People would ask how Ruaraidh Wilson could possibly defend certain individuals, and the methods by which he did so were often so infuriating that they could start to comprise a strong argument for vigilantism. However, as a cop, he made you raise your game. If you got a conviction against him after he had worked his voodoo, you were not going to lose one wink of sleep dwelling on the possibility that you didn't get the right man. Thus a lawyer like Wilson was crucial to ensuring that justice was done. At least that was what Catherine kept telling herself: it was what sometimes stopped her getting out of bed, driving across town and burning down his house in the middle of the night.

Her colleagues must have got some kind of reciprocation from their sensitivity during Dom's wild years, right enough. Wilson had access to a lot of very privileged information, and his ability to negotiate secret deals was legendary. The case against one villain might collapse, then a few months later, another would fall right into the police's hands. Nobody would ever be able to join the dots, however. Like a great magician, the point when you thought you had worked out how he had done it was the point when you were furthest from the truth, exactly where he wanted you.

'See, you say "mysterious", but I always interpret that word as "suspicious". Enlighten me.'

'Don't waste your ire on it, Catherine,' he told her between drags, cigarettes being the only vice he allowed himself these days. 'It won't do any good. It wasn't even your case, so keep your powder dry for when it is.'

'That's just it, though. I've got a dead drug dealer in Gallowhaugh and Gary Fleeting's well in the frame for it. Even if it wasn't him, his boss Frankie Callahan is thigh-deep in something right now, I'm sure of it.'

'I think we can both agree we'd be happier putting Fleeting away for murder than Class A possession. Maybe it's a case of "what's for you will no' go by you".'

'Aye, and maybe there's something going by me right now, as in over my head. I want to know what I'm missing before I start putting a murder case together.'

'I'm pretty sure if you had put *this* case together, it would have flown,' Dominic said. He wasn't trying to sound patronising or sycophantic, but he didn't sound convincing either. He was trying to lead her off the scent.

'Bollocks. There was nothing wrong with that bust. The t's were crossed and the i's all dotted. That decision wasn't taken regarding the likelihood of securing a conviction. It was political. Why did you drop it?'

He took a long draw on his fag, staring out at the rain, acting like this was becoming a bore, but she could tell it was because he didn't want to look her in the eye.

'It's not at my discretion to say,' he finally told her.

Catherine responded with a small shrug and a growing silence, making out she was resigned to leaving it there. She wasn't, however. He was going to tell her more, because she knew just which button to press.

'That's as may be,' she said with a sigh, 'but if you don't give me something, I'm going to have to conclude that it's not entirely unrelated to the fact that Gary Fleeting and Frankie Callahan are both clients of your father.'

'Oh piss off,' he replied sourly. 'My dad has represented just about every gangster in Glasgow at one time or other. Hardly an astronomical coincidence.'

'Aye, but this is the first time one of his clients was being prosecuted by his son. All of a sudden the charges disappear. I'm not saying there was anything improper: I'm sure your side got something from the deal. I'm just surprised you—'

'You've no idea what you're talking about,' he interrupted curtly. 'You've some fucking nerve as well, considering all the pressure was coming from your end.'

Catherine's satisfaction at having procured a response was utterly swamped by her dismay at what it told her.

'My end? Someone in the police brought pressure to drop the case? Who?'

He gave the slightest shake of his head, its subtlety inversely proportional to its gravity.

'It wasn't my decision.'

'Not your decision? I thought you were prosecuting it.'

'So did I. But you're right. All of a sudden the whole thing went political and it was out of my hands.'

'Who brought the pressure, Dominic?' she pushed again.

'I'm not supposed to know, and I'm sure as hell not supposed to say.'

He did know though, and he clearly wanted to say. He looked as pissed off about it as she was. Unfortunately, his fag was almost down to the stub and both their court cases were starting in a couple of minutes.

'Come on,' she urged, putting a hand on his forearm. 'We're on the same side here. If I'm going after Frankie Callahan, it would benefit both of us if I knew who might be tying my shoelaces together while I'm not looking.'

His eyes flashed angrily.

'You don't need to give me the motivational speech. I had pricks like that ruffling my hair when I was growing up.'

He took a final draw and flicked the cigarette into the wall-mounted bin.

184

Shit, Catherine thought. That was it. Gone.

They went back inside together, Dominic striding purposefully through the lobby as though trying to put distance between them. Catherine guessed she wasn't even going to get a polite goodbye, but he suddenly stopped outside his court and glanced to the side, as though checking who might be nearby.

'It's very secret, very sensitive,' he said. 'I'd love to tell you, and I'd love to be prosecuting Frankie Callahan, but I can't give you that name. What I can say is that it was not so much pressure as a plague.'

With that, he turned and strode briskly through the doors as though the court offered sanctuary in case she might pursue him.

Way above her pay grade right enough. Way above his too, which was presumably why he couldn't—or rather wouldn't—tell her.

Then she realised that he just had.

Not so much pressure as a plague.

Thank you, Dominic.

A plague of Locust.

RUN TO GROUND

Since Ingrams had a pistol stashed in some hidey-hole under the Land Rover, it wasn't a surprise that he had a well-stocked toolbox under one of the benches in the back. Having checked beneath the front of the vehicle and declared that the axle was intact, he produced a short-handled hacksaw and set about cutting away the thick lower trunks

185

of the hedgerow, freeing the wheel arch.

Jasmine dabbed with a hanky at a small wound to the left side of her head. She had suffered several light scratches from the glass, little diagonals on her arms no worse than might be inflicted by a toddler's nails, but the one to her scalp was deeper and stubbornly refusing to clot. She thought it must have been when she banged her head on the door frame, but she could feel a lump from that blow a couple of inches higher than the cut.

These minor injuries felt like merely an inconvenience, a mess to clear up that was barely related to the real damage she had suffered. The shimmering fragments of glass seemed disproportionately trivial by way of wreckage, too. It felt like a hole had been blown in the very fabric of the world as she understood it, and none of the existing evidence could truly testify to its enormity.

Everything should stop for now, she believed. There should be about two dozen police converging on this place, closing off the entire area while they commenced their investigations. She should be delivered into the safe hands of a massive machine, her role now reduced to that of witness while more capable and empowered agencies took responsibility for whatever had engulfed her.

Instead, it appeared, the world around her was indifferently getting on with itself. Ingrams in particular seemed concerned with nothing more pressing than the need to free his vehicle from the hedge. Something about his pragmatism was deeply offending her.

Several cars passed in either direction. They all

slowed to have a look, a few getting as far as winding the window down ahead of presumably offering assistance, but Ingrams calmly waved them all on. He clearly didn't want to have to explain anything to anyone, which prompted a further horrified deduction from Jasmine.

'You're not calling the police?' she asked incredulously, as he held open the driver's-side door and indicated that she should climb back in.

'I'd rather not, no. I think it would be difficult to make a statement about what happened without mentioning that I had a gun, and that might lead to certain complications for me.'

'Complications? What about men with shotguns? I'd anticipate that having my head blown off might complicate things quite a bit. It's not my problem you're mixed up in stuff that means you've got guns stashed under your car. No, actually, today it *was* my problem, and that's all the more reason I want the authorities involved.'

Ingrams let her babble for a moment, then started the engine by way of overruling her objection. He pinned her with that stare as he spoke.

'First of all, once again, gun, singular. Second, also once again, you're the one who's mixed up in something. And third, if it wasn't for me having my gun, singular, we'd both be dying from shotgun wounds right now. I'd consider it an act of courtesy and gratitude, therefore, if you didn't respond to my saving your life—twice, plural—by dropping me in it with the cops.'

Jasmine said nothing for a while, seething. She wasn't feeling much gratitude, as she still wasn't buying the theory that this was something that was

187

happening to her rather than him. The guy could shoot a gun out of a man's hands, she realised. That meant he had chosen not to kill or even wound the gunman, but merely scare him off instead. Why?

Complications. Mess to clear up. Difficult matters to explain to the police. What kind of man was so reluctant to involve the authorities under circumstances like *this*? And what would he say if she insisted? She needed to know where she stood, and whether where she *should* be standing was as far away from Ingrams as possible.

He interpreted her silence as the end of the discussion and began negotiating the Land Rover away from the hedgerow and off the grass verge.

'I need this investigated,' she said, as calmly and resolutely as she could manage. She required it to sound both reasonable and decisive. 'If you're right, and it was me they were after, then I need protection. I'm sorry that it's going to make things awkward for you, but I have to go to the police.'

Her heart was leathering it again, almost as much as when she'd been under fire, and it wasn't going to slow much until she heard his response, which didn't come soon.

It was Ingrams' turn to say nothing. He edged the vehicle forward on to the tarmac and accelerated gradually, warm air blowing through the frames of the shattered rear windows. With him not making a further verbal appeal, she began to wonder what he might do to obstruct her.

'I can protect you,' he said eventually. 'Better than the police. I'll come back to Glasgow with you, help you look into this.'

Yeah, right, was her first impulse, then she

188

thought of DS McDade and of Sergeant Collins, of how much she had wanted them to take her seriously, then of that sinking realisation that they would only assist her inasmuch as she was, at best, tangential to their interests. Ingrams was offering one-on-one assistance. However, she tempered her temptation by asking herself what reason she had to believe she wasn't merely tangential to his interests right now too. What motivation did he have to get so involved, beyond keeping the police out of his business?

'I thought you said this had nothing to do with you. That you know nothing about any of it. Remember that patter?'

'I do know nothing about any of it, but it's clearly got something to do with me now. Your boss goes missing and there's a file with my name and the address of the refuge lying open on his desk. You come and see me by way of following this up and all of a sudden we're getting shot at. I want to know where I fit into this. Plus they damaged my Land Rover. I'll be hitting them up for the excess.'

Jasmine thought about it for a while, dabbing at her head some more with the hanky. The blood was still spotting, and now she could feel a hard little lump at one end of the cut, something embedded just under the skin. Wincing a little, she dug at it with a nail and tugged it loose. It came away into the hanky amid a few strands of hair. She picked it clear and held it between her thumb and forefinger. It was a tiny lump of metal.

'I think my head took a chunk out of your door,' she said sceptically. 'Sorry.'

'Shotgun pellet. Must have been a ricochet.

Technically, you've been shot in the head and survived. Congratulations.'

She dropped it as soon as she heard the first two words, horrified. It disappeared into the footwell and rolled beneath her seat among a thousand fragments of glass.

'Okay,' she decided. 'No cops. You can come with me, but no guns either. Singular or plural.'

'This is Glasgow we're talking about,' he replied, his accent sounding all of a sudden like he belonged to. 'I'm not going there without one.'

'Then you're not going there with me. In my experience, men with guns attract men with guns.'

'Your experience? Your experience of being around men with guns amounts to the past hour.'

'Yes, and one hundred per cent of my experience has involved me ending up getting shot at by other men with guns.'

'And as you just saw, they're a lot less lethal if you can return fire.'

Jasmine knew he was right, that she was being irrational, but even the memory of how the pellet felt between her fingers made her squirm and shudder.

'Just tell me there'll be no more guns,' she said. 'Lie to me if you have to.'

'I won't lie to you,' he replied, though he left it at that.

They didn't speak for another mile or so. They came to a large roundabout, which was when it occurred to Jasmine that they weren't going back the way they had come, but had carried on their original course.

'Aren't we going back to the refuge?'

'I'm going to get the part I need for the

shredder.'

'I thought you said you needed a new shredder altogether.'

'I was being shifty and evasive, remember?'

'I don't mean to sound needy or inconsiderate, but in light of recent developments, can't it wait?'

'No. It's important if I'm going to help you. Rita's used to me taking off at short notice, but if I leave work unfinished, she'll worry about me. I only ever want her worrying about running the refuge.'

Jasmine marvelled at the concept of anybody actually worrying about the welfare of someone as scary and dangerous as Ingrams, then it occurred to her that maybe he did a little more for Rita than she had let on.

* * *

As she pulled the Civic into the office car park, Jasmine could see a telltale shimmer of broken glass on the concrete.

'That's Jim's surveillance van,' she told Ingrams. 'Looks like it's been tanned.'

They had reached Glasgow around half-seven, Ingrams requesting her to take them straight to Sharp Investigations.

It had been close to five before they left the refuge. Ingrams had finished off what he was working on, then driven off again to retrieve some things from home. He returned inside forty minutes with a black canvas bag slung over his shoulder, the contents of which she did not wish to speculate upon. As it hadn't taken him long to make this round trip, she wondered why they

191

couldn't just have gone there en route, which was when she deduced that he hadn't wanted her to know where he lived.

She had waited in the garden, on a wooden bench in the shade, watching Ingrams work. He was shredding the branches of an overgrown hydrangea he had spent the morning taming with a hedge-trimmer. He gathered the chippings in a plastic bucket and transferred them in batches to a hopper in preparation for mulching, his actions always briskly industrious but unhurried.

She saw Rita again only briefly, immediately upon their return.

Ingrams had parked the Land Rover around the back, where she wouldn't see that it was damaged. Rita had heard the engine and come out to meet them. It looked like a welcoming gesture until Jasmine discovered its true purpose, which was to tell her to stay outside the building so that the women wouldn't have to remain in their rooms. She was polite and almost apologetic, but Jasmine heard the steel behind her quiet tones and recalled Ingrams' caution that Jasmine had been wrong if she thought she'd made an ally. Ingrams disappeared inside with Rita for several minutes, during which he presumably explained a few things and eluded quite a few others.

Jasmine filled him in on the drive north, her blow-by-blow being a means of stretching the very little she actually knew over the longest number of miles. After that she kept prattling about herself because she was so uncomfortable with the absence of any conversation between them. She'd catch herself wittering on, wondering why she was telling him this stuff, some of it personal bordering

192

on inappropriate: all about her mum and how she came to be working for Jim.

Ingrams seemed considerably less unnerved by silence, but he didn't seem to mind her talking, as he would ask her something every so often and set her off again. He wasn't going to oblige her by way of reciprocity, though. Occasionally she'd chance her arm, hoping some kind of bond was being forged or even that she might just catch him off guard.

'You're actually from Glasgow?'

'Originally. A long time ago.'

'Did you know this Glen Fallan guy? Know *of* him?'

'No.'

Now Ingrams climbed awkwardly out of the Honda and stretched, his height emphasised by the low-slung vehicle. He ambled slowly towards the van, twisting his neck and loosening his limbs, then bent over to peer through the broken window.

'It's a surveillance van, supposed to blend in and not be noticed,' he said. 'How did they know it's his?'

'Maybe they didn't. But it's been parked in the same spot night and day for the best part of a week.'

'Anything leap out at you as missing?'

'I don't think Jim keeps anything in it. Never leaves the cameras inside if he's not using them.'

'Whatever they're looking for, they're being very thorough.'

Jasmine unlocked the building's rear door and held it open for Ingrams. He proceeded inside with a cautious and surprisingly light step, which prompted the upsetting understanding that whoever had broken into the van could still be inside the office.

They climbed the stairs in silence. Jasmine kept expecting Ingrams to take out a gun, then when he didn't, admitted to herself that she was actually wishing he would. Why had she asked him not to bring one? And why hadn't he just overruled her and told her not to be so bloody stupid?

To her great relief, they found the office door closed and locked. Jasmine was about to stick her key into it when Ingrams restrained her hand. He crouched by the lock and examined it.

'Scratch marks,' he said. 'Fresh ones. It's been picked recently. They've been here.'

'Why would they pick the lock? Why not just kick the door in, like they just smashed the van window?'

'You're supposed to be dead by now. A break-in at your place of work would be a big arrow for the Tyneside cops looking into the shootings. A nondescript van getting tanned after being left unattended for several days would be less of a flag.'

'Yes, but what else could they expect the cops to connect it to? Unless they thought that me getting shot in your car would suggest I was just in the wrong place at the wrong time. In which case, why would anyone think that a guy who keeps guns in his car would make a more plausible target for a shooting, I wonder?'

'No comment.'

Jasmine unlocked the door and reached inside to turn on the lights. There was no immediate indication of a break-in, and certainly she felt no sense of someone having been there remotely comparable to the sense of *no one* having been

194

there that had so spooked her on Monday. The place looked very much as she had left it, enough for her to wonder how you distinguished between fresh scratch marks around a lock and innocent older ones from misdirected keys. Perhaps nobody had broken in, and perhaps it had just been some chancer who'd tanned Jim's van.

'What have they taken?' Ingrams asked, as Jasmine scanned her surroundings.

'To be honest, I don't know what's normally here well enough to know what's missing, never mind what they might be after.'

She looked at the desk, and the neat piles of folders she had stacked up. They were where she'd left them, but one thing did strike her right away.

'The Glen Fallan file is gone. It was at the top because I was copying down your contact details. Apart from that, I couldn't say.'

'What about the computer?' Ingrams asked.

Jasmine switched on the PC, surprised to feel a tingle of anticipation as she did so. She could list any files that had been accessed since it was last booted up, and finally they'd have something solid to work on.

The machine beeped in a low-tech, unfamiliar manner. She looked at the screen, which was mostly black with a couple of lines of white text, the lower of which said: 'Please insert boot disk.'

'Shit,' said Ingrams.

'What does that mean?' she asked.

'That they've formatted your hard drive. Erased everything. They don't want anybody to be able to work out what this is about.'

'It's backed up, at least. We won't know what they were looking at, but the information is retrievable.'

'Well, that's something. Have you got the FTP login?'

'The what?'

'Doesn't matter. If you've got Jim's email address and the host, we can . . .'

Jasmine looked at him apologetically. She had no idea what he was talking about.

'Never mind,' he said patiently. 'What else were you planning to look into? You said on the way up that there was another case that Jim had been working on separately.'

'Anne Ramsay. But according to the cop who was here, it was a dead end. Poor woman whose parents and brother went missing a quarter of a century ago. Definitely a dead end for us, though: we don't have any contact details. I don't have the folder and the computer files have been wiped.'

'You don't have the folder? They took it, then?'

'No, it wasn't here before. I think Jim must have taken it. Oh, wait, though. I do have her number. It should be on the phone. She called here looking for Jim. Said he had told her he expected to have some news early this week. McDade guessed he was going to let her down gently. He told me Jim would have known it was wrong to take her money.'

'Why would Jim have taken the case file with him if he was going to let her down gently? He must have thought there was something he could find out. And if you're going to let someone down gently, you don't give them several days' notice to get their hopes up. This is where we should start.'

Jasmine looked at the screen again, the cursor blinking expectantly in the absence of a bootable disk.

Blink. Blink. Blink.

She thought of other blinking white dots on black screens, of monitors and alarms, and something inescapable finally ran her to ground. She realised she had been trying to stay ahead of it for hours, keep her mind busy, hope to avert it with information or just sheer activity, but she was out of road. Her eyes filled up and the tears began to spill.

'What is it?' Ingrams asked, his voice soft but not solicitous, like it wasn't his place to enquire too deeply.

'Jim,' she said, struggling to keep her voice steady. 'He's not just my boss. He's my uncle; well, my mum's cousin. All of this: the shooting, the break-in, wiping the hard drive. It means he's dead, doesn't it?'

She stared up at him from Jim's chair, searching for what she might read in his expression. Ingrams said nothing, because he had nothing to offer. In his face she could see that he had known the truth of this way back, probably the moment that shotgun took out the windows.

She bent forward, her head resting in her hands, trying to disguise her sobbing from this comparative stranger but powerless to prevent the grief from seizing her as she accepted the truth of it all. She felt so cold, so isolated. This should be news she was receiving from a caring source, someone to hold her in these moments. Instead it was bereavement by way of deduction and inference. Bereavement at a remove: the acceptance not merely that Jim was dead, but that he most likely had been for days, and she was only now finding out.

Everything she had feared when she felt that instinctive disquiet in this office on Monday morning had been proven true. In recent times, it seemed, *all* her worst fears came true. Yes, it's cancer. Yes, it's spreading. No, it's not treatable. Yes, it will only be months.

Yes, it looks like tonight will be the end. Yes, she's gone now.

Yes, Jim's dead too.

Ingrams said nothing, remaining a few feet away. She didn't know whether she hated him for standing there in indifferent silence or was grateful to him for keeping his distance and not intruding.

'Who are you?' Jasmine asked, her voice reduced to a rasping whisper.

'We need to get you a place to stay,' was his reply. 'If they've been to where you work, they probably know where you live. It won't be safe there.'

Jasmine had a vertiginous sense of events threatening to overtake her, of becoming a piece of flotsam swept along by this tide. She felt like she had nothing to cling on to, apart from Ingrams, and she barely knew who he was.

'I need my phone charger,' she said, a single practical thought bubbling up with undue prominence as her mind searched for ways to give her back some degree of control.

'We can pick up a new one in the morning. Meantime we'll find a hotel.'

'I don't have any money,' she said apologetically.

'I do.'

'Why would you help me?'

'Rita would boot my balls if I didn't,' he replied.

She accepted that for now, as she was in no state to dig deeper, but they both knew it was bullshit.

They went first to a big twenty-four-hour supermarket where she picked up some toiletries and a change of clothes, then Ingrams booked them two rooms in a hotel by the Clyde. It was big and corporate and faceless, a good place to blend in and not be noticed.

Upon his advice, bordering on insistence, she ordered some room service. She didn't think she was hungry, but ended up demolishing a club sandwich, having remembered that she had barely eaten all day. As soon as she had finished the last of it, tiredness struck like a net thrown over her, pulling her down to the bed.

Sleep didn't come immediately, though. More tears came first. Finally, alone and unwitnessed, she could let go, let it all go.

She was crying for Jim, and crying because his loss was making her feel such an echo of the death of her mum. But somewhere within her pain and sadness there was a tiny seed of reassurance, because the loss of Jim wasn't as bad. Nothing would ever be as bad again.

EXPLOSIVE INFORMATION

Catherine and Laura found Bob Cairns in a café on Robertson Street, just off the Broomielaw on the banks of the Clyde. It was an old-fashioned and unapologetic greasy spoon joint, the sort of establishment you increasingly only found tucked away in the back streets, so that there was almost something illicit about it. Not that the consumption of saturated fats was in any danger of going out of fashion in these parts; just that it had become more of a dirty little secret, something the city didn't want to wear on its sleeve.

Bob was sitting at a booth, his back to an expanse of PVC upholstery so riven with scratches, scars and stitching that it resembled a Glasgow hard man's face. As they walked in, Catherine thought she could smell cigarette smoke, but it was just the immediacy of her mental association; either that or the years since the ban hadn't been long enough to quite clear it from the place. There was actually something reassuring about this kind of establishment still being here, just as there was something reassuring about finding a polisman like Bob Cairns sitting in it. You knew that the men with faces resembling the upholstery were still out there, so you needed cops of Bob's ethos and generation to maintain a kind of equilibrium.

Not much for the skinny latte and blueberry muffin, our Bob. He wasn't eating his way towards an infarct either, though: wholemeal roll, no butter, *grilled* bacon, grilled tomato and brown sauce. He was still a fit man for close to sixty, though there was undeniably more of him these days than there had once been. Catherine had heard he'd missed work yesterday too, which was virtually unheard of. Guys his age, especially the super-dependable ones, you always feared that bit more for whenever you heard they were ill.

There didn't appear to be much wrong with him today, though. He had his phone sitting on the table next to a steaming mug of black tea, an alert, slightly restless air about him as he tucked into his breakfast. It was a look Catherine recognised: a cop who knew that something was in the wind and was impatient for his cue.

He didn't smile when he noticed them; just gave a subtle nod of the head by way of beckoning them to join him. He wouldn't necessarily have known they were coming here this morning, but he would have been expecting Catherine at some point. Bill Raeside had relayed to her that Cairns had some fresh information regarding the McDiarmid murder, but in typical Cairns style, he preferred to pass it on face to face rather than over the phone, and preferred to do so in a place like this rather than anywhere so boringly convenient as a police station.

Catherine knew she had to indulge him. As she explained to Laura, on the surface it might appear unnecessary, but when you looked a little deeper, there were many subtle ways in which it was quite the opposite. For one thing, with old-stagers like Cairns and Fletcher, you had to play their game a wee bit in order to keep them sweet, especially when you outranked them. Guys like that needed their due, and respected you more if they believed that you genuinely understood what they brought to the table. If you didn't know what they were worth, they thought you were an idiot, and generally they'd be right. So if they asked you to meet at a grotty caff rather than just give you the gen over the phone, you didn't moan about it.

'A little deference goes a long way,' she told Laura. 'And the corollary is doubly true. Officers with that much experience, that many contacts and that level of understanding of the system have an

201

unofficial rank, regardless of what it says on their warrant card, and you'll pay a heavy price if you don't recognise it. Get on the wrong side of them and while they might not make it their job to screw you over, they would certainly regard it as one of the perks.'

In an age of electronic policing, there was also much to be said for meeting colleagues from other squads and other divisions face to face whenever the opportunity presented itself. Loath as the likes of Cairns would be to call it that, it was a valuable exercise in networking. It meant you didn't just pass on little discrete quanta of information pertaining only to specific inquiries, like worker ants meeting in a line. And perhaps most importantly, it was more conducive to a little quid pro quo. When Cairns had goodies to hand over, he liked to sound you out for what might be available in return.

'Glad to see you're feeling better,' Catherine told him, having ordered up a couple of coffees. 'When I heard Bob Cairns had called in sick, I thought it was one of the signs of the end of days.'

Cairns looked quizzical for a moment, then realised what she was on about.

'Naw, I'm fine. It wasnae a health thing: more a kind of family emergency. My youngest had a problem with her digs. She's at uni in Preston, starting final year. She stayed on over the summer doing a research project. Anyway, the wee place she's in is right by the river, which is lovely until the fuckin' thing bursts its banks. Ground floor is under two feet of water noo.'

He took a mouthful of tea. Catherine noticed him eyeing his phone as he did so.

202

'You expecting a call?'

He rolled his eyes as if to say 'and how'. He wasn't for giving anything away yet, though.

'Heard you had the bold Abercorn trying to peek at your homework over the Jai McDiarmid murder,' he said. 'Have you worked out his angle?'

'I'm wary of even thinking so,' she replied. 'It's often when you reckon you've worked out Abercorn's angle that he's got you exactly where he wants you.'

It was a calculatedly neutral reply. Catherine wasn't giving away to anybody that she suspected Abercorn was protecting Frankie Callahan, and certainly not to a stalwart of the Drug Squad. Never mind Abercorn's angle, she wondered: what's yours, Bob, and what are you hoping I'll toss back in return for this morning's tip?

Relations between the Drug Squad and Locust were as strained as they were complex. Cairns and Fletch were enjoying an Indian summer to their long careers—Starsky and Hutch meets Jack and Victor, as Raeside put it—and earning plenty of plaudits from their peers. But their boss, Gerry Milligan, was almost as adept at posturing and politicking as Abercorn, so they were getting free rein while it suited him. The head of the Drug Squad knew that having them bring in bodies and make seizures was making his outfit look as good as Abercorn's long game was making Locust look bad, but that didn't mean he was kidding himself that it was effective or sustainable. There was a lot of strategy in play, and Catherine wasn't passing either side a chip unless she knew precisely how it would affect the game.

'He give you the mosquito speech?'

'No. I'm starting to feel left out.'

'Or maybe he thinks you're twenty-first-century enough to understand. His kind of polis.'

He had a devilish glint in his eye, which gave away that he was trying to wind her up. She fixed him with a stare that warned him he'd have to try harder than that.

'I believe you thought you might have something for me?' she suggested, albeit doubting he'd hand it over quite yet.

He glanced at his phone again and surprised her with a widening of his eyes and a slightly distracted preface of 'A-a-a-y-y-ye', drawn out to last several syllables. It was as though he was so intent on whatever he was waiting for that he'd forgotten to dangle her on the hook for the usual duration.

'I gather you've not had a stirring public response to your appeal for witnesses regarding the late Mr McDiarmid?'

'You've got to buy a ticket,' she said, by way of acknowledging that her expectations had been low. 'What can you do? It's Gallowhaugh. Somebody can get slashed in broad daylight in front of thirty folk but no bugger saw a bloody thing.'

'Witnesses do talk to *some* people, though,' he replied enticingly. 'I've got a source—a good source—who tells me that Paddy Steel's people are out shaking the trees. Seems someone came forward to tell Paddy they saw a black van emerging from the Langton Drive end of the wee lane parallel to the Shawburn Road on Sunday night at around the time McDiarmid's body was dumped.'

'This'll be the Paddy Steel who made out to me that he and McDiarmid were barely nodding acquaintances and he had no idea what the murder was about.'

'Aye. And I heard he was wearing a bulletproof vest at the time.'

'A black van,' she said. 'Anything more? A guess on make or model?'

'Ford Transit.'

'Of course,' said Laura. 'Had to be the vanilla of vans. At least it wasnae white, eh?'

'Ah, but the thing is, it wasnae black either.'

'What?'

'Paddy Steel's numpties are out looking for the A-Team, but my source spoke to another witness, who remembered a *dark blue* van going into the same lane at the Capletburn Drive end, around midday.'

'Dark blue would look black near midnight under the street lights,' Catherine observed. 'Thanks, Bob.'

'For what it's worth,' he acknowledged.

He resumed work on his bacon roll, his eyes straying to the phone briefly once more.

'You're looking at that thing like it's going to lay an egg,' Catherine said.

'Or blow up in my face,' he admitted.

'How so?'

Cairns took a gulp of tea.

'I've got this tout, an *extremely* well-placed tout, who's been an invaluable asset but precisely the high-maintenance, pain-in-the-arse Pandora's box you'd expect as the price. He's as fly as he is ambitious, and let me tell you, this boy takes the piss out of playing both ends against the middle. It's always a good rule of thumb that it's okay being used as long as you know you're being used, but in his case you can never be quite sure *how* you're being used, and that makes me nervous. Anyway, he's due to call. Overdue. It's something big, I'm pretty sure. The more he fucks you about, the bigger it is.'

'Any hints?'

'Just that it's something he's expecting to go down today. It'll be drugs; it's *always* drugs. He wouldn't give me any more, made out he didn't have the details yet. The bugger knows fine, but he loves keeping you on tenterhooks. Gives him a stiffy to think you're hanging on his every word. Coy bastard as well: likes to keep things ambiguous until the last possible moment, probably so he can keep changing his story as the situation—'

Cairns cut himself off at the sound of his phone finally ringing. It barely got through one chime before it was at his ear. He got up from the booth and wandered out of the café, away from the sounds of chatter and the hiss of the coffee machine.

'What I wouldn't give for that number,' Catherine remarked, watching Cairns as he nattered in the doorway. 'Not that his source would talk to anybody else, but I'd love to know who it is.'

'Not as much as Dougie Abercorn,' suggested Laura, prompting Catherine to smile.

Cairns ended his call and returned only a couple of minutes later, looking as animated as Catherine could ever remember seeing him.

'Could have a situation,' he said, breathing heavily through his nostrils. 'Could be fucking with me, but could have a situation. In fact, he's double fucking with me because he knows I know he could

206

be fucking with me, and he also knows I cannae ignore the fact that we could have a situation.'

'Bob,' she said firmly. 'You're havering. What's the script?'

'He said there's a package in the left luggage at Central station. Said it was likely to prove explosive.'

'A bomb at Central?' Catherine said. 'Is he placed to know something like this?'

'This bastard? You never know. But he didn't say it was a bomb. "Likely to prove explosive": those were his exact words. I told you, he never gives you anything straight. It's always wrapped up in shite and barbed wire. Whatever it is, I'm not taking any chances. We need to evacuate.'

*   *   *

Evacuating Glasgow Central station on a weekday morning was no trivial matter; it wasn't like you could just hit an alarm somewhere and get everybody to muster at an assembly point. Not only did they have to close the station, but they had to stop all the trains heading into it. This took the cooperation of the Transport Police, as well as authorisation from Scotrail, which Catherine, as detective superintendent, had to procure using her sternest yes-I'm-serious telephone manner.

Nobody who had regularly travelled into Central by train would be particularly surprised or alarmed at finding themselves sat there unmoving, parallel to Bridge Street, a frustratingly few hundred yards from the platform. However, what might tip them off that something extraordinary was afoot was the fact that they couldn't pass the time as usual

207

staring across towards the Citizens Theatre and reminiscing about childhood trips to the panto, because their view was blocked by half a dozen other stationary trains. And those were just the ones on final approach; further services were being halted at every major junction, with trains held at commuter stations all the way down each line.

Catherine didn't have to worry about them, though: they were somebody else's problem, safely contained by the simple expedient of switching a few signals to red. Clearing several hundred people out of the station itself was a bit more logistically complex.

With no time to waste, they had to pull in every officer who could get there inside five minutes, which meant there was no room for egos or quibbles over rank and demarcation. They were all bobbies now, Catherine and Laura stewarding passengers towards the exits and checking for strays alongside the uniformed PCs.

As the PA system urged them to vacate the premises and follow the instructions of the police, Catherine noted that the travelling public had become 'passengers' again. She recalled the time during her late-eighties adolescence when, literally overnight, the announcements began referring to them instead as 'customers', in a conspicuously ideological manipulation of the language. 'Customers boarding the train'; 'Customers awaiting the express service to Carlisle'. You didn't tell kids that people on a train were customers. It was such a cumbersome distortion as to make it an insultingly obvious and rather craven act of Thatcherite compliance. She couldn't recall when they went back to being passengers again, but was

208

glad that they had. You could tell passengers to get their arses out of the station in case it got blown up; 'customers' suggested that if they'd paid their money, they could take their chances.

Their task was more than just a matter of clearing the platforms and sweeping everyone out from the main concourse. There were now more shops, pubs and restaurants in Central station than there had been on Calderburn High Street when Catherine was growing up. There were sandwich shops, newsagents, hairdressers, chemists, a currency exchange, fashion accessories, a florist, a greeting card store, an M&S food hall and even a jeweller's. It was an upscale one at that, rather pretentiously called Coruscate, and found itself the subject of some rather jaundiced speculation on the part of Laura as they approached the premises.

'A jeweller's in a railway station? One-stop guilty conscience shop for the man with more to atone for than the florist can cover. Fleeting moment of thinking about the missus on the way home that's supposed to make up for never thinking about her the rest of the time.'

This would normally have provoked curious speculation as to what misadventures had coloured Laura's past love life, but right then Catherine couldn't think past how it might apply to herself.

A few months back, she had come perilously close to forgetting Drew's birthday. She had been away overnight, at a meeting in London, so she'd unknowingly dodged the awkwardness of not having a card or present for him first thing that morning. It only occurred to her when she was killing time in Terminal Five, waiting for her flight home. She saw this gadgety watch and reckoned

Drew would love it. She was aware she hadn't been wife of the year of late, so thought she should buy him it just to prove she was thinking of him. Mind you, she thought, his birthday was coming up soon, so perhaps she should buy it and wait until . . . Oh God.

He did love the watch. They'd had a curry delivered, split a bottle of wine and had sex; great sex. Hurried, lustful, oh-Jesus-it's-been-ages sex, then slow, tender, delicate and ever-so-slightly fetishistic sex. Drew was dopily happy, while Catherine felt the most precarious relief at her narrow escape. She vowed privately she wouldn't get so caught up in herself any more, and that it wouldn't take a special occasion for her to buy him a wee present or even just to say sod it, let's have takeaway, wine and a shag on a school night.

Promises, promises.

It didn't take much to clear the punters from the shops; as soon as they saw the mass movement outside the windows, most of them came pouring forth to find out whether whatever was going on was about to bugger up their journey. The staff were the ones who required more of a strong hand and a stern tone, particularly with regard to communicating that no, they didn't have time to secure displays of merchandise, retrieve the keys, set their store alarms, lock the doors or roll down their overnight shutters.

The assurance that there was going to be nobody free to roam the station other than cops didn't prove universally mollifying. By the time the last of the shop staff had been herded out of the main exit on to Gordon Street, Catherine had agreed that they would be corralled separately and

210

be the first allowed back into the station, in order that none of the local neds could rapidly improvise a large-scale freebie pick-and-mix.

They set up cordons either end of Gordon Street, clearing all civilians back on to the pavements of Union Street and Hope Street. This left Gordon Street itself as a staging area for police vehicles, the latest of which to arrive was the sniffer-dog unit. The van was waved through to the taxi rank, sheltered beneath the glass canopy abutting the first floor of the Central Hotel, where Cairns was waiting, his phone to his ear.

'EOD are on their way,' he told Catherine, meaning the Army Explosive Ordnance Department. 'I'm gaunny look like such a dick if this turns out to be nothing. Paranoid side of me cannae help but wonder if this is all my tout's way of burying me.'

'You're a bit long in the tooth for stage fright, Bob,' she told him, gentle chiding as a form of moral support. He did seem very nervous, though, which told Catherine she ought to be too.

Cairns briefed the officer in charge of the dog handlers, telling him to task one dog to sniff for drugs, the other for explosives. The dogs were trained for both, but they needed to know as soon as possible which substance they were dealing with.

'The likelihood is it will be the former, but we have to rule out the latter,' he advised. 'The information was specific to the left-luggage facility, so we'll start there, but if we come up blank, we'd better widen the search.'

The two handlers fitted their animals with the bright blue harnesses that communicated to the dogs that it was time to go to work. They

211

proceeded inside through the main archway, Cairns setting off a few moments behind them.

After a couple of paces he stopped and turned to Catherine.

'You coming?' he asked.

'Sure,' she replied, though she felt a little apprehensive.

She wondered about this instinctive reluctance. Was she concerned that he was inviting her to ride shotgun so that she would find herself sharing the blame if it turned out to be a false alarm? Then she passed the hollowed-out World War II bomb that stood just inside the main entrance and remembered a more prosaic reason for why she might not fancy a trip to left-luggage.

Trying to stay calm and professional, her mind sought out a distracting thought, then promptly wished it hadn't found one.

She and Drew used to meet at the bomb when they were first going out together, coming off of different trains. She could still remember how it felt to watch the crowd and suddenly see him appear, walking towards her. The age difference seemed smaller as they got older, but he really did seem like her toy boy back then: Drew twenty-two and she thirty-one. They both thought their relationship was frivolous and uncomplicated, neither sizing the other up with a view to long-term suitability: in her case because he was just meant to be a bit of diversion, a rebound fling; and in his because, well, he was twenty-two. That was what took the pressure off and let her just enjoy being with him. It was fun. *She* was fun.

Then.

He hadn't come home last night. He called

212

around seven to say that some of the London office were booked into the Mal in Leith, and he was going to do likewise so that they could all have a late one. She had told him sure, enjoy yourself, make the most of it. The irrational side had receded; she wasn't scared of him getting tipsy and lunging for someone else—or not *as* scared. But she felt the news that he wasn't coming home as a blow. He wasn't doing it to get at her, but her guilty conscience couldn't help but interpret it as a deserved punishment, thinking that if she had been a little nicer to him of late, he'd have taken that last train.

The station was like she had never seen it, a real zombie-movie scene. No people, no trains, no movement. No silence, however. An alarm was going off over at the row of shops to the right of the platforms. One of those self-important fusspots had ignored their instructions and set the security system, then one of the uniforms must have tripped it when he put his head around the door to do a final check.

The left-luggage facility had enjoyed an upgrade a couple of years back, fitted out with new self-operated lockers that were opened using an electronic keypad. Customers could set their own four-digit code instead of carrying a key around with them, which meant that if they forgot it, it was a simple matter of the attendant on duty coding an override, thus saving on cutting replacement keys.

Once inside the left-luggage area, the contrast in the conduct of the two dogs could barely have been more pronounced. One of them was sniffing methodically up and down with the guarded air of a dog sitting by a dinner table trying not to come

213

across as too optimistic in its hopes for a few leftovers, while the other zeroed in on a particular locker and began pawing at it like there was a bitch on heat inside, sitting on top of thirty kilos of fillet steak. Catherine wished she had been paying more attention to which one had been primed to sniff for which substance.

She got her answer when Cairns sent not for the EOD, but for the attendant to override the electronic lock.

The attendant looked anaemically pale with fear, and it was to avert the threat of him being physically sick that Catherine corrected Cairns' omission and informed the guy, 'It's okay, it's just drugs.'

And by God was it drugs. Cairns rolled out a mid-size charcoal-coloured fibreglass pull-along suitcase and placed it on the floor. He snapped open the catch and flipped up the lid to reveal that it was packed tightly with dozens upon dozens of bricks of brown powder wrapped in parcel tape.

'Jesus,' said the dog handler, whose charge was having to be held back. He squatted down next to the beast and it seemed to get the message.

'Jackpot,' Catherine observed. They wouldn't know until they got it tested, but she strongly suspected this was pre-cut. In that form and that quantity, it was unlikely to be just waiting to be divided straight into several thousand tenner bags. 'I think we've just intercepted several months' worth of a major player's supply.'

'Aye,' Cairns mused. 'I'd call that explosive.'

'Do you have any idea who this lot was meant for?'

'Nothing concrete, but we'll find out soon

enough, because whoever was expecting to pick it up will throw some size of tantrum.'

Cairns told the dog handlers they could stand down, explaining to the one looking for explosives that this possibility had now been ruled out.

The other dog wasn't quite ready to jack in its shift. It was now sniffing enthusiastically around the base of another locker, one that it had rather astonishingly managed to open.

Upon closer inspection, this was down to the lock having been damaged and the door rendered unlockable. The locker itself was empty, as anything unlockable was bound to end up around these parts.

'There's been drugs in here at some point,' the dog handler said of the broken locker. 'I'd guess that isn't the first suitcase full of gear that's been stored here.'

'No,' agreed Cairns with a grin. 'But I'm willing to bet it's the last.'

He let out a sigh that turned into a laugh, a combination of relief and elation. It proved infectious. Catherine laughed too. This was a result. A hell of a result.

*   *   *

The suitcase was escorted out by two Drug Squad officers and driven off in a van with a couple of motorcycle outriders for added speed and security. Catherine gave clearance for the trains to resume and the cordons to be dropped, with the shop staff allowed a head start as agreed.

As they marched on to the concourse, she saw the jeweller's manageress suddenly up the pace and streak through the pack into the lead. She was outstripping the rest despite the encumbrance of her stiletto heels, like the fastest yummy mummy at a sports-day parents' race.

It was Catherine's guess that this was whose alarm was still reverberating around the station. On another day, she might have been inclined to go over and issue a rap on the knuckles for blatantly ignoring police instructions, but she thought she'd let it slide. It felt like a good morning to be a police officer, and there was no pressing reason to sour the mood.

The manageress disappeared into the shop but the alarm failed to cease ringing. She re-emerged only a few moments later, looking as shocked as she was angry, and hurried across to where Catherine stood next to Cairns, subjecting them both to a breathless, spluttering and livid rant, the gist of which proved that even on a day like today, every silver lining had a cloud.

Her name was Maraidh Morgan, and it turned out she had followed police orders unquestioningly and *hadn't* set her security system. Inside Coruscate, however, there was a permanently alarmed cabinet displaying their stock of ultra-high-end watches, and the reason it had gone off was because somebody had taken a power saw to the thing and cleared out the lot.

THE ABANDONED

They arrived at just after one o'clock, as arranged. The address quoted turned out to be a red

216

sandstone terraced house in Clarkston, to the south of the city, in a quiet neighbourhood a couple of streets back from the main road. There was a little girl playing in the front garden, strapping two plastic dollies side by side into a toy pushchair. She had black hair in pigtails and was wearing the skirt, shirt and tie of a school uniform.

Jasmine said hello to her as they opened the gate, but she said nothing and took off inside while they walked along the flagstoned path. The front door was open, and they could hear the little girl's voice telling her mum that someone was coming.

Jasmine rang the bell anyway, and waited in front of the stone step. She could see inside along the hallway and found herself wondering: what's wrong with this picture? The confusing answer appeared to be: nothing whatsoever. It looked like a shopping-catalogue picture of domestic contentment. Handsome building, tasteful decor, one cute wee moppet just started school, a stair gate and framed photos testifying to a curly-topped younger brother completing the family unit.

A door opened at the far end of the hall and Anne Ramsay emerged from an airy-looking kitchen. As she did so, a silver Volkswagen Passat pulled up in front of the house and its driver emerged briskly, as though racing to be first to reach them.

Perfunctory greetings and introductions were exchanged around the front door before Anne directed them towards the kitchen. She let Jasmine and Ingrams pass so that she could talk to her husband, asking him with a near-accusatory curiosity what he was doing home at this hour.

'I told you I'd wrap up early so I could be here

for this.'

'Yeah, but there really wasn't the need. I told you I'd be fine.'

Jasmine detected an unusual kind of tension between them and quickly identified it. It was the tension between two people who didn't want to admit to themselves or to anybody else that there was any tension between them. It wasn't aggro, wasn't simmering resentment or grudges or huffs, but once you had noticed it, it was *all* you noticed.

The husband's name was Neil Caldwell, Jasmine noted from some envelopes on a kitchen worktop. He was wearing a shirt and tie but didn't look natural or comfortable in them. Anne Ramsay, for her part, was dressed down but still contrived to look rather buttoned up. She was in loose trousers and a T-shirt but struck Jasmine as being as better suited to office attire as her husband was to the informal.

'So, what do you have for us?' he asked rather urgently, before Jasmine or Ingrams had been offered a seat around the kitchen table.

There was the crust of a jam sandwich still sitting on a plate, recently abandoned perhaps by the wee girl. Three Hot Wheels cars sat in a short queue near the middle of the table, like the sugar bowl was a roundabout.

Anne gave her husband a perplexed look, perhaps telling him to back off, and suggested they take a seat. Jasmine preferred to remain on her feet when she made her opening remarks, as it made her feel less pathetic.

'First of all, let me apologise. Jim Sharp was supposed to be in touch earlier this week, but the reason he hasn't been is also the reason we're here.

Jim didn't turn up to work on Monday and we don't know where he is.'

Anne looked initially crestfallen and then a little concerned.

'He's gone missing? Have you told the police?'

'The police have been informed,' Ingrams replied, 'but unless there are suspicious circumstances, they have no remit to investigate.'

He phrased it well, Jasmine thought. Technically, both of his statements were true.

'And you think it's connected to the work he was doing for me?' Anne asked.

'As his associates,' Jasmine replied, 'we're pursuing various lines of inquiry, starting with examining all his current open jobs. Most of those have been well documented at our end, but the reason we've had to trouble you is that unfortunately Jim seems to have taken your case files with him.'

She recalled Anne's anger on the phone earlier in the week and adopted a tone she hoped sounded both sincere and businesslike.

'I appreciate that this might be difficult for you, or maybe just tedious, but we need you to outline for us what it was you hired Jim to look into.'

Anne gave a broken sigh; large on the intake, like she was gearing up for an expression of extreme disdain, then after a short pause, the more measured exhale of someone who was showing admirable and pragmatic restraint.

Neil didn't seem to read it that way, though.

'Why don't I go over this with them?' he suggested to her, in a way that was supposed to sound solicitous and considerate, but which Jasmine could tell Anne only found annoying.

'I'm fine,' she insisted, a little tersely. Jasmine's guess was that she was anything but, and Neil knew this, but nothing he offered to do was going to help. 'I'll talk them through it. You go upstairs and get the, you know, dookit thingy. And keep an eye on Megan, make sure she doesn't have any reason to wander in here, okay?'

'Sure,' he said, almost grateful to have a task.

Jasmine expected Anne to sit down, but instead she leaned against a worktop, her arms folded.

'If you're planning to record this or write it down, start now, because I'm only doing it once.'

Jasmine felt a moment of the kind of panic she usually felt when she was out with Jim: of being underprepared and conspicuously found out as a fraud. She didn't have a Dictaphone or even a notepad.

Ingrams came to the rescue by placing his phone down on the table and briefly working the touch screen. Jasmine realised she had a similar function on her own mobile, but stopped herself from duplicating his actions because she thought it would be obvious to Anne that she was just copying him. She at least remembered to put her mobile to silent. Having set the office phone to divert to hers, she didn't want any ill-timed interruptions.

'My parents were Stephen and Eilidh Ramsay,' Anne began, her tone slow, deliberate, well rehearsed. 'My dad was a statistician for a chemicals company outside Milngavie and my mum was a primary school teacher. We lived in Bishopbriggs, or at least I did from about nine months; before that my parents rented a flat in Partick. My mum was from Paisley and my dad

220

from Kilsyth, where his parents still lived.'

She sounded dispassionate, like she was talking about someone else's family, or even someone else's ancestors. Maybe she had laid this out a few times too many, or maybe this was her way of keeping her distance from the flames.

'This time twenty-seven years ago, August 1983, I had just started school. I was four. It was a doubly exciting time for me, because we had a new baby. My wee brother, Charlie, was four weeks old. It was . . . a Friday night.'

Jasmine picked up on the pause. It wasn't something Anne had any trouble remembering; she was taking a moment to steady her voice, check she wasn't going to start breaking down when she went on.

'I went to stay the night with my gran and granda, my dad's parents. It was so my mum and dad could go out for their dinner, get a wee bit of time together, because everything had been chaotic with the new baby and everything. Plus I always loved going to my grandparents. I stayed there a lot, usually a Friday or Saturday so my mum and dad could get a night out and a lie-in. I didn't understand their end of it back then, but I sure can now.'

'You've got two yourself?' Jasmine asked, then for a terrible moment feared she was about to be told some tragedy concerning the little boy in the pictures, who was nowhere to be seen.

'Megan and Charlie.'

She said this latter with an awkward smile, the hint of a lump in her throat.

'Megan's four and Charlie's three. He's at nursery, and Megan's just started at primary school. I had some time in lieu so I've taken it this week so that I could help break her in. They're only in until twelve for the first month. Neil's sister will be picking her up the next few weeks.'

'What is it you do?'

'I'm a solicitor. Harley and Pryde on Albion Street. Used to be in criminal but I moved to conveyancing a couple of years back as it's just less depressing. Anyway, that's neither here nor there.'

'And your husband, is he a lawyer too?'

She gave a short, dismissive laugh. Jasmine wasn't sure if she was ridiculing the idea of her husband as a lawyer or Jasmine for suggesting it.

'No, Neil's an IT consultant.'

She said this as though it should explain a great deal. To Jasmine it certainly explained why he didn't look comfortable in a shirt and tie, but evidently it ought to cover many other shortcomings.

'Anyway,' Anne said, like she was frustrated to have been sidetracked, but only in the way that it was frustrating to have a cold-caller on the phone when you're halfway through cleaning a really rancid oven, 'my brother Charlie went with my parents that night because he was being breastfed. He was a very quiet baby, I recall. Just lay there asleep most of the time, which was why they must have reckoned they could take him to a restaurant. Or a hotel, rather.'

'They were staying the night at the hotel?' Jasmine asked.

'No. They just went to this hotel restaurant, the Campsieview Hotel outside Lennoxtown. They were going to have dinner and go home to Bishopbriggs, then come and pick me up again on

222

the Saturday morning.'

Anne's mouth opened but she stayed silent for a second or two. She had to swallow before forming the words: 'They never came back.'

She spoke slowly and deliberately, like she was trying to remember a speech rather than voicing what was going through her head right then.

'My grandparents reported them missing later that day. According to the hotel, they left the restaurant about twenty-five to eleven, with Charlie in his carrycot. My mum was breastfeeding, so she wasn't having any alcohol, and she couldn't drive yet because she'd had a Caesarean four weeks previously, so my dad wasn't drinking either.'

Jasmine couldn't fathom the significance of them not drinking, but it was incanted like a prayer, so it had to mean something to Anne personally.

'They were seen one more time,' she stated, and now her voice really was wavering. 'Saturday morning, around eleven o'clock, at Bothwell services on the M74 southbound. The witness came forward to the police once the story had broken in the local media; something he hadn't thought of as significant at the time. He'd seen two people matching my parents' description putting a carrycot into the back seat of a car. It stuck in his mind because he had offered to help and they'd been quite brusque in their refusal. It was the last time anybody saw them.'

Anne opened her eyes wide, as though trying to clear them, the way you did when you had just about avoided tears.

'And were the police satisfied that it was your

223

parents this witness had seen?' asked Ingrams. 'Not just some couple with a carrycot?'

She nodded resignedly, as though she had spent many years contemplating the ways in which this might have turned out not to be the case. 'It was quite a distinctive car. The witness said it was a lime-green Audi 80. That's what my dad drove. I don't really remember it, but it's in some old photos, sitting in the drive. And they did used to have a bit of a palaver fitting the carrycot in the back seat. It was in the days before proper babies' car seats, and according to my gran, my mum insisted on jamming it in sideways so that it was wedged lengthwise between the back seat and the passenger seat.'

'What else did the police discover?' Jasmine asked.

Anne took a breath, a smaller version of that same broken sigh. Anger, frustration, then self-discipline, keeping a lid on it.

'Nothing. Nothing whatsoever. Nobody had seen them between Friday night and late Saturday morning. It was as though they packed themselves into the car and drove off the planet, somewhere south of Hamilton. It became a big story in the papers for a few weeks, although I was too young to really be aware. Certainly too young to understand why my parents would . . .'

At this, her words dried up, and Jasmine saw tears spilling down her cheeks. She felt intrusive and voyeuristic, as well as achingly discomforted at the glimpse this offered her of her own future. If after a quarter of a century Anne still felt this kind of pain, then it wasn't going to get easier for Jasmine any time soon.

'I'm sorry,' Anne said, ripping a sheet of kitchen towel from a holder on the worktop and dabbing at her face.

Jasmine knew from harsh experience that there was nothing helpful or sensible to say at this point, and so said nothing, despite the pressure she felt to fill the silence. Fortunately, Neil came in and filled it for them. He placed a black box file on the table and went across to comfort his wife.

Anne waved him away with a hand before he could touch her. There was a rigidity to her body language, no room for misinterpretation. Not in front of the detectives. If ever.

'You'll have to excuse me,' she said to them. 'Neil will have to take it from here. I'm going to take Megan and wander along to pick up Charlie,' she told him.

Neil nodded understandingly as she walked hurriedly from the room. He stood awkwardly for a moment, unsure where to put himself; *apologising* for himself. Then as though recovering a sense of purpose, he opened the box file and stood back, inviting them to look through its contents.

It was full of newspaper clippings, some wrapped in clear cellophane mini-wallets, others pasted on to coarse paper like items in a scrapbook.

Scrapbook didn't seem an appropriate word, Jasmine thought. Scrapbooks were for nostalgia, for treasured memories. Perhaps that was why Anne couldn't bring herself to give a name to the box. It had mostly stayed closed, she surmised, as even the oldest of the clippings were only slightly yellowed, the newsprint and pictures clear and not faded. It wasn't a box Anne took out and looked

225

through, then: more a repository where these things were shut away, but nonetheless she had felt a compulsion to preserve them.

'As you can see,' said Neil, 'it was a big story for a few weeks. Anne's grandparents collected this stuff obsessively; then the obsession passed to Anne herself. The tabloids kept it bubbling for a while by entertaining every attention-seeking chancer who happened to see someone with a carrycot and a green Audi. Sometimes I doubt they even worried about the make or colour that much. Then it trickled its way down the news agenda until being consigned to history.'

Jasmine flipped through the box, handing pages to Ingrams as she discarded them. There were clippings dating from the nineties and into the new century, sometimes small news stories and sometimes full-page features. She saw a double-page spread from 2003, folded up inside a cellophane wallet. It included a family photo of Anne with her parents, a tiny head shot of the baby inset. Opposite these were computer-generated images of how all three might look now, the new technology being the angle on which they had hung this two-page rehash of old news.

Above a sidebar was a shot of Anne playing in her garden only days before the disappearance, included because it showed the brand new green Audi 80 sitting at the side of the house. Inset into this one was a recent head shot of William Bain, the last person to see the Ramsays before they disappeared. There were a couple of quotes from him too, but understandably he had no more to say in 2003 than twenty years before that. It had been a chance encounter whose significance was only realised after the fact.

'Every so often something emerges that allows the press to rake through it all again,' said Neil. 'In the early years, as you can see, it would often be an alleged sighting, usually abroad. Somebody on holiday in Greece or wherever would see a wee boy of roughly the right age with a couple who might vaguely resemble Anne's parents. Summer's a quiet time for news, so they could fill a page or two by recapping everything, turn it into a feature. They never think about the pain they're causing.'

Ingrams pored over a couple of these 'Ramsay disappearance revisited' spreads, the same sparse facts rehearsed and the same photos rerun, ten years but no substantial differences between the articles. The only thing that had changed was the witness's head shot, the guy looking older and greyer, his reluctant and rather bleak fifteen minutes of fame evidently delivered in instalments over twenty-seven years.

The most recent piece was only a couple of weeks old, a half-page flashback feature from the *Daily Record*, hung on the news that a private investigator had been hired to look into the case. There were a few non-committal quotes from Jim and even a couple from Neil, but nothing from Anne. None of the pieces had comments from Anne.

'She's been offered plenty of money over the years for an interview, but she's not prepared to put herself through it. It comes around nearly every year, same time. It was Jim's idea to tell them about hiring him. He said they'd leave us alone if they had a new angle, and he was right.'

'What happened to Anne?' Jasmine asked.

'After the disappearance.'

'She was brought up by her grandparents.'

'Must have been difficult. A terrible thing to have to come to terms with so young.'

Neil gave a small nod but looked away. He thrust his hands into his pockets, seeming to physically withdraw and leave them to the file, even though he remained exactly where he was.

Jasmine reached into her own pocket.

'That's my phone,' she said to Ingrams. She stared at the screen, angling it so that Neil couldn't see that it was blank. Ingrams could, though, and looked at her quizzically. She held it to her ear and pretended to answer, quickly explaining to nobody at all that she couldn't talk right now and would get someone to call back.

'Tron, that was Caroline at Galt Linklater about the Turner case. Can you go and give her a ring? The notes are out in the car.'

Ingrams assented and got up, a sheaf of cellophane-wrapped pages still in his hand.

'Do you mind if I hang on to these a minute?' he asked.

Neil shook his head, barely engaged. Ingrams could have asked to borrow the microwave and got the same response.

Ingrams left the kitchen, but as he did so he gave Jasmine a stare that indicated he was only cooperating on the understanding that this would be explained later.

The explanation was simple. Neil was clamming up because they had started skirting territory that men didn't open up about around other men.

'How long have you been married?' Jasmine asked him, once she was sure Ingrams had withdrawn outside.

'Six years now,' he said neutrally. He then offered a smile, like it had belatedly occurred to him that his flatness had given something away.

'Not all plain sailing, I'd guess,' Jasmine ventured.

'What do you mean?' he asked defensively, ready to robustly rebuff any attempt to impugn the perfection of their relationship. Jasmine had been banking on it.

'Nothing. It's just, I used to go out with a guy whose parents had both died when he was ten. Car accident. Utterly devastating. I mean, *ten*. He must have felt so lost. He was brought up by his mum's sister. I liked him, but he never really let me close, you know? I mean, we joke about all guys being reluctant to commit, but in his case it was the real deal. It wasn't just me. Nobody got close, in case he lost them.'

Jasmine watched Neil's expression soften, the defences drop and an engagement enliven his features, an eager recognition that she was talking about something he was uniquely qualified to understand. She took it as a great compliment to her acting ability and improv skills, given that she was completely making it up.

'That was Anne,' he said quietly, with a bittersweet smile. 'Only ten times worse. She didn't just have your standard orphan's abandonment issues to contend with, because it wasn't merely about something that happened to her parents. It was something her parents did to her. They were last seen heading southbound out of the city on the M74. Where were they going? And more importantly, why were they going there without

229

her? They were supposed to be picking her up around then, on the complete opposite side of the city. Imagine having those kinds of unanswered questions in your head your whole life.'

'You must have been pretty tenacious. I'm guessing she pushed you away a few times.'

He gave a short, dry laugh of recognition.

'Suffice to say, I must have been the most anxious bridegroom in recorded history. I remember thinking to myself: why does the registrar have to speak so slowly? Hurry up and make it official before she bails on me again.'

Jasmine gave him an encouraging smile.

'We met at uni. She was at Glasgow and I was at Strathclyde and we had some mutual friends. We went out for about six months and then she broke it off over the summer. When I say she broke it off, technically I was the one who said let's finish this, but she kind of engineered it: she was increasingly horrible to me until I'd had enough. We got back together a couple of years later. She had gone out with a few guys in the meantime, one of whom I vaguely knew. He told me a very familiar tale. So when the same thing started happening again, I called her on it.'

'Brave move.'

'Desperate move. I was crazy about her. Still am. It was touch-and-go for a while, kill or cure. Turned out to be cure, just. She admitted to herself what was going on. She said it helped to externalise it; unfortunately, she's only ever able to externalise it in retrospect.'

'At the time she can't admit to herself why she's doing it?'

'That's it. She gets horrible to me because part

of her thinks I'm going to leave and she just wants to get it over with, while another part wants to know I'll never leave no matter how horrible she is.'

'Can't be much fun for you.'

'Over the years we've got better at anticipating the triggers, but sometimes they come at you sideways. It's a lot less fun for Anne, so I try not to feel too sorry for myself.'

'What triggered it this time?'

Neil paused, looking intently at her for a moment, considering and then discarding the option of denying that such a situation was ongoing right now.

'It's been a slow burn. We both knew it was coming, but awareness of it isn't like a magic talisman. Megan turning four back in April kind of started it off. That was the age Anne was when it happened. Megan starting school was always going to be a tough time. It's supposed to be one of the big happy milestones as a parent, but secretly we were both dreading it. We talked about it, though, and came up with a plan.'

'Is this where Jim Sharp comes in?'

'Partly. Megan was in nursery: same one as Charlie is in now. We knew that one of the bonuses of her starting at the local primary school was that we wouldn't have to be paying her nursery fees any more. Anne had often talked about hiring a detective to look into the case, because the police had been worse than useless. I was against it because I thought it would just keep the wound open indefinitely. Who knows how long you could be paying somebody, especially when they have a vested interest in keeping the investigation going.

No offence.'

'None taken. It doesn't work like that, though. Jim wouldn't string anybody along.'

Jasmine almost skipped a beat, realising she'd had to check her tense and hoping it hadn't been noticeable.

'I know. He came recommended. Anne asked around her own law firm and a couple of others. We decided we'd spend what we had previously been paying for Megan's nursery fees on hiring him. Anne agreed we would give it a few weeks but not get hung up on the whole thing. It was kind of symbolic, almost: like we were paying somebody else to worry about it so that we could enjoy this time.'

'But then Jim told her he would have some news for her this week.'

Neil nodded stoically. This development had clearly precipitated a whole new storm of hurt and frustration: aggravating everything it had been supposed to salve.

'Anne said she wouldn't have any expectations, but hopes are something else. She stopped believing in miracles a very long time ago, but she's spent her whole life looking for something that would give her soul peace. She even went to see this Bain guy a few years back, not long after Megan was born. Being a mother unleashed a whole lot of emotions for her. I don't know what she was hoping to get from him, but it became important to her that she have contact with the last person ever to see her family.

'I went with her. It was horribly awkward. Kind of embarrassing. The guy really had nothing he could tell her, but at least he was honest about it.

232

Unlike the psychics: we've had a few of those sniffing around over the years. They really are the scum of the earth. I'm telling you this so that you understand my position. I know part of Anne is still on a quest, but it's my role to protect her from anyone who would exploit that.'

*   *   *

Making her way back along the short garden path, the box file under her arm, Jasmine felt a liberated relief at being out of the house. On the surface it looked like the perfect family home, inhabited by the perfect family, but there was something stifling about the place, like Anne and Neil were fairy-tale characters gripped in temporal stasis by an evil spell. Time went on around them, but they were trapped for ever, unable to escape this thing that held them.

She thought of her own mum and perhaps for the first time, instead of merely missing her, she felt grateful that she'd got to have twenty years of her company, her love. She felt grateful also that she'd had the time to mourn, and appreciated as a blessing the certainty that her mother was gone.

As she climbed into the car, Ingrams held up a small square slip of paper, like a tear-off sheet from a telephone notepad.

'This was inside the plastic wallet next to a "twenty years on" feature from 2003. It's William Bain's contact details.'

Jasmine didn't see the significance.

'Yeah. Anne Ramsay went to see him once. He didn't have anything to tell her. What about it?'

'His home phone number is on your list.'

Ingrams gestured to the back seat, where she had left the hand-written sheet detailing the office phone's incoming and outgoing calls.

'Jim must have spoken to him recently,' he said.

'Probably just retracing the initial investigation in order to be thorough. He's not going to suddenly remember something crucial after twenty-seven years.'

'And yet Jim said he'd have news. Call him. Tell him you're a reporter. Set up an interview.'

Jasmine got out her mobile and dialled the number.

'Don't tell him your real name,' Ingrams added, as it began to ring at the other end.

'Why not?'

'Because it's Sharp.'

'Oh, of course,' she realised.

She didn't have time to be embarrassed, as a gravelly older male voice came on and offered a curious 'Hello?'

'Eh, Mr Bain? My name is Sharon James, I'm with the *Evening Times*,' she added, hoping she'd remembered correctly that it was the *Record* who had already run a recent story. 'I'm doing a piece on the Ramsay family disappearance, and—'

'Two hundred,' he interrupted gruffly.

Jasmine glanced at Ingrams and remembered how irritating people could find it when you kept asking them about something they knew little or nothing about. Bain must have become mightily pissed off over the years at receiving precisely this kind of enquiry. She doubted this was actually the two hundredth similar request, but she could understand why he had adopted such a posturing tone.

Then he made her feel like a rube with the clarifying addition of one single word.

'Cash.'

'Two hundred . . . pounds?'

'I've been over this for you people time and again for twenty-seven year. It's about time yous made it worth my while.'

'Ehm . . . if you hold on, I'm just going to have to run this past my editor.'

She muted the phone and was about to explain to Ingrams, but he was way ahead.

'Tell him one fifty; two hundred if he agrees to a photo.'

'I don't have two hundred pounds.'

'Have you got a camera?'

'There's lots back at the office.'

'Then let me worry about the money.'

PLAYED

Despite the size of the drugs seizure, Maraidh Morgan couldn't complain about her robbery being made a low priority by the police in the twenty-two hours since.

'In terms of manpower, I've never seen such a response to a break-in,' Zoe Vernon put it, leaning on Catherine's desk.

Zoe was finishing off a banana, possibly her third, and also quite possibly Catherine's. She had brought one along for a mid-morning snack but couldn't remember if she'd taken it out and put it on her desk or left it in her bag. Zoe grazed on fruit all day, making it hard to identify any given item as being part of any specific meal. She was the kind of girl who was so fit it actually made you tired just thinking about what kind of training regime she observed to get that way. A major bonus was that if required, she could run down a fugitive suspect like a Kenyan hunter ran down a gazelle, but the price was that she regarded all fruit left lying around the place—even on someone else's desk—as windfall.

'Bordering on the disproportionate,' Catherine agreed.

'I heard Cairns was going mental. Pretty embarrassing for us, I suppose. Have to be seen to make amends. We evacuate the place and somebody walks off with, what was it, a hundred and forty grand's worth of watches?'

'Rolex Oysters, Ulysse Nardin, Baume and Mercier, Cartier: best of gear, as they say.'

'Anything on the store CCTV?'

'Baseball cap, head down at all times. There's a partial face at one point. Cairns is passing it around. The thief brought the power tool in a sports bag. We're waiting to get a look at the station footage, but the theory is that he hid in the shop next door during the evac, then nipped out their back door and in through the rear entrance to Coruscate. In and out in seconds. Hid out around the back of the shops after that, or possibly inside one of them, and then slipped away when the punters were allowed back in.'

'So it was a planned job? He knew what was going to happen?'

'Looks that way. This is the real reason Cairns has rounded up the cavalry. It didn't just happen *on* his op, it happened because of it. This is about

Cairns' source. He said the guy was an Olympic-standard exponent of playing both ends against the middle. Whoever he is, he set this up. He had good intel on the drugs, but he was getting his end. That's why he threw the word "explosive" into his message.'

'He knew Cairns would evacuate the place.'

'Meaning he—or more likely somebody working off his tip—would be in position at the station, ready to take advantage. It puts Cairns in a very awkward lie. This source has proven very valuable, but how much can you let him take the piss? Nobody likes getting played, even as the price for a haul that large.'

'I heard they're estimating it could be worth three million.'

'We'll tell the press seven,' Catherine said, eliciting a wry smile from Zoe. 'This wasn't a one-off, either. Looks like they were using the left-luggage facility as an escrow holding point. It's a way of doing a large-scale drug deal without the risk of anybody getting fingered handing over or receiving the merchandise. We're guessing the wholesaler leaves the shipment there and then supplies the locker number and combination to the buyer once payment has been received.'

'Got you,' Zoe said. 'So then the buyer pitches up and walks away with the suitcase without either party having to be in the same room at any point. Vendor could get off a train from London or wherever, make the drop, then get the next train back again, minimum exposure.'

'Depending on what stage of the transaction had been reached, this could get very messy. There's bound to be quite a "he said, she said" between the wholesaler and the buyer over who owes who.'

' "Likely to prove explosive",' Zoe quoted, opening up another interpretation of the informant's carefully chosen words. 'Any word on who the buyer was likely to be?'

Catherine thought of Frankie Callahan's distracted calm, his controlled management of her visit, a man not wanting any complications; a man with something major in the offing.

She could see Laura through the glass, striding towards Catherine's office with that serious, determined look on her face. It was good to have someone working alongside you with that level of application and commitment to the job in hand, but if the lassie didn't lighten up a wee bit now and again, she was going to start worrying.

Laura had spent most of the previous day diligently probing for holes in Gary Fleeting's alibi, going at the task like it was her predestined purpose in life. The guy had baited and patronised her with what he believed at the time to be impunity. Instead he had just made it Laura's sole ambition to put him away.

Laura tracked down the one-night stand, a girl called Lyndsay McLaughlin. She admitted sleeping with Fleeting, but it was the sleeping part that was a problem for his alibi. Lyndsay said she woke around two in the afternoon, so couldn't confirm Fleeting's claim not to have left until after one.

The Bay Tree was starting to show gaps in its foliage too, as far as it covered Fleeting's evening. All the diners Laura spoke to confirmed that they had seen him working behind the bar, but they were less certain about whether he was still there around the time they were leaving. One did say he

238

was fairly sure Fleeting served him during last orders, but admitted to having had quite a few by that point. Pissed revellers did not play well in court as witnesses, no matter what they did for a living or how posh their postcode.

Laura swept on towards Catherine's office with an impatient sense of purpose. She looked like she had news.

'Just the woman I wanted to see,' Catherine hailed as Laura reached her office doorway. 'We need to go back and ask Frankie Callahan a few more awkward questions.'

'I think that's going to be a problem,' Laura replied.

WITNESS

The door was answered by a hard-faced middle-aged woman in hospital blues. Jasmine pondered briefly whether William Bain would turn out to be considerably older and more infirm than the most recent photo suggested, but then she noted the laminated badge pinned to the woman's chest. It was issued by Hairmyres Hospital in East Kilbride and identified her as 'Margaret Bain, Maternity Ward'.

She stepped aside to let them in but kept the door open as she pulled a light jacket off the end of the nearby banister.

'I'm just going on shift,' she explained. 'I'd make yous a cuppa tea, but I'm cutting it close. He's in the living room.'

Jasmine was about to assure her it was fine, but

239

she was out of the door and away with all haste.

They stood in the hallway for a few moments, wondering whether Bain would appear to greet them or should they feel free to proceed unaccompanied. Ingrams looked the place up and down, almost bashing his holdall against the wall as he turned around in the narrow hallway. He had a camera slung around his neck, a tripod and spare lenses in the bag.

They had picked these up from the office, after which they stopped in at the Silverburn shopping centre. They grabbed a quick bite to eat there, and Jasmine purchased a notepad and some pens in order to look more like a reporter. While they ate, Ingrams gave her a few suggestions for what she should ask, then led her off to a men's fashion store, where he bought a black peaked cap.

He had pulled it down low and tight over his head just before they got out of the car at Bain's address. Jasmine asked why he thought it would make him look more authentically like a photographer, but she got no answer.

Ingrams had paid for the food, like he paid for the hotel, and had fronted up the cash to pay Bain too. She was as grateful for his money as she was grateful for the assistance of someone who appeared to know what he was doing, but what made her uncomfortable—even more than being in some scary stranger's debt—was that she still couldn't work out what was in it for him. He'd claimed he wanted to know how he fitted into the picture, particularly as the picture now involved death, attempted murder and conspiracy to destroy evidence, but he had equally insisted that his part was tangential, that Jasmine had been the

240

target back in Northumberland. As far as she could see, this equation didn't add up. It was missing a variable.

The Bains' house was a 1950s-built ex-council semi, the kind of place that could look deceptively small on the outside but surprisingly roomy within. In Bain's case, the deception was reversed, largely because the place was so cluttered. There was no empty space on any horizontal surface, every flat object accommodating a smaller one above. Stacks of magazines provided a platform for piles of DVDs, or in some gloomier corners, piles of VHS tapes. Sun-faded cardboard boxes towered and interlocked like brickwork along walls and beneath tables. It was quite definitely the home of somebody who never threw anything out, and as the cash-stuffed envelope in Ingrams' bag testified, never gave anything away either.

There was a smell of chips throughout the place too; not the enticing aroma of vinegar, but the slightly choking stale odour that hung around after cooking. It made her wish she hadn't eaten.

Bain sat in an armchair in front of a disproportionately large telly tuned to Sky Sports News. He turned down the volume by way of acknowledging their arrival, but didn't switch off the set. He looked early sixties but was possibly younger, given that he didn't appear to be a long-term *Men's Health* subscriber. He was fatter than the photos had suggested, the slight jowliness of his face only hinting at the extent of his middle-age spread. Jasmine scanned the walls and spotted a few photos among the piles of junk. No kids. Just him and the wife. Looked like they'd lived here for decades.

241

'You got the money?' he asked.

Ingrams handed it to Jasmine as he crouched down over the bag, busying himself with the tripod. Bain barely gave him a second look. He checked the money and saw that the full two hundred was there, then placed the envelope on top of a side table; or more accurately on top of a folded newspaper on top of a ketchup-smeared dinner plate on top of a side table.

'Fire away,' he said.

'Do you mind if I just snap a few while you talk?' Ingrams asked, reverting to that strange, artificial-sounding accent.

Bain assented with an indifferent wave of his right hand.

'I've read all the clippings,' Jasmine began. 'And I appreciate you've been over this story many times before, so I'd like to take that all as read and approach it from another angle.'

'Any angle you like, hen. It's no' gaunny make much difference because the facts are the same any way you look at them.'

'Where were you going yourself that day?'

'Fishing. I was heading down to a wee place I know in Galloway.'

'Catch anything?'

'Cannae remember. I don't think I've ever thought about it, in fact. See, when you're asked a hundred times about one thing that happened that day, you forget everything else.'

'What did you stop at the services for?'

'Petrol, and I nicked into the toilets at the wee café place. I was walking through the car park when I saw them with the carrycot.'

'How did they seem? Were they calm, agitated?'

'Aloof,' he responded. 'You know, preoccupied.'

'And you offered them help getting the carrycot into the car.'

'Aye. They seemed to be having a bit of bother. I just asked if they were all right there and they shrugged me off. Never really gave it much thought at the time. Folk can be a bit stressed around weans. You shouldnae take the huff.'

'Have you a weak bladder?' Ingrams interjected, looking at Bain through the lens of Jim's camera.

'Whit's that got to do with anything?' Bain asked.

'From here to Bothwell services must be about twenty minutes, tops. Just wondered why you had to pee so soon.'

'I don't know. Probably forgot to go before I set off,' Bain offered, aiming a disgruntled look towards Ingrams.

Jasmine was feeling pretty disgruntled towards him too. It wasn't going to help matters if he pissed Bain off.

'Why do you think the incident stuck in your mind?' she asked. 'I mean, it was a few days later before the story broke.'

'I couldn't say. I'd probably forgotten about it by the time I was a mile doon the motorway. Then when I read about these folk being missing, it just kinda flashed up in my mind, total recall. I guess that's why the polis do those reconstruction things, isn't it?'

Ingrams moved a little closer with the camera and asked Bain if he wouldn't mind standing up and turning around to look out the window for a few shots.

'Want something a bit more interesting, you

know? Looking towards the past sorta thing. If we just do a head-and-shoulders it'll make you look like a criminal.'

Bain laughed a little uncomfortably but posed as asked.

'That your car, the Astra?' Ingrams asked, indicating the silver vehicle in front of the house.

'No, it's the neighbours'. Margaret's away in ours.'

'We're the Civic.'

Bain sat down again and Ingrams retreated back in the room, attaching the camera to the tripod.

Jasmine was about to ask her next question when Ingrams got in ahead of her.

'You confirmed to the police that the couple were driving a green A-reg Audi 80 and that the baby's carrycot was purple. Is that right?'

'Aye. Nice motor in its time, that Audi 80.' He gave Jasmine a knowing smile as he made his bid for a point of identification. 'Not as nice as thon Audi Quattro in that programme aboot the lassie back in time, but nice all the same.'

'What reg is your neighbour's Astra?' Ingrams asked.

Bain reeled slightly in his seat. He turned his head but his chair was facing away from the window and was in any case too low down.

'I'll take that as a don't know. Let me try you with an easier one. What colour is our Civic?'

Bain squirmed for a moment then went for blue as a gambit.

'Try red. You looked at it two minutes ago and you can't remember. So how did you manage to recall what colour the carrycot was from a brief encounter several days earlier?'

244

Bain was seething, and Jasmine feared he was about to order them out of his house. Instead he sighed and seemed to calm himself.

'I remembered the colour because it reminded me of a toy pram my wee sister used to play with,' he said, staring daggers at Ingrams. 'And my memory was a bit sharper twenty-seven year ago than it is the noo, okay? Now why don't you just stick to taking your photies, son, and let the wee lassie do her job.'

Jasmine gave it a moment for the tension to settle. She shot Ingrams a questioning look as he squatted behind the tripod, but like Bain all she got was an eyeful of lens and peaked cap. She looked at her list of questions suggested by him, all fairly neutral and unchallenging, and wondered what he was playing at. Then it hit her that this was a script, and for his own reasons he had only shown Jasmine her own lines.

She hit Bain with a warm and apologetic smile and ploughed on, giving the part her all now that she understood it.

'What made you come forward?' she asked him. 'I mean, a lot of people would have just thought it was nothing to do with them, maybe told themselves they hadn't really seen what they thought they had.'

'Sense of duty, I suppose. I'd read about the poor wee lassie that was left, and, well, you've got to do your bit, haven't you? Too many folk just look the other way these days. That's what's wrong with this country.'

Bain sat forward in his chair, raising a finger for emphasis.

'I mean, just to be clear, this is the first time I've

asked for money to talk aboot this. I've never gone to the papers: they've always come to me.'

He folded his arms and sat back again, content that he had made his point.

Ingrams let loose a derisory snort of laughter.

'Something funny, son?' Bain asked, rising aggression in his voice.

'Wee bit, yes.'

'Well why don't you speak up and say it to my face, instead of acting the smart cunt from behind your tripod over there?'

'Sense of duty?' Ingrams said, peering over the top of the camera.

When he spoke again, his accent had changed.

'You're the kind of guy that wouldnae let somebody else smell your farts for free if you could charge for it.'

Bain got to his feet, bristling with anger, but there was a confused caution about his face too.

'I want the pair of you oota here. Sorry, hen,' he told Jasmine, 'but I'm no' listening to this in my ain living room. And I'll tell you this, smart-mooth, if I was twenty years younger, I'd kick you up and doon the street like a wet tracksuit.'

Ingrams stood up from behind the tripod, rising to his full height and taking off the peaked cap so that Bain could finally see his face properly. And that face had transformed. It was the same man, but there was a cruel, glowering darkness to his expression that rendered Jasmine retrospectively terrified to have spent the past couple of days in his proximity.

The effect on Bain was even more dramatic. He spluttered, his breathing gone awry, and his legs seemed to buckle, causing him to slump back down into his chair.

'You,' he croaked, his mouth flapping like a landed fish. 'You're supposed to be deid.'

'I got better. And I reckon twenty years ago you'd have shat it from me, same as you're shiting it now. Street-fighting was never really your forte, any more than was helping oot the polis through your "sense of duty". Credit fraud, sure. Bit of reset. Moving smuggled fags by the vanload. But coming forward as a witness? Come on, Wullie, you never did *anything* without a back end for yourself.'

'That's all behind me,' he pleaded. 'Has been for twelve year, since I finished my last stretch. I work at B and Q. I'm straight noo.'

'But you weren't straight then. That poor wee lassie you said you were just doing your bit for, she's spent her whole life thinking her family abandoned her. Twenty-seven years asking herself why they would do that, torturing herself because of what you told the polis. You were never at Bothwell services that day, were you?'

'I was, I swear. And you're right, there was an angle in it for me. I came forward because I thought it might turn out handy to run up a wee bit credit with the polis. I was walking a thin line in those days.'

'You're talking shite, Wullie. I made up the bit about the carrycot being purple. I don't know what colour it was, and neither did you. Yet when I pressed you about it, you dreamed up a wee ad hoc explanation for why you remembered. Trust me, you're walking a much thinner line by lying to me, especially when it's so fucking *obvious* you're lying.'

247

Ingrams began walking towards him, just a couple of slow steps. Bain looked forlornly at the door and at Jasmine, though what the hell he thought she could do was anybody's guess.

It *was* obvious he was lying, which begged the question why he wouldn't just admit it. The answer, Jasmine realised, was that something scared him more than the man in his living room.

He shook his head, saying, 'I swear, I swear, I swear,' until it became a near-tearful whisper, a mantra of desperate supplication.

'I believe you,' Ingrams said, eliciting a tiny degree of relief but a greater quantity of concerned doubt. 'Not about seeing the Ramsays,' he clarified. 'You've been lying about that for twenty-seven years. But there's one thing you're not entirely lying about. You said you've never asked for money to talk about this, and I believe you about that. The papers came to you, you never went touting to them, because you never wanted to draw any scrutiny down upon your story. But today isnae the first time you've been paid for telling it, is it?'

Ingrams collapsed the tripod and slowly, very deliberately began unscrewing it from the base of the camera. Jasmine couldn't begin to imagine what he might be planning to do with it, but Bain was clearly doing nothing but.

'Who told you to lie, Wullie?'

'Believe me, son,' he said, shaking his head gravely, 'you really don't want to know.'

Ingrams had finally detached the tripod. He placed the camera carefully down into the bag and gripped the aluminium stand in his right fist.

'Believe me, I really, really do.'

248

Jasmine looked from Ingrams' fist to Bain's face, expecting to see greater panic, but instead he wore a bitter, ugly grin. It was the vengeful smile of the beaten man who knows that whatever he is about to surrender is booby-trapped.

'I'll tell you who paid me,' he sneered. 'A right nasty, ruthless piece of work. More brutal, more greedy and more twisted than any gangster in the city. Fallan, his name was. Detective Inspector Iain Fallan. Though I believe you referred to him as Dad.'

IDENTITY

Jasmine could see Bain watching them through his living-room window as they walked silently towards the Civic, perhaps reassuring himself that they were leaving. It looked like he was on the phone. She wondered which side of the law he was calling, and understood that they'd better get moving or they'd soon be finding out.

She set her phone back to its normal profile, from silent, and as she did so she noticed that she had a voicemail message. She retrieved it as she walked around to the driver's side and got into the car. It was a call for Jim, relayed from the office phone. She felt a rising in her chest as she heard the words 'This is a message for Jim Sharp' preface the recording, but her pulse fell again as it turned out to be from Scottish Gas, something about a heat-loss survey. Jim must have been getting loft insulation or maybe a new boiler. Jasmine could feel herself threatening to choke up, like when she took calls from Mum's old friends who hadn't heard, or when mail arrived for her. For some reason, a magazine subscription had been the worst, because it spoke to something Mum had enjoyed, the life she ought still to be living.

Neither of them said anything as she started the engine and pulled away. Ingrams didn't enquire after the phone message and seemed reluctant even to aim any looks her way. It was hard to imagine anyone ever describing her passenger as vulnerable, particularly given what she had just learned and witnessed, but she definitely got the impression that his defences were down. There was something contrite and regretful about him, his face bearing very little resemblance to the snarling demon who had just menaced Bain.

She had seldom been comfortable in his presence since they met, but for the first time it seemed like he was uncomfortable in hers. Jasmine wasn't having it, though. It was a small car, with no room between the front seats for an elephant.

'So I take it we can drop the pretence that you are anyone other than Glen Fallan?' she asked.

He still didn't speak for a while, long enough for her to think he was either in the huff or genuinely wounded about this.

'I used to be,' he eventually replied, his voice low and distant, like he had dragged the words up from somewhere very deep inside. He didn't seem inclined to elaborate.

'Did Jim know the truth about you?'

'Yes.'

'Shit,' she said, gripping the steering wheel tighter as an outlet for her temper. 'And you never said a thing.'

'He hadn't been in touch. I wasn't lying when I said I hadn't heard from him since last year.'

'Why was he looking for you before?'

'I can't tell you. I'd be breaching Jim's client confidentiality.'

Jasmine sighed, though she'd have preferred to scream.

'And would it be breaching his client confidentiality to speculate as to why he had your file out? What's your connection with all this? Why did you drop everything to come up here with me? No more lies. Tell me the truth.'

'I dropped everything because somebody was shooting at us. I came here with you because I want to find out why. I don't know what my connection is to this, but if we're going to work it out, we need to focus on what we *do* know.'

'What we *do* know? I don't even know what to call you. Is it Tron? Is it Glen? What kind of a name is Tron anyway? As in the daft sci-fi movie? As in the steeple?'

'As in the theatre. Something . . . happened to me there.'

'What?'

'It was where I decided I didn't want to be Glen Fallan any more. Nobody's called me by that name for twenty years.'

'And would you care to tell me what occasioned this epiphany?'

'I wouldn't say it's germane to the matter at hand. What is more relevant is that Bain's statement being bollocks changes everything. Without it, the Ramsays' last sighting is leaving the Campsieview hotel in Lennoxtown the night before.'

'Why would the police be distorting their own investigation?'

'*A* policeman was distorting the investigation. And if you had had the pleasure of my late father's acquaintance, you'd appreciate that it's not a given he was doing it from the inside.'

'So Bain wasn't just goading you with that? Was your dad really a bent cop?'

'Let's just say his corrupt side was among his more positive attributes, and leave it at that.'

Jasmine caught a glimpse of his face as he said this, slowing the car to a halt at some traffic lights. There was no wry humour to his expression, only a steely bitterness.

'What is crucial,' he went on, 'is that my father would have known what an impact Bain's statement would make on whoever was conducting the inquiry. It completely altered the timeline for the Ramsays' disappearance, not to mention the geography.'

'Do you reckon Jim had worked this out?'

With all their cards on the table, they had pressed Bain about Jim's investigation. Bain admitted Jim had been to the house to talk to him, but said he had stuck to his story.

'Bain was never going to crumble in front of Jim like he did in front of me, but if Jim was trying to deconstruct the investigation, it must have occurred to him how much hinged upon Bain's contribution. It shaped the entire thing to the extent that it was responsible for creating the mythology that developed around the case. Last sighting late night at a hotel, people just shrug, think poor bastards must be dead in a ditch, or driven their car into a canal. Last sighting broad

252

daylight at a motorway services, that suggests a journey. All those reports that kept the story alive down the years, people telling the papers they may have seen the Ramsays abroad, that all stems from Bain's lie.'

'So there's a good chance Jim was asking himself what the picture would have looked like without it. Why didn't the police ever do that?'

'Presumably they had little else to go on, and no reason to disbelieve Bain.'

'Apart from him being a petty crook?'

'That may actually have made him a more credible witness. There was no angle in it for him, as far as the police were aware: no reason why he would come forward and involve himself in this just to lie.'

'Yet you worked it out right away, soon as you recognised his photograph in the papers.'

'I didn't work it out right away, I just had my suspicions, based on a more in-depth knowledge of Mr Bain's character than the contemporary investigators may have enjoyed.'

'Why didn't you tell me?'

'I didn't want to prejudice our wee interview, and I needed what they call a Method performance from you, to put him at ease.'

'I know what a Method performance is. I'm better trained as an actor than as an investigator.'

'You're a trained actress?'

He seemed pleased by this, an undisguised delight playing across his face. Jasmine wished she could scrutinise it closer to see whether it was actually amusement, Ingrams perhaps thinking 'well that would explain a lot', but she had to keep her eyes on the road.

253

'I don't want to talk about it. As you said, we have to focus.'

'Sure,' he agreed. 'And you made a good point before. If my old man was looking for a stooge, he could have come up with plenty who were more ostensibly respectable than Wullie Bain.'

'Maybe Bain had other attributes that balanced it up,' Jasmine suggested.

'Aye. Like knowing his place and not being particularly inquisitive. Wullie was never the kind of person to ask too many questions if you put money in his hand.'

'Did you know him well back then?'

He stared ahead, evidently no keener to elaborate upon this than she had been about her abortive acting career. But then he took a breath and answered.

'I started off as a debt collector for a gangster called Tony McGill. I say gangster, but Tony never really had a gang. In my experience, organised crime in Glasgow was never very organised. But representing Tony's interests, you crossed a lot of paths, made a lot of connections. It was like Facebook for criminals. And I never forget a face.'

He spoke this last statement not with pride or menace, but with the most bitter self-recrimination.

In the silence that followed, Jasmine felt her anger at his deception recede as she began to glimpse the true nature of what underlay it. He had abandoned his name in an attempt to leave his former self behind, but remained burdened by Glen Fallan's sins. And with that in mind, she belatedly understood the act of self-sacrifice he had just committed on her behalf.

'Bain didn't recognise you until you forced him to. You could have kept your identity secret, but you gave it up in there to help me.' She swallowed, feeling a lump rise in her throat as she often did these days whenever someone surprised her with a kindness. 'Thank you.'

'I didn't give it up in there. I knew I was giving it up when I decided to come back to Glasgow with you. It was only a matter of time after that.'

'Still, I appreciate it.'

'You may want to save the thanks until you find out what else comes with the package.'

'Why did you decide to come back here with me?' she asked, figuring she'd chance her arm while his defences appeared to be down.

He stared at her for a moment, his expression unreadable.

'I've made a lot of enemies in my time. Left a lot of UXBs in my wake. I've learned to react to the warning signs whenever one might be threatening to go off. Who was the call from?' he added, changing the subject so conspicuously as to unambiguously close its predecessor.

'It was for Jim, but it was nothing. Gas Board, doing some kind of survey. I think they were trying to flog him a new boiler.'

'Is that another number accounted for on your list, then?'

'I forgot to check.'

'May I?' he asked, lifting Jasmine's phone from where it was resting in front of the gearstick.

'Sure.'

Ingrams reached into the back seat and retrieved the list, then thumbed his way to Jasmine's call log.

'Yep. There it is: outgoing call. Here's a thing, though. Did you know Bain's number appears on the incoming list as well as the outgoing?'

'I hadn't spotted that, no. Guess he could have been returning Jim's call or checking a missed number. It's also possible I duplicated it by mistake,' she admitted. 'I was trying to be methodical, but it's not my natural métier.'

Just then, Jasmine's phone rang in Ingrams' hand.

'Shall I?' he asked.

'Please.'

Ingrams answered. She heard a few neutral 'okays' and 'sures', then, more curiously, he told the caller: 'Well, Jim is actually out of the country at the moment. Yes, unexpectedly. But he mentioned this to me before he left, so I'll be over first thing tomorrow. Maxwell Road, isn't it? Okay, see you then.'

'Who are we seeing on Maxwell Road?' Jasmine asked.

'Scottish Gas. Industrial and Commercial department. Guy was trying one more time before he left for the night. He was calling to inform Jim that the heat-loss images he enquired about are ready for him to pick up.'

'What are heat-loss images?'

'I don't know, but the ones Jim requested are twenty-seven years old. I don't think he was buying a new boiler, do you?'

FIRE-DAMAGED

'How do you like your drug dealer?'asked Cal O'Shea. 'Rare? Medium?'

'*À point*,' Catherine replied.

'You're in luck, then.'

Everything was soaking. Catherine stood in a puddle an inch deep stretching all the way across the floor of the Top Table depot. It was a single-storey but high-ceilinged industrial unit on the outskirts of Hamilton, close to the East Kilbride expressway. The tableware side of Frankie Callahan's catering supply company used it as a central distribution point: tablecloths and napkins were brought here after being laundered, then racked up in hoppers ready for resuply.

It was a testament to the quality of Top Table's linen that it had proven sufficiently fire-retardant as to have played its part in preventing the place burning to the ground, despite petrol having been liberally doused about the premises. According to one of the firemen, the collapse of several hoppers and subsequent spillage of hundreds of yards of cloth had smothered a significant proportion of the flames and prevented serious structural damage to the building.

Clearly they were going to have to ditch most of this stock due to fire and smoke damage, but Frankie wouldn't be losing any sleep over it. What with being dead and all.

There were three corpses inside the building; the firemen had discovered two of them partially buried under piles of linen. They were all charred

257

and wet, but Cal declared the burns largely superficial. 'Which will be a big comfort to them,' he added.

The two partially buried bodies belonged to Frankie Callahan and Gary Fleeting. They were discovered face down, each having been shot several times.

The third body sat upright, tied to a chair with bungee cord. He looked like some macabre king of fire, surveying the scene before him from his metal throne.

'Stab wounds to the thighs, more shallow cuts to the chest, several slashes across either cheek,' Cal informed them. 'Looks to me like they were torturing him when they received a surprise interruption. Callahan and Fleeting were both shot in the back to bring them down, then took two each in the back of the head to finish them off. Professional. Execution-style. The guest of honour took a double tap to the head also, so it wasn't a rescue mission. We found his wallet in the pocket of a jacket dumped over in the corner by the back door. According to the driving licence, his name was Thomas Miller. That ring any bells?'

Catherine looked at the blackened and ruined face, exit wounds having blown his features apart. His own mother wouldn't recognise him, God help her.

'Tommy Miller,' she said. 'Quintessential Glasgow fly-man. All things to all men.' She turned to Laura. 'One might even say an adept at playing both ends against the middle.'

'You reckon this was Bob Cairns' source?'

'Frankie and Gary here appear to have believed so. I think this may answer the question of whose heroin we confiscated yesterday. Bad day all round for this pair. Lose three million quid's worth of drugs in the morning, then get shot dead and set fire to later on.'

'Aye. That would fuck me off,' Laura said, mimicking Callahan's intense sincerity. 'It would fuck me right off.'

She looked down with contempt at what was left of Gary Fleeting. Sure didn't look so pleased with himself now. There would be no more 'wee durties' happy to 'take it all ways' from him.

'Who would have done this?' she asked. 'The wholesaler, maybe? Could be the drugs got lifted before payment was made and they weren't prepared to just write it off against tax.'

'Can't see it. It's too soon, and too extreme. The amount of heroin Frankie Callahan was moving each year, it would be bad business sense to react like this. They'd want to work something out, a compensation payment or some other make-good. When your handover strategy involves leaving the merchandise unattended, you'd have to think there would be some kind of agreement in place to cover this sort of scenario.'

'This happened with no questions being asked. Both of them shot in the back before they could even speak, then Tommy here taken out because he was a witness. Whoever did this just wanted them dead. That suggests a simpler motive.'

That was when Laura noted the significance of the supply firm's delivery fleet, pointing out two of them parked on the depot's forecourt.

They were both dark blue Transit vans.

There had been a dark blue Ford Transit seen entering the lane where Jai McDiarmid was

259

abducted, and a similar vehicle seen exiting the same place around twelve hours later when his body was dumped. Paddy Steel's people had been looking for a black one, but it was hardly a stretch to imagine they would eventually make that small chromatic leap.

Catherine was starting to hear Moira Clark's voice in her head.

'The press talk about gang wars, drug wars and turf wars,' Moira once told her. 'And gangs, drugs and territory *are* factors in these incidents, but they're never the primary cause. Round here, folk don't plan very far ahead when it comes to violence. They don't go in for campaigns and strategies. Vendettas, aye. Feuds, absolutely. Tit-for-tat. Grudges. Vengeance. Always remember: this is Glesca.'

As if she needed any further confirmation of this hypothesis, her phone began to ring, its screen identifying the incoming caller as Detective Superintendent Dougie Abercorn.

LOST IN THE SWAMP

'I'm not trying to piss in your chips here,' said Abercorn. 'I realise you think you're close to a result on this, a big result, but I'm getting a very strong vibe that something about this may not be quite what it appears. I'd advise you not to rush into anything.'

But then he would say that, wouldn't he, given the way developments had left him floundering. Something not what it appeared? More like something wasn't in Abercorn's script, and he wanted to stall her while he got back on to the right page.

He told her they needed to talk, urgently, and dangled the intrigue carrot by requesting that they do so at his office, 'for reasons of discretion'. If she hadn't been to the High Court the other day, she'd have told him to stick it, but given what she now knew about Abercorn pulling strings for Callahan, she decided to play along, reckoning that for once she might get more out of the exchange than he would.

She would confess to a guilty satisfaction at seeing that his office was smaller than hers, but then she realised this was probably an optical illusion arising from the fact that it was so claustrophobically cluttered.

She was almost disappointed in him. She had this image of Abercorn as being such a sleek operator that his office would be pristine beyond the point of anal: not a paperclip out of place, not a single stray sheet on his desk, just a state-of-the-art laptop and a framed photo of a wife and kids that weren't actually his, just there for show to make him look more human.

'I'm not rushing into anything,' she replied. 'Especially with my prime suspects in the McDiarmid murder currently lying on slabs down in Cal O'Shea's laboratory.' She wrinkled her nose in distaste, realising she could smell on her jacket an odour unsettlingly redolent of barbecue. 'Suspects, I would add, that you made a point of trying to ward me away from earlier in my investigation.'

Abercorn ignored this and directed her

attention to a mugshot among the piles of documents scattered about his desk. There was a black-and-white computer image clipped to it, showing a CCTV still from yesterday's robbery.

'This is the partial shot we've been circulating of the guy who robbed Coruscate,' he told her. 'He's been identified as this man, name of Liam Whitaker. He's a time-served thief and housebreaker, but the clincher is that he's a known associate of Tommy Miller.'

'We brought him in yet?'

'He's gone to ground.'

'With a hundred and forty grand's worth of jewellery, no wonder.'

'Not jewellery,' said Abercorn. 'Watches.'

'What's the difference?'

'These extremely upmarket watches are very popular among the higher echelons of the criminal fraternity.'

'The blingest of the bling?'

'No, you won't find them actually wearing one. Way too valuable for that. They *hold* their value; in fact even appreciate sometimes. They're an investment, for money-laundering purposes. Instead of having two hundred grand sitting around the house waiting for the Proceeds of Crime Act to come along and swoop it up, they have it sitting there in the shape of high-class watches worth ten and twenty grand a pop. Collector's items. And when they want to liquidise some capital, they can sell them, legitimately.'

'This isn't telling me anything new. I had already worked out that Cairns' tout must have planned to exploit the evacuation. This just gives us an idea of how much it was worth his while.'

'He wasn't only Cairns' source,' said Abercorn quietly, almost confessionally. 'That's the whole thing. He was our tout too, one of our CHISes. We were quietly keeping tabs on Callahan's operation, but unbeknown to us, Miller was double-dealing the information. Guess it gives new meaning to the term *Covert* Human Intelligence Source.'

Catherine felt her eyes widen and tried not to indulge a sense of perverse satisfaction.

'Which he knew he could get away with because he had sussed that you weren't acting on it,' she said. 'Not directly, anyway.'

'Well, that's one way of looking at it, yes. We didn't realise until today, and Cairns remains none the wiser.'

'Is this why you got the charges against Gary Fleeting dropped?'

Abercorn's mouth flapped silently for half a second, betraying his disquiet that she should know this. He tried to regroup but she could tell he was rattled.

'We have to make some unpalatable choices and swallow down some very bitter pills. I know what gets said about us, about me. Letting Off Criminals Under Secret Trades. Guys like Cairns are everybody's hero because they swat a few mosquitoes. It takes a lot more work for a lot fewer plaudits when you're trying to drain the swamp.'

And there it finally was. But he wasn't finished.

'We're after the big players. Gary Fleeting doesn't even register, and Frankie Callahan is a speck of dust. Folk here think the world starts and ends in Glasgow. We're developing a picture of a massive, highly complex distribution system, not just UK-wide, but cooperating with forces overseas from Moscow to Marrakech.'

He indicated the mountains of files and documents threatening to collapse and swamp him like those tablecloths swamped the flames consuming Callahan and Fleeting.

'Look at this shit. What do people think we do all day? Dream up new ways to get in the way of "real" police work? We're trying to map the reach of a supplier who is a major node in this network. I couldn't afford to have Callahan's operation derailed at that point for the sake of putting a nothing like Gary Fleeting away for a five-stretch. What would that achieve?'

'I think James McDiarmid's mother might have a forthright take on that question.'

'That's making the assumption that Fleeting killed him. I'm just not as convinced as you that this is all quite what it looks like.'

'What it looks like to me is pretty simple,' Catherine retorted. 'Gary Fleeting killed James McDiarmid over a girl, or who knows, there was no love lost: maybe the girl was just an excuse. A few days later, Tommy Miller tips off Bob Cairns and he intercepts Frankie Callahan's next heroin haul. Frankie and Gary suss the source of the leak and go all *Reservoir Dogs* on Tommy Miller, but while they're at it, one or more of Paddy Steel's people shoot them and set fire to the place in revenge for McDiarmid. What part doesn't add up?'

Abercorn produced a clear plastic document wallet from a drawer beneath his desk and handed it to her, a white A4 sheet visible within.

'It's the early lab analysis on yesterday's heroin seizure,' he said. 'The stuff's pure shit.'

'Pure shit, as in totally uncut?'

264

'No, as in shit. Garbage. Worthless. It's mostly talcum powder and gypsum. There was only enough heroin in it to attract the sniffer dog.'

Catherine skim-read the report, confirming what he was saying.

'So this wasn't Frankie Callahan's shipment?'

'There was a shipment due, according to our sources, and previous shipments have been transferred using the left-luggage store at Central, but clearly that's not what Bob Cairns intercepted yesterday.'

'So was it just a decoy left by Tommy Miller to clear the station for the robbery?'

'I don't think so. Cairns would have cut his balls off, and Miller would have known that. Miller believed he was giving Cairns good intel.'

'But then if no heroin shipment went missing, what were Callahan and Fleeting doing cutting lumps out of Tommy Miller?'

'I don't know. Like I said, something here is not what it seems. Add to that what you know about Paddy Steel, who by your account was out jogging with a bulletproof vest on earlier this week. At a stretch, I can maybe see him sanctioning a revenge hit on Fleeting, but taking out someone as prominent as Frankie Callahan as well? Why would he want to escalate things to that level? I think there's something else going on here, something we're not aware of.'

There was also, Catherine was sure, something he wasn't saying either. He had this torn look, like he was unsure whether to give anything away. Abercorn was normally more poker-faced, but lately the game was threatening to get out of his control.

'What else do you have?' she demanded. 'Come on, you're standing there like a wean that's shat his nappy.'

He gave an uncertain sigh, biting his lip for a moment.

'Okay,' he conceded. 'I know you think that we're always cadging information without giving anything back. I wasn't withholding this, I just wasn't sure it was relevant; I'm still not. Could be unrelated, though working here, you stop believing in coincidences.'

Christ, enough preamble. He really grudged giving you anything.

'Spit it out,' she said.

'Does the name Glen Fallan mean anything to you?'

She let it ring around her head but it shook loose only the merest fragment.

'I vaguely remember hearing the name *Iain* Fallan from older colleagues. Wasn't he murdered?'

'Iain Fallan worked CID over in Gallowhaugh back in the seventies and eighties. He was found dead in his car one night, killed by a single stab wound to the back of the head. The killer was never caught. There was no indication of forced entry, so it was assumed that he was killed by somebody he trusted enough to have them sitting in his back seat.'

'Another cop?'

'Fallan was notoriously corrupt. He had allies and enemies on both sides of the law. His son, though, only followed in one set of his father's footsteps. He was a debt collector, enforcer and hit man, initially for Tony McGill, but later for Stevie

266

Fullerton, after Tony went inside. You won't find much of a file on him. He wasn't your normal Glasgow gangland bam. He was as stealthy as he was discreet, and he understood enough about the police to avoid ever being caught. He seldom left a body, just made people disappear. Made a *lot* of people disappear.'

'This is all sounding very past tense. If he was so good, what happened to him?'

'Poetically enough, one day he was the one who just disappeared. It was twenty-one years ago, summer of 1989. He was rumoured to have been murdered in his home, out in rural Lanarkshire. According to gangland lore, it was Stevie Fullerton and his people who did it, in revenge for Fallan killing Stevie's cousin over a girl. Classic criminal infighting.'

Catherine couldn't see where this was going. Fullerton was a pretty big player these days, but she had found nothing to suggest he was at war with Frankie Callahan, or even Paddy Steel.

'So how does this colourful wee snippet of local history relate to my investigation?'

'Because I've got it from very strong sources that Glen Fallan is looking in pretty good nick for a dead guy. He showed up yesterday at the house of an ex-con and occasional tout by the name of William Bain.'

'An occasional tout? Couldn't he just be fishing for a few quid?'

'My source says Bain was terrified. Claimed Fallan made no secret of who he was, though Bain wouldn't say what he wanted. Fallan was with a young girl, late teens/early twenties, driving a red Honda Civic. He wrote down the plate. We traced it to a Jasmine Sharp, who it transpires showed up at Partick police station on Monday to report a missing person: her uncle, Jim Sharp, private investigator and ex-cop.'

*   *   *

The state of clarity and purpose in which Catherine had entered Abercorn's office was a mere memory by the time she left it again. She felt confused and frustrated, and not a little angry. She wasn't sure quite what had gone on in there, but had the suspicion that whatever it was, she had come off worse. That was classic Abercorn. Even though he had ostensibly been giving her something, she still felt like she'd had her pocket picked. She should have known, though, and that was what made it worse.

Head games: that was all this was. Abercorn had been blindsided by Callahan's murder and he was trying to run interference in order to buy himself time to catch up.

The major dealer he was monitoring—not to mention pulling serious strings to keep him in play—had been gunned down under his nose, leaving him with nothing else to follow. Was Abercorn worried his jacket was on a shaky nail? If she wrapped up these murders, and the McDiarmid one that had precipitated them, was he afraid that the brass might think they had been mistaken to prefer him over her for the Locust job? Was he that paranoid? That petty? Or, in true Abercorn style, was he concealing some other agenda that she was oblivious of?

Any way up, she wasn't going to let him derail

268

her. For what else was that Glen Fallan nonsense all about, other than an attempt to send her on a wild goose chase?

Clark's Law still stood. The lab report on Cairns' heroin haul posed some very odd questions, but it didn't change the dramatis personae. It was still about Gary Fleeting and Jai McDiarmid, Frankie Callahan and Paddy Steel, Liam Whitaker and Tommy Miller.

She was walking slowly through the car park, taking her time in order to clear her head with some air, when her mobile rang, heralding a call from Cal O'Shea.

'I've some rather disturbing news with regard to our special fried gangsters,' he said, his typically arch elocution failing to conceal a note of concern.

Jesus, what now? Catherine wondered.

'They're still dead, I take it,' she said, figuring if she set the bizarre-bar that high, she could handle anything below.

'Most certainly, yes,' he confirmed. 'But that is just about the only aspect that remains what it appears. The fire broke out at around two in the morning, isn't that right?'

'The fire brigade logged the call reporting the fire at Top Table at around two forty-five. Why?'

'All three of these men had been dead for several hours before that. Callahan and Fleeting were killed yesterday evening, around eight; Miller at least two hours earlier than that. Furthermore, they all received most of their wounds post-mortem. The lack of internal bleeding indicates that Callahan and Fleeting were shot in the back several hours *after* being shot in the head; similarly the stab and slash wounds to Miller, who was long dead before he was tied to the chair.'

'You're saying it was staged?'

'It's quite possible none of them were alive when they were brought to the warehouse. The place was supposed to burn, but the perpetrator or perpetrators were better hit men than they were arsonists.'

'Why stage something if you're planning to burn it down?'

'To prevent me discovering what I just have. You were supposed to find a fire-gutted warehouse containing three charred bodies from which it could nonetheless be deduced that two had been taken by surprise and shot in the back in the act of torturing the third. And had whoever did it not made a grave miscalculation regarding the flammability of table linen, we'd have been none the wiser.'

Catherine hung up and stood perfectly still next to her car. It was one of those times when she imagined she could sense the planet spinning beneath her feet. She felt just a tiny bit less connected to the world, her stature a little shorter, the surrounding buildings a little taller.

Nothing was what it appeared. Bob Cairns had been led to a suitcase full of dust. Frankie Callahan had not lost a shipment of heroin. He and Gary Fleeting had not been torturing Tommy Miller. There was a decades-dead assassin walking the streets. And most bizarrely of all, it could well be that Dougie Abercorn was actually trying to help.

DARKEN THE MEMORY

Once again Catherine found herself gatecrashing someone else's breakfast, though given the time since she'd blearily grabbed her own, it felt like it ought to be closer to lunch. She smelt freshly brewed, *proper* coffee, saw baskets of croissants and pastries, while waitresses skipped past bearing steaming plates of bacon, haggis, kippers, scrambled eggs. Diners mostly in business attire were enjoying leisurely chats, sitting with the morning paper if they were alone, or in the case of one quartet, conducting a breakfast meeting. It all looked terribly grown-up and civilised.

Catherine had managed a slice of toast and half a cup of tea in between clearing spilt Ready Brek, wiping faces and mediating a protracted and passionate dispute over who was getting the free toy that would be so prized as to be lying forgotten under the fridge this time tomorrow, while her sole ally in all this was standing at the worktop on the other side of the kitchen, hastily grabbing mouthfuls of cornflakes as he cleaned yesterday's mud from two junior-sized pairs of trainers.

It wasn't always quite so fraught and frantic, especially not on a Saturday; normally the chaos level was a constant but the pace was more relaxed due to the greater flexibility of Drew's working patterns. This morning, however, he had a flight to London to catch, which meant departing early enough to account for the M8 traffic, as well as leaving sufficient time to drop the boys at his parents' en route. They generally tried to avoid both having work commitments on the same Saturday, but sometimes it was simply inescapable. At least there was no school pick-up to worry about later.

The atmosphere between her and Drew had been less tense last night. By the time they got the boys settled, they were both content to sit on the settee in front of the telly for a couple of hours. *Cobra* was on Sky Movies, an irresistibly awful piece of eighties trash, a subgenre they shared a passion for. Catherine found the moral simplicity and facile resolutions more of an escapist fantasy than any sci-fi movie, while Drew lapped up the cartoonishness and gratuitous violence because the games he worked on espoused the same guilty-pleasure ethos.

They had sat and giggled over it like a couple of old friends. Catherine found this both a reassurance and a bit of a disappointment at the same time, because she didn't want to settle for it, and certainly didn't want Drew to think she had. They were old friends, but they were supposed to be lovers too.

There still wasn't much she could do about that, even if they hadn't both needed to be up at dawn. She didn't mind snuggling chastely against Drew on the sofa, but she didn't want to be held, didn't want to be naked. When she thought of Drew naked, she pictured him all burnt up like Callahan and Fleeting, sensed his vulnerability, his mortality. And God, that smell had been about her all day. Even after a shower, she could smell it from the laundry basket, adhering to her clothes.

There were things you couldn't just wash off at the end of the day.

272

There's this dark place you go. You're angry on the road to that place and you're unreachable when you get there. But what's hardest is you're numb for days afterwards.

I always come back though, Drew. Please wait for me.

Catherine spotted them in a corner, furthest from any windows. Neither of them appeared to be saying very much. Fallan was sitting with his back to the wall, with a clear view of all exits. He had noted her entrance but was pretending he hadn't. Perhaps he didn't view her as a threat.

Jasmine Sharp was slight and pretty in a fresh-faced, girlish way. Catherine knew from her details that she was twenty, but she could pass for a schoolgirl, or maybe that was simply because she seemed so small next to Fallan. Catherine suspected she could look a lot different if she wanted to. Jasmine wore no make-up and her hair was tied back, something of laundry day about her. Catherine had wondered why a girl with a flat on Vicky Road would be staying in a hotel only a few miles away. Now she knew.

She had the look of a fugitive.

Catherine approached the table. The girl turned to look at her, but Fallan remained intent upon his black pudding and scrambled eggs. Nonetheless, he spoke before she had the chance to open her mouth.

'How can I help you, Officer?' he asked, without looking up from his breakfast, and without any hint that he had any intention of helping her. The only thing he truly wished to communicate was that he had recognised her for what she was the moment she walked through the double doors into the

273

room.

'Glen Fallan, I presume?' she asked. 'I'm Detective Superintendent Catherine McLeod, CID.'

She extended a warrant card towards the table, a prompt for him to look at it and by extension herself. He did, his eyes rising neutrally to take in the card and then to meet hers.

He didn't acknowledge the name, but he didn't deny it either.

'And you must be Jasmine Sharp.'

The girl gave her an uneasy smile and a cooperative nod. She wasn't so used to playing it cool around the polis.

'Mind if I join you?'

'I think it's residents only,' Fallan replied.

Catherine ignored this and pulled out a chair.

Jasmine tutted, which Catherine interpreted as proof that she was learning fast from her mentor with regard to the attitude one presented to the police. Then it became clear that it was Fallan who was the target of her irritation.

'What?' he asked.

'Took me three days to get you to admit that, and now complete strangers are just walking up and calling you it.'

A waitress came over and asked Catherine if she'd like some tea or coffee. The percolated coffee smell was tempting, but she opted for tea, some wee girlie part of herself still viewing it as a special treat to get a steel pot and a jug of milk in a restaurant.

'I'll bring a fresh pot for everybody,' the waitress said, oblivious of the tension at the table or simply helpless but to ignore it.

Fallan glared at her as she withdrew, in annoyance at her unwitting complicity, but only once her back was turned.

'I take it Mr Fallan has been going by an alias?' Catherine asked.

'Tron Ingrams,' Jasmine said helpfully, a lack of guile in her expression making it hard to tell whether she was too naïve to be protective of this information or merely trying to discomfort Fallan.

What *are* you two doing together? Catherine wondered.

'My name *is* Tron Ingrams,' he said. 'Glen Fallan is a name I left behind more than twenty years ago.'

'It's a lot easier to leave behind a name than it is to leave behind a past. Especially a past like yours, *Mr Ingrams*.'

'How did you find us?' asked Jasmine, a little concerned.

'Us *public* investigators have access to some useful resources,' she replied, intending to put the girl further on the back foot. 'For instance, you'd be amazed how many times your number plate gets scanned these days.'

The waitress returned with a large pot of tea and began to pour.

As she did so, Catherine found herself suddenly staring with horror at Fallan, briefly helpless to disguise her reaction as she realised that she had met him once before. She had seen his face and heard his voice this morning, but neither had piqued more than the minimum search of her memory she habitually conducted whenever she met anyone with a connection to the world of crime; a search that had turned up no results.

It was the smell of the tea that did it, the sense most closely connected to memory. His face, his voice and even his posture were rapidly reassembled in a specific context: sitting at another table, a quarter of a century ago, drinking tea while she watched him in fear and hatred.

She couldn't reach for her cup because she was concerned her hand would tremble conspicuously.

Fallan eyed her briefly, aware of her previous stare. Had he recognised her too? Unlikely. He would barely have noticed her at the time, just one more scared face, the kind he must have seen dozens of every day.

The memory came crashing over her like a wave. Fallan had been in her parents' kitchen, along with that horrible little grey man she still saw some nights in her unquiet dreams: a wispy-haired walking corpse who smelled like he lived in an ashtray.

Sitting at her parents' table. Drinking her parents' tea.

Taking her parents' money.

Catherine fought to control herself. A reservoir of hatred had been breached, something she thought had been locked down and secured long ago. She could do with a drink of tea, but she still couldn't trust her hands; either to remain untrembling or to refrain from throwing the scalding liquid into Fallan's face.

'What are you doing back in town,' she asked, trying but failing to quite keep the venom from her voice. 'Here to pick up again where you left off?'

Fallan said nothing. The girl was less adept at waiting out an awkward silence, however.

'My uncle's gone missing. He's also my boss.

The police weren't providing much assistance, so he's been helping me.'

'People disappearing? Yes, he'd certainly be an expert on that.'

Fallan calmly finished off the last of his breakfast and put down his cutlery, then looked Catherine in the eye.

'Is there something we can help you with?' he asked, his tone communicating that if there wasn't, he would strongly prefer to be left alone.

'James McDiarmid. Frankie Callahan. Gary Fleeting. Tommy Miller. Any of those names familiar to you?'

Fallan took a sip of tea with affected gentility.

'Nope.'

'All four of them have two things in common. They all have connections to drug trafficking and organised crime, and they have all died violently in the past few days. So in the same week that I get four dead criminals to play with, it turns out that Glen Fallan is back from the grave. Dead gangsters, Glen Fallan. Glen Fallan, dead gangsters. From what I gather, they tend to go together, like bacon and eggs, coffee and cream, guns and bullets. Can you understand why I might be inclined to connect these two developments?'

'When did they die?' he asked.

'McDiarmid Sunday, the others Thursday.'

'I was in Northumberland on Sunday,' he said. 'Came up here on Wednesday.'

'He's been with me the whole time,' said Jasmine.

'Even during the night?' Catherine asked. It was a distasteful thought, but she needed to know.

'No,' Jasmine insisted, looking equally appalled.

'And you can't vouch for him on Sunday either, because you hadn't discovered your uncle missing yet. Do you have any idea who this man is? What he's done?'

'I know he saved—' Jasmine began, but cut herself off in response from a look from Fallan telling her not to go there.

'If the detective superintendent has specific questions, feel free to respond, but otherwise don't rise to the bait.'

Fallan spoke to Jasmine like Catherine wasn't even there. She decided to respond by speaking like Jasmine wasn't either.

'Why are you really back in town, eh Fallan? If you're not shagging the girl, then the altruistic behaviour has to be a cover for something else. You here to settle old scores with Stevie Fullerton? Or maybe you and Stevie have had make-up sex and now you're helping him clear away some of the competition.'

'I've not spoken to Stevie in twenty-one years and I've never heard of any of the people you just mentioned. Who were they?'

'Frankie Callahan, one of Glasgow's biggest heroin pushers. Gary Fleeting, his right-hand man. Tommy Miller, drug dealer, thief, fence and tout. Jai McDiarmid, drug dealer and close associate of Paddy Steel, also a major peddler of smack. Jai was beaten, possibly tortured, then shot in the head and his body dumped out the back of the tanning salon he owned. The other three were all double-tapped, execution style, and left in a warehouse near Blantyre.'

'I'm a wee bit out of touch when it comes to my Glasgow gangsters,' Fallan replied with a blank

278

shrug. 'I'll say this, though: it doesn't sound like Stevie's style. He didn't go starting wars. Stevie was always about the business, didn't like unnecessary aggro.'

'So did it constitute necessary aggro when he tried to kill you? Oh no, hang on, that was more probably personal, wasn't it. What with you offing his cousin.'

It was the first time she felt like she'd landed a blow. Fallan looked distinctly uncomfortable, sending an anxious glance towards the girl.

Catherine finally reached for her cup and took a sip of tea to celebrate. If her hand trembled, he didn't seem to notice.

'Of course, strictly speaking, that's just speculation,' she added, offering them both a cold smile. 'Jazz Donnelly's body was never found. He just disappeared. That was *your* style, wasn't it?'

Jasmine was looking at Fallan and he was suffering under the heat of her gaze.

'Like you said,' he replied in a low, quiet and conspicuously controlled tone, 'it's speculation. And it doesn't fit with you finding four bodies, does it?'

He seemed content to have batted this back to her, then something evidently occurred to him.

'The MO does have a certain ring of familiarity,' he said, and she instinctively knew a barb was coming: a sting in the tail or a flat-out lie, but undeniably some kind of fuck-you. 'We'd be talking a bigger gang than Stevie's, though. We'd be talking the biggest gang in Glasgow.'

'And who is that then, according to a man who claims to be twenty years out of touch?'

'Better ask somebody older, hen.'

NAMING THE SINS

They sat in silence for a long time after the policewoman left. It was one of those silences that you know is going to define your relationship for ever after: depending on what broke it; depending on the next thing Ingrams finally said. And it had to be something *he* said, had to be him that broke it. It was his choice now whether he wanted to close the door on what had just been discussed, whether he thought she had any right to know.

They were starting to clear tables. Breakfast finished at ten, and it was five to. There was still tea in both their cups, barely lukewarm now, undrinkable.

'I didn't recognise her,' he said. 'McLeod. The cop. I didn't recognise her.'

'Should you have?'

'She recognised me.'

'Well, she knew all about you, probably has a file.'

'No. I saw it: the moment she recognised me. She wasn't expecting to, and then flash, there it was. I couldn't miss it. Pure hate, a lifetime of hate.'

'Why? Because she's a cop?'

'More personal than that. More specific. But I don't know what, and that's the thing. I hurt so many people. Far more than I can remember; and far more than I could even notice.'

It took all of Jasmine's courage to ask, but she knew she couldn't not know.

'You hurt . . . women?'

He looked her in the eye.

'Yes,' he said, not flinching from her gaze. 'Not directly. But I hurt them, women and children, without a doubt. McLeod could have been somebody hiding behind her crying mother while I threatened her father. One of the countless witnesses you don't even see because they're never going to tell anybody.'

Jasmine swallowed. This was the hardest conversation of her life, asking questions she didn't want to ask, of a man who didn't want to answer, but both of them understood that the chalice couldn't pass either of their lips.

'And the other things she said . . .' Jasmine began, but she could not put a name to those things. Could not ask him: 'Did you kill people?'

And yet she knew that in her stumbled few words, she had.

'It's a myth told about old-school criminals that they don't hurt the innocent,' he said. 'We already know that's not true. But aside from what they might excuse as collateral damage, they like to tell themselves that the rule is you don't hurt non-combatants. You're only *fair* game if you're *in* the game. But the truth is that your definition of a combatant eventually becomes anybody who stands between you and what you want.'

Ingrams looked away, his gaze towards the windows but his mind's eye somewhere much further distant, somewhere Jasmine suspected she'd never like to see.

He closed his eyes for a moment, then opened them and looked at her with that vulnerability she'd glimpsed in the car just after they left Bain's house.

'I'm not an evil man, Jasmine. But I'm not a good one either. McLeod was right. You can leave a name behind, but you can't escape who you are. Coming back here, seeing the fear on Bain's face, the hatred in that policewoman's . . . it's made me realise I can't separate one life from another. I need to put a name to my sins, and I need to wear that name.'

'So you're Glen Fallan again?'

'Yes.'

'Good. Tron's a stupid name.'

STOLEN GLANCES

Laura's mobile rang as they walked back to their car, parked directly adjacent to the main entrance of the Bay Tree restaurant. The Bay Tree sat at a T-junction on the main road through Thornton Bridge. During evenings and lunchtimes there were normally cars trailed all along the secondary road parallel to the side of the building, the restaurant's cottage origins denying it the luxury of a dedicated car park. It was mid-afternoon, but they'd still have managed to find a space closer than their previous visit no matter the hour. The place was closed for business today, and until further notice.

The staff had all been hanging around, looking a little lost. There was no work for them to do, but they evidently felt they had to be there, perhaps as a show of willing, or maybe just to find out whether they would still have jobs.

Catherine and Laura's inquiries found that

neither Callahan nor Fleeting had turned up on Thursday at all. According to Callahan's wife—a peroxide moll from Central Casting who was fair chewing the scenery in playing the grieving widow, perhaps in case anybody doubted her genuine sadness at being left with a two-million-pound mansion and God knows how much more in other saleable assets—Frankie had left their house at eight o'clock on Thursday morning. He hadn't said where he was going, but it was the last time she ever saw him.

Eight o'clock struck Catherine as a purposefully early start, the start of a man with a busy day ahead of him. A big day, perhaps. Heroin shipment day, even.

Fleeting was last seen in his favoured boozer, the Raven's Crag, the night before. According to the landlord, he drank in comparative moderation and jacked it in well before last orders. Once again, the behaviour of a man with important things to do the next day.

'It's Anthony Thomson,' Laura announced, glancing at the screen. 'Why do they call him Beano, by the way?'

'Because of his rank,' Catherine explained. 'He's a detective constable.'

Laura's screwed-up expression indicated that this hadn't shone much light, but Catherine wasn't spelling it out any further.

Catherine climbed into the passenger seat, Laura tarrying outside a few moments, muttering acknowledgements as she took the call.

'Preliminary Forensics are in on the Top Table vans,' she reported, slipping behind the wheel. 'They found traces of blood in one of them: O neg.

283

It's a match for Jai McDiarmid.'

'Supporting what we've said all along,' said Catherine with a frustrated sigh, as the evidence flipped back on itself one more time. 'Maybe it's not that we're missing something; maybe just the opposite. Maybe this is precisely what we thought it was, but there's something else in here that doesn't belong, and that's why it doesn't add up. Callahan and Fleeting were definitely gearing up for something important, and now it's all but established that Fleeting killed McDiarmid. So what if this is just what it looks like: tit-for-tat drug killings?'

'Except we now know the scene at the depot was staged,' Laura reminded her, rather balefully.

'But what, really, does that change? What if Steel's people did it, and the reason they staged it to look like Callahan and Fleeting were torturing Miller was that *they* were the ones torturing him? Or at least to disguise the fact that *they* killed Miller, and Callahan and Fleeting had nothing to do with it? Maybe Paddy Steel and Tommy Miller *both* knew something about that decoy heroin shipment. Because that, to me, is the key: that's the rogue element that's throwing everything else off.'

Laura didn't reply. She just stared out through the windscreen with a pained expression, as though none of what Catherine was saying made any more sense than why people called Anthony Thomson Beano. She went to put her key in the ignition, then just stopped and slumped back in the driver's seat, like she had lost all will.

'Are you all right?' Catherine asked her. She had stopped herself doing so about half a dozen times already today, Laura having been even more sullen and withdrawn than usual, but she couldn't let this one go.

Laura looked across at her, concern and apology written across her face in equal measures.

'I did something wrong,' she said. 'Something I shouldn't have, but a victimless crime, you could say. Nobody would have needed to know, nobody would be any the wiser, eh?'

'Except?' Catherine prompted.

'Except that it meant I found something out, and I now cannae say what without saying how.'

It was like talking to Duncan or Fraser. Promising them they wouldn't get into trouble because you needed to know, but aware that a sanction might nonetheless be obligatory.

'Come on, you can tell me. You're halfway there.'

Laura made a nervous face, a change at least from the gloomy one that had permeated her day.

'It was Thursday morning, at that café. After Cairns got his call. You remember you went outside to get a better signal, eh?'

'Sure,' Catherine encouraged. It was less about the signal and more about the background noise in the busy café. It had been her job to call Scotrail to order the closure of the station and demand that they stop the trains: not something you could afford any ambiguity over resulting from a clatter of crockery or a shriek of laughter in the background, nor something you wanted to sound like a half-arsed idea you'd just had over a bacon roll and a double espresso.

'Well, while you were out there, Cairns nipped to the toilet before all the action kicked off. He left his phone on the table.'

285

Laura bit her lip.

They both knew the next part. She didn't have to spell it out, though she did feel she had to excuse it.

'You'd said to me a few minutes before, you know, what you wouldn't give for that number.'

Catherine withheld a host of unhelpful responses, grateful again to her sons for training her to handle such situations.

'I know it was wrong, I don't need any lectures on the ethics of it. It's just I feel like I've been treading water since I got here. Not living up to anybody's expectations. I needed something in my locker. I wanted to be able to pull a rabbit from a hat, eh? Of course, soon after, I realised it was a bloody stupid thing to do, not least because this was a rabbit I couldn't show to anybody. But the thing is, I need to show it to you. I saw the report on Tommy Miller yesterday, and the mobile number listed as being his wasn't the one that called Cairns.'

'Did you get a name?

'No, I just looked up the last incoming call. The phone hadn't identified it as an established contact: just a number.'

Catherine felt the familiar relief of recognising a squall unlikely to escape the bounds of its teacup. She wouldn't be leaving her mobile lying about near Laura, right enough, but still, there was a simple enough explanation.

'It's most likely Miller had more than one mobile,' she reasoned. 'Especially if he was playing so many angles.'

'It's not so likely he would have been picking up last night, though, eh?'

Catherine felt her eyes bulge.

'I tried the number from my desk,' Laura confirmed. 'Got a hello. I asked, "Who is this?" and they hung up right away.'

'But Miller was definitely Cairns' source. Abercorn confirmed they knew he was touting to Locust as well as to Bob.'

'I don't doubt he was. But that's not who phoned Cairns while we were with him in that café on Thursday morning.'

Catherine's head was starting to implode. If Cairns had a second informant in play, it was a very fly move to let everyone believe his source was Miller: what better way, in fact, to protect the remaining one than by making people think his info came from elsewhere? But if it wasn't Miller who tipped off Cairns about the shipment, how come Miller's pal Whitaker was in place ready to tan the jeweller's?

'I *am* sorry,' Laura intoned sincerely. 'I'm not habitually sneaky, just a daft moment of impulse. I didn't feel I'd got off to a very good start here in Glasgow, but this is hardly gaunny rectify that, eh?'

Catherine could see tears forming in her eyes.

'You're doing fine. What gave you the idea you've made a poor impression?'

'Just . . . low confidence, I suppose. Not feeling quite myself.'

'Is it the change of city? Why did you apply for a transfer?'

Laura paused, longer than it had taken her to fess up to snooping Cairns' phone.

'Bad break-up,' she said.

Catherine could tell the brevity was down to knowing she could only get out a few words at a

287

time without crying.

'Bad relationship.'

There was bitterness to this second issue: self-doubt, regret, pain, and so much anger.

Laura looked her in the eye, just for a quarter of a second: long enough to let her see it.

Catherine reached out a hand and clasped it around Laura's clenched fist.

'You're doing fine, hen,' she said quietly. 'You're doing fine.'

Then the windscreen shattered.

Catherine shuddered bodily in fright as thousands of pieces of glass suddenly filled the air around them. She looked briefly at Laura, then behind, aware that the rear windscreen had gone too.

She caught a microsecond's glimpse of a man in a mask levelling a pistol through the rolled-down window of a red car, then ducked as he pulled the trigger again.

They flattened themselves as low as they could across the front seats, hearing further rounds zip above their heads, pinging into metal and smashing the side windows. The Rover lurched on its suspension cradle as two of the tyres were hit, then she heard the gunning of an engine and the squeal of rubber on tarmac.

Catherine was shaking with fear, pinned to the seat as though the earth had swapped its gravity for Jupiter's, but she knew she had to garner what she could witness from the retreat. She forced her head up in time to see the car for a second before it disappeared around the corner and was lost.

It was enough to notice two things. One, that the number plate had been taped over, and two, that it was a nineties-model Honda Civic.

BEYOND THE VISIBLE SPECTRUM

They were met in the reception area of the Scottish Gas building on Maxwell Road by a man in a light-grey suit who introduced himself as Eric McGranahan, head of the Industrial and Commercial department. He was quiet-spoken and friendly, striking Jasmine as a man at ease with himself, a species that had proven thin on the ground in recent days. He looked early sixties, around Jim's age, so it was no great surprise (though privately a little sad) for Jasmine to learn that he and Jim were old friends.

'Jasmine *Sharp*?' he emphasised when she gave her name.

'Yes. Jim was my uncle. Well, my mum's cousin.'

'*Was?*' he asked, looking momentarily concerned.

'I just mean, my mum's no longer with us,' Jasmine clarified, retrieving the situation.

'Oh aye, I think Jim mentioned that. I'm sorry.'

'Sure.'

'Would have been around the turn of the year?'

Jasmine nodded. He was out by a couple of months, but she felt that if she spoke right now, her voice would choke up.

'Aye, last time I saw Jim must have been not long after. It's one of those things, you always mean to get together more often, but what with work and everything . . . and b'Christ, you know what Jim's like with work.'

289

Jasmine gave him a smile of recognition, some little part of her still daring to hope that they were wrong about all of this and that she'd see Jim again one day soon.

McGranahan escorted them up to the Industrial and Commercial department, which was situated on the third floor. The layout was mostly open-plan, stretching from the western outer wall to the eastern, with a row of enclosed rooms running the length of the building, partitioned off with aluminium and glass. McGranahan had his own private office in one of these, but he led them past it to a double-width apartment four doors along. It had a white screen on one wall and a data projector suspended from the ceiling towards the other end. Glass ran the length of the room, affording a view into the open-plan area, with venetian blinds providing the option of darkness and privacy. Opposite the glass on the windowless facing wall was a deep cabinet split horizontally, an arrangement that reminded Jasmine of the poster bins in a card shop. The top half displayed dozens of large frames, hinged for browsing, and the bottom half a grid of pigeonholes, each containing a rolled-up document. The office also accommodated a light-table, a photocopier and two very wide desks, upon one of which sat eight cardboard tubes.

'This is the map room,' McGranahan explained. 'It's a bit of a relic now that everything's all computers and sat nav, but knowing us, it'll be another ten years before we get around to finding another use for it.'

He nodded towards the room-length cabinet.

'We'll probably donate that lot to the People's

Palace or some other museum.'

'What are they?' Jasmine asked. She could only see the outside edges of the frames, but the one at the front looked like a map.

'Street maps of Glasgow. The ones on top denote the sections of the grid, and in the corresponding boxes underneath are the bigger-scale equivalents, showing the layout of all the gas mains. There's multiple versions of most of them, going back fifty-odd years, showing where the street layouts have changed.'

Ingrams wandered over to the desk bearing the cardboard tubes.

'Are these the images?' he asked.

'That's them, aye. I had our poor secretary Josephine down in the bowels of the building looking them out. I couldn't believe how long it had been since we started doing them. If you'd asked, I'd have guessed ten years ago. It's actually more than thirty, though Jim only wanted the first two.'

'What exactly are they?' Jasmine asked.

McGranahan walked over beside Ingrams and popped a red stopper from one of the tubes, pulling a rolled-up sheet of glossy paper from inside. He unrolled it and laid it out flat, which was when Jasmine noticed the sliding clamps at the edges of each table, there to hold such large documents in place.

The sheet was roughly a foot and a half deep by four feet wide, and upon it were four dark horizontal strips, each running almost the full width of the document. When Jasmine stepped closer, she saw that they were black-and-white aerial photographs, but something about them was very odd. They were almost like negatives, so much blackness dominating the image.

'They're an infrared aerial survey of the Glasgow area, taken in overlapping latitudinal strips. We do them every five years. It lets us identify premises that are losing heat, which shows up as white on the photographs. If they're a customer, we advise them on ways to reduce this and burn less gas.'

'Is that not a bit turkeys-voting-for-Christmas?' Ingrams suggested.

McGranahan smiled.

'Aye, if you were to look at it purely on a raging capitalist running-dog level.'

'But I suppose this was before "Tell Sid".'

'Then or now, waste is never good business.'

'Did you say it was *two* surveys Jim requested?' Ingrams asked.

'Aye. Four of these sheets per survey. Each one took four or five nights' flying to complete. There's minor inconsistencies because of small temperature variations, but you can only see it if you look closely at the overlaps. They do them at the same time of year, for purposes of comparison. Always December. Needs clear nights, so the view isn't occluded, and cold so that you get a stronger heat contrast. The red-stoppered ones are the first survey, from December 1978, green stoppers are the second, from December 1983.'

Jasmine and Ingrams shared a look. These were the two surveys taken either side of the Ramsays' disappearance. One five years before, the other four months after.

'Did Jim happen to say why he was interested in them?' Jasmine asked. 'It's just, he only mentioned to us to pick them up if you called while he was away.'

'No, he didn't. I'm curious myself. He phoned last week to ask, first time I'd spoken to him in months. When I asked what he wanted with them, he said it was one of those things he could only tell me about once it was concluded. He did promise he'd be doing that over a few pints, but he was definitely being a bit coy, which only served to pique my more morbid suspicions.'

'What's there to be morbid about?'

'Now, I don't want to be giving away my dark secrets,' McGranahan said with a teasing smile, which betrayed that he'd be crushingly disappointed if they weren't interested in him doing just that. 'I remember telling Jim about these once, being my rather pitiful offering in response to all the gruesome stories he was able to tell me about his time in the polis.'

He began scanning the strips, his eyes moving left to right. He didn't point with his finger, but it was clear that he had found whatever he was looking for.

'Identifying the properties on here is a real pain in the arse. You've got to cross-refer with the maps and cross-refer again with the records to find out an exact address and whether they're a customer. You're talking about thousands of properties. So back in the early days, we'd save it until the summer and get a student in to do it as a holiday job. Summer of '89, the young guy we had in examining the 1988 survey was a right warped individual who happened to notice this.'

McGranahan reached into a drawer below the desk and produced a huge magnifier, the glass

inset on plastic runners for sliding back and forth.
He placed it over a section of one of the strips and
stepped back to let them view it. In the centre,
Jasmine could see a grid of tiny white vertical lines,
set in six or seven long horizontal rows.

'What is it?' she asked.

McGranahan gave her a wicked grin.

'The Necropolis.'

THE BIGGEST GANG IN GLASGOW

'I imagine I'd be underselling it if I said you could
probably do with a drink,' ventured Sunderland.

He was waiting outside her office when she got
back from being checked out by Samira Arora, the
police casualty surgeon. It was purely procedure, a
cursory once-over that would normally have been
carried out by the station's first-aid officer, but
Samira was in the building anyway, and everybody
was in a bit of a froth. The only injury Catherine
had sustained in the shooting was a bruise to the
elbow where she'd rattled it off the handbrake
when she dived for cover.

'I'm okay,' she said, the shock having passed and
long since been replaced by outrage.

'Yeah,' Sunderland mused. 'I was okay after
getting shot at as well; bank robbery back in
ninety-seven. Next day somebody tapped me on
the shoulder in a queue at the supermarket and
within seconds I had them in an armlock, pinned to
the floor. It was a sixty-five-year-old woman who
was trying to tell me another till had opened up. I
don't know what Samira said, but I'm prescribing

you a pint for relief of post-traumatic stress.'

'I think Laura's in more need of some TLC than I am. Why don't you ask her?'

'I already did. She's coming too, as soon as the doc's finished with her.'

'I'm not going anywhere until they bring in that bastard Fallan, which I can't believe hasn't happened by now. Christ, how hard can it be? We know where he's staying and we know what he's driving.'

'Not going to happen,' Sunderland said flatly. 'He hasn't been found because your orders were countermanded. By me,' he added, folding his arms.

'Countermanded? Why?'

'That information is strictly on a need-to-be-drinking basis. Come on, get your coat. It's not as if you're driving, is it?'

*   *   *

Sunderland set down their drinks, neither of which stayed on the table for a full second. Catherine took an immodest few gulps of beer, feeling just a little better by the time she had swallowed.

She knew Sunderland was doing this as a courtesy, an acknowledgment of what they had been through. The likelihood was that he hadn't even been working today, which added to his personal solicitousness and the gravity with which such an incident was treated. What didn't add up, however, was his admitting he had blocked her order to bring in the chief suspect.

'So I gather you had a wee encounter with the not-so-late Glen Fallan,' he said.

295

'An encounter?' Catherine snapped back. 'That's not the word I'd use.'

'I was talking about your breakfast meeting.'

'Oh. Well, forgive me, Graeme, if my impressions were superseded by more recent events. Why is he not being huckled, right now?'

Sunderland took a long pull on his pint, a little froth adhering to his top lip. Catherine vaguely recalled a moustache misadventure of a decade back. It hadn't suited, though in Catherine's opinion the list of men it did was about the same length as the list of great Scottish cricketers. The guys in Drew's office all grew them for 'Movember' last year, but Catherine did a deal to match her husband's sponsorship if he didn't join in.

'Because it wasn't him.'

'Wasn't him? He was in that girl's car. And he'd taped over the plates too, my own stupid fault for letting slip it was how I'd found them.'

Sunderland shook his head.

'On a wee hunch, I made some inquiries as soon as I heard. Turns out a red M-reg Honda Civic was stolen from an address in Rutherglen overnight. Jasmine Sharp's motor is an N. That's why the plate was taped. It wasn't Glen Fallan shooting at you this afternoon, but somebody wanting you to think it was.'

'The theft of a red Civic isn't hard proof. It could be coincidence.'

'This is why you need a drink, Catherine. Get the shock and anger out your system and think rationally. It would be a *hell* of a coincidence.'

'Okay, so what was the rational basis for this wee hunch?'

'I knew Glen Fallan. Not well, but well enough

296

to know he's never made an attempt on anyone's life.'

'You're denying he was a killer? He all but admitted as much to my face.'

'I'm not denying it at all. I'm saying I know it wasn't Glen Fallan shooting at you today, because you're still alive. Glen Fallan doesn't make *attempts*. If he wanted you dead, we wouldn't be having this conversation. Come on, Catherine: a guy pulls up behind you in the street, in broad daylight, in the same kind of motor you already associate with him, and starts shooting holes in your car. Not exactly discreet.'

Catherine caught up.

'The shooter wanted to be seen,' she said.

'The word is out that Fallan's back in town, and he was never short of enemies. You spoke to him this morning. How did he seem? What did you ask him about?'

'Seem? Big. Guarded. Scary. The strong, violent type. I asked him about Callahan, Fleeting, McDiarmid, Miller. He said he didn't know who they were.'

'Did you believe him?'

'Yes,' she admitted. 'I pretended to him that I didn't, but it was obvious. He's here about something else. He's with this young girl, as you know, Jasmine Sharp. Works for her uncle's PI outfit, except, get this, *he's* gone missing. Retired cop. Jim Sharp. That ring any bells?'

'Yeah, he was CID over in Clydebank. Good cop. A workaholic, though. No surprise he went private. Guys like that *can't* retire. And he's gone missing?'

'Apparently. She reported it Monday. Says

297

Fallan's helping her look for him. He's going by the name Tron Ingrams these days. I can't work out what his angle is, but then I know next to nothing about him.'

'Well, unless you work out what his game is, and unless it affects you directly, I wouldn't be in a hurry to get involved. Tread very lightly, and make no assumptions about him: positive or negative. Anybody with a past like his who's subsequently stayed off our radar for more than twenty years is either very much reformed or even more dangerous.'

'There was one thing he mentioned,' she remembered. 'Think he was messing with my head, but he made reference to "the biggest gang in Glasgow". Said I should ask somebody older about it. Do you know who that is?'

'Aye,' said Sunderland, his features suddenly that little bit more alert. 'Us.'

INFRARED AND SONIC BOOM

Jasmine found a space for the car across the road from the little row of shops at the end of the cul-de-sac, occupying the ground floor of a corner-block tenement. The parking was denoted by white lines at thirty degrees to the kerb, angling the vehicles like hands of cards either side of the street. It had been rendered a dead end by a phalanx of concrete bollards terminating its decades-old connection to the adjoining road and necessitating a circuitous approach to reach it. It was a mostly residential neighbourhood, hence the paucity of free spaces and the greater paucity of life on the street. It was not so far from Jasmine's lately unoccupied flat, in a part of the South Side where you did find these isolated wee pockets of shops like they had broken off from the glacier of the city centre and drifted away.

They were headed for a map supplier, as directed by Fallan. Jasmine couldn't help but wonder at the irony that he had searched for the shop using his mobile phone, and then satellite-navigated to the place using the same device, but had assured her that the humble artefact of non-digital printed cartography was not yet redundant. They were going to pick up Ordnance Survey maps of the Greater Glasgow area, drawn to a scale that was as close a match as they could find to the heat-loss photographs. They were also going to purchase a couple of magnifiers and some highlighter pens, then commence what could prove to be the world's longest game of spot-the-difference.

Jasmine was not heartened by the information that the students hired by Scottish Gas to analyse the surveys for heat loss were typically employed for eight weeks, though the number of locations they had to identify was considerably greater. Fallan reckoned this would take only a couple of days. It would be painstaking, eye-straining and stultifyingly tedious, but Jasmine was still grateful for the project, as it represented purpose, progress and a greater distance before they ran out of things they could do. After that lay a place she feared, a place where she was alone without her mum, without her uncle, without a job, without a goal and without any money.

'You okay?' Fallan asked as they crossed the street. 'You seem kind of spooked.'

'It's the idea of all those bodies glowing. I can't get it out of my head.'

Decomposition, McGranahan had explained: the chemical reactions involved in the gradual breakdown of the bodies gave off heat, enough to be detectable to the infrared camera through six feet of earth and several thousand more of clear air.

Jasmine checked her stride, walking a little faster in response to the sound of an approaching car, a silver Vectra. It would have to slow down anyway, she was aware, as it was a no-through-road, but drivers could be complete dicks, like when they wouldn't slow to let you out even as they approached a red light. He'd be heading back again *tout de suite* too, as there were no spaces to be had.

'It gets worse,' Fallan told her. 'Some of those cemeteries had been closed for decades when that survey was done, yet they were only glowing a wee bit dimmer than the rest. It seems your light really does shine longer after death than it does while you're alive—but you can only see it in infrared, and it helps if you're flying in an aero—'

He stopped mid-word, something about him instantly altered to a heightened condition of alertness, like an animal that had sniffed something on the breeze.

Jasmine was aware of his head turning, then a microsecond later of being gripped around her waist and thrust forward between two of the angularly parked cars. She tumbled to the ground, clattering her elbow against the side of a Peugeot

300

and her knee on the tarmac. As she fell, she heard something crack in the air above her head, and the simultaneous sound of an object embedding itself in the stone of the tenement alongside, dust puffing out in a wispy breath from the resultant hole.

She was being shot at, again, and unlike most things in life, it didn't get any easier from experience. The fear, in fact, was cumulative, as though everything she had felt in Northumberland was instantly recalled and everything she felt now was supplementary to it. She felt frozen on her hands and knees, terrified to move, terrified not to.

Another crack followed, accompanied by a shattering of glass and a second impact in the stone of the building, then another, and another.

Why was this happening to her? She hadn't done anything wrong. Where were the police? Where was her mummy? Where was Uncle Jim? Where was Fallan?

He was gone, no longer alongside her, but she could hear him scrambling close by, and from her perspective, sprawled on the deck, she saw that he was one car away.

Daring to look behind her, she could see the wheels and skirts of the Vectra that had been heading towards the bollards, now sitting stationary, engine idling.

The shooting stopped, but Jasmine's relief lasted only a second and a half before she recognised the sound of the Vectra's door being thrust open. The gunman was about to get out and come looking for them.

Before he could, she saw Fallan suddenly spring from the balls of his feet, diving towards the

301

pavement, where he rolled beyond the last of the parked cars into clear space. He came up into a low crouch, both hands raised, a length of metal glinting between them in the late-afternoon sunlight.

She waited for the blasts, but they never came. The only bang was that of the door slamming closed again, followed by a whine from the Vectra's engine as it commenced a high-speed reverse. Jasmine followed its progress from an ant's-eye view, seeing its wheels and chassis retreat backwards for a few seconds, before a squeal of rubber and a new gunning of the engine accompanied a precise one-hundred-and-eighty-degree spin, allowing the car to make good its escape up the forward gears. It was the manoeuvre Fallan had attempted in his Land Rover on Wednesday, but this time executed perfectly.

She stayed down until she was sure the Vectra was definitely gone, by which time Fallan had made his way over. She saw a flash of metal once more as he slipped a hand into an inside pocket.

As he helped her to her feet, she looked around, to the shops, to the junction cut off by the bollards and to the other side of the road it abutted. She could see a woman walking a dog about forty yards down on the right, well out of sight of where the action had been, but there was nobody else around: nobody running to ask if they were okay, nobody cowering in doorways, nobody calling the cops on their mobiles or, more likely, recording the thing on video. A cul-de-sac wasn't the ideal place for a drive-by, but that apart, the gunman had chosen his moment perfectly. Once again, it was as though it hadn't happened, the world obliviously getting on with itself.

This time, however, she was unambiguously grateful for Fallan's intervention.

'So you did lie to me,' she said. 'About not bringing a gun. Please ignore me if I say anything daft like that again.'

'No,' he corrected her. 'I said I wouldn't lie to you, and then you didn't ask. I didn't bring a gun.'

He reached to the inside pocket and produced his phone.

'What, can you get a bullets app for that thing now?'

'I guessed I was dealing with more shite-bag than shooter. Didn't like it up them on Wednesday and I figured it was one of the same folk. Gave him the impression I had a gun and he skited pronto.'

Jasmine was still shaking as Fallan led her into the map shop, though she was unsure whether it was a good or a bad thing that she felt she was recovering quicker than when she'd been shot at three days ago. She didn't feel like she was going to vomit, albeit she hadn't been spun around in a Land Rover on this occasion, on top of dodging the hot lead. Maybe it was indeed true of this as it was of everything: there's nothing like the first time.

She exited the shop before him, stopping around the corner to examine the bullet holes while he paid for the maps and the magnifiers. They'd been lucky the Corsa wasn't alarmed, as it had lost its windscreen as well as both driver's-side windows.

She put a finger to the tenement wall, feeling the need to prove to herself that it had been real, the events of only a few minutes ago already threatening to fade into unreality via some self-defence mechanism in her subconscious. She felt the edges of the holes, disappearing deep into stone that had weathered more than a century of Glasgow winters, shuddering a little as she thought of where else the bullets might have ended up embedded.

'What kind of gun did he have?' she asked as Fallan came back around the corner, a cardboard cylinder under his arm. 'It sounded weird, quieter than before but as if the sound was right above my head.'

'I didn't get a long enough look to ID the piece, but he was using a suppressor.'

'Is that the same thing as a silencer? What were the noises I heard then?'

'Sonic boom: bullets breaking the sound barrier. Chose a quiet spot for the hit, put a muffler on the automatic, but he didn't know to use subsonic ammunition. Knew his limitations, though; or at least knew enough about me not to fancy his chances if I was returning fire.'

'He knew how to drive better than you, I'll give him that.'

'That didn't escape my notice,' Fallan said, gazing back thoughtfully towards the tyre marks the Vectra had left during its handbrake one-eighty.

'So,' she ventured, 'given that you don't have to explain away having a gun, can we call the police this time?'

'Are you kidding?' he replied. 'I thought you said you noticed how he drove.'

'What's that got to do with it?'

'That *was* the police.'

THAT GOLDEN RULE

'I owe you an apology,' Fallan told her, as Jasmine brought the Civic to a halt, having reversed into a neat little space just outside her tenement with practised expertise and not a little relish. It was a small comfort, the reassurance of something familiar, and she'd take her reassurance wherever she could get it right now.

It was the first thing Fallan had said since shortly after getting back into the Civic, when he had told her she might as well go back to her flat as to the hotel, on the grounds that the latter was no safer now. If McLeod could find them, he reasoned, then so could anyone else in the police.

What he hadn't said was how he knew that it was cops who were stalking them, beyond the fact that their would-be killer back outside the map shop had been pretty tasty behind the wheel.

Jasmine wasn't going to argue. Staying in the hotel was adding to this sense of her life being on hold, that she had been pulled away from everyday reality into some sort of limbo beyond which her future was unclear. She wanted to stand under her own shower, even though it alternated between just too hot and just too cold; wanted to wrap her hair and her body in her own towels, even though they never felt quite dry during the months when the radiators were off. She wanted to eat a microwave-baked potato and drink half-flat fizzy water from the two-litre value bottle sitting in her kitchen.

'For what?' she asked, turning off the engine

305

and withdrawing the keys.

'Well, not an apology: a clarification. It isn't you they've been trying to kill. It's me. Though I think you're the bonus ball.'

'How do you know this?'

'Same reason Jim had pulled out my file and was planning to come looking for me again. Whoever's behind this knew my father, and both they and Jim believed I can connect them to this.'

'Would "this" be one of those UXBs you talked about?'

'A very big one, yes. Something I said to McLeod came back to me when I saw that guy pull his handbrake turn. I was being facetious at the time, as I tend to get a bit petulant around self-righteous polis, but I think that's what this is actually about: the biggest gang in Glasgow.'

Fallan gathered up the heat-loss scrolls, the OS maps and the magnifiers and followed Jasmine into the close. As she put her key into the lock of her third-floor flat, she paused a moment to wonder just how badly the world had fallen out of kilter since the last time she crossed this threshold, that she was now purposely avoiding the police while inviting a self-confessed murderer into her home.

Fallan made straight for the kitchen and began unrolling photographs on the table, weighing down the corners with cutlery. Jasmine put on the kettle and was relieved to see that the one-third-full carton of milk in the fridge was still in date. It had only been three days, but it felt like she'd been gone a month.

'My dad's nickname was Nine-Bob,' Fallan said. 'Not among the polis: that's what the villains called him.'

'Nine-Bob?'

'As in note. As in "bent as".'

'I see.'

'Except, well, there's bent polis and there's bent polis. It's not an easy job, I'll admit that. It can be a non-stop war, in fact, so you have to choose your battles. You fight the fights you can win, and you fight the fights that most need fighting. You can't fight on every front, and what the more pragmatic cops soon grasp is that you don't have to make every thief and fly-man your enemy. You need treaties. You need alliances.'

'Some crimes being worse than others,' Jasmine said.

'They'd never admit it publicly, but they understand that if they're cracking down on one thing, then that means a blind eye might need to get turned to something else. Of course, they'll complain that the top brass keep changing their minds about the league table of badness. Back in the early eighties, drugs had just started to top the charts.

'As I told you, I worked for a gangster in Gallowhaugh by the name of Tony McGill. The Gallowhaugh Godfather, the papers called him, and he loved that. He saw himself as old-school, liked to indulge in the notion that he had some kind of code of honour that the new breed didn't observe. It was a tripartite code. One: don't hurt non-combatants.'

He gave her an arch look, acknowledging that they'd covered the truth of this one.

'Two: never grass to the polis; and three: don't deal drugs. Tony made an ostentatious virtue of observing number three, but only out of necessity, because he couldn't source a supplier. Those who could were a threat to his power base. Hence he tended to be flexible in his interpretation of number two. His golden rule was more along the lines of "don't let anyone *know* you grass to the polis".'

'He informed for your dad?'

'It was a mutually beneficial arrangement. Above all, polis need results. They need numbers: arrests, seizures, convictions. Tony helped my dad and his colleagues keep their figures high. He gave him bodies, stashes and weapons that he could present to his superiors to show what a good job he was doing. But the benefit to Tony wasn't just in my dad ensuring that the polis turned a blind eye to his own activities. It was in my dad's interests to keep Tony top of the heap and his competitors at bay. I thought that just meant locking them up.'

Fallan stared down at the strips of images. His thoughts seemed far away, perhaps back in the time that was reflected there in infrared, a map upon which he might well see the sins of his own past picked out in tiny white lines.

'You should be aware,' he said quietly, regretfully, 'that I was once kinda Luke Skywalker to Tony McGill's Emperor Palpatine. Difference was, I did take my father's place at McGill's right hand, a few years after my father was dead. That's how I know about this, although it's never easy to sort the fact from the fiction. Among criminals, folk are tight-lipped about the big truths and garrulous with bullshit. Tony didn't like talking to me about my father, but he let slip a few things, and there were stories I'd hear from folk who never knew my dad had been in the polis, far less who he was.

'A recurring rumour was that the polis had got rid of people. Both sides of the law were aware of these stories, and actually some reckoned it was the polis who started them. If the cops were trying to put the wind up some wee shaver, they'd allude to this, make him think he had worse things to worry about than a night in the cells, and all of a sudden they got a lot more cooperation. Similarly it served Tony well to let his enemies believe that he had polis in his pocket who could make you disappear if you became a problem. Like I said, it's hard to sift the truth from the bullshit, and I'm not sure I believed any of it back then, but here's the thing.'

Fallan gave a burdened sigh and glanced again at the heat-loss photographs, his eyes focused near the top of the sheet.

'Polis and crooks alike—and your uncle Jim would have known this—when they alluded to this rumour, they always couched it in the same terms: "a one-way trip to the Campsies". Now, for two points and a Blue Peter badge, which range of hills would you have to drive along the foot of to get from the Campsieview Hotel in Lennoxtown to Stephen and Eilidh Ramsay's house in Bishopbriggs?'

QUIET LITTLE VOICES

'Is he still asleep?' Stephen asked his wife.

He had rolled the window down, since the

Audi's fan was doing nothing but circulate warm air. The air outside was no cooler, but it just felt less stuffy inside, and on such a full stomach he'd been wary of feeling sleepy. The problem was, as he knew from experience, opening the front windows mostly blasted air into the back seat, and he didn't want Charlie caught in his own private wind tunnel.

Eilidh leaned around to check, one knee on the passenger seat, her shoulder bumping his on her way past.

'He's sound,' she reported.

'Just worried about the draught.'

'It's mostly above him. Plus the hood of the carrycot is deflecting it.'

'Noisy, though.'

'You know Charlie. He could sleep through anything.'

'He's a wee star that way,' Stephen reflected with a smile. 'Night and day's difference from his big sister.'

Annie had been murder. It was probably exacerbated by their stumbling incompetence as first-time parents, but they just could not get that wee lassie to sleep for more than a couple of hours at a time, or stop crying for even a quarter of that, until she was about three months. She was hardly the most passive-natured wean even now, which had undoubtedly been a factor in the four-year gap before they had another. Stephen had often worried that a second child would get short shrift, Annie having eaten substantially into her sibling's allocation of parental patience before he got there.

Charlie, however, was the kind of baby that probably made other first-timers convince

310

themselves they were parenting geniuses. He went off to sleep easily, stayed zonked out for hours at a time, and sat there contentedly when he was awake. Stephen would have said Charlie was happy to just watch the world go by if it wasn't that he knew his visual acuity was insufficiently developed for him to see much more than blurred blobs, but damn if those blurred blobs didn't seem to hold his attention.

Eilidh had breastfed him in the car before going into the restaurant, their hope being that he would nod off shortly afterwards and allow them to enjoy their dinner together in peace. Instead, he had lain there in his carrycot on the floor by their table, gazing in quiet fascination at whatever his little eyes were making out, before finally dropping off sometime around dessert.

'What did we do to get such a contented baby?' Eilidh asked, settling back into the seat, her elbow resting on the open window.

'Maybe we were due it as compensation after the last one. I mean, I love her more than life itself, she's the apple of my eye, but there's no denying she's a hard shift.'

'The more complex and high-functioning the machine, the more maintenance it needs,' Eilidh replied. 'That's what I tell myself anyway. If it turns out she's a wee dafty, I'll be feeling very short-changed.'

'I'll be feeling astonished. She's as smart as she is argumentative. Remember that time we were out for a walk and you pointed out a horse, and she was insistent that it was called a cow.'

'She was about eighteen months,' Eilidh recalled, laughing. 'She'd got confused because

311

they were on facing pages on that picture book I used to read with her, but there was just no way she was backing down.'

'She's going to be a lawyer, that one,' Stephen said. 'Either that or the dictator of some small Central American republic.'

'And what about her wee brother?'

'Charlie's in no apparent hurry. He's watching very carefully before he makes any decisions.'

Stephen glanced over at Eilidh, who was smiling contentedly to herself.

'It's been a lovely evening. Just hope your parents haven't been run rings around.'

'They love it. They'd have her to keep. But yeah, it's been just what we needed. Could do with a pint, right enough. Maybe have a can when we get home. That peppercorn sauce on the steak was lovely, but a bit salty.'

'Should have drunk more water.'

'I know, but I get bored of it. Bit of a scunner that you can't drive when you're not drinking anyway.'

'Them's the rules after a Caesarean.'

She put her hand on his thigh, reaching across the handbrake.

'It's not without its benefits, though.'

'You serious?' he asked, perhaps just a little too eagerly. It had been a good couple of months after Annie's birth before they'd had sex again, though the fact that Eilidh had had an episiotomy was in practice the least of the reasons. For all Charlie was a good baby, he was still a baby, which meant Eilidh was knackered much of the time, and to be honest so was Stephen, meaning he had all but forgotten that this time there was no physical

312

restriction why they couldn't.

Eilidh responded by drawing her hand further along his thigh towards his groin.

'You sure you never drank anything?' he asked.

'I'm a bundle of hormones,' she said, giggling. 'Far more disinhibiting.'

Stephen stepped on the accelerator for a moment.

'Right. If we get a speeding ticket, it's your fault. I cannae wait to get you home.'

'And I don't think I can wait that long.'

'What?'

'Look where we are,' she said. 'Must be two minutes away. Why don't we, just for old times' sake?'

'But Charlie's on the back seat. I don't want to move him. It's always murder wedging that thing in there.'

'Not on the back seat. It's a warm night. There's a spare blanket. Like we used to.'

'We'll be home in twenty minutes.'

'Hormones, remember? I might have changed my mind in twenty minutes.'

'Deal.'

It was a spot he knew about because he used to come here on his bike as a kid. The place was only a few miles from his parents' old house, the one he grew up in, before they moved to the semi in Kilsyth where they lived now. He'd spend all summer out cycling around with his pals, finding out where every last back road, track and pathway led.

There was more fencing back then, because the quarry was still in use. That was how he and his pals had discovered it, in fact: the sound of the

313

blasting. He remembered hearing the bangs from his bedroom at home and wondering where they came from. Then one day he found out, the 'Danger: Quarry' and 'Keep Out' signs reading like 'Free Sweeties' to a bunch of ten-year-olds.

By the time he was taking Eilidh there when they were courting, the blasting had long since ended. There was a farm track you could get your car down, skirting the broken fences where Stephen and his pals had first worked out what lay beyond the forbidden boundaries.

Stephen drove slowly. You had to be careful at night because, with whole sections of the fence pilfered for its wood, there was no barrier to the quarry's edge.

He and Eilidh had first come here as teenagers, for the tranquillity of the spot, somewhere to sit and talk of a summer afternoon when they only had the money for a bottle of Irn-Bru by way of entertainment. Then, a little later, it became more favoured for evenings, not least because his parents were hyper-vigilant about leaving them alone together in the house, terrified their son would get his girlfriend pregnant.

It was never the most beautiful view: just a wide horseshoe of rock, earth, scrub and puddles. What made it seem spectacular was the sense of altitude, accentuated by the sheerness of the walls, seeing bare rock plunge so far, so straight.

Stephen and his pals used to lie close to the edge and watch the workies obliviously getting on with it below. As long as you kept still, they never saw you; it was the place he learned how seldom people ever look up.

Eilidh checked on Charlie while Stephen got out

the spare blanket that was in the boot. His mum had knitted it especially for swaddling the new baby. He wondered what she'd think if she knew they were using it for an outdoor quickie on the same patch of grass where they'd enjoyed many, many outdoor quickies throughout adolescence.

Eilidh really wasn't kidding about being hormonal.

'Just be careful of my boobs, they're a bit tender,' was about the only thing she said, then she pretty much launched herself at him. It was just as much of a quickie as their first excitable efforts. The combination of erotically poignant memories, the illicit thrill of it being outdoors and the fact that it had been more than a month since the last time meant neither of them lasted very long.

They lay there afterwards, under the stars, enjoying the warmth. It never felt this warm so late in the evening in Scotland. It was like being abroad on holiday. The air smelled different: more aromatic, a hint of barbecue on the breeze even though the nearest house must be a mile away.

Stephen knew it was one of those moments he'd always remember. They'd talk about it when they were seventy; embarrass Charlie with the tale of it when he was old enough.

Then they heard an engine, and saw a pair of headlights bobbing and snaking their way into the quarry below.

CLARITY

To her surprise and considerable delight, Catherine found Drew at home when the car Sunderland had organised dropped her off.

He wasn't long in the door. She found him in the bedroom, unpacking the overnight bag he now didn't need. His meeting in London had wrapped up early, and though he was supposed to go out for dinner with friends and crash at a hotel, he had enquired about changing his flight instead, and got lucky with whoever he spoke to on the BA desk.

'With the boys at my mum's overnight, I realised that if I could make the six thirty-five, with a fair wind I could be home by half eight and manage a quiet wee night in, just the two of us. Maybe phone out for a curry.'

She felt herself just melt. Frantic phone calls and a mad scramble just to have curry from the local takeaway when he could be relaxing in trendy bars then eating somewhere sophisticated in London.

She loved that about him: that he was impulsive, but only impulsive about her. Mostly what she loved about him rushing home like this, however, was simply that it was about him unquestionably still loving her, despite what a nightmare she could be.

She stepped into his arms, aching to be held. He would have been naturally expecting a kiss, but she just enveloped him, clinging on tighter and tighter, tears beginning to stream down her face. Drew was doubtless surprised (and probably a little chuffed)

316

that his gesture was going down quite this emotionally, but he had no idea just what it meant right then, and nor was she telling him. Not tonight, and not until she'd got to the bottom of it. He'd only worry.

Eventually she pulled away enough to turn her head and give him his kiss, but he got a lot more than he was expecting on that score too.

Only moments before, she would have thought that the last thing she could manage right then was sex. She was so tense, so shaken, so angry, unable to keep a single thought for more than a few seconds. But as soon as he held her, she felt better, felt calmer, felt centred. And then she felt need.

They hauled each other's clothes off: hurried, impatient, clumsy.

He made to go down on her. Another nice gesture, but not tonight. She needed him to fuck her. Sometimes what they did together she thought was best described as lovemaking: tender, delicate, selfless. Sometimes it was erotic, sometimes it was fun. This was fucking.

Hurried, impatient, clumsy: she accidentally pinched the tip of his penis as she pulled him into her. It caused him to let out a little howl, but the bonus effect was that it retarded his ejaculation, taking him a long time to come. Good. She came quite quickly, but she didn't want him to stop. She wanted him to keep fucking her, and she all but screamed at him to do so, liberated by the knowledge that the boys were at their grandparents' overnight.

They both showered while they waited for the takeaway, eating it on their laps in front of *Commando*. They didn't get to the end. Catherine was lying with her head rested on Drew's chest, and sometime around Rae Dawn Chong's rocket-launcher mishap, his hand moved to rest on her breast. She hadn't put a bra back on, just a T-shirt, and as her nipple tightened and rose in response to his touch, she felt his penis do likewise through his shorts. She took him in her mouth for a while, then told him to fuck her again, right there on the couch, just because they could.

Catherine showered again, briefly, but it was long enough for Drew to be asleep by the time she made it to the bedroom. Giggling in the afterglow, he had remarked how 'that must have cleared your head' and predicted that she would be asleep in no time.

He was the one who went out like a light.

Catherine lay for a while in the darkness: calm, relaxed but her brain still alert. Drew was right about the first part: the reason she wasn't sleeping was that her head *was* clear. Very clear.

She had been seeing things that weren't there, distracted by trying to make connections between phantom elements, although in mitigation, she'd been given a few nudges towards doing that.

She had been drawn to Fallan by her anger and a long-burning hatred. She'd have put his face on the gunman no matter what car he pulled up in. Her powers of deduction, judgement and basic police sense had been bypassed by emotion, and now she could see that it was just plain daft that an accomplished hit man would do everything but wear a sign identifying himself, while firing a full magazine into a car only a few yards away without hitting either of the occupants.

Nobody was trying to kill her, but somebody was

definitely trying to knock her off track. Somebody wanted her going after Fallan, not because they had it in for him, but because it would keep her eyes off her true target.

It had to be someone who knew Fallan had resurfaced. More than that, it had to be someone who knew about the red mid-nineties Civic, and not only knew about it yesterday, but had the wherewithal to quickly locate and steal another one. Finally, it also had to be someone who knew she had been to see Fallan, who knew that she was aware not only of what he was driving, but of what he was capable.

Sunderland's single, cautious, defensive word echoed in her head.

'Us.'

Who was it that had told her about Glen Fallan in the first place, and thereby thrown a rogue piece into the puzzle so that she couldn't make any of it fit? Someone with a lot of hidden connections with organised crime in this city, someone who had wise old heads like Fletcher wondering at what point the line between gaining somebody's trust and being in somebody's pocket started to blur.

Detective Superintendent Douglas Abercorn.

LISTENING TO FEAR

Jasmine turned over in bed and looked at the clock, its green LED lights reporting that it was twenty past two. Her heart was thumping in her chest, her body energised and alert, and it was only this sudden start that even told her she'd been asleep. It couldn't have been for long either, perhaps the descent into an unconscious state being what precipitated her regression to the events outside the map shop.

She felt like she'd dreamed about it only for a split second before coming to; the memory of external sounds and images only a faint echo. It was the internal sensations that had truly jolted her, as though her mind and body were working through feelings and responses that had been deferred at the time by other survival mechanisms.

Prior to that, she had lain awake and frustrated, tossing and turning as the hours drew on and sleep did not come despite her exhaustion and the familiarity of her own bed. Part of it must have been down to the shooting, so many mental and physical systems suddenly supercharged and then only slowly coming down again. Her brain, for one thing, seemed in no state to rest, but nor was it proving any use at analysing any of the things that had been thrown at it. There were just too many of them, and she was too tired—and her brain too skittish—to concentrate on any single problem, jumping randomly from one to the next. It was like trying to sleep while someone was changing channels on a radio.

Two questions in particular kept prompting her for answers that she couldn't give.

One was that Jim, like she and Fallan, believed the truth might lie buried in a shallow grave somewhere in the Campsie Hills, where the Ramsays had been in the wrong place at the wrong time to witness something nobody was supposed to see. However, even if Jim found the bodies, what would this prove that posed such a threat that he had to be killed for it?

A DNA match with Anne Ramsay could identify the bodies and thus demonstrate that their disappearance had been murder, but that wasn't going to offer any clues as to whodunit. Even if Fallan could make a connection between his late father and some cops still working today, there would be nothing to say that they'd been involved in this.

There had to be something else, but she wasn't going to find it tossing and turning sleepless in the dark.

The other, more unsettling question concerned the fact that she was even alive to be asking it, and only Fallan could possibly offer any illumination on that one.

With her heart still thumping and a dryness in her throat, she decided to get herself a drink of water fresh from the cold tap. As she crossed the hall, she saw from a glow around the door that the kitchen light was on, and entered to find Fallan still at work with the maps and the magnifiers. The kitchen clock now read two thirty, and he didn't appear to have moved from where she'd left him when fatigue had deceitfully enticed her to bed almost four hours ago.

She really wouldn't want this man as her enemy. He was a machine.

As she let the water run, draining the tepid stuff out of the system first, this last observation prompted her to broach the subject that was troubling her most.

'Back at the map shop this afternoon, how did you know we were about to get shot at? That car was behind us when you reacted, and prior to that you hadn't given it a second look. Then all of a sudden you're throwing me out of the way just in time. It was like you'd eyes in the back of your head. Same as on Wednesday.'

Fallan stared at her, as though weighing up whether she was worthy of a response, and for a long second she thought she'd come up short.

'Fear,' he said eventually. 'I listen when it speaks.'

Jasmine looked quizzically at him, not understanding, and simultaneously worrying that this was what he'd suspected.

'I felt fear too,' she explained herself, 'but *after* he started trying to kill me, when I knew there was a threat. You seemed to know before. How does that work?'

'I don't mean conscious, specific fear, I mean subconscious and strictly non-specific. Something you feel, not something you think: a peremptory feeling that tells you urgently and unequivocally that you are in danger. You never get that? A sudden, unarticulated sense that something about your immediate environment is disturbingly wrong?'

Like having a killer sitting in her kitchen, Jasmine thought but didn't say. Instead she cast her mind back to the start of all this, and that precipitous assault by a feeling of unease.

'Yes. Monday morning, when I went into the office. I knew something was wrong but I didn't know *how* I knew.'

'That was fear talking. Conscious thought occupies only a small proportion of the brain: most of it is taken up with processing input from the senses, input you are not aware of processing.

322

Most of our conscious thought is rooted in language, which evolved fairly late in the day and is like a flashy but clumsily written piece of software compared to the rest of the operating system, which ticks away silently and makes sense of the information it's getting much, much faster. The part of your brain that tells you to run because your early-warning system detected a predator or an avalanche was there a lot longer than language and responds a lot more immediately.'

She remembered assessing her surroundings in Jim's office, the tiny clues that she had looked for after the fact in order to explain what her subconscious mind had deduced in a flash.

'So what information told your brain we were about to get shot?' she demanded.

'I'm not sure. Car not slowing down as it reached a dead end; maybe something else about the way it approached; a glimpse of what could have been a gun but which my mind ignored until it combined with other information: I don't know. I could try to retro-analyse, but that's the whole point: it wasn't a response to rational analysis, it was a response to something in the brain that we tend to ignore *because* of rational analysis.'

'You sound like this is something you've thought about a lot.'

'Comes with the territory. We don't listen to fear properly. We feel it, but we try to explain it away, because we relate it to our conscious thought, render it in language. Most of the time, when we rationalise it, we're looking for reassurance, for reasons why that feeling was a false alarm. *We're looking for reasons why it's going to be okay.* For a great many people, I've been the reason it *isn't*

323

going to be okay. Listening to my fear is the reason I've lived this long.'

Jasmine looked at the strips of landscape mapped out on the table and wondered how many little white lines on subsequent surveys were down to the man at her table. Then she feared she might well up with tears as she remembered about the littlest white line of all: tiny, lifeless but still glowing somewhere on those photographs. A four-week-old baby, incapable of witnessing anything and incapable of ever telling anybody.

That was when she saw it: a woman in theatre blues, a laminated badge clipped on to her chest.

'Bain's other half,' she said.

'The nurse? What about her?'

'She's not a nurse. She's a *midwife*.'

'What difference does that make?'

'You said it right outside their house: if your father was looking for a stooge, he could have come up with plenty of better candidates. So what got Bain the gig?'

'His missus worked in a maternity ward,' Fallan said, getting it.

'Bain's number appears on both the outgoing and incoming lists. It's not a mobile: it's the phone in his house. So what if the incoming call wasn't *Bain* phoning Jim: what if it was *her*?'

LOCUST IN FLIGHT

Abercorn's black Mondeo took a left on Albion Street and turned on to the Trongate. Catherine was two cars back, further concealed, she hoped, by the disguise of being in Drew's car rather than her own, though she didn't know whether Abercorn was aware of what she drove privately.

He certainly wasn't aware of her presence, but that was the beauty of it: as a police officer, you're the last person to suspect that *you're* being followed.

It was a simple left turn, but one that Catherine always felt as a bit of a jolt, as though too much had changed from one street to the next for them to meet on the perpendicular. You went from the Merchant City with its upmarket urban digs, trendy pubs and chic eateries, the aspirational Glasgow of tourist brochures and lifestyle supplements, straight to this neglected-looking stretch of bargain shops, grotty boozers and greasy spoons, Glasgow's own portrait of Dorian Gray. It had been like this for as long as she could remember: like a withered appendage at the end of Argyle Street, where the chain stores and logos gave way to hand-written posters full of stray apostrophes.

That was Glasgow, though. It scrubbed up well, it knew how to put its face on, but there was always a more gritty reality just a street away. It wasn't hidden, but most people could simply choose not to see it.

It was coming up for two. She had been following him for around five hours, but she was good at this: the waiting part. It wasn't an easy skill to develop, but once you had it, it never left you. It was a state of mind, a mindfulness of being.

You had to accept that nothing might come of it, that you could be wasting your time. You had to avoid visualising what you hoped to witness, or even wondering what would constitute an act or sight *worth* witnessing. You just had to wait and see, wait and see.

Of course, this was made a little more challenging by the fact that Catherine was engaged in an unauthorised surveillance of a fellow officer, and that there was a limit to how much time she could dedicate to such a one-woman operation, but that again was something she'd had to make her peace with before commencing. She accepted she might see nothing, and just as important, she accepted that there might be nothing *to* see.

At the moment, though, she was optimistic that she was finally on to something. When you've been watching someone drive all day, you can notice small tells, subtle changes to how they are handling their vehicle. In the case of Abercorn right then, it was similar to someone driving over the alcohol limit: he seemed just that bit more careful and deliberate about everything. Or maybe it was simply that, after a day largely spent around the city centre, he was finally heading into Apache territory.

He drove east along the Gallowgate, past the Barrowland and round the dog-leg up to Tollcross Road. His pace was steady and careful, keeping his distance from the car in front. He couldn't have made himself much easier to tail. There were no evasive manoeuvres, no doubling back on himself or sudden non-indicated turns. Only his route was questionable, and only in retrospect. He turned left off Tollcross Road before it became Hamilton Road, heading north past Tollcross Park and east again on to Shettleston Road, only to come back south through Mount Vernon and end up travelling east again on Hamilton Road. Could be he knew about a traffic issue, could be he changed his mind about his route, but Catherine was aware that if he had any suspicions about the black BMW two and sometimes three cars back, then an unnecessary U-shaped detour would be a good way to confirm them.

He'd need to have spotted her way back, however, and that didn't strike her as probable. She had kept a minimum one-vehicle cover, and with him never getting an eyeball on her face or her plate, if he even noticed that there was a black BMW somewhere behind him, it was unlikely he'd assume it was the same one.

Certainly, as he continued on his route eastwards, parallel to the M74, he never gave any indication that he had seen something that was going to make him change his plans. Steady, careful, deliberate, unhurried, anonymous, and quietly purposeful. He drove on past where Calderpark Zoo used to be, along the dual carriageway until the coarse grass and crash barriers gave way to pavements, trees and red sandstone on the outskirts of Uddingston.

Catherine felt a tingle in her gut as the Mondeo indicated offside, which would take him down towards the river. There was an address she knew down there, a handsome property guarded ostensibly by electronic gates and CCTV, but more effectively by the reputation of its owner. It wasn't the only house in the street, though.

She told herself, therefore, not to want it, not to visualise it, but a possibility such as this was too tantalising not to raise her pulse.

She had to pass Abercorn and keep going as he

waited for a break in the oncoming traffic. She kept him in her sights, though, checking her rear-view and preparing to respond. He made his right turn a few seconds later; some obliging driver must have given him a flash. Catherine executed a swift U-turn in response, the breadth of the road allowing her to pull the BMW around one hundred and eighty degrees at still a decent clip.

She accelerated eagerly towards where the Mondeo had turned, feeling for the first time a little anxious that her quarry would not be visible after she made the next left. She'd briefly lost him a couple of times today, but remained calm and played the percentages, reacquiring him in each instance roughly where she might have expected to. What made this different was that she had succumbed to the temptation of considering a desired outcome.

Just wait and see, she told herself. Wait and see.

Catherine reached the junction maybe only thirty seconds behind Abercorn, but when she turned the corner, she could see no vehicles in motion on the road in front of her.

Wait and see. Wait and see.

She kept driving, urging her mind to think of where she might re-acquire him, but conscious that her mind wasn't going to listen until she had passed a particular address.

Before she even reached it, she spotted the Mondeo: parked on the left between a big X5 and a two-seater Mercedes, Abercorn still inside.

Catherine passed him again, carrying on along the street at a little over twenty. She allowed the earlier tingle to become a thrill, the possibility she had entertained passing from the tantalising to the tangible. It felt like a very long hundred yards, a very slow ten seconds, but she waited until she had covered what she considered a respectable distance before pulling in, making sure she could still see the Mondeo in her passenger-side wing mirror.

She recalled Fletcher's words of a week ago.

I'm just saying, be wary of Abercorn until you know what game he's really playing. And more importantly, whose side he's on.

Letting Off Criminals Under Secret Trades.

Dougie Abercorn, head of Locust, had just pulled up outside the home of one Stevie Fullerton.

PHANTOMS

They intercepted Margaret Bain as she walked towards the hospital's main entrance, ready to begin her shift. Jasmine felt like some doorstepping journalist, waiting around to ambush an unsuspecting woman on her way into work, which reminded her that this was what Margaret Bain had believed her to be when she visited her house. Jasmine didn't imagine her husband would have told her the truth about her and Fallan any more than he'd have told her the truth about why they were there.

In the event, there was more waiting to be done. Margaret looked askance at their approach, taking a moment or two to work out why she recognised them.

'I'm not allowed to talk to reporters,' she said.

329

'You need to go through the trust.'

Jasmine didn't know whether this was true, but they weren't there to interview her in her capacity as a trust employee, and she strongly suspected Margaret knew that.

'We're not reporters,' she said. 'We're private investigators. We work with Jim Sharp. We know you spoke to him.'

That got a reaction: the worried look of someone whose fears have just been confirmed.

'And he's gone missing since,' Fallan added.

'I'm due on shift in two minutes. I can't talk to you.'

'We'll wait for your break,' said Fallan, in a manner that conveyed she could expect to still find him waiting if she hid on the ward until midnight. 'It's about the Ramsay baby.'

Her mouth opened just a little, but no words issued. Then she made a frantic, frustrated gesture with her hand and walked off towards Maternity.

'Could be here a while,' Jasmine said, once Margaret had hurried out of sight down a brightly lit corridor.

Fallan shook his head.

'First break, she'll be here. She can't *wait* to talk. Her conscience is bothering her: that's why she called Jim.'

Jasmine could face some more waiting; having spent most of yesterday getting eye strain playing infrared spot-the-difference, this would be an easy shift. They now had a shortlist of possible locations, some of which admittedly could turn out to have been sheep or cattle.

Fallan was right. Margaret Bain reappeared after a couple of hours, looking both solemn and

330

anxious, and led them outside, where she could have a cigarette. They walked a short distance to the edge of the car park, out of earshot of the other smokers in their hospital gowns, some still attached to drip stands.

'I didn't know,' was the first thing she said, having sucked a couple of times on the cigarette like it was Entonox. 'Please believe me, I didn't know.'

Jasmine wanted to reassure her that they weren't there to pass judgement, but remembered what Fallan had said while they waited.

'Let her talk. Don't fill in any awkward silences. Don't make her feel better about herself. The thing that's going to do that is telling us the truth.'

'I didn't even realise there was anything *to* know until Mr Sharp came to the house,' she went on. 'I heard him arguing with Willie, accusing him of lying about seeing those folk at Bothwell services all those years ago. I know Willie was never the most honest man in the world, especially back in those days, but that was the first time anyone had ever suggested he might not have been telling the truth about that. I didn't even connect the two things at the time, never mind as the years went on.'

She took another drag on the cigarette and exhaled it in a drawn-out sigh.

'Me and Willie weren't married in those days. We were engaged, but we weren't living together. The thing is, I didn't even know Willie was the witness in that story until years later, when one of the papers did a piece on it. He never said anything to me about it at the time. Didn't say anything to anybody, in fact: in Willie's circles it wasnae a good

331

idea to advertise the fact that you'd been talking to the polis, you know?'

Jasmine nodded but said nothing.

'It would have been the Sunday, the day after Willie says he saw them; though bear in mind at this point he hadn't come forward to the polis, let alone told *me* anything. He went to the polis a few days later, claimed he had seen a news report that jogged his memory. This particular Sunday, though, he got me to do him a favour.'

She looked away, towards the hills and countryside to the west, as though she could see there the path she'd taken and wished she could change it.

'All right, so I wasn't the most honest person in the world either in those days,' she admitted. 'It was just a fraud, that's all. I'd done it before, always swearing off it later. I was terrified I'd get caught, but you can always do with the money, can't you, and anyway, I reckoned: what's the harm? It was a victimless crime. That's what I told myself, anyway.

'Willie asked me to add a birth. See, it's all computerised these days, but back then, all you needed to register a baby was a parents' hospital card, which the maternity ward would issue, and for the birth to be recorded on the official hospital list, which would get forwarded to the registrar's office as a legal requirement.

'That Sunday, Willie asked me to get hold of a parents' card and to forge an entry in the birth list. I initially said no, but the money was too good. It was two thousand pounds, a fortune. We were getting married, trying to save up for the wedding and a honeymoon and setting up home together.

'I thought it was the usual: an identity scam. When I'd done it before, Willie sold it as a package, and that's what he told me was happening that day as well. See, once you've registered a fake birth, you've got this phantom identity you can use for all sorts: claiming child benefit for a non-existent child, getting a false passport, God knows what else. I never asked.'

She took another drag, another glance towards Renfrewshire like it was the land of past regrets.

'I said I thought it was just the usual, but I was lying to myself. You didn't get two grand for that. I knew it was more than the usual, but I didn't stop to ask any questions. I didn't think about much beyond making sure I pulled it off without getting caught. It didn't cross my mind for one second that there was a real baby involved in it somewhere. Not until your man Mr Sharp came to the house.'

'You called him, didn't you?' said Jasmine. 'It showed up on the office phone records. Did you tell him what you've told us?'

She nodded.

'It was a week past on Wednesday. He came to see me at work, same as you. Wanted to talk away from Willie, I suppose.'

'What else did you tell him?' Fallan asked. 'Did you give him a name?'

'I couldn't. I don't remember the name. It was a boy, that's all I know. No first name either. You don't need that for the hospital card—just the parents' names. It's in case they've not made up their minds.'

'You don't remember?' Fallan asked doubtfully. 'This one wasn't the usual. You got two grand.'

She looked ashamed, like she might be about to

333

cry.

'It was nearly thirty years ago. And it wasn't just the once or twice I'd done it before.' She winced, troubled and embarrassed by the memory. 'There were a lot of names: I did it six times over the years, maybe seven. I can't remember. I'm sorry. I can tell you what I told Mr Sharp, though. If you go to the registrar, you can look up male births registered for that date. Not from this unit, though,' she added. 'It was the Victoria I worked in back then.'

SECRET TRADES

Catherine was starting to worry that she had been spotted. She couldn't see much more than the passenger-side flank of the Mondeo in her wing mirror, but it did give her a clear view of the full width of the pavement in front of Fullerton's house, and Abercorn had not yet crossed it. He must still be in the car, but if so, what was he waiting for?

She cursed her own overcautious patience. She should have pulled in fifty yards sooner, into that big space between the blue Corsa and the grey A5. She'd have been able to see right into the Mondeo from there, not blocked by the big builder's van that was four vehicles back. Or perhaps she hadn't been patient enough, and should have driven a bit further before doubling back. That way she could have parked on the opposite side, facing Abercorn's vehicle from a safe distance.

Wait and see. Wait and see.

She wanted to twist in her seat and check if a change of position afforded any better view past the builder's van, but she knew she couldn't, mustn't take her eyes off the wing mirror. The whole purpose of her day, and perhaps the whole key to this investigation, was concentrated upon the image reflected in that little round-cornered rectangle of glass, so she remained focused entirely upon it, barely daring to blink. Which was why she almost hit the ceiling when a fistful of knuckles chapped the driver's-side window, only inches from her ear: three short raps.

She turned around in fright, rapidly transforming into shock, horror and ultimately bafflement as she was confronted by the sight of Dougie Abercorn, an admonishing frown on his lips but a wry hint of amusement in his eyes.

Catherine climbed out of the BMW, feeling her cheeks burn, at a loss for what she might offer by way of explanation. All that came to mind was 'It's not what it looks like', which was particularly hopeless because it was obvious to both parties that it was exactly what it looked like.

'Nice ride,' said Abercorn drily.

'It's my husband's. How early did you spot it?'

'As a tail? It wouldn't be fair to say.'

'No need to be polite. Christ, I thought I was good at this.'

'I don't doubt you are, but the reason it wouldn't be fair to say is that I had countersurveillance running: two other cars specifically checking I wasn't being followed to this address. You had no chance.'

Catherine didn't know whether to feel relieved that it hadn't been down to her own incompetence or all the more appalled to know that several other officers had been watching her go off the reservation.

'Team One clocked that I had a tail, and that's why I went up past Tollcross Park. It was so Team Two could race ahead and do a reciprocal to get a look at you, see who you were.'

'Why did you carry on to your destination, then? Or did you take me to Stevie Fullerton's house as a joke? And why are you running countersurveillance?'

'It's no joke, and though I'm running countersurveillance because I've come to Stevie Fullerton's house, it's not Stevie I've come to see. Why don't you join me? I think you'll find it instructive.'

He gestured to her to walk towards chez Fullerton, whose electronic gates were swinging open up ahead.

'I have to say you're taking this rather well,' she said apologetically.

'Running Locust, you get pretty thick-skinned. Besides, you're not the only one to think there's a bent-polis scenario in play here. You just went after the wrong cop.'

'And which would be the right one?'

'That's what I'm hoping Liam Whitaker can help us ascertain.'

'Whitaker's here? With Stevie Fullerton?'

'Hence the countersurveillance. He's been in hiding since the robbery, as you know, but not just to avoid arrest. He's in fear for his life, specifically from the police. Stevie Fullerton has been sheltering him for a couple of days. He got in touch through back channels; Stevie's wise enough to know you can't hide for ever, and mercenary enough to spot an opportunity. We've had access on the understanding that Whitaker's whereabouts is not disclosed to the police at large: not until certain matters have been resolved, at which point he'll be our witness.'

'*Had* access? You've seen him already?'

'Yesterday. Sunday. I'll have to vouch for you, because you weren't part of the deal, but understand this much: when this is over, Whitaker walks.'

'Fine with me. But what does Fullerton get out of this "opportunity"?'

Abercorn tapped his wrist. Catherine thought he meant that they had to hurry along and there wasn't time to discuss it. Then she worked it out.

'The price of doing business,' she remarked distastefully.

'Letting Off Criminals Under Secret Trades,' Abercorn replied.

*   *   *

Whitaker reminded Catherine of a recently released hostage, though his captivity was not yet over. He was wearing clothes that didn't look like his own, he had a three- or four-day growth on his jaw and the slightly dazed look of someone who had gone a long time without sleep followed by a sustained period of little else. His nails were bitten to the quick, and having chewed his way through all of those, he had moved on to the dead skin around the tips of his fingers, gnawing distractedly on the edge of a digit any time someone else was speaking.

337

Fullerton had absented himself after escorting them to Whitaker's temporary quarters. He had given Catherine a finely scrutinising look, asking himself whether he recognised her. She was fairly certain the answer was no, and equally certain that it would be the opposite from now on. He trusted Abercorn, evidently, as only the most cursory assurance was required by way of vouching that she would not betray Whitaker's location. Perhaps Fullerton was just sufficiently confident that they would not be allowed to leave with Whitaker in their custody, nor back to do so without a warrant.

'Tell Detective McLeod what you told me,' Abercorn prompted.

They sat in a rear-facing room with the blinds tipped partially shut. Whitaker had informed them that he had not stood in sight of the street since being driven here, his journey spent lying across the back of an SUV. Catherine thought it was an overreaction; he was hiding from possible sightings, not dug-in snipers, but then she remembered who had fed Whitaker the Coruscate job, and what had happened to him since.

'Whit, go over it again?' he replied. He was clearly not someone with whom police cooperation sat well, even when it was the only way to safeguard his future.

'You'll have to go over it a lot more times before it buys you a get-out-of-jail card, Liam,' Abercorn told him. 'And if any discrepancies start to appear, we've got a problem. Talk.'

He had a nibble on a knuckle and began.

'It was Tommy gie'd me the shout. Says he could guarantee that Central would be getting cleared oot on Thursday morning. Don't know how he knew, but that was Tommy for ye: fingers in a lot of pies. He was in with a lot of people, but very discreet: he could be doing a wee bit of work for Frankie Callahan without Frankie knowing he was in with Stevie here as well, for instance. I mean, I was his mate for years and I'd hear things and think: whit? I didnae know Tommy knew *him*, you know?'

Abercorn arched his eyebrows at Catherine, by way of acknow-ledging that yes, they did know, what with Tommy touting to different police officers without either of them being aware of it.

'We'd talked it inside oot, and I'd been into Central and walked myself through it a few times. It was all set. Thing is, Tommy never got in touch on Wednesday. Never heard fae him, couldnae get haud ay him. Tried him again Thursday morn. Still nothin'. I thought maybe it was aff, but I went to Central anyway, just in case. Tommy could be like that: he could drap aff the radar. I thought I might be wasting my time, but at those stakes it was worth a punt, you know?'

'At six figures, yes, probably worth hanging around Central on the off chance,' said Catherine.

'Anyway, as you know, turns oot Tommy's on the money. There's an announcement on the tannoy and they're evacuating the place, so I sticks to the script. Soon as I heard the announcement, I nicked into the card shop, and while everybody was starting to file out, I dived in between these two display gondolas like I'd planned: they were back to back, leaving a wee crawl space to hide in. I heard the polis come in and make sure everybody was leaving, including the staff, while I just sat tight. Once everybody was gone, I bailed oot the

339

back door, into the wee enclosed area behind the shops where they keep their bins and packing crates and that, then in through the back of the jeweller's. In an' oot, matter of seconds. Bang, bang, bang.'

He had an uncertain look and helped himself to another bit of dead skin from his index finger. He should have been recalling a moment of triumph, but he was reaching the part where it all went wrong in a way he couldn't have anticipated.

'The plan was to slip away once the crowds came back in. I was at the far end of the enclosure behind the shops, waiting and keeping an eye out. I was expecting to see the bomb squad or whatever coming in first, but instead I heard a car coming up the ramp, you know, past platform eighteen?'

Catherine nodded. There was a horseshoe of road just beyond the escalator leading down to the low-level trains. The entrance was on Hope Street, and allowed cars to drive right up alongside platform eighteen to drop off passengers, then come straight back out again.

'There was two guys and a dug. Polis. I keeked over the top of the fence and ducked doon again. I was shiting myself in case the dug sniffed me oot. Dug wasnae there aboot me, but. One of them led it away intae the station while the other yin stayed at the motor with the engine running. He went tae the left luggage, then a coupla minutes later I heard him coming back. I had another wee keek and saw he was carrying this big fuck-off rucksack. Piles back intae the motor and zoom, they're away.

'I'm thinking: result. Punters'll be getting let back in any minute. Instead, next thing I see is mair polis and mair dugs headin' intae the station, like the big search has only just started.'

Catherine recalled the sight of the sniffer dog, snuffling eagerly at that other locker, even able to open the door because the lock had been knackered. She thought of the witness accounts of Callahan and Fleeting on Wednesday night and Thursday morning, two men with a job to do. There had indeed been a shipment waiting for them at Central Station, but it had been removed. Then a few hours later, so were they. For ever.

'I was with Cairns when he got the tip,' she told Abercorn. 'For reasons I can't disclose, I know for a fact that the call didn't come from Tommy Miller.'

'He had a second source? You think Cairns got played?'

'No, I think *I* did. By Cairns. I got a message he had information for me regarding the McDiarmid murder: wanted me to meet at a café two minutes from Central, first thing Thursday morning. It was so that I'd be on the spot, buy into it. I even phoned Scotrail for him, gave the order to shut down the station. The call he got was for show, for my benefit; or it was to let Cairns know everything was in place. Either way, it must have come from one of the guys Liam here saw.'

Something else fell into place as she spoke this aloud. The call had definitely come from a cop. He had picked up when Laura dialled the number, but not when Catherine had tried dialling it this morning. On the later occasions, she was calling from her mobile, but Laura had called it from her desk. All outgoing calls from the station showed up as the same switchboard number, so the source must have thought it was Cairns phoning him.

'Which brings us to the purpose of my visit,' said Abercorn, reaching into his jacket. He produced an A5-size envelope and pulled from it a stack of photographs. Catherine recognised most of them as cops, with a few villains and a few nobodies thrown in for control.

Whitaker screwed up his face as he pored over them, looking anxious and frustrated. He dallied over one or two of them, but was reluctant to commit. Catherine caught Abercorn's gaze as Whitaker came to the head shot of Cairns' big buddy Fletch, confirming their mutual suspicion that he had to be the top candidate, but Whitaker failed to pick him out.

'I told you,' he said to Abercorn. 'I only caught a glimpse. A couple of these guys look vaguely familiar, but that's all I could say.'

'What about CCTV?' Catherine suggested. 'The station's full of cameras.'

Abercorn gave her a sour look, like she was missing something obvious.

'Drug Squad took all the CCTV files off of Scotrail on Thursday,' he said. 'Can't see them handing them over to Locust in a hurry, but when they do, you can bet there will be a few gaps. Cairns—and whoever he's working with—has had several days to edit them.'

Abercorn directed Whitaker's attention back to the photos.

'Come on, think. You were there the whole time.'

'Aye, hiding, remember? The motor was parked facing away from me, so I never saw the driver's face at all. The other guy, I'm telling you, I stuck my heid above that fence for a quarter of a second

342

each time. I'd just tanned a hunner and fifty grand's worth of watches. If they'd looked up and seen me, I was fucked. Older guy, that's all I could say for sure.'

Abercorn looked away towards the partially covered windows. There was nothing to see: Catherine could tell he was just trying to contain his frustrations.

'Well, we do have another avenue we can pursue,' he said.

'Which is what?'

Abercorn nodded to the door.

'We'll leave the pictures with you, Liam,' he said. 'Give you time and space, see if it helps not to have us breathing down your neck.'

They exited the room into the dim hallway, but Abercorn evidently wasn't speaking further until they were out of the building altogether. These walls had very interested and very untrustworthy ears.

'Bob Cairns has been a cop in this city for over thirty years,' he said quietly, back out on the pavement. 'He's got friends in every division, trusted contacts at every level. We start asking questions and it'll get back to him in no time. He's got *at least* two accomplices in this who will also have their ears to the ground and whose identities remain a secret. I'd bet the farm on one of them being Fletcher.'

'Me too.'

'There's also at least one other, and we don't know how far or how high this might go.'

'Please tell me there's a "but" to this.'

'Oh, there is. But you won't like it.'

'Hit me anyway. What's your other avenue?'

'I think we need to go back and play nice with Glen Fallan.'

'He knows nothing about this,' Catherine assured him. 'Trust me, this is coming from someone who would like nothing more than for him to be implicated.'

'But this isn't what we'd be asking him about. I dug a little deeper into his father's record. Iain Fallan was in CID over in Gallowhaugh. Wild times: a law unto himself, fair to say. Saw himself like a frontier sheriff.'

'You going to tell me Bob Cairns was his deputy?'

'Among others. Including Bill Raeside.'

Catherine felt her cheeks flush with dismay, the anger of having been played coming back for a second pass.

'Raeside owns an Alsatian dog. He was also the one who relayed the message that Cairns had information and wanted to meet. I saw his photo in there, but Whitaker didn't look twice. Anyone else?'

'Yes,' said Abercorn, looking weighed down by a burden that was about to be doubled rather than shared. 'A young DC by the name of Graeme Sunderland.'

NAMES ON A PAGE

The registry office was on Martha Street, just around the corner from the Strathclyde University student union. Jasmine must have passed the place twenty times without paying attention to what it was; in fact, she remembered getting off with a guy up against its locked doors late one night/early one morning, before heading down to George Square for the night bus home. She'd been at the union with friends to see Twin Atlantic. She had got talking and dancing with him, before having a very enjoyable snog in which he had acquitted himself well by way of keeping his hands respectably in place around her shoulders.

Scott, she thought his name was, or possibly Sam. She later learned that he was sixteen and still at school: a fifth-year at Glasgow Academy. Never mind looking like a student, he had looked older than her. The kids that went to the private schools always did, right enough. Better clothes, or maybe just better breeding: going back several generations without anybody ever missing a meal. That was a year and a half ago, and Jasmine still got carded now. She'd taken his number and meant to call him, but it was just before Mum got sick; or rather, just before they got the diagnosis.

Seeing the spot where they'd kissed and the sight of the union building looming above John Street, she realised she had spent so long worrying about the future that she seldom gave much thought to the world she had lost. It wasn't just Mum that had been taken from her. Saturday nights, boys, friends, gigs, the student years, the dreaming years, they had all gone too. She could have *some* of those things again, though, couldn't she? If she got through this. If people stopped shooting at her.

Fallan explained what they were looking for, and the man on the desk was friendly and helpful, almost to the point where Jasmine was starting to become suspicious. Then she realised that she had simply recalibrated her expectations of such things after several days of dealing with people being awkward, evasive, confrontational, and occasionally murderous.

He looked like he might have been in the place since it was built, someone who fitted into his job and his environment so comfortably that she expected that anyone familiar with the place would find it hard to imagine one without the other. He was one of those distinguished old guys who are impossible to picture as young men, and probably wasn't much different then; he had a grace about his manner and a lightness on his feet that must have endured for many decades.

He disappeared off to the archives and re-emerged about ten minutes later bearing a couple of slightly yellowed pages. He was about to place them down on the desktop when he suddenly looked unsure of himself, a searching expression on his features.

'You're the second party to be making this inquiry of late,' he said. 'I just had a wee bit déjà vu and remembered I had looked out these same pages for another chap, maybe just a week and a half ago.'

She and Fallan shared a look. Jim.

'It was the Victoria, wasn't it?' he confirmed.

'Yes.'

'Aye. Sunday the twenty-first of August 1983. Definitely the same. Eight births: three girls and five boys.'

Jasmine got out a sheet of paper and began writing down the names of the boys and their registered parents, ordered alphabetically. It was another list to work through, like the one still folded up in her pocket detailing the office phone calls. That felt like an ancient artefact by now, the first step she had taken on this journey. This new list, however, would be what guided her to the end. This list contained the answer she was looking for, via one of these names.

Before she had finished copying them out, Fallan put a finger down decisively on the last one.

'Him,' he said.

'How do you know?'

'Trust me, I know. You don't work for Tony McGill for years without that name becoming familiar. I'd admit the name isn't entirely exotic for these parts, so it *could* be a coincidence, but I seriously doubt it.'

'It's not,' Jasmine realised, pulling out the call log and unfolding it.

It was near the top of the outgoing numbers, and therefore among the last calls made.

'I assumed it was just another firm Jim did work for,' she said. 'Jim must have called him up after seeing his name on this list.'

'He wouldn't have broached it over the phone,' Fallan reasoned. 'Not something like this. He must have made an appointment to see him. That's why he told Anne Ramsay he'd have news for her after the . . .'

Jasmine was faintly aware of movement at her side, someone coming through the swing doors a few yards away. She read the look of sudden alertness on Fallan's face and felt something inside turn to icy dread in anticipation of whatever events were about to rapidly unfold out of her control.

She wasn't thrown to the floor this time, and nor

347

would any bullets be flying. From the look on Fallan's face, he'd have been happier if there were.

TWO PORCUPINES MAKING LOVE

They sat around an eight-legged table in a small conference room inside the city chambers, its windows giving on to the continuation of John Street that ran through the buildings. Abercorn had procured use of the room at zero notice, from some contact of his at the council. Catherine didn't know if it was just availability that had dictated his choice of venue or whether he was hoping to engender some kind of sense of civic duty and spirit of mutual cooperation in their guests.

In the case of Fallan it might be a bit of an ask. He looked like his surroundings were constricting him, a predator in the zoo, restive and bristling. If they were going to get anything from him, they were going to have to get it fast. The girl would be a better bet, but Catherine had the impression it would be difficult to isolate her from her companion. His body language was very protective towards her; hers more trusting of him than perhaps she even realised.

'Saturday afternoon, back of two, Laura here and myself were shot at several times by a gunman in a red nineties-model Honda Civic.'

Catherine watched for their responses. Fallan was unemotive; still and calculating. Jasmine Sharp looked a little startled; surprised and clearly puzzled.

'We know it wasn't you,' Catherine went on. 'But

348

someone wanted us to think it was.'

'Funny,' Fallan said. 'A couple of hours after that, a gunman in a silver Vauxhall Vectra shot at us. Difference was, our guy wasn't doing it for show. He intended to kill us. Someone tried to kill us both on Wednesday too, down in Northumberland, I'm disinclined to think these incidents were unrelated.'

Catherine had heard nothing about this, and a look to Abercorn confirmed he was equally uninformed.

'We were unaware of that,' she said. 'Why didn't you report it?'

She wasn't expecting a guy like Fallan to tell her. He didn't disappoint.

'I realise the police are busy people,' he said with a dryness that lacked all humour. 'Don't like to bother them with trivia.'

Catherine ignored this.

'These two incidents on Saturday *were* connected,' she said. 'I think we were supposed to get shot at and then a little later you were supposed to be too dead to offer an alibi. The intended conclusion was that you were trying to stop us looking into certain matters, only to be gunned down yourself, taking a number of awkward questions with you to the grave.'

'What awkward questions? Like who killed those guys you were asking about?'

'Among others.'

'How did you survive?' asked Laura. 'See, at first I thought our guy was just a bad shot, but he'd actually need to be quite a good shot to fire off so many rounds without hitting either of us. Were you armed?'

349

'Yes,' Fallan said. He gave the three police officers time to formulate a question before adding: 'With a mobile phone.'

'He pretended it was a gun,' explained Jasmine. 'It scared the guy off.'

'I think my reputation preceded me.'

'Or your father's,' Catherine suggested.

Catherine felt Fallan's reaction like a change in the weather inside the room. She had definitely just plucked the lyre of Orpheus, but the question was, what would emerge from Fallan's personal underworld?

'You know this was cops,' he said flatly. 'How?'

'Among other things, you told me.'

'The biggest gang in Glasgow,' he confirmed.

'Why would they want you dead? You haven't poked your head out for twenty years and all of a sudden they're shooting at you. What have you two been looking into?'

Jasmine began to answer, but Fallan laid a hand on her arm and spoke over her.

'I'll show you mine if you show me yours.'

Abercorn gave her a look of assent. Catherine was planning to open up anyway, but it told her how high the stakes must be if even he thought it was time to lay his cards on the table. Either that or he had already calculated that Fallan and the girl had more to tell them than the other way around.

'What do you remember about a policeman by the name of Bob Cairns?' Catherine asked, conscious that she was being almost Abercorn-like in turning an apparent disclosure into a request for information. She hoped Fallan didn't reciprocate or they could be here all night.

'A good friend of my dad's. Used to come round the house all the time, sit up drinking, telling stories. When I was wee, listening to them talk made me want to be a polisman when I grew up. I liked him.'

He gave a shrug, as if this was all he could say and he needed Catherine to offer more. Then his tone darkened.

'Of course, this was when I was too young to know any better. Too young to realise that for all he could talk tough, he was a shitebag who turned a blind eye to what was going on in our house because otherwise he'd have had to stand up to my dad.'

'Stand up to him over what?' asked Laura, whose urgency betrayed her suspicions.

'Exactly what you think,' replied Fallan, looking her in the eye and holding her gaze for an uncomfortable few moments.

Catherine couldn't say what he saw in there, but some kind of understanding definitely passed between them.

'I take it he's still around, then,' Fallan said to Catherine, 'still peddling his salt-of-the-earth old-school Glesca polis shtick. Or is he retired?'

'CID retire at fifty-five,' Abercorn said. 'He's almost there. Can you think why he'd want you dead?'

'If it's him, then I *know* why he wants me dead. But as far as I can see,' Fallan said, turning back to face Catherine, 'you still haven't shown me yours.'

Catherine paused for a moment, then gave him a solemn nod, her way of conveying that she wasn't playing any games.

'Okay, here's the Cliff's Notes,' she began. 'Last

351

Thursday morning, Bob Cairns asked me to come and meet him because he had information regarding the murder of a mid-level drug dealer named James McDiarmid. While Laura and I were with him, he got a call, ostensibly from a source named Tommy Miller, regarding a potential bomb threat that resulted in the evacuation of Central station. No bomb was found. Instead, we recovered what appeared to be a very large consignment of heroin intended for Frankie Callahan. At the same time, Liam Whitaker, a thief and friend of Tommy Miller, took advantage of the evacuation to steal a hundred and fifty grand's worth of watches from the Coruscate jewellery shop inside the station.

'We subsequently discovered that the "heroin" was worthless dust, but Whitaker witnessed two other cops enter the station first, and leave with a rucksack that we now believe to have contained the drugs Frankie Callahan was waiting for. By the end of that day, Callahan, his fixer Gary Fleeting and the source Tommy Miller were all dead, the scene set up to look like the two drug dealers had been gunned down while torturing the source. Miller wasn't the source, though: the call came from someone else, whom we can reasonably assume to be one of the police officers Whitaker saw removing the real heroin.'

'What was the information?' Fallan asked. 'The reason Cairns needed you to meet him?'

'He'd heard that Paddy Steel's people were out looking for a black Transit van in connection with Jai McDiarmid's death. He also said he had another source who reckoned the van was dark blue.'

'Forensics subsequently found McDiarmid's

blood in one of Frankie Callahan's dark blue catering supply vans,' said Abercorn. 'It was parked outside the depot where Callahan, Fleeting and Miller were found dead.'

'And prior to that,' Fallan said, 'did you have any other corroboration of that information?'

'No,' Catherine realised. 'Now I come to think of it, Cairns was the only source of that information. Though if it was a fit-up, how would they get McDiarmid's blood inside one of Callahan's vans?'

'Easy,' said Fallan. 'If they're the ones who killed McDiarmid.'

'But why would they . . .' she began to ask, before she saw *precisely* why. 'A phoney tit-for-tat. They murder McDiarmid, knowing Fleeting will be in the frame because McDiarmid was sleeping with Fleeting's girlfriend. Then there's a motive for Paddy Steel to have killed Fleeting and Callahan.'

'And the reason they need them dead is so they're not around to ask what happened to all their heroin,' suggested Abercorn. 'That question was supposed to be covered—or at least shrouded in mystery—by the discovery of the decoy suitcase. Which was why Miller had to die too: he knew there was a real shipment coming into the station that day. And why Cairns went overboard on the search for Whitaker: he wasn't supposed to be there.'

'The big question is who *else* was there,' Catherine told Fallan. 'Who were these other cops? We came to you because we know Cairns worked with your father. We want to know who might be in on this, and how far up it might go. Cairns' mate from the Drug Squad, Fletcher, is top

353

of our list, as they've worked together off and on for as long as anybody can remember, although not back in Gallowhaugh. We know your dad also worked with Bill Raeside and Graeme Sunderland. Those names ring any bells?'

Fallan nodded solemnly, sitting back in his chair. There was a lot going on behind his eyes, only a fraction of which she expected him to share.

'Bill Raeside—or Wullie, as he was in those days—was the shitebag's shitebag. Born to do as he's told. Never a trigger man, but he'd be happy to reap the benefits and provide logistical support.'

'Raeside was the first officer on the scene when McDiarmid's body was discovered,' Laura recalled.

'More than that,' Catherine admitted. 'He made sure Locust weren't informed, and specifically suggested to Sunderland that I be given the case.'

'What's Locust?' asked Jasmine.

'My department,' explained Abercorn. 'Organised Crime Special Task Force. Why would he specifically suggest you take the case?'

Catherine fumed as she admitted that once again she had been played.

'They must have guessed that an apparent motive concerning petty gangland feuding would suit my sensibilities.'

She felt Fallan's gaze.

'They thought you wouldn't look a gift horse in the mouth,' he said, and clearly understood why.

Oh Moira Clark, where are you now? Catherine thought.

'A suggestion to which Graeme Sunderland duly assented,' said Abercorn. 'How did *he* fit in, way back when?'

Fallan was silent for a while, and before he

finally spoke, he gave out a very quiet sigh through his nostrils, one you really had to be listening for to notice. He looked conflicted, and Catherine suspected that whatever he said next wouldn't be the whole truth.

'Sunderland won't be part of this,' he said eventually. He spoke with conviction, but his evident determination to close the issue invited all the more scrutiny.

'How do you know?'

He paused again, and Catherine imagined she could see him blanking out the lines of a document in his mind before handing it over.

'My dad, Cairns and Raeside were a tight wee crew. Worked together for years. Sunderland was the new kid, dumped into Gallowhaugh on his first CID posting. He would have been exposed to some of what they got up to, but only to see if he had a taste for it. He wouldn't have been allowed to know about the heavy graft; just petty stuff he was in no position to do anything about. He didn't have a taste for it, though. He got out again fast. He's the one I blame least.'

'Blame least for what?' asked Laura.

'For turning a blind eye to what they could plainly see in my house. My father was a brutal man, a very brutal man. You don't become what I did if you're brought up by Ned Flanders. They all pretended they never saw what was going on, even when it was staring them in the face, because they were too scared to confront him. I was too scared to stand up to him as well, but I was a kid. They were supposed to be upholding the law, protecting the vulnerable. Some fucking detectives. Sunderland was the only one who at least seemed ashamed of his cowardice. He's not your man, believe me. Too young, for one thing.'

'Too young for what?' Catherine asked.

'You said Cairns is pushing retirement. Raeside must be too. I think you're looking for someone else who isn't going to be punching in for much longer.'

'Fletcher again,' Catherine said, Abercorn returning her gaze by way of concurrence.

'How much heroin are we talking about?' Fallan asked. 'Realistically.'

'Three million wholesale,' said Abercorn. 'That's what Frankie Callahan was paying per shipment, according to our sources. Pure and uncut.'

'Sounds to me like they've cooked up a wee scheme to boost their pensions,' Fallan suggested.

Catherine recalled her words to Abercorn a week ago, about Cairns and Fletch.

There's a lot of cops just like them. They've done their thirty, they're approaching retirement and they're skint despite working hard all their lives, yet every day they see these chancers driving about in their pimped four-by-fours, spending money like water.

She felt like the walls of the room were expanding away from her, once again the world's dimensions altering so that things around her no longer quite fitted the way they used to. Nothing was certain any more. Clark's Law was in tatters, the good guys were very, very bad guys, and here she was on the same side as not only her bête noire from Locust, but one of the few people on this earth towards whom she harboured genuinely murderous feelings.

It seemed, under the circumstances, way past time that he showed her his.

'You said someone tried to kill you on Wednesday, down south?' she asked.

Jasmine nodded eagerly; Fallan just stared.

'Bob Cairns threw one of the very few sickies of his entire police career on Wednesday. As you put it, Mr Fallan, I'm disinclined to believe these incidents are unrelated. This thing at Central station took planning. It took care, patience and above all, discretion. So with all that on his plate, on the day before the big operation, why would Bob Cairns be driving down to Northumberland in the hope of killing you?'

'Because it's no use having a share in a three-mill drug score if you're going to spend the rest of your life in jail.'

Fallan looked to the girl and gave her a gesture as though to say 'the floor is yours'.

Catherine felt an anxious pang of anticipation, wondering whether this ceding of control meant he was coming through with the quid pro quo.

The girl said her piece.

Was he ever.

SINS OF THE FATHER

Ruaraidh Wilson stood with his back to them, staring out on to St Vincent Street through his office's imposing triptych of towering windows. Catherine was reminded of his conduct in court, turning his back thus while he mentally composed a rebuttal in that most unusual of circumstances: a

357

question or an answer he was not expecting.

He rested his hands on the ledge, bowing his head, the action slightly hitching the tails of his jacket. Catherine had thought it was something he only wore in court for show, and was a little surprised to find him thus attired even in his chambers, like an actor permanently in character. He was someone who had affected a middle-aged look since his twenties, a man out of time, if not a little out of fashion. He was not flamboyant or ostentatiously eccentric in his appearance; merely a little odd. He was a man *apart* from fashion, an intellectual who simply wouldn't waste his time or his brainpower engaging in such superficialities. Or maybe his brainpower had engaged sufficiently to deduce that this might be a wise and imposing impression to give.

Usually, when he turned around, you could tell he had a response he was pleased with because there was an eager energy about his features, even if part of that response would involve pretending to look sorrowful, angry or confused. When he turned around right then, he merely looked old.

Old and suddenly very, very tired.

'It's about his son,' Catherine had said to Wilson's secretary. She had felt a little guilty about this, aware of the awful conclusion he would reach when informed that there were police here with this message. It was necessary, however. They needed to get instant access and couldn't give him time to make any phone calls. Jim Sharp had called to make an appointment and hadn't been seen since.

Her conscience was slightly assuaged by the thought that being forced to confront his worst fear would make it a little easier for Wilson to deal with merely the runner-up.

Wilson didn't appear as though he was handling that one very well either.

He had looked dismayed at the sight of five people piling into his private office when he was perhaps expecting two, but that also was necessary. Catherine wanted to instantly convey that no matter his power, skill and connections, this was not something he would be able to contain.

It had also been made pretty clear to her that Fallan and the girl were not prepared to sit this one out, and given what they had uncovered, she felt they had earned their ticket in.

Wilson leaned against the windowsill, as though the four feet to his desk and the ample mahogany breadth of it were not a comfortable enough distance from his besieging visitors.

'I didn't know at the time,' he said.

'We're hearing that a lot,' said Fallan.

'Sincerely, I didn't.' He put a hand to his face, three fingers delicately cradling his forehead. 'I used to worry myself sick that this day would come, but as the years went by, I thought about it less and less until I'd become almost convinced it never would. I used to have half an idea of what I'd say to him, but now I just don't.'

Wilson's eyes filled, rheumy and bloodshot.

'He's still my son,' he said, his face contorting in the spasms of a sob.

Catherine gave him a moment but resisted offering a sympathetic face.

'We need to know what happened,' she said firmly.

Wilson composed himself, taking out a white

359

cloth handkerchief and wiping his face.

'I did it for Wilma,' he said. 'My late wife. It was all she wanted, a child. When you're younger, it's not something you worry about *not* having; you just assume it'll happen. Christ, the lengths you go to in order to make sure it *doesn't* happen . . .'

He shook his head wryly.

'It just didn't happen for her. For us. She had several miscarriages, and the doctors said each one made it less likely she'd carry to term in the future. They said it was getting dangerous for her, in fact. She became very depressed, very withdrawn. We decided, of course, that we'd apply to adopt, but we were on a long waiting list.'

He closed his eyes and turned his head, as though trying to shut out a memory, or maybe something that lay in his future.

'Fletcher McDade was a friend of mine. We played golf together. I'd told him about Wilma.'

'McDade?' said Jasmine suddenly. 'He's Fletcher? He's Cairns' pal?'

'Since they were cadets at Tulliallan, as far as I know,' Catherine replied. 'What about him?'

'Never mind,' Jasmine said, glancing towards Wilson. 'It can wait.'

Catherine wondered why the girl hadn't made the connection before, then realised they had never referred to him by his surname. Nobody ever did: he was Fletcher or Fletch to everybody on the force.

Wilson looked grateful for the interruption; all good lawyers knew how to benefit from a recess when they were in a hole. This was one even he wasn't digging himself out of, however.

'Fletcher came to see me in the middle of the

night. I thought someone had died. Well, they had, but not the person I was told. Fletcher said some young girl had taken an overdose, some poor junkie, and they'd found a baby in the flat. He told me the child was barely a week old, that the girl had delivered it at home, out of her box on smack, and had only left the house after that to score. The birth had never been registered. The mother was dead and nobody knew about the baby.

'He said they could fix it so that the baby was registered as ours and nobody would ever know otherwise. It would go to a good home and we'd have a son and we'd never have to have that talk. He'd never need to know he was adopted and we'd never need to worry about someone else knowing and telling him. Amazing how simple it looks when it's the middle of the night and you're desperate and deluded.'

'Weren't you concerned that people would notice your wife hadn't been pregnant?' Catherine asked.

'Wilma hadn't been out much in a long time,' he said. 'As I mentioned, she had become very withdrawn, very depressed. And very much larger. I believe they call it "comfort-eating" these days. That night, she came downstairs when she heard us talking. When Fletcher told her, she didn't need asking twice. We didn't think we were doing anything more wrong than skipping the queue, bypassing the red tape of the adoption procedure.'

'When did you find out otherwise?'

'By the end of the week, the story was all over the news about the Ramsays. I tried to deny it for a while, told myself it was a coincidence, but inside, I knew. I dug around discreetly, found no record of any woman dying from an overdose that night or even that week.'

'Did you challenge Fletcher?'

'Delicately. He eventually admitted there had been no dead junkie, but he said it wouldn't benefit me to know more. "We're just making the best of something that can't be changed." That was how he put it. I left it at that; I knew he was right. I didn't want to know more, and it *couldn't* be changed. I couldn't take the baby back from Wilma by that point, and I never told her. It was my burden to carry.'

'Put you in a compromising position, though, didn't it?' Catherine suggested. 'Police officers knowing this about you.'

He shook his head ruefully.

'No. I was the one who had power over *them*. At worst, all I had done was participate in an illegal adoption. I don't know what happened to the Ramsays, but I knew Fletcher and his colleagues had more to lose if the truth ever emerged; not that I would ever have allowed that to happen. It would have been devastating to Wilma and, as time went on, to Dominic.'

'Is this why the police were so understanding during Dominic's wild years?' Catherine asked. 'Were strings being pulled, favours called in?'

'I wasn't leaning on anybody, not with this. I think Fletcher and certain others felt a responsibility towards Dominic, hence their intercessions. There was certainly plenty of guilt to go round. It was my fault Dominic was off the rails, though. It wasn't an easy burden to carry sometimes. You say it won't matter that he's not your own blood, and it doesn't, it really doesn't, but when you're under stress, you can think unworthy thoughts. There was often tension between us, and I'd vacillate between riding him hard and overindulging him out of guilt.

'You might think there's a certain irony in that he took measures to distance himself from me, publicly rejecting me, in fact. Maybe there is, but that doesn't make it hurt any less. We've actually been getting on much better these past couple of years, since his mother . . . since Wilma died. I think he'd also come to realise that this game isn't as morally simple as he used to believe.'

'Why didn't the police just leave the baby on a doorstep, or at the hospital?' Jasmine asked.

'Because it would have been investigated,' Catherine replied. 'Connections would have been made. Stephen Ramsay's parents would probably have been able to identify the child. This way, Charlie Ramsay effectively disappeared from history.'

'Until now,' Jasmine stated, causing Wilson to visibly wince. 'Until my uncle found out the truth. What happened to him?'

'I thought I had dodged a bullet,' Wilson said. 'I saw the piece in the paper a couple of weeks back, about Anne Ramsay hiring a detective. Not long after that, this Jim Sharp bloke called up and asked if he could come in for a chat. I knew what it was about, and naturally I feared the worst. I called Fletcher to let him know. He told me it would be okay: that this detective was an ex-cop and he would have a word, straighten it out. I assumed he had, as I never heard from Sharp again.'

'Neither did we,' said Jasmine darkly.

'Can we trust Wilson not to go and act on this?'
Jasmine asked anxiously. 'He could be making
phone calls right now.'

They had adjourned to a nearby bar and
restaurant on St Vincent Street where Abercorn
had advised they could get a private room. Jasmine
had gone there once for lunch, celebrating the end
of term. She'd spent far more than she could
afford because they were divvying up the bill, and
Charlotte Queen had been in the group. Jasmine
would have been happy with a bowl of pasta and a
pear cider, but Charlotte had been ordering
oysters and champagne, forgetting that not
everybody's daddy was a millionaire; and that not
everybody even had a daddy.

Jasmine knew so little about hers, only that he
was dead. Her mum wouldn't talk about him, and
steadfastly discouraged the subject. The most she
would say when asked was that she had made some
big mistakes from which she was lucky to escape,
and that having Jasmine had been her salvation.
'My gift from God,' Mum always called her, even
though she wasn't religious.

Jasmine had tried to piece together a picture
from sparse and sketchy clues: overheard remarks
among relatives, unguarded things her mum had
said either in distracted moments or later, when
the drugs were taking hold, though in those
instances, disinhibition had to be balanced against
unreliability. All she knew was that her mum had
grown up in a bad area of Glasgow and allowed

herself to become involved with some dangerous people on the rationale that if she was in their camp, they would protect her from other dangerous people. She had relocated to Edinburgh while pregnant with Jasmine, in order to make a fresh start. Like Jasmine, she had trained to be an actress, but had settled for the role of drama teacher and, of course, mother.

'I trust him,' said Catherine. 'He can't contain this, but if he wants some control over when it breaks, and the chance to sit down with his son in the meantime, then he'll cooperate.'

Catherine was trying to look reassuring, but Jasmine felt instinctively wary. The policewoman had always been civil enough towards her, but this constant sense of latent hostility emanating from her towards Fallan all but crackled like ozone in the air, and Jasmine couldn't help feeling some of that was coming her way by association.

'Cooperate is pushing it,' said Abercorn. 'He'll comply, but he won't do anything to assist us unless it helps keep him in the clear.'

'No doubt,' Catherine agreed. 'But at least he'll be neutral. The one good thing about him being a material witness is that at least it won't be him defending the bastards when we get them to court.'

'We're a long way from that yet,' Abercorn cautioned. He turned towards Jasmine. 'What were you going to tell us about Fletcher?' he asked.

'He came to the office last Tuesday,' she replied, 'saying he had heard about my missing-person report, and he was looking into it because he knew Jim from the job. The thing is, now that I remember, he seemed to get a bit of a fright when he first entered, like he was surprised to find me there.'

'He was coming to tan the place,' Fallan opined. 'Clear out the files connecting Jim to the Ramsays. He—or one of them anyway—came back and finished the job once you were gone.'

'His manner was odd, too,' Jasmine said. 'Very serious, full of a thousand questions, then all of a sudden getting flippant and telling me not to worry about it.'

'He was sounding out how much you knew,' said Catherine, 'and must have satisfied himself that you weren't going to be a threat.'

'Daft wee lassie that doesn't know what she's doing,' Jasmine said with a shrug.

'They still followed you, though,' said Fallan. 'The next day, to make sure. And it didn't set their minds at ease when they saw that not only were you continuing your investigation, but that I was your first port of call. Bad enough the ghosts of the past rising again, but rising again when there's a three-million-pound payout in touching distance. I think I'll take back my earlier apology. I don't think either of us would have been collateral damage on Wednesday. When they saw us together, they needed us both dead.'

'But why would you be a threat at that stage?' Jasmine asked. 'You couldn't connect them to the Ramsay disappearance, only to your father.'

'But my father wasn't the only person they were afraid of me connecting them to.'

'Who, then?' Catherine demanded, her tone mirroring Jasmine's own surprise and impatience.

'Three million quid's worth of heroin isn't going to be much good to three retired cops unless they fancy spending their autumn years selling tenner bags in pub lavvies. There's got to be a buyer lined up.'

Fallan turned to address Abercorn.

'You're the organised crime expert,' he said. 'What's Tony McGill up to these days?'

Abercorn grimaced a little, as though having to dig deeper and more obscurely into his mental files than he'd been expecting.

'Served the best part of two decades after getting busted in Liverpool having just bought enough drugs to service Motley Crue for a century. He always claimed it was a set-up, but then so did OJ.'

'He *was* set up,' Fallan replied. 'Just not by the cops, as his personal mythology maintains. But that's ancient history. What about now?'

'He got out six years ago. His son, also Tony, you know him?'

'Teej. Living proof that talent often skips a generation.'

'Yeah. He took charge of the family business, with Tony senior pressing the remote control from inside. It wasn't a golden age, fair to say. After all those years there wasn't much of an empire for Tony to return to. He was over sixty when he got out. He's sixty-seven, sixty-eight now. Not exactly an up-and-comer.'

'Gangsters aren't like CID. There's no statutory retirement.'

'Certainly old Tony still sees himself as a bit of a player, but everybody else sees him as a bit of a joke. Yesterday's man. Still got a lot of connections, but the folk who know his name are getting older and fewer. Still got the same old problems, too. Doesn't have a line of his own to a supplier. Worst of it is, his big fears all came true while he was inside.'

'He who controls the spice controls the universe,' said Fallan.

This eighties movie reference elicited a tiny smile from Catherine, despite herself, but was evidently lost on everyone else, Jasmine in particular.

'Those who did have a direct supply were able to steam in,' said Abercorn. 'Even if McGill hadn't been in jail, he'd have been helpless to prevent his power base getting swept away. All his old stomping grounds—Gallowhaugh, Shawburn, Croftbank—he's still got a name there but no real power.'

'And who has?' Fallan asked.

The answer literally gave Abercorn pause. He looked sharply at Catherine for a moment before they answered pretty much simultaneously.

'Frankie Callahan.'

'Old-school crooks, old-school polis,' Fallan mused. 'Old alliances enduring and old habits dying hard.'

'Old habits such as covering their tracks and vanishing the evidence,' said Catherine. 'We know everything but we've got nothing. These guys are going to be very hard to take down.'

'Then we get them to take themselves down,' Fallan said gravely.

'How?' Catherine asked, with the cautious curiosity of someone who knows there's an answer to her question but is less certain she's going to like it.

'Way I see it,' Fallan replied, 'you guys can't go

368

through most of your normal channels because you don't know where you might be tripping over one of their connections. So that means you're going to have to outsource this to Sharp Investigations: let Jasmine and me handle it.'

Catherine eyed him with admonishing scepticism.

'This would need to give us something admissible,' she warned him. 'It's not going to take Ruaraidh Wilson to blow us away in court if your plans involve somebody getting tied to a chair with Gerry Rafferty playing in the background.'

Fallan put on a look of hurt innocence that paradoxically made him look like the most demonic person Jasmine had ever seen. And that was before he told her what he had in mind.

'Oh, no, it wouldn't be just *my* talents that we'd need to make this fly.'

A ONE-WAY TRIP TO THE CAMPSIES

Jasmine could hear footsteps in the corridor outside, and steadied her breathing in response, preparing for her cue. She had to pitch it just so. There were no rehearsals for this, no retakes, and there would be no second show to get it right.

She could display anxiety but not fear; the time to be scared would come later. Frantic anxiety, rather than despairing. Supplicant. Contrite. Helpless. Just like on the phone.

'Mr McDade, I'm so sorry, I'm just so sorry,' she had said. 'I didn't know who else to turn to. I know you told me to leave it to you, and I should have, I really should have, I know that now. But I just . . . I was so worried for Jim. I've got nobody else. I had to find out what I could, but, God, it's just been so awful. People shooting at us and this *Fallan* guy, this *psycho* . . .'

She'd even managed tears at this point; the sound of them anyway.

'Hang on, calm down, hen. Calm down. Keep it together. What's happened?'

'Too much to say. I've got myself in way over my head. I've found out some things and I'm really, really scared. This guy you told me about, Glen Fallan, he isn't dead. I thought he was someone else at first, and I thought he was going to help me, but he's everything you said, and there's people trying to kill him and now he's been arrested and I've got nobody if they come after me, and there's these photographs and I don't know—'

'Woah, steady the Buffs. Stay calm. He's been arrested?'

'Yes. He tried to shoot these police officers, and he took *my car* to do it, and now I'm scared they'll think I was involved. I know you said to sit tight and stay out of this, but I think everything that's gone on is connected with whatever's happened to my uncle Jim. Have you found anything out?'

'I've made a few inquiries. Nothing as dramatic as you, by the sounds of it. Did you say something about photographs?'

'It's these infrared photographs that Jim ordered. Overhead shots of the landscape, north of Glasgow, mostly the Campsie Hills, taken in late 1983. The guy he ordered them from said that they show up body heat, even from cemeteries. I think Jim was trying to find where some bodies might be

370

buried, and I think somebody might have killed him to prevent that. I'm scared they're coming for me next. But if I give the photos to you, you'll be able to look into it, won't you? You'll find out what's going on, and find out who's doing this, and I'll be safe, and—'

'Keep it together, hen. Don't worry. It'll all be okay. Are the photos with you just now?'

'Yes. I'm at Jim's office. I thought it was the safest place because they've already burgled it. Can you come and meet me here? Please? Quickly?'

'You sit tight, hen. Sit tight. I'll be with you soon.'

And now he was in the building, only seconds away. Was this the beginning of the end, or the end of the beginning? she wondered. The former, she hoped. She had to escape this place of stasis, this state of life on hold.

She cast her mind back seven days, everything that had passed since flickering past in a blur. Her surroundings were the same but the world looked different; the eyes that viewed that world, those surroundings, altered far more.

Some things had not changed, however. Once again she was sitting in Jim's office, contemplating his absence and what deeds might lie behind it. Once again Detective McDade was on his way here, intent on removing evidence and about to encounter someone he was not expecting.

'Remember, you'll be covered at all times,' Fallan had assured her.

Why did people think putting more guns into the equation made things *safer*?

The office door opened and McDade walked in.

There were no lines scripted for this part: just

371

the appropriate expression on her face and the composure of her body language as she stood by the window, expectantly cradling the cardboard scrolls.

She stood there helplessly, offering them towards him, clutching them just a little too tight so that they bunched together and one threatened to spill to the floor. McDade strode over swiftly to relieve her of them, which was when he felt cold steel against the base of his skull.

'Hands up and to the sides,' Fallan commanded. 'You've got a Heckler and Koch Mark 23 plus suppressor pointed right into your brain stem, and unlike your effort on Saturday, this one's armed with subsonic low-velocity ammunition, which will very quietly bounce around back and forth inside your skull until your brain is mush.'

Or at least that was what Fallan told him. It was, in fact, a length of pipe, but that mattered little, as there would be a silenced automatic in Fallan's hands in only a few seconds' time.

'Where's your piece?' he asked.

McDade went to reach inside his jacket.

Fallan moved the pipe and pressed it into the base of McDade's spine instead.

'Slowly,' he warned. 'Barrel between your fingers. And in case you were thinking you might have a window here to try something because I won't shoot you in the head, you'd be right. I need you alive. What I don't particularly need is for you to be able to walk. Ever again.'

McDade very slowly removed a silencer-fitted handgun from his jacket, holding it as instructed. Fallan took it from him and quickly examined it, ejecting the magazine for a moment then slamming it home again.

'You'll be Fallan's boy, then,' McDade stated evenly. 'Not quite as under arrest as I'd been led to believe,' he added, eyeing Jasmine with accusatory malice.

'Tramping about where I'm not meant to with my dainty little feet,' she said, reminding him of his patronising words the last time he was standing there.

'I don't think you can really take the huff with Jasmine,' said Fallan, 'considering what you came here to do to the girl.'

'And what you did to my uncle Jim.'

'I don't know what you're talking about. I came here to have a look at these photos you told me about.'

'With a silenced Beretta?'

'She told me people had been shooting at her. It was for her protection.'

'Aye, I forgot: you're polis. You're all about doing the right thing, aren't you, Detective Inspector McDade?'

'It's Detective Sergeant. And I suggest you put the gun down. I realise there's some dangerous people on your case, but I can help you with that.'

'I don't doubt it,' Fallan told him. 'Which is why you're about to take us on a wee jaunt to the Campsies. See, the thing is, we already know the truth about what you've done, so it's not lies and denials that will stop it being a one-way trip for you.'

'What will?' he asked nervously.

*   *   *

373

They took Jim's surveillance van. Jasmine went first, told by Fallan to check that the path was clear and to have a look at the car park, making sure McDade hadn't been followed.

'It's just his car out there,' she reported. 'A silver Vauxhall Vectra.'

Jasmine got the van open while Fallan escorted McDade to the vehicle and directed him to the driver's seat. Fallan then took his place on the passenger side and Jasmine climbed into the back.

Fallan dangled the keys for McDade to take, keeping the Beretta pointed at him with his right hand.

'I know off hand about twenty parts of the body where I can shoot you a couple of times without it seriously impairing your ability to drive,' he warned.

'Where are we going?' McDade asked.

Fallan had explained the choice of vehicle by telling McDade that it seemed 'appropriate, a wee tribute to absent friends'. In truth, it was because they had already set up a couple of cameras inside, as well as sound-recording equipment tuned to receive signals from the transmitters they were each wearing. They were also both carrying digital voice recorders, and Jasmine had set her phone to audio-memo mode as well, as another backup. They wanted to catch every word and every nuance. It wasn't just a matter of soliciting an admission, but about getting him to reveal irreparably damaging knowledge, facts only the guilty could know, and the biggest of those would dictate their destination.

'You're going to take us to the Ramsays, then to Jim Sharp,' Fallan told him, as McDade started the engine.

'I swear, I don't know what you're talking about.'

Fallan pressed the end of the silencer into a fleshy part of McDade's thigh.

'Don't tempt me. We know you were there when the Ramsays were killed. We know Dominic Wilson was born Charlie Ramsay. We know you brought the baby to your pal Ruaraidh. We know you're his go-to guy on this, the guy he phoned when Jim called up asking awkward questions. Wilson told us all this himself, so get the pedal to the metal.'

McDade gave a quivering sigh, fear, anger, shock and resignation all readable in his response. He put the van into gear and began to drive.

'Aye, I suppose you're wondering why Wilson didn't call you after *we* came asking awkward questions. Couple of reasons, really. He didn't know he was effectively ordering a hit when he phoned you about Jim. More importantly, though, he understood he had nothing to fear, because we're not hell-bent on dropping him in it. Or you, necessarily.'

McDade shot Fallan a guardedly curious look, then returned his eyes to the road.

'How so?' he asked, accelerating up a slip road on to the M77.

'Because we're not here looking for justice. A bunch of old men going to jail isn't going to bring back Jasmine's uncle Jim.'

'What?' Jasmine asked, with vocal shock and heartfelt outrage. 'This isn't what we discussed. I bloody well *am* looking for justice.'

'You won't find it, though. It's a chimera, it's

Peter Pan's shadow. Even if you can get hold of it, you'll discover it's got no substance, and it's nae use when you're paying the rent.'

'So what *are* we looking for?' she asked, indignant sarcasm dripping from her emphasis.

'Compensation,' he replied, addressing McDade. 'See, I once read how there's certain cultures who believe that if you murder a man, your punishment is that his family become your responsibility. It left a profound impression on me. It's a principle I've embraced. When you killed Jim Sharp, you took away not just Jasmine's uncle, but her livelihood as well.'

'You want money? So why are we going to the Campsies?'

'Mutual assurance. See, here's how it's gaunny play. There's a shovel in the back of the van. You're gaunny take us to where the bodies are buried and you're gaunny dig them up for verification. They won't be in the best of nick, but Eilidh Ramsay was wearing an engagement ring with a diamond, a ruby and an emerald set in gold. I'm figuring, what with you all being filth, you wouldn't have been stupid enough to steal it and put it into circulation, so it should be still there. Jim will be easier to ID, obviously.

'That gives us proof of what you know. Maybe we'll even take a few wee snaps of you in action. After that, it's time for financial reparation, and you're going to be giving till it hurts, as they say. Once we've got the money, you and Cairns and Raeside can come back and move the bodies so there's no way we can hurt you and no more reason for you to hurt us.'

'And what if I *don't know* where these people are

376

buried?' McDade asked, with earnest anxiety.

'Then we still go up the Campsies, except you use the shovel to dig a big hole, I put two in your head and bury you there, and we go through all this again tomorrow night with Bob Cairns or Bill Raeside.'

'Christ,' McDade muttered, sounding broken. 'How much do you want?'

'Three hundred thousand. Two for Jasmine, one for me.'

'Three . . . ?' he gasped, giving a hollow laugh of incredulity. Jasmine didn't rate his acting. 'You're forgetting you're dealing with polis, not gangsters, Fallan. We're skint. We're gaunny be living off pensions in a year or so.'

'Aye, I'd sympathise, if it wasnae that I was talking to this jewel thief who saw you walking out of Central station on Thursday morning with a very big bag of uncut heroin. My sources tell me Frankie Callahan was paying three million per shipment. Now, obviously you'd have to be charging Tony McGill less for the drugs per se, maybe two mill, but once you factor in taking out the competition for him as well, it's got to be up to at least two point five. Maybe two point four so it's a three-way split of eight hundred each. Or is there somebody else?'

McDade visibly seethed, his knuckles whitening as he gripped the wheel.

'Nobody else.'

'McDade, Cairns and Raeside . . . and now Fallan again, just like the old days, eh? Except this time Fallan's not taking an equal share of the payout. Just a kick in the arse over ten per cent. That seems fair enough, doesn't it? So once we've

377

seen the bodies, you're going to make some calls. We want it tonight. All of it.'

'We don't have it.'

'Bollocks you don't,' Fallan said, sticking the silencer into McDade's groin. 'The station job was Thursday morning and it's now Tuesday night.'

The van wobbled a little between lanes on the motorway, then came back into line.

'You think Tony McGill hands over three million quid just like that?' McDade asked.

'No, I'm guessing there's instalments, but if you'd any sense, the biggest one would be upon initial delivery. A third, maybe? Twenty per cent?'

'Twenty-five,' McDade admitted with a sigh.

'There you go, then. Three hundred easy, after which you're away clean with the rest, without having to kill anybody else. Just view it as Big Fall getting his share first. Aye, a pay-off from Tony McGill: just like the good old days. I don't really remember you, though. Mind you, you weren't Gallowhaugh CID, were you? You were Drug Squad. How did that work?'

'What do you mean?'

'I mean what was the quid pro quo? Drug Squad: I'm guessing Tony was good for information, got you plenty of arrests, dope-on-the-table stuff. It's your end I can't suss. Normally it was about turning a blind eye, but with Tony there were no drugs to turn a blind eye to. That was his whole deal: the man keeping drugs out of Gallowhaugh. What did you do for him? Was it just about getting rid of problems, eliminating the competition, same as now? Did you kill the Ramsays for him? What did they do wrong? How did that go down?'

'It wasn't like that,' McDade said, his voice trembling with emotion. He almost sounded tearful. 'It was nothing like that. You called it the good old days, well it fucking wasnae. It was the worst of times. You're not too young that you don't remember. It was wild, brutal. We were stretched so thin you could practically see through us. We had to do the odd deal with the devil, accept a few least-worst solutions.'

'Taking folk up the Campsies and killing them doesn't sound least-worst to me.'

'Look who's talking,' McDade said bitterly.

'I never swore to protect and serve, or whatever you chancers claim. You were supposed to be the good guys.'

'Compared to the shite we were up against, believe me, we were the good guys. Still are. Nothing was black and white in those days.'

'Describe the shades of grey for us then.'

McDade dropped down a gear as he approached the off-slip for Royston and Springburn, taking them north of the city, towards the Campsies. Jasmine thought she saw his left hand hover around his jacket pocket, and worried for a moment that he might have a second gun concealed there. Fallan appeared to have noted it too, and didn't seem concerned.

'There was an accident,' McDade said. 'There was this wee ned, right hard ticket. I knew he had information about a supplier up in Maryhill, but I was getting nothing out of him. I mentioned it to Bob and he said they could help. They being him, your dad and Bill. Said they'd talk to him in the back of a van, you know?'

Fallan's face darkened.

379

'I'm familiar with the practice. Saw the aftermath getting dumped out up the Spooky Woods in Gallowhaugh plenty of nights. Sometimes they could still just about walk. Our taxes in action.'

'Well, this guy was a tough nut to crack. Too hard and too stubborn and too stupid to give it up. It went too far.'

McDade swallowed, genuinely troubled by the memory of a moment when everything had changed and could never go back to how it was.

'We're left there with a deid guy in the van. What could we do? I knew this place, though. A quarry up the Campsies, only recently closed down. Lot of loose earth, broken stone, and completely enclosed, nobody to see you. We buried him up there.'

'What was his name?'

'McGeoch,' he said softly. 'Scotty McGeoch.'

'He wasn't mourned much, I take it?'

'He was reported missing, but the folk missing him had a big list of suspects for who might have got rid of him, and we werenae on it.'

'Result,' said Jasmine drily.

'It was a nightmare,' McDade retorted.

'But a recurring one,' suggested Fallan.

McDade nodded regretfully.

'Not long afterwards there was this bastard, and I mean utter bastard, Vinny McLellan. You remember the name?'

'I knew the family.'

'Well, he was literally getting away with murder because everybody was too scared to testify against him. Raped a lassie who had been a witness, just to give her a taste. He was an animal and we put him

380

down. Justice was done. Nobody would have blamed us, though that didnae stop me blaming myself, for a long time. You stop worrying about being caught, but it's not an easy thing to live with. You tell yourself you have to, though, that it's your burden to carry.'

'I know you never get away with murder,' Fallan reflected.

'Trouble is, it gets easier. You must know that as well. Especially when it's scumbags you're dealing with.'

'What about schoolteachers and chemical statisticians?' Jasmine demanded.

'It wasn't like that,' McDade said again. 'There was a guy called Jai Kerrigan, did a lot of work for Tony. Became one of his inner circle. You remember the name?'

'I remember he disappeared one day and was never seen again.'

'It's not true that we got rid of people for Tony McGill. Just a rumour he allowed to fester. But this was different. It was in a lot of people's interests. Jai had gone behind Tony's back and was trying to stitch up a deal with the Cassidy family to distribute heroin in Gallowhaugh. The ramifications were huge, and the fallout would have been very bloody: we'd have been up to our knees in corpses. It was a surgical strike, you could say.'

'A rational transaction?' Fallan suggested.

'It made everybody's lives a lot easier, and in many cases a lot longer. We took him to the quarry: me, Bill, Bob, your dad and McGill. He insisted on being there. Fannied about, milking the moment, until your dad ended it. Shot Jai through the head. But then we heard this scream, a woman's scream. We looked up—it was this really warm, clear night—and saw these two people looking back down. Don't know what they were doing there: shagging maybe. Their car was parked close to the edge of the quarry but we never noticed anything because the lights and the engine were off and because generally you just don't look up.'

McDade gave another rueful sigh: another moment he couldn't change.

They were heading out of Bishopbriggs now, on the road to Kirkintilloch.

'They ran for their car because they knew we'd seen them, and started it up in a crazy hurry; engine over-revved and the wheels must have been spinning on the grass. We were panicking. Your dad fired a shot. I mean, fucking one-in-a-million shot. You could never repeat it if you tried for a month.'

He shook his head, his eyes on the darkness and the cat's-eyes ahead.

'Must have blown out a tyre at just the right moment—or just the wrong moment. The car slewed to one side, got yanked like it was on a rope, and went over the edge. Hit the ground bonnet first, flush-on. Neither of them were wearing seat belts; probably never had time. They were both dead by the time we had run over to the car. Came straight through the windscreen, the pair of them, on to solid stone. Never had an earthly. We're standing there in a daze, not knowing whether to be appalled or relieved, and that's when we heard it: the wean, greetin'.'

'How did he survive?' asked Jasmine.

382

'Carrycot was wedged in that tight, and the wean was swaddled up in a ton of blankets. He was fine.'

'Apart from having just been orphaned,' she observed.

'Aye, well,' said McDade grimly. 'There was nothing we could do about that. Or rather, there was. We could make sure he would be looked after, given to a good home.'

'And you looked out for him ever after.'

'Always. Always. A lot changed that night. You cannae just walk away from a thing like that. Well, some folk can,' he added, casting a resentful glance at Fallan. It took a moment for Jasmine to deduce that McDade wasn't alluding to Glen himself, but to his father.

'What happened to the car?' Fallan asked, presumably with a professional eye for such detail.

'McGill got it towed away and scrapped. Or more likely salvaged for the back half of a ringer. He's another one that wasnae exactly chastened by the event.'

'And you *were*?' Fallan challenged. 'That's how you were able to still shoot gangsters and ex-cops nearly thirty years later?'

'We *were* chastened. We didn't walk away from it all right away—your dad and Tony McGill were still baw-deep in each other's business, and your dad was a hard man to say no to.'

'Plus you wouldn't have wanted him thinking you might turn on him.'

'No, he knew we were all way too scared of him to do that.'

'Jolly lucky break for you chaps that somebody murdered him, then.'

'I know nothing about that,' McDade said, with

383

a vehemence Jasmine instantly believed. 'Nothing. But after he died, things changed. It was a fresh start. I did the job: straight. We all did. No more Wild West stuff, no more backhanders.'

They were well into the countryside now, at least a mile from any source of light pollution. Jasmine could see insects dancing across the beams of the headlights, on full because there were no vehicles coming the other way. McDade turned off down a single-track road, its entrance concealed by trees, somewhere you'd need to know really well not to miss in the dark.

'We did a difficult job and we gave it our all, because we owed that. Put in the hours, put ourselves between the scum and the psychos and the ordinary folk just trying to get on with it. And we watched guys like Stevie Fullerton and Frankie Callahan and the Cassidys and Christ knows how many others grow more and more rich and more and more untouchable; more and more *respectable*, while we cleared up the bodies and waded through the misery that kept them all there.'

She felt the gradient immediately. They were heading down, the road bumpy and winding. McDade took it slow, as though worried he'd snap the axle on a hole or a rut. He'd driven this road before, all right, knew its turns, knew its traps. The full-beam lights picked out walls of scrub and scree either side, crushed rubble and hard-packed earth beneath the wheels.

'Meanwhile we're struggling to pay mortgages and tuition fees and respite care, ending up with most of our pensions and savings spoken for before we even retire. Bill Raeside gave thirty years, lost his wife to cancer, what does he get?

384

Spent my whole career fighting this supposed war on drugs, and where are we? More people doing them than ever, more people selling them than ever, and our seizures are estimated to be about one per cent of what's actually making it through. Was it worth it? Worth all our efforts, worth so many folk dying, killing each other? Fuck no. So yeah, we decided we were having something back. A few more dead lowlifes were barely gaunny tip the scales.'

'What about dead ex-cops?' Jasmine asked. 'Jim Sharp put in the time and the hours you did, lost his marriage and missed out on half his kids' lives because he was so dedicated. Where's his slice of this heroin deal?'

McDade brought the van to a very gentle halt. Jasmine could see sheer walls of stone in the headlights fifty or sixty yards ahead. There were trees and bushes dotted about the fringes where twenty-seven years ago there must only have been earth and weeds. She wondered what buried sins their roots had tangled around for anchorage.

'Jim dredged it all up again,' McDade said, bitterness overwhelming his regret. 'Just when we were ready to secure our futures, he had to go and exhume the past. We'd done our penance, served our time. We spent a quarter of a century paying for what happened to the Ramsays.'

'Let's go and ask them if they forgive you,' said Fallan.

McDade got out of the car slowly, opening the driver's-side door with exaggerated care to the point of reluctance, Fallan keeping an eye on him as he exited. Then, once he was on his feet, McDade just disappeared, lunging to his right so

385

that he was out of sight behind the metal walls of the van.

At the same time, the van's rear door was hauled open and Jasmine was confronted with the sight of a man pointing a single-barrelled pump-action shotgun at her. He looked wide-eyed and jumpy, which made her twice as scared and all the more compliant when he ordered her out. Raeside, she estimated: never a trigger man, according to Fallan, but because of that, even more dangerous under these circumstances than somebody who was comfortable with such a weapon in his hands.

She edged her way out, Raeside stepping backwards away from the rear to give her space to walk into, his eyes always on hers. The moon was full and the clouds few, the van's headlights bouncing off the horseshoe walls for further illumination.

Once she took a couple of paces on the dusty earth, she could see Fallan. He had a gun to his head, held by a middle-aged man who'd look tall next to anybody else. Cairns. He must have appeared at the passenger-side window while Fallan was watching McDade get out.

She could see a car now, tucked away behind some trees. They'd got here first and lain in wait, knowing this was the destination. She now understood a further reason why McDade had been driving so slowly into the quarry: it was to give his colleagues time to get into position.

'We've been polis three decades,' said Cairns, answering her unspoken question. 'I mean, don't get me wrong, you're not the worst actress we've ever come across, but do you think we don't recognise a trap when we see one?'

She thought of McDade's hand hovering over his pocket, wondered if his phone had been in there: an open line, letting Cairns and Raeside hear what was going on and where they were headed. Maybe they had followed the van discreetly from the start, waiting out of sight as McDade walked into the office and played his part. And maybe it had been McDade's task to lead them here to this place one way or the other.

McDade reappeared at the front of the van, a clear plastic bag in his hand. He approached Fallan cautiously and took hold of the Beretta he was holding out, gripping it through the cellophane and inverting the bag like he was picking up a dog turd.

Fallan let out a grunt of self-reproach.

McDade handed Raeside the bagged Beretta and took hold of the shotgun, keeping it trained on Jasmine.

'I take it that was the weapon you used to kill Frankie Callahan, Gary Fleeting and Tommy Miller?' Fallan asked.

'Aye,' said Cairns. 'And now it's only your prints that are on it.'

'Quality fit-up. My old man would have been proud.'

'Nothing personal, son. Just the way things have worked out.'

'Naw, sure. Fletcher there was telling me all about it on the road up. I was that moved I was near greetin'. It's almost an honour to be part of it.'

'Don't saddle up the high horse around us, son,' Cairns hissed. 'We'd have a long way to fall before we'd even be in sight of you.'

'Prove it, then,' Fallan said. 'Let the lassie go.

She's got nothing on you. You can move the bodies. She's too scared to do anything. Pay her off: she takes some money, she's part of this.'

'I don't need money,' Jasmine pleaded. 'I'll keep quiet, forget about everything. I just don't want to die.'

There was a painfully tense silence. At least they were thinking about it.

'He's got a point,' said McDade. 'If she disappears, it's another missing person that could lead back to the Ramsays.'

'What?' asked Cairns. 'You think "could lead back to the Ramsays" is less of a risk than leaving somebody out there who knows everything for fucking definite?'

'At least don't kill her until she's told you about Campbell de Morgan,' Fallan said. 'Because that might have a strong bearing on your decision.'

'About who?' Cairns demanded.

'Campbell de Morgan,' Jasmine repeated clearly, for the benefit of everybody listening. 'He was a surgeon, gave his name to these tiny red spots that can appear on your skin. Do you know what they signify?'

'No, what?' Cairns asked impatiently. 'Cancer?'

'They signify absolutely nothing,' she replied. 'I only mention them by way of contrast: you know, in comparison to the tiny red spots on all of your skins that signify you've had police marksmen training laser-sighted rifles on you since you got here.'

The three cops looked at each other and saw the little red dots on each other's foreheads, which had moved there from less conspicuous places since Fallan gave the code word.

An electronically amplified voice hailed them from the rim of the quarry, where the marksmen were positioned.

'Put down your weapons slowly, place your hands on your heads and get down on your knees,' it commanded.

Cairns and McDade let out gasps of disbelieving exasperation, but all three of them complied with the order immediately, smoothly and demonstrably. These were men who implicitly understood the equation governing risk to civilians and margin of doubt in the minds of trained police shooters. One involuntary twitch and they'd be dropped. This was over.

'What was that about not recognising a trap when you see one?' Jasmine asked Cairns, backing away from where the three men were now kneeling on the earth.

Cairns didn't even look at her by way of response. He only had eyes for Fallan.

'How about that,' Fallan said. 'Me, bringing down the bad guys, just like my old man always didn't.'

'Your old man?' Cairns asked, then spat on the ground. 'I suppose, under the circumstances, I might as well let you know now. It was me that killed him.'

He spoke with real venom, true conviction.

Fallan stared down at him pityingly.

'I'm not the kind of guy who can always tell when somebody's lying,' he said. 'But I can tell you're lying about that. You were too big a shitebag, and you haven't changed. Anyway, I've got to go, and there's a guy on his way down wants a word with you. Something about locusts and

389

mosquitoes, I think he said.'

FAMILY (I)

Catherine wouldn't normally allow anybody to smoke in the car, but she was making an exception. Dominic Wilson was so jumpy that she feared he'd throw open the rear door and dive out while the vehicle was in motion if he didn't have a cigarette to occupy himself. Catherine was in the back with him, Laura at the wheel, her little dark cloud just a shade lighter these past few days. She'd been quieter, though; more reflective, but when she did speak, she was less deferential. She seemed to have developed a strange fascination with Glen Fallan, which Catherine was less happy about, but anything that helped bring out the detective Catherine had heard about from her colleagues on the east coast would be tolerated.

'How's Ruaraidh?' Catherine asked, a sensitive question, she appreciated, but for all that a good distraction from Dominic's anxiety over the coming rendezvous. She chose her phrasing carefully, too, avoiding the words dad and father, as their status was now more than a little ambiguous.

'He's on holiday,' Dominic replied. 'Took off to Malaysia with this woman he's been seeing. Everybody assumes he's hiding from the press, but I think he's hiding from me. The weird thing is, I don't actually feel angry with him. I mean, like, I actually feel less anger with him than ever before, and I'm not quite sure why. Maybe I'm still just

390

numb from shock, but that's not how it feels.'

'I was there when he was initially confronted about it,' she told him. 'And the one thing there's no ambiguity about is the depth of his feelings for you.'

'Yeah. I think the reason I'm not angry is I kind of feel sorry for him. I can't decide whether he did a good thing for bad reasons or a bad thing for good reasons. And without getting too anthropic about it, his decisions made me who I am and I can't change it. It's a serious head-fuck. Been over and over it in my mind, but I haven't reached any conclusions.'

'What about the PF's office: have they?'

'Oh, the one thing that's for sure is that he'll walk away clean. I'm staying out of it, though. Recused. Thinking of taking a holiday myself. I'm glad to be clear of what's going on just now anyway. Someone will be able to write a PhD one day about the horse-trading that's going on with regard to who's getting prosecuted for what on this one.'

'Deals within deals and compromises within compromises,' Catherine suggested.

'You've no idea. The big balancing act is between bringing an acceptable form of resolution while keeping certain cans of worms closed. Everybody's got an agenda. You guys never got the drugs, did you?'

'Not a chance,' Catherine admitted. 'Disappeared untraceably into Tony McGill's gossamer web, probably within hours of the station job.'

'Yeah. Cairns, Raeside and McDade aren't helping to hang him either, which surprised me. I'd have thought they'd stake everything on deflecting as much blame as they can his way.'

'Scary gig being a polisman in prison,' Catherine said. 'They'll have a lot of enemies, so they'll need allies on the inside. It's in their interests more than ever that Tony McGill enjoys an Indian summer to his criminal career.'

Laura brought the vehicle to a halt outside the Ramsays' house. Catherine imagined she could detect Dominic's anxiety levels surging in response to the finality of the engine being switched off. He seemed in no immediate rush to get out of the car.

'I'm so nervous about this,' he said, perhaps oblivious to how staringly apparent this was.

'There's nothing to worry about. I met her a couple of days ago. She's lovely.'

'*I've* met her too,' he retorted, 'about a dozen times. Prosecuted her clients back when she was in criminal law. That's what's so freaky. This is very different.'

'You spoke to her on the phone, though, didn't you?'

'For about an hour.'

'Well, there you go.'

'I know, I know. It's just, face to face . . . I'm excited. This will be good,' he coached himself. 'I've got a niece and a nephew, did you know that? Got aunts and uncles too; cousins. My family was so small, so enclosed.'

He reached for the door handle: finally, she thought, plucking up the courage to open it, but he stopped and looked at her again.

'Did I tell you it turns out I'm a Catholic?' he asked.

She shook her head.

'I was christened, apparently, at three weeks. Irony is, I've got a season ticket for Parkhead.'

'What's ironic about that?'

'I decided I was a Celtic fan when I was about twelve just to annoy my dad, because he was such a Rangers man. A very prominent Rangers man, in fact: all brown brogues and dignity. Turns out the whole time I was actually Tim to the brim.'

'Enough procrastinating,' Catherine told him. 'On you go.'

The front door swung open even as they were walking down the garden path. It was Jasmine Sharp who opened it, performing the counterpart chaperoning role on behalf of her client.

Jasmine ushered Catherine and Dominic into the living room, where Anne Ramsay was standing, clasping and unclasping her hands. She looked just as anxious as Dominic, but expectantly so rather than apprehensive. Catherine noticed the kids' toys scattered about the place but an absence of actual kids. Must have been parcelled off to Granny's, as this would have been a confusing moment for them to witness.

Anne didn't say anything. She almost did, opening her mouth for a second or two, but words didn't come; words couldn't deal with this. Then she took a couple of steps towards Dominic and pulled him to her, the tears flowing before they'd even touched. His body was shaking with her sobs as she clung on to him, his own arms visibly tightening around her as something inside him let go.

Catherine looked silently at Jasmine and gestured towards the door. Anne's husband, Neil Caldwell, read it too, and joined them in the hall, where Laura was waiting.

'Is she okay in there?' Jasmine asked.

'Absolutely,' said Neil, his own eyes a little watery. 'Absolutely. She's been like a kid on Christmas Eve the past few days, waiting for this moment, but happy, you know? At peace.'

He got out a paper hanky and dabbed at his eyes and nose.

'We're both so grateful to you for what you did,' he said to Jasmine. 'And so sorry about your uncle.'

Jasmine nodded her acknowledgement. Catherine could tell she was holding back tears of her own.

'And get your bill in right away,' Neil told her. 'Don't stand on ceremony. The best money we've ever spent.'

'Never mind about the money,' Jasmine said softly. 'It wasn't about that.'

Catherine recognised that the girl was a little overcome.

'She'll send you an invoice,' she said. 'I'll make sure of it. Gratitude and warm wishes don't pay the rent,' she told Jasmine with a friendly smile.

The girl nodded, a wry look of self-reproach on her face.

'Yeah,' she agreed. 'Glen said something similar.'

Which quite wiped the smile off Catherine's face.

*   *   *

'You know,' Laura said, twisting the key in the ignition as Catherine pulled on her seat belt, 'all it takes is somebody to just mention that man's name

394

and you look like you're going to punch a wall. It's a bit scary.'

Catherine glanced back towards the house, where she could see Jasmine still chatting to Neil Caldwell at the open front door.

'Not as scary as I find Fallan,' she replied. 'We're talking here about a man whose reputation is so grim in certain circles that last week he frightened off an armed gunman using a mobile phone.'

'Yeah, but it looks to me like these days he's on the side of the angels.'

'My fear is more derived from his abilities than which team he's currently playing for, because that can change: what he's capable of does not. Once a killer, always a killer,' she added, with a conviction borne more of fear that it was true than of certainty.

'It's no wonder. The more I hear about his dad . . .' Laura gave a shudder. 'A pure psycho.'

'Yeah, well, there you go,' Catherine replied. 'Like father, like son.'

Laura's hand had been hovering over the gearstick, but she withdrew it and turned to look at Catherine.

'You really hate him, don't you?' she asked. 'I mean, not just fear. True hate. Did you know him back when, before he disappeared?'

Catherine let out a sigh, buying time as she gathered her thoughts. She wasn't going there, not with her DI, and not now. Laura deserved an answer, though, because what she had said was true.

'I encountered him fleetingly, a long time ago,' she replied. 'He was a nobody, a small cog in a very nasty machine, so oblivious or indifferent to the damage being done that he doesn't even remember. I don't hate him for that. I hate what he represents.'

Laura took this in and seemed to understand what Catherine was trying to say, but she didn't look entirely satisfied. Nor did she look any longer like someone who was going to keep her thoughts to herself.

'But does he not also represent the possibility that we don't have to be defined by the worst things that happened to us?' she asked, sounding like she needed to believe this was true. 'Does he not represent the chance that we can change?'

FAMILY (II)

By the time of Jim's funeral, the weather had turned, heavy squalls of rain soaking people who had left for the outdoors unprepared due to the periods of watery sunshine in between. For the first time in months, the rain felt cold, and there was a bite in the wind that warned Jasmine that summer was quite definitely at an end.

She didn't fear the winter. It couldn't bring anything worse than what she had endured last year, the least of whose depredations had been the coldest weather in four decades.

They'd had to wait for the post-mortem and all the attendant investigations to be completed—for Jim's body to finally cease being an instrument of the law, even after death—before they could bury him. Or rebury him, rather, somewhere fitting, the sod cast this time by those who loved him and mourned him.

Jasmine had stood among them, missing him, remembering him, loving him, though she thought that this time tears would not come. She had cried already, she thought, cried enough; known Jim was dead long before anyone else here, and forced herself to confront that as a reality.

She was wrong, however: as she saw the grief on her cousins' faces, she saw reflected back the grief she had suffered this past year, and cried once more. She was mourning Jim, and still mourning Mum, but would admit that she was crying just a little for herself. She was allowed to do that now: she didn't need to worry that it meant she was crumbling, that she wouldn't cope.

While the rest of Jim's immediate family began drifting away towards the warmth and shelter of the waiting car, his eldest daughter Angela came over to Jasmine and they stood by the grave, the rain pitter-pattering on their umbrellas like the departing susurrus of quiet, respectful voices.

'I wanted to say thank you,' Angela said. 'On behalf of . . . I mean, my mum as well, and everybody.'

Jasmine felt a little confused as to what she might be being thanked for, and it must have registered on her face.

'Without you, we wouldn't have had this. A chance to say goodbye, to all come together. To *know*. God knows the Ramsays never got that.'

Jasmine gave her a sad smile and a hug by way of acknowledgement, her thoughts going back a few days to the service she had attended for Anne's parents, Stephen and Eilidh. People had thanked her then, too: total strangers, these middle-aged men and women with decades of hurt in their eyes turning to sincerest gratitude for having been released from this prison of not knowing.

For the first time in over a year, she had stopped feeling like a lost little girl. All these older people, a generation apart, were acting like she was the one who had taken care of them, like they saw this woman standing there whom it took Jasmine a while to recognise as herself.

'Look,' said Angela, 'there's another reason I need to speak to you. We had the reading of the will. Jim left the business to us, to his children, collectively. It wasn't that specific a stipulation, it just got covered among a more general directive. The thing is, it's not worth anything except as a going concern. The office is rented on a lease and there's not a lot of assets worth liquidating: an ageing computer, an old van, a bunch of surveillance equipment and some office furniture. I mean, he *was* the business: a one-man show. Until he brought you in.'

Angela cast a tearful eye to her side, where her father's coffin lay waiting for the mounds of earth either side to be shovelled over him for ever.

'We've discussed it and we're all agreed that it should be yours if you want it. We've no doubt it's what Dad would have wanted, especially if he'd known what you just did.'

Angela filled up again, her face creasing once more with grief.

'Just . . . think about it and let us know,' she said, her voice cracking at the end.

Jasmine nodded solemnly and Angela walked away to where her husband Mark was waiting, holding open the rear door of a black funeral car.

The red Civic was parked somewhere in the caravan of mourners' vehicles along the narrow one-way road that snaked through the cemetery, striking an almost inappropriate note of vivid colour among the black cars and black clothes. Everyone was heading to a nearby hotel for more hugs, tears and sausage rolls. Jasmine would catch them up in a little while.

She walked among the graves, looking at dates going back a century. Rows of little white lines, giving off their secret heat. One of them was her mother's, if she could get her bearings and find it. Yes, she remembered now: just along from the mausoleum of some Victorian businessman. She hadn't been back here since the funeral, partly because she didn't want to revisit such a scene of pain, but largely also because she didn't see the point. It wasn't a place to remember her mum, because she'd never *been* here with her. It was just where her body lay, no more infused with her essence, with all the things that made her herself, than that quarry had been infused with the essences of Jim or the Ramsays or anybody else who had been buried there.

Still, she always felt guilty about not going, like it was some kind of daughter's duty she was neglecting.

The headstone was there now. She remembered getting a letter about it, with an acknowledgement that the fee had been paid through some kind of insurance. It should have given her a more pressing impetus to return to the cemetery, but at the time she just wasn't strong enough. This would be her first time of seeing it. She suspected it would upset her, in particular the dates: the finality

399

of that second one, bracketing a life and rendering all its deeds and possibilities finite.

The dates did not upset her, though. She was too distracted by the name, because in its unaccustomed formality, it looked like a mistake.

Her mum was Beth: that was how she was known to friends and colleagues, to anyone she ever stopped to talk to on the street when Jasmine was dawdling at her side, tugging Mummy's hand to move along.

Beth, always Beth. Letters would say 'Elizabeth' sometimes, if it was something official or junk off a mailing list, but neither Beth nor Elizabeth was actually her first name. As Jasmine remembered now, that was her middle name.

Jasmine assumed that she just preferred Elizabeth, but realised that she must have gone by her given first name once, because Jim would call her by it occasionally. He'd refer to her as Yvonne, then correct himself, like Mum used to when she referred to her old pals by their maiden names.

There it was: written in stone. Yvonne Elizabeth Sharp.

And that was when Jasmine shuddered, like the cold rain had run off her brolly and poured straight down the back of her neck.

The Fallan file.

CLIENT: YES.

There had been no invoicing details. That was because Jim was doing it for nothing. He was tracking down Glen Fallan for her mum, and he'd found him, but that wasn't all.

Jasmine recalled Jim's upper-register hand-writing on the notes and saw now how she'd misunderstood it, assuming that it referred simply

400

to Jim having got in touch with Ingrams. What it had actually said was 'INGRAMS CONTACTED YES', and a date.

Glen Fallan had been to see her mum shortly before she died.

FORGIVENESS

Catherine was lying awake again. It was close to three o'clock on Sunday morning, and what was making it worse was that somebody would have to be up with the boys at seven, and it was her turn. Drew had got up yesterday, albeit Catherine didn't get a lie-in then either. She and Laura had been due to go and pick up Dominic to escort him to the Ramsays', and Drew had sorted the boys with breakfast and taken them swimming so that she would have time to make herself presentable.

She had woken around twenty past two and couldn't get back to sleep. Why couldn't she sleep?

It had been a good day. A tiring day, in all the best ways. When Laura brought her back home, it wasn't yet eleven. It was a clear, sunny day. Cooler than it had been, with a breeze that promised autumn, but way better than anyone living in this part of the world had ever come to expect for late August.

She and Drew had taken the boys to Loudoun Castle for the rest of the day, down in Ayrshire. They had been going there for a couple of years, and despite Catherine's natural aversion to theme parks, she always found it curiously relaxing and a little quaint: its verdant setting making it seem all the more like a place where old amusement rides were put out to pasture. The boys adored it, of course, and every time they came back, it seemed they had each grown tall enough to be allowed on one more attraction than last time.

After that, they had gone out for dinner, the four of them, to the little Italian place round the corner where the staff had made a fuss of the boys since birth. Could have been there she made her misstep, taking a large espresso after dessert. Surely not, though: it had been around seven. Coffee only did this to her normally if she had one at the end of a meal out without the kids and was drinking it after ten.

She didn't have any trouble getting to sleep; in fact had slipped away so pleasantly it was like she was on opiates.

She and Drew had made love, and this was definitely making love. It had been very tender, very intimate, very *slow*, and very quiet, apart from towards the very end when she couldn't help herself. Drew had threatened to put a pillow over her face lest she wake the boys, which had made her giggly and thus only added to the intensity of the orgasm and her vocal appreciation of it.

She felt a long way from sleep now. Not worried or anxious, but the way she felt when there was something unresolved between them, a matter that they hadn't had the time or the inclination to discuss. There was nothing wrong between them, though, nothing she was turning over in her head.

That was just it, however. It was something that wasn't between them. It was something she kept hidden, in the heart of that place Drew knew she went, angry on the road there and unreachable

402

when she arrived.

They had talked plenty today, making the long walks between different areas of the park, while the boys ran ahead, zigzagging back and forth across the paths. She had apologised for becoming obsessive, and Drew had acknowledged that it wasn't something that happened all the time, just that it had come on the back of a difficult couple of months.

He said he understood that it would always be part of the deal that she would be withdrawn at times, as there were certain things he was grateful that she didn't bring home from work with her. However, he argued, there were times when she was clearly carrying a burden she shouldn't try to shoulder alone.

She had talked a little about Fallan, enough to offer him something by way of explanation, but same as with Laura, she hadn't talked to either of them about the real reason he disturbed her, the real source of this wellspring of hatred.

Lying awake once again in the dark, she kept thinking of what Laura had said, about how people didn't need to be defined by the worst things that happened to them, and about how perhaps they could change.

She started replaying today's conversations in her head, trying to capture the thing that would not let her rest, the bird that was loose in her attic.

'So this guy Fallan helped you?' Drew had said.

'He wasn't helping me. He was helping himself, and helping Jasmine Sharp, though I'm not quite sure why. I was just an auxiliary beneficiary.'

'But either way, he was on your side. Doesn't that open the door just a wee bit to forgiving him?'

403

Drew suggested this warily, afraid he'd get his head bitten off even though they were standing among dozens of people, watching the boys on a merry-go-round.

'I'm just saying,' he clarified. 'You've never told me what went on with your family back then, and I respect that you don't want to, but it still twists you up inside even now. It's easy for me to say, I know, but a lot of people maintain that forgiveness can be liberating.'

'He's not looking for forgiveness. I don't think he even remembers.'

'But what are *you* looking for? It's not him that needs forgiveness. Maybe it's you who needs to forgive.'

And there it was, the bird, ceased flapping around and temporarily come to rest. Motionless for the moment, but that didn't mean it could easily be captured, nor that it couldn't take wing again and resume bouncing off the walls.

Maybe all she needed was to open a window. That wouldn't be simple either, though.

Drew was right about one thing and wrong about another.

It wasn't Glen Fallan that Catherine needed to forgive.

FOUR WORDS

The wind had picked up in recent days, all the more blustery on the higher ground of Northumberland, where it was claiming the first dry leaves. The colours weren't yet turned; grass

404

still growing on the roadside verges enough for cutting work to be slowing down the traffic. It felt between seasons, between times: something not quite over, something else not quite begun.

As she drove up to the refuge, she could see Fallan to the side of the house, holding a leaf-blower in one hand like it was a dust-buster. He wore dark green camo trousers and a sleeveless T-shirt, just as he'd been dressed when she first met him. She didn't think the outside temperature would ever have much bearing on his gardening attire, as he seemed the kind of man for whom hard graft was enough to keep him warm.

She felt nervous almost to the point of nausea at the sight, his very familiarity and an instinctive warmth at seeing him again now adding to the turbulent mix churning inside her. She'd felt less apprehensive the first time she came here, and no more confident of being told the truth.

He didn't smile when he saw her, but he did stop what he was doing and walk across to greet her. There was warmth in his expression, but worry too, like he was pleased to see her but somehow not happy she was here.

No preamble, she thought. She'd never get through it; it would only make the main event more enormous.

'I found bank statements,' she began, and from his expression she could tell he was not even going to attempt to pretend this could mean anything else. 'My mum's, from 2007 onwards. She was receiving payments every three or four months from a company called Morningstar. I called the bank and they told me the installments went back twenty years.'

Jasmine paused, trying to keep her voice steady, trying to hold her nerve.

'Morningstar is an anagram of Tron Ingrams,' she stated, as blankly as she could manage.

Fallan said nothing. He folded his arms as though he was suddenly feeling the cold, that rarely glimpsed expression of vulnerability about his face and his posture.

'I know you went to see her, not long before she died,' Jasmine continued. 'That first time I came here, to the refuge: you knew who I was all along, didn't you?'

Fallan nodded solemnly.

'I knew the second I saw you sitting there with Rita in the kitchen,' he admitted.

Jasmine looked beyond the house, away to the north, away from Fallan. She had to take her eyes off him in order to ready herself, but she could smell that scent of him again, of the outdoors and of fresh sweat and recent ablutions.

She took a breath, then despite the breeze threatening to swallow her faltering voice, from somewhere found the strength to say the most difficult four words of her life.